# Silver Bow's Tab

# Silver Bow's Tab

## The Jalisco Incident
## Part 1

**Rivers Coffman**

*To my wife, Sarah, who encouraged me*

*with a shrug and a simple statement.*

*"Go for it."*

# Prologue

Charlie gasped as he regained consciousness in the old grain warehouse. The gasp wasn't much; his left lung had collapsed from the bullet that tore through it. He'd been shot in the back between the plates of his armor, and the slug took a hard left turn and exited just under his armpit. His right arm wouldn't move and felt like it was on fire with the amount of pain pulsing through the limb. His mouth was full and his lips were covered with the dirt and grain on the floor. The pain radiated all along the right side of his head, neck, and lower torso. Shrapnel from that grenade. Thankfully, his shredded arm managed to protect the most vital parts of his body. The grenade had landed in a pile of grain next to him and sunk to its base before it detonated. There was no other way he would have survived at that range.

He took shallow breaths as he lifted himself up to his feet with his only good arm, his vision blurring from the lack of blood and oxygen. He dragged his boots in the dirt and grain with every step as he made his way to the outer wall of the destroyed grain warehouse and saw the outer edge of Yongsan in the distance. The city was ten kilometers away. From the looks of it, it had just started to rain. It was December 27, and Yongsan was in the middle of spring and the wet season. With the blood in his mouth mixing with the dirt and grain, Charlie gritted his teeth and took more shallow breaths with each step.

With only one functional lung, one functional arm, and sheer determination to survive, he got one step closer. Another. Another. His shredded arm dripped with blood, and he realized he needed to use a tourniquet before he bled to death. He fell to one knee and grabbed it out of his armor's individual first aid kit, IFAK, and groaned loudly as he tightened the band until he felt pins and needles. With the blood flow stopped, he cried out as he stood, knowing that he couldn't get off his feet again.

His body howled at him. Every step took mental and physical effort. He could feel the shrapnel tearing his flesh as he moved, causing blood to slowly ooze from his wounds. Even with his pricy armor, there were still many gaps that had allowed the grenade to render his flesh like a woodchipper, and he was almost certain that the only thing keeping him alive was the armor's undershell, which had fast-acting coagulants that sealed open wounds.

After what seemed like an eternity stumbling in the rain, his vision blurred more and he started to become muddleheaded. His heart was working overtime to give oxygen to his body as it strained from exertion in its severely weakened state. The bleeding had mostly stopped, but the loss of blood and oxygen continued to weaken him. It was a positive feedback loop. Movement required oxygen and oxygen required more blood to flow. With only one lung, he was practically experiencing a slow and painful asphyxiation.

He stopped and tried to breathe as hard as he could with the collapsed lung to give himself as much oxygen as his body would allow. He reached for his IFAK and pulled out a small autoinjector full of epinephrine. Epinephrine, or adrenaline, would give him the last push he needed to get to the edge of Yongsan. He could see houses in the distance, probably only a kilometer or two away. He jammed the autoinjector into a gap between the armor plates on his abdomen and felt reinvigorated as the adrenaline gave him that little extra push towards survival.

He moaned with pain. Every step required more focus, more energy, more willpower. The houses drew closer with every agonizing step. He wanted to collapse and simply die, but he pushed himself further and further, far beyond what he ever thought was possible.

He tried to replay the events in his mind to keep it distracted from the pain, but the more he thought about it, the more he realized that he had been betrayed and left to die. It wasn't accidental friendly fire or that a firefight had broken out between the Pit Vipers and the sellers. He wasn't a target of opportunity…it was premeditated.

From where the bullet had struck him between the plates in the back, there was only one person that could have made that kind of shot at that distance and had that kind of angle. He closed his eyes forcefully as a mixture of blood and spit dribbled off his lips. It couldn't be. There was no reason for her to shoot him in the back…was there?

The grenade. There was no denying that the grenade came from behind him as well as he used the crate as cover. He distinctly remembered hearing his brother shout "This will finish it!" mere moments before the grenade landed.

*Why would they do it? Wh-why?*

Though it may have kept his mind off the pain, it also kept his mind and eyes away from what was in front of him. His toes caught the lip of a rock, and he fell. His right arm disobeyed all commands, and he had no time to force his left arm to brace him before he fell into the mud. The air swiftly exited his one good lung as a few pieces of shrapnel dug deeper into his flesh, causing him to cry out weakly.

He pulled his head upward and saw that he was only a couple hundred meters away from civilization. He was so close. He had to somehow tap further into his strength and will to find safety and help. He used his left arm and pushed himself up with all his might and put his legs underneath him, one at a time. His mangled and blood-covered right arm dragged in the mud, and despite him using a tourniquet to stop the blood flow, his nerves shrieked at him with searing pain as the mud and dirty rainwater sloshed into the open wounds. It wasn't until he felt mud that he realized that right ring and middle fingers had been sheared from his hand. The flesh and bone had slowed the shrapnel just enough to allow the metal to only embed itself in his skull behind his ear rather than going into his brain. "Lucky" was an understatement.

He pushed onward with all of his reserve strength as the adrenaline wore off. His muscles began to atrophy with the lack of oxygen as he slowly climbed the steps to the first house. He weakly leaned against the doorframe and pressed the call button on the access panel, but no one came or answered. He managed to put his left hand into a fist and pounded on the door a few times, but only silence answered him.

*Please…someone be home at the next house…*

Charlie descended the slick steps with as much care as he could. His vision began to fail him again as everything became blurry while he ascended the steps to the next house. He felt sleepy. The final stages of blood loss. Despite his suit mitigating the wounds, he was still bleeding, and the constant strain and exertion only made his heart pump harder—which made him bleed more. At the second house, the result was the same.

*Please…*

He descended the steps with a slight stumble, but he used the handrail to keep himself upright. If he fell over in the rain now, he'd die. Mercifully, there was a small chain-link fence at the front of the next house, and he used it to support himself as much as he could. Since it was on his right, he couldn't hold on to the fence with his destroyed arm. He took a few steps, then leaned against it to regain what little strength he had. The four steps up to the front door for the third house might as well have been a mountain. His legs burned from the lack of oxygen as calcium rushed to the fibers. By the second step, his legs shook as if he was trying to beat a personal best in squats.

He finally reached the top of the steps and leaned heavily on the small entryway wall that led up to the door.

*Please…*

He managed to keep himself upright, but his entire body's weight rested against the door. He was barely able to press the call button. This house was his last hope. The blood loss, the numbness, the exhaustion all told him that he would never make it to the next house. He was so weak that just leaning against the door required all of his focus and effort. Then, finally…

"Uh, yes? Hello?" a woman asked through the access panel's speaker.

"Help…" Charlie weakly muttered.

"Who are you? What do you want?" she asked apprehensively.

"Help…" he repeated as his vision grayed.

The door flew open with a hiss and Charlie fell to the floor. Before he lost consciousness, he could hear the woman shriek with horror and say, "Stay with me! I'll get an ambulance!"

# Chapter 1

Eri used her wrist to wipe the sweat from her brow. Her hands were covered in dirt and grease and the drier air of the late Corinth summer made the shop feel like an oven being opened in front of her face. While Corinth's summer was in its last month, her friends in Athens were enjoying a pleasant and mild winter. Every day in the Corinth summer working as a maintainer made her want to move back to Athens, but the tourist town had little use for someone who worked on engines. Any shop that worked on engines consistently had wait lists for new maintainers and she did *not* want to wait tables on the beach while she waited years for an opening.

"I'm just sayin', Eri, this could be your chance to finally do somethin' rather than constantly fixin' cars and winterizin' a whole bunch of yachts. These guys need someone who can work on ship drives."

"*A* ship drive, not multiple," Eri replied with a sigh.

"Whatever," Ash exclaimed, "ya always said ya wanted to work exclusively on ship drives, and now's your chance!"

Annoyed, Eri stared at her sister through the side of her eye. Something was off, she could feel it. For the past two years, Ash had dragged Eri with her everywhere and refused to let Eri go to another city or system without her. She was glad that her half sister wanted to foster a more constant relationship, but any time Ash pushed to stay together, it just reminded her that all of it was catalyzed by their parents' murders.

"Please," Ash pleaded, "just take a look. The worst they say is no and the worst we say is no, but I want ya to be able to do what ya love."

"Then let me respond to their posting," Eri replied.

"Well…that's the thing. They also need someone for freight security and my time in the militia would probably give me an in as well. Wouldn't that be great? The two of us together, traveling the Frontier?"

"You already have a good job here working as a mobile bank vault guard," Eri said.

Her taller sister groaned in frustration and turned away. Eri thought she was being dragged along on another job hunt that would ultimately make them move again for Ash's sake. Ash had already apologized to her twice before about having to move so they could pay rent, but this time seemed different. Ash was insisting on Eri getting the job that she desired as the catalyst for their departure from Corinth, not Ash suddenly losing a job or a bad breakup with a boyfriend.

The prospect seemed appealing enough to Eri to at least consider it. Corinth was not the kind of place that was best suited for people who wanted something more. It was the kind of town that offered dead-end jobs that only paid well because other people left as soon as they had the opportunity.

The duality of a mining town. Good pay with a great culture, but not much else. Despite that issue, Ash's insistence on applying to the freight job made Eri suspicious of her sister's true intentions. Eri wondered if Ash wanted to get away from Corinth because she had discovered her boyfriend was cheating on her with other women. It was becoming a pattern for Ash to leave a town or city whenever she had a bad breakup.

"Why do you want this job so badly?" Eri asked in frustration.

"Well, I wanted to make it up to ya," Ash said meekly, "I dragged ya along with me to Athens four days away from Yongsan just after ya finished your certification for maintenance engineerin'. If it hadn't been for me getting' fired and unable to pay rent, ya'd probably be in a dream job. I just…I just wanted to give ya the chance I took from ya."

Eri pursed her lips and managed to smirk. Ash didn't want this for herself, she was sacrificing a decent job for her sister's dreams. Eri wasn't entirely convinced though. She knew there would probably be others better qualified than her that were applying. Freighters were willing to pay lots of money for certified maintainers to keep their ships in top shape and to control power if they ever needed to fight or escape pirates.

*Pirates…*

The greatest threat to economic stability and prosperity in the Frontier were the roving bands of pirates that often killed entire crews for a simple pittance of cargo or to salvage or sell the ships they captured. Would she be willing to work on a freighter and risk getting killed—or worse—by pirates?

"I don't know…" Eri managed to say.

"Please, Eri," Ash pleaded, "at least give it a chance. Ya never know what kind of pay they may be givin' and what kind of ship they'll be flyin'."

"Woo, yay," Eri began sarcastically, "I can't wait to be on a really nice ship when I get killed by pirates."

Ash scoffed and waved dismissively, "Look, I was in the Yongsan militia flotilla for years before Dad died—pirates are *heavily* exaggerated in the Frontier. It's all Feddie propaganda to get people to come back since they lost the war. The people that mostly get hit by pirates are drug runners staying away from major hyperspace lanes. As long as these guys stay in the major lanes, we'll probably never run into pirates."

Eri breathed in deeply through her nose. Ash was probably right, given her experience, but she didn't like the idea of never truly having a home and just paying rent on an apartment that they'd probably use for only three weeks out of the year. She just wanted stability.

The past two years had been tough and chaotic, and the last thing she needed was to completely uproot herself again. The one thing stopping her from outright refusing was the thought of finally working on a ship's drive core. She hadn't touched one beyond winterizing the occasional millionaire's travel yacht since her maintenance engineering certification test.

"Alright, fine," Eri conceded.

"Awesome. When do ya get off work?" Ash asked.

"I get off at four."

Ash shook her head, "Damn, that asshole making ya work ten-hour days again?"

"Don't remind me," Eri muttered as she went back to working on the car in her bay.

"Alright, I'll come pick ya up at four and we'll go meet them."

Ash ran out of the shop with a gleeful spring in her step despite all the armor and ammunition she carried. Eri tightened a bolt to spec, the torque wrench squealing to notify her of proper newton measurement. She wiggled the wrench free as she heard Ash's truck start and drive away.

*She better hope that I don't regret this…*

When four o'clock arrived, Eri washed her hands and gestured over her tool to get it to wake up. The holographic amber screen came to life over her wrist. She selected the app that allowed her to clock out, but before she submitted her hours, she heard an all-too-familiar bark.

"Eri, I need you to stay a couple more hours. I've got two customers who want power cells replaced."

Eri growled quietly as she looked up from her tool. Her boss, the shop's owner, trudged over to her. "Listen, these two are willing to pay overtime rates, I just need you to stay for two hours."

"I'm not staying, Juan!" she yelled, "I've been here for ten hours already, and I have things to do tonight. If you want to service those customers, fine, but I'm not staying any longer."

"Eri, please," Juan pleaded, "you'll get double-time overtime."

"You said that last week and then you stiffed me with time-and-a-half. You're lucky I don't report you to the Labor Board."

"All I'm asking is for you to be a team player tonight. I'll even give you Saturday off."

"Hold on," Eri said angrily, "you already gave me Saturday off because it was my friend's wedding, remember?"

"Oh, yeah…right…" Juan said as he scratched his head in embarrassment.

Eri waited for Juan to respond, but he never muttered a word.

"So, are you going to give me tomorrow off as well?" Eri asked in anticipation.

"Absolutely not," Juan replied in disgust, "you already have a ton of work to fill your entire day tomorrow."

"So you were ready to give me a day off, but when you heard that I was going to have a day off already, you back off and ask me to still work as usual?"

"C'mon, Eri, be a team player and help me out here," Juan said quietly to keep the customers' attention away from the argument. Eri glared at Juan. "Besides, who else is gonna hire you? Everyone in town is laying off maintainers."

Eri's anger boiled to the surface. She knew Juan was lying. Other shops were desperate for a certified maintainer. The only reason why she took the job with Juan was because he worked on ships and he let her winterize them.

"You know what? You're a piece of shit. I quit!"

Eri pressed submit on her tool and stormed out toward Ash's truck, which was patiently waiting outside the shop.

"Hey!" Eri yelled to the customers as she walked out, "This guy's an asshole who won't hire more workers and overworks the ones already working for him." Juan held up his hands, his face contorting to appear innocent. "By the way, he's overcharging you by twenty percent." Eri turned back to Juan and gave him a rude gesture.

"What the fuck was that about?" Ash asked as Eri slammed the door shut. "And stop slammin' my doors!"

Eri breathed deliberately to calm herself while music played softly through the truck's speakers. "I quit. I'm just fucking done with him. He wanted me to work two more jobs replacing power cells. Said it was only two hours. It would have taken at least three and a half…"

"So…you're saying ya want the freight job?" Ash asked with a smile.

"Let's see how it goes first. There's a couple of shops that have tried to hire me in the past. I'm sure if the freight job doesn't work, they'll hire me in a heartbeat…and they're unionized."

Ash smirked and started the truck. "Alright then, ya can shower and change and then we'll meet with the freighters."

After a ten minute drive, Eri went inside their prefab apartment and showered. Sweet relief fell down her face alongside the tepid water. She felt free, liberated. Juan may have paid well and gave her the opportunity to work on ships, but he still treated her and the two other maintainers at the shop terribly. She was the only certified maintainer in the shop and Juan was able to skirt around regulatory authorities by requiring her to sign off on all work. The system meant that she was constantly at the shop approving work while the only other certified maintainer, Juan, was able to go home.

"You don't have a spouse and kid, so you should help out more" was practically Juan's mantra at the shop. He made sure that he always had single or unmarried employees so he could force them to work longer hours without getting fined by the Labor Board. Juan, in short, was a slimy owner who took every advantage he could to make a profit and used laws as a cudgel rather than as a boundary.

Eri emerged from her room with her hair tied up and still damp. Ash waited in the living area with her security uniform still on, armor and all. Eri glared at her taller and older half sister.

"What?" Ash asked finally.

"Are you seriously going in your uniform?"

"Why not?"

"Ash," Eri began, holding back a laugh, "they're going to see right through you and see how hard you're trying to impress them. You're going to have the exact opposite effect that you're hoping for. The freighters will see you as a poser. Just wear street clothes and open carry your gun if you think you have to show off anything."

Ash sighed through her nose to demonstrate her annoyance with her sister. "Fine," she said, "but I'm not gonna put my hair down." Eri heard Ash removing her armor and rifling through her closet. After a short while, Ash returned to the living area wearing street clothes with her pistol in a thigh holster. "Alright, let's go."

Eri took the tie out and let her damp hair fall to her shoulders. Her naturally wavy brown hair dried better in the Corinth summer. They jumped into Ash's truck, and Ash groaned as Eri put the truck's roof down so she could dry her hair.

"Quit complaining," Eri replied, "you know my hair dries best like this."

"Ya wouldn't be sayin' that if you had straight hair like me," she said as she tucked her ponytail behind her back, inside her shirt. Ash put on sunglasses to protect her jade green eyes from the blinding sun and headed toward the intended destination.

"So where are we going?" Eri asked loudly over the wind.

"Ray's," Ash said plainly.

"The dealership?"

"Yup."

"And you don't see anything wrong with that?"

"The job postin' said that their ship is just parked out back behind the dealership and they don't work for Ray."

"Wait!" Eri yelled as she turned to Ash, her wavy hair blowing violently in the wind. "Isn't there a scrapyard behind Ray's?"

"I dunno," Ash replied with a shrug.

Eri already didn't like the sound of this job prospect. If the ship was behind Ray's Astral, that meant the ship was more than likely poorly maintained, and she had her work cut out for her. The truck pulled into the dealership and drove to the back ,where the sisters found a half-completed ship and two men, both extremely dirty and sweaty, who were placing an outer panel to the hull. It was a Kandahl AG-53, an underappreciated classic first introduced about fifty years ago.

The ship was at the top of a large mound of dirt that elevated it above the road, and the approach up to it was littered with crates stacked on each other. A few of the crates were open in the hot Corinth sun, but many others were closed. By Eri's estimation, the crates were more than likely parts and supplies used to help restore the ship, waiting to be used by the ship's owners.

It was an odd sight. In the middle of this scrapyard was this mostly intact ship, and the few other ships present were tucked away in the farthest spots, rusted beyond repair. The Kandahl AG-53 sat between tall piles of scrap metal as if it had been built from the very scrap within the yard. Eri hummed with apprehension.

"See? Nothin' to worry about," Ash said with a wink.

"It's still mostly unfinished," she retorted.

Eri took a closer look as she got out of the truck, her hair now perfectly dried. The ship's exterior seemed to be mostly repaired and replaced. The outer hull panels were unpainted and shiny. The rear cargo ramp had been lowered, and she could see that the interior was in desperate need of repair and restoration. Parts of the interior were rusted or simply nonexistent. The paint on the interior was heavily chipped and peeling from the walls. The AG-53 may have been a good choice, but the sheer amount of necessary work made her think the freighters might be in over their heads.

"Can I help ya?" the first man asked as he wiped his face and hands with a towel.

"Yeah, I'm Ashley Erikson, the one who responded to your job postin'. This is my sister Erina Bezek, she's a certified maintainer."

"Pleased to meet ya," the man said with a typical Frontier accent and an outstretched arm to Eri, "I'm the ship's captain, Francis Flores."

Eri shook Francis' hand and took in his towering height. He was a full head taller than Ash, and she was as tall as the average man. He must have been forty-five centimeters taller than Eri. She only came up to the man's chest.

Francis was of medium olive complexion with black hair and brown eyes. Body hair drenched in sweat poked out from underneath his shirt collar and seemed to end only at his neck and face. He had a scruffy but kempt beard of a modest length that complimented his dark black hair. He smiled, showing his white teeth and shook their hands firmly like a businessman.

"How did you two find a Kandahl AG-53?" Eri asked. She couldn't help but inquire about the story of the beautiful ship under heavy renovation.

Francis opened his mouth, but the other man interrupted with an authoritative but bored voice. "Do you think you're going to impress me with that company-supplied service pistol and that store-bought nylon thigh holster?"

Eri looked around Francis's tall, but slender frame. At the end of the ship's chassis, the second man was crouched and welding a hull panel to the frame with a torch. He stopped and lifted his welding mask to reveal an incredibly dirty face. He dropped the tools and removed his gloves, then lowered the zipper on his coveralls as he approached them to allow air to cool him.

"No, I just like to open carry when I'm off duty," Ash lied.

"Sure you do," the second man said sarcastically while he walked toward Ash. He stopped in front of her, leaving some room for him to examine her. His head looked down at her feet and then up to her face. He scoffed with contempt. "Let me guess: militia before you started working for a security company?"

"Yeah, Yongsan," Ash replied plainly. Her sister and the man were practically the same height.

"Well, you won't fool either of us if you think you're going to impress…especially when you claim that you open carry. You don't have a round chambered in your sidearm." Ash stiffened.

He turned his head and gazed at Eri for a moment. She noticed his eyes were a deep and vibrant blue like the ocean far out beyond the coast. His expression was extremely serious, cold, and full of calculation.

"Please excuse my cousin, Charlie," Francis said with a slightly annoyed tone. "The first officer may have terrible manners, but he's one of the smartest and toughest guys you'll ever meet. He'll be the security chief once we have a crew together."

Charlie's eyes lingered for a moment on Eri, then flicked back to Ash. He closed the gap between them and Eri could feel how uncomfortable Ash felt, despite both her and Charlie being the same height. Ash leaned back and looked away.

"How many fights have you been in, Ashley?" he asked as he crossed his arms.

"Like…firefights?"

"No, dogfights," he replied with sarcastic annoyance.

"Well…none," she replied sheepishly.

"What kind of guns do you possess?" he asked.

"I've only ever had issued weapons," she replied as she looked down.

"Why?"

"Too expensive. I've been savin' up to get one of my own though."

Ash continued to look at her feet as he nodded.

"At least you're being honest now," he remarked. "You should always assume that people can see through your bullshit."

He continued to look at her. There was a long silence between them with Ash becoming more and more obviously nervous with each passing moment. Eri glanced at the tall captain, but he just watched intently, as if Charlie's silent examination and interrogation meant something.

"Well, if you don't have a weapon, then you definitely won't have any armor," Charlie finally said. "Let me ask you, Ashley: why would I hire you when I could just hire a merc?"

"Because it wouldn't just be another job for me," she answered. "Eri is my sister, and if ya hire her, I'd do everythin' I can to keep her safe, more than just some merc gettin' a paycheck."

"But with your lack of experience and training, how much will that matter?" he asked.

Ash looked away. "I don't know."

Charlie swiftly exhaled through his nose like a bull, seeming unimpressed by what he saw with Ash, then made his way to Eri. The afternoon sun hit his right side, causing a slight glare to appear on his hand. His hand wasn't black from dirt—it was metal.

"If you had a budget of two hundred thousand shen," Charlie began as he walked around Francis and squared himself directly in front of Eri, "what kind of drive core and generator would you put in an AG-53?"

Eri pulled her index finger's knuckle up to her lips as she thought for a moment. "What do you plan on doing with the ship? You're practically rebuilding it from the ground up."

Charlie's eyes narrowed as he thought about her question. "Let's say I want to put in the strongest shield generator for this size ship and arm it with six railgun turrets, two nose-mounted beam cannons, and two side-mounted missile bays…what would be your answer?" he asked.

Eri thought again. "Well, you have many choices, but if you want the very best for that price and not go overbudget, you'd need to get a Lestour E-7 and accompany it with a Bestok D-453, preferably one that was built before Lestour was bought by Sunstreak."

Charlie's eyes began to wander all around Eri like the examination he'd just conducted on her sister. Finally, his eyes met Eri's hazel ones. His gaze pierced directly into her, the silence between them palpable. In the awkward pause between them, she noticed small details on his face; the welding mask unfortunately concealed much of his head. The right side of his face showed numerous scars, and his right ear had a small chunk removed from the edge.

*What's he thinking?*

Charlie's deep blue eyes lifted away from hers and he glanced at Francis. "I like her," he said with an approving smirk. He turned away and started heading back to his workspace. Charlie then rearranged himself and said, "Erina can stay, but I need to see more with Ashley."

He then put the welding mask back down in front of his face. Eri couldn't quite put her finger on it, but there was a hint of some accent in Charlie's voice when he mispronounced her name. He said it with emphasis on the Er and had a soft I rather than a hard, emphasized I.

"I guess I answered correctly," Eri concluded uneasily to Francis.

Francis leaned in. "That's probably the best compliment ya could get from my wordy cousin," he whispered with a wink. He then turned back to Charlie and shouted, "Why don't ya put that shit down and show Erina—"

"You can just call me Eri," she quickly corrected him.

"Eri, the shuttle?"

"Another time," Charlie retorted, "I need to get this panel welded today or we'll be behind schedule…again. Besides, I have a doctor's appointment in an hour."

"Charlie, let me do the fucken panel and show Eri around, god damnit. You'll still have time to see the doctor as well."

Charlie stopped and yanked off his welding mask. He pressed his lips together as he removed his gloves again and unzipped his coveralls to his navel, revealing a plain tank top soaked in sweat. He shimmied himself out of the top of his coveralls to reveal more than just a prosthetic hand, but an entire arm.

Before stem cell regeneration treatments became easy to manufacture and worked effectively, cybernetic prosthetics were common, but that was over fifty years ago. Now, unless you lost the limb for too long of a time before treatment or had a medical condition, you could repair and regrow anything within a fraction of the time it used to take. Limbs were bo longer lost completely unless untreated for a few days. Broken bones took days to repair, not weeks or months. She wondered what could have caused him to lose the arm completely.

Eri's mouth moved on its own and she gaped at the cybernetic limb until Francis stepped between her and Charlie.

"Don't look at it too much," Francis whispered loudly, "the arm is a very touchy subject with him."

Eri nodded at Francis as she heard Charlie say, "Just because the war made you deaf and you can't hear yourself whisper, doesn't mean *I* can't hear you."

Eri held back laughter. She couldn't quite put her finger on it, but there was something about Charlie that made her appreciate his blunt nature and utter lack of decorum. She saw Francis roll his eyes before he turned to Ash.

"Ya and I can discuss a few things while Charlie shows her the shuttle," he said with a smile.

Eri could see Ash's sudden lack of enthusiasm. Charlie's demeanor and words had definitely damaged her ego and self-esteem. Charlie did not wait for Eri and walked around the other side of the Kandahl. She ran to catch up with him. As she approached, she was able to study him closer. For a man, he was average, or barely taller than average. He had short, dark hair of an indescribable color turned almost black by sweat. The straps on the welding mask had created indentions all throughout his hair, making it look incredibly unkempt and dirty.

As she started to walk alongside him, she noticed a few tufts and streaks of coarse gray hairs lightly interspersed throughout, and the edging behind his ear was broken up by scars. Until that moment, she had not noticed the scars interspersed along his jaw and neck. It was difficult for her not to look at Charlie's prosthetic, but it was clear that the designer did their best to match his other arm.

While Francis had the tall, lean, and slender body of a runner, Charlie had more of a build akin to a martial artist or a boxer. Where Francis had dark and course body hair throughout, Charlie had significantly less hair that was finer and lighter in color. Where Francis had a short and scruffy beard, Charlie was clean-shaven. Though Francis said they were cousins, the only similarity between them was their skin tone, though Francis's was darker. If the captain had not mentioned their relation, she would have never guessed it.

"How long have you been working on ships?" he asked.

"I haven't done much with ships, to be honest," she replied.

Charlie grunted with approval. "Not one to oversell yourself?"

"Better to be honest," she said with a shrug as she looked down at her feet. She did everything she could to avoid looking at his arm.

"Let me ask you then," he said as he looked at her through the side of his eye, "how did you know the E-7 and D-453 would fit in the engine room?"

Eri looked away for a moment and then looked at the eye gazing at her. "My dad loved ships. He always wanted to refurbish a classic model and journey the stars when he retired. He wanted me to help him restore a Daniels R-6. The R-6 and the AG-53 pretty much have the same size engineering compartments."

Charlie nodded slowly with approval. "You and I had the same idea for drive core and shield generator. Unfortunately, I don't know whether that shows my knowledge is better than I thought, or if it demonstrates your lack of knowledge."

"I wouldn't say it's either, to be honest," she replied.

Charlie stopped and faced her. "Explain," he demanded.

"The E-7, especially the pre-buyout E-7, is well-known for its performance and reliability and the D-453 is a well-tested compliment to it. Many freighters and yachts this size use that combo. If money was no object, I would have other recommendations."

"Indulge me and tell me what you would pick if we didn't have a budget."

Eri looked away from him for a moment as she thought.

"More than likely, I would recommend one of those new Nebula YT-92s that came out last year for the drive core, though I don't know if it would actually fit. I'd have to look at the manual."

"And for the shields?"

"If the YT-92 was around the same size as an E-7, I'd go with a Sunstreak RS-105. They claim that the RS-105 has better protection against particle beam weapons despite it being the same size as a D-453."

"Fair enough," he replied as he brought his metal hand up to his chin. "What do you know about weapon systems?"

"I know how to maintain and repair them when things go wrong, but they weren't ever something I studied a whole lot," she answered with a shrug. "If you have any question about drive cores, I'd probably answer it, but shields and weapons aren't really my specialty."

"Honest again," he remarked. His eyes narrowed. "When did your father die?"

Eri's eyes widened mostly because of the neck-breaking change of subject. "How did you know…" she asked slowly and with apprehension.

Charlie exhaled sharply through his nose as he continued toward the shuttle, "You said everything in the past tense. No one talks about their parents in the past tense when discussing their plans for retirement unless they died before that happened."

Eri realized at that moment that Charlie listened carefully and with intent. Francis's assessment concerning Charlie's intelligence was not unwarranted; his brain clearly never stopped thinking. Even an explanation as innocuous as hers had meaning to him.

"A little over two years ago," she answered somberly.

"I don't mean to open old wounds or offend," he explained plainly, but cordially. "I apologize if I did. I was just curious."

"No, it's alright," Eri lied.

Charlie glanced at her for a moment, then returned his eyes forward.

"Here it is…*Fire Arrow*," he said with discernable pride as he pointed to the small red ship in front of the AG-53.

"Oh, you are using a Daniels Dart as a shuttle…that's kind of clever, to be honest."

"Take a look around. What can you tell me about her?" he asked.

*This is a test. What small details can I see?* She scanned the length of the hull, noticing a slight bump where the drive core sat inside its slender frame. She saw that the three gimbled machine guns that the manufacturer affixed to the nose from the factory had been replaced with two static railguns. *Fire Arrow* also had a strange pod attached to the top just over the cockpit. She didn't know what it was, but it was definitely something important. She began to physically inspect the ship by walking around, looking underneath, and touching various panels. She stopped and turned back to Charlie, who had silently followed her through the whole inspection.

"New drive core, custom-fitted shield generator, new armaments—my guess would be a torpedo tube is up at the top—and increased armor."

Charlie stood there like a statue, his hands clasped behind his back. He slowly tilted his head.

"…and?"

Charlie's response confused her. *What did I miss?* Her eyes darted back and forth to see anything else different with the shuttle. She couldn't find anything, but Charlie's demeanor suggested that she had missed something, and was giving her a chance at redemption.

After a short while, she looked down at her feet and muttered, "I don't know."

Charlie remained static. Eri could not help but look up to see his response. He silently looked at her, his attitude remaining completely neutral.

*Did I pass the test? Was all of this to see if I was bullshitting him? Why won't he say anything?*

Without saying a word, Charlie turned around and started walking toward Francis and Ash, who were having a cordial discussion. Eri followed at a distance. She failed—she must have. She wanted to ask, but any time she thought about it, her mouth refused to move. She suddenly felt dread. As Charlie approached Francis and Ash, he put his arms back into the coverall sleeves. He stopped to whisper something to Francis, and then walked up the cargo ramp into the AG-53 without saying another word. By the time she joined Francis and Ash, they were shaking hands.

"Well, we appreciate the opportunity," Ash said in poorly veiled defeat, "we hope to hear from ya soon." Ash looked at Eri and smirked, clearly trying to hold back her disappointment, "Let's go home, they need to discuss it."

Eri looked down at her feet. "I think I ruined it for us," she admitted after Francis was out of earshot.

Ash put her arm around Eri and led her to the truck. "Don't worry about it. Who knows? Maybe they just wanna iron out the details. After all, we were probably the first people to respond to the job ad. They posted the openin' this morning." The two got into the truck, Eri closing her door slowly. "Besides, if anyone messed it up, it was me. Francis told me that Charlie is the one that has final say on hirin' or firin' people. Ya heard what he said about me…" Ash drove for a short while in silence, then took a sudden right. "Fuck it, let's go to *Akhmed's*. Ya and I both don't have work tomorrow and ya should relax before heading to Athens for Huang's weddin' on Saturday."

Eri smiled as the two headed to the bar. If there was one thing she really enjoyed doing with Ash, it was throwing darts while having a few drinks. They entered the bar and noticed all the regulars had filled up the bar top. The sisters sat down at one of the corner booths. Before they could even start talking, the waitress came by and delivered two glasses.

"Ya know me so well, Ish'e," Ash said to the waitress.

"And what will you have tonight, Eri?" the waitress asked with a smile.

"I'll have what she's having," Eri replied as she pointed to Ash's usual mixer.

"Okay, I'll just bring out another for ya, Ash."

Ash nodded and watched Ish'e leave. Eri grabbed the second mixer and raised her glass for a toast. They clinked their glasses and both took large gulps.

"Eh, fuck those guys anyway. That Charlie guy is a *giant* asshole," Ash exclaimed over the bar noise, "you'll probably get a better job workin' for one of the shops around here."

Eri smiled slightly knowing that Ash was doing what she could to help lighten the mood. "I liked what they had planned to do with that AG-53 though. Whatever they're going to transport, they won't be messing around."

Ash looked away for a moment, seeming to ponder something. "Fuck 'em. Let's play some darts."

# Chapter 2

Charlie watched Erina intently as she scanned *Fire Arrow*. He could tell from their short conversation that she was fairly knowledgeable and wasn't just an ordinary maintainer. He couldn't quite put his finger on it, but there was something about her that made his intuition go wild. There was an X-factor with her that he hadn't quite placed. If he didn't hire her, her potential would be wasted. He grasped his hands behind his back, watching the tiny details in her eyes and body language just as he was taught so many years ago.

He saw her eyes stop briefly over the extra armor panels that he had affixed to the hull, the rather obvious torpedo tube, the custom-fitted shield generator, the weapons, and the drive core. After seeing those, her eyes danced around on one more pass to see if she missed anything. Besides seeing the custom interior that he had made, she had spotted all the changes.

"New drive core, custom-fitted shield generator, new armaments—my guess would be a torpedo tube is up at the top— and increased armor," she finally replied.

*Impressive. Let's see if the alterations were too obvious or if she is as detail-oriented as she appears.*

"…and?" he said to bait her.

She immediately turned toward *Fire Arrow*, and he could see fear and confusion on her face as her eyes raked from side to side to see if she had missed something.

*Impressive, but has some self-confidence issues. She seemed so confident before…*

Charlie could see in Eri's eyes that her confidence diminished completely. His eyes narrowed as he watched her slowly look down at her feet.

"I don't know."

*Interesting…*

Charlie didn't say a word. He made his considerations regarding Erina as he marched to his cousin.

*She clearly has talent—or in the very least works hard with her trade—but her confidence wavers when presented with something unknown. Out in the galaxy, you need a maintainer that can keep their cool under stressful situations; however, that can be trained. Her knowledge seems extensive and she is honest, something in short supply in the Frontier.*

Charlie then realized that Eri had not said a word and was following at a distance.

*She's shy. Though she may love to talk about drive cores and such, she's still shy at heart and can't bring herself to ask me if she passed my little test. If given time to think, will her answer be different?*

Charlie finally pulled himself out of his thoughts when he realized that he was almost on top of his cousin Francis and Ashley, the militia woman who had tried too hard to impress them.

*She on the other hand…I'll need to see her shooting abilities before I make my decision.*

Charlie placed his hand on his cousin's shoulder.

"Write up a contract for Erina, but keep it quiet for now," Charlie whispered in the captain's ear. "I'll test the tall girl tomorrow."

Francis had turned his head slightly to hear his cousin's whisper, but he didn't show any obvious indication he heard. Thankfully, Charlie saw the small changes in his expression that told him that Francis understood. He strode up the cargo ramp and up the aging stairs to the living section of the ship to grab a fresh change of clothes. On his way out, he saw Francis putting on a welding jacket and welding mask.

"Don't worry about the weld," Charlie told him, "I'll take care of it when I get back from the doctor. Besides, your welds are shit."

"Well aren't ya just full of nice fucken compliments today," Francis retorted sarcastically. "I'm so glad that my dear cousin Charlie is here to gimme sweet nothins to boost my confidence."

Charlie stopped at the bottom of the cargo ramp and stared blankly at Francis. "The welds will keep the ship from having catastrophic leaks into the vacuum of space. Do you think that I'd let you make a shit weld on the hull and endanger the lives of the crew just to preserve your fragile feelings?" Charlie chuckled as he walked away. "I'll take care of that last little bit when I get back."

"Love ya too, dickhead," Francis sneered as Charlie disappeared around the corner toward *Fire Arrow*. He walked to the Daniels Dart and lowered the main ramp before heading into the ship and turned on auxiliary power for the drive core. He then marched back to the small bathroom module he had placed into the ship. Before he entered, he raised the access ramp for privacy.

Originally, the Dart was designed for small, one-day jumps between planets and space stations, but Charlie had managed to turn the ship into a shuttle that, if the need arose, could travel for four days at FTL before refueling. With the added longevity to its flight time, he would need something more than just a simple toilet.

He had extended the small toilet room into a full-fledged bathroom with a sink, shower head, and drain. When the shower was needed, the toilet would disappear into a hidden compartment and turn the small module into a shower. He had also added shallow cabinets to keep toiletries, towels, and such for him and other people to utilize on a multi-day trip if needed.

Charlie quickly showered and changed his clothes. He walked over to the locker by the helm and opened it with his left thumbprint and his passcode. The locker snapped open and he retrieved his knife. He was going to see the doctor, so having his pistol on him would be a poor decision, even in a more gun-friendly town like Corinth. Doctors always treated their offices like some sacred temple where nothing could enter without their permission, and it always rubbed Charlie the wrong way.

Charlie grabbed his dirty clothes and coveralls and took them back to the AG-53. Inside the empty engineering compartment where a drive core should be, there was nothing but random items, including the bag for his and his cousin's dirty laundry. After disposing the laundry, he exited the unpainted ship and turned left, where their car was waiting for him. He got inside, turned on the car's power cell, and drove away.

He arrived about twenty minutes later and waited patiently to be called into the back. When he was called, he followed the nurse to another room where she took his vitals and other medical information. He waited again for a long while, but the doctor finally arrived with a courteous knock on the door.

The man walked in and closed the door, not even acknowledging his patient, instead walking to the folder full of information.

"Mister…Menillo," the doctor finally said. "You said that you experienced a migraine a few days ago that was accompanied by a short hallucination. Can you please describe them to me?"

Charlie sighed with frustration. He hated explaining the same thing more than once. "Like I told your nurse: I started experiencing the worst headache that I've ever felt. It honestly felt like someone was digging around inside my skull with a hot knife. While that happened, I saw some sort of hallucination. A man I've never seen before just saying nonsense."

The doctor looked at Charlie blankly, but Charlie could see the small details in his expression and body language. The man seemed moderately concerned, and after skimming through Charlie's medical records, his concern grew.

"Usually," the doctor began, "I would tell someone to come back if it happened two other times within six months, but I have some worries about this given your medical history." The doctor grabbed the thick folder of information and held it as he approached Charlie. "You have had multiple cases of being hospitalized because of head trauma and you survived a…grenade?"

Charlie nodded to confirm.

"You have experienced a lot of trauma in your life so far, and many men like you who were in the revolution that experienced frequent head trauma have come into my office within the past few years. I want to do some thorough tests and see how much damage your frequent head trauma has caused."

"Wait…" Charlie said, "Are you saying I may have…brain damage?"

"Sometimes brain damage is minor and people live with it through a long and prosperous life without ever feeling its effects until an advanced age," the doctor explained. "But people who experience *frequent* head trauma, especially at such a young age, can develop something called traumatic encephalopathy syndrome, or TES. Depending on the extent of the damage, TES is either treatable or fatal. To make matters worse, you have Garner's disorder, and GD will prevent the more experimental treatments that have shown to reverse some of the damage caused by trauma."

"Let me guess," he said with annoyance, "the experimental treatments use long-term neuro-SCR therapies."

"Yes, sir," the doctor confirmed.

"So for me…it's either fatal or just enough to prevent further damage rather than reverse it…" Charlie said it more as a statement than a question, but the doctor confirmed with a nod. "How long does TES take to kill me and what exactly happens?"

"One step at a time," the doctor said with his hands raised. "It's better to be patient and cautious rather than jump to conclusions at this point. I only mentioned TES because it is a significant possibility with your history, but we won't know anything until we get some imaging done. I'm going to send you over to Corinth General Hospital for that. More than likely, neurology won't see you for a couple of days, and then they'll tell you the results."

"Thanks, Doc," Charlie murmured with disbelief as the doctor handed him a note with information, directions, his recommendation for imaging of his brain, and a prescription for strong headache medication.

Ash left the bar earlier than usual. For the first time in a while, Eri had managed to beat her older half sister to the point of making her go home in defeat. She claimed that losing wasn't the reason, but she just wanted to go home early. Eri didn't buy it.

Ash's dart throwing seemed very off that night. More than likely, she was distracted by the afternoon meeting with the freighters. She also left her keys with Eri. Ash often left in the car and Eri walked home alone an hour or two later.

Eri continued sipping on her fourth mixer in the booth as she slowly scanned the room. She noticed over in the smoking section that there was a familiar black arm at a table on the opposite side of the bar illuminated by the embers of a cigarette.

*How long has he been here? Did he follow us?*

Eri slowly got up and made her way over to the smoking section. Charlie was taking a long drag on his cigarette when she noticed he held it differently than everyone else around him. While they held the cigarette between their middle and index finger, Charlie pinched it between his thumb and middle finger. As she got close, a small puff of smoke exited his mouth before swiftly re-entering. He turned to look up at her and exhaled through his nose. The smoke slowly exited his nostrils like a horse's breath in winter.

Charlie's appearance was very different from earlier. He wore a simple shirt that was possibly a size too large for his frame. His hair was no longer disheveled and she could see that it was a strange mix of blond, brown, and black with the few coarse hairs of gray interspersed. She had never seen a hair color like that. He had a cowlick at the front that stood straight and tall, but he simply worked his styling around it, using it as a kind of part for his hair and swooped it to one side.

Next to him on the bench was a large overcoat, something she never saw people wear in the Corinth summer except for the occasional bounty hunter. That was typical with that job to the point that many people didn't wear long coats or dusters so they wouldn't be mistaken as a bounty hunter.

Eri didn't know what to say in the moment, but she knew she had to say *something*. It was clear that Charlie was waiting for her to begin the conversation.

"For someone as smart as you, I didn't expect you to be a smoker," she managed to utter.

*What the* hell *did I just say?*

"Probably one of the worst conversation starters I've ever heard, but if that's how you want to start our little chat, I suppose that would be mildly sufficient."

"You could have started the conversation if you had something better to say…"

Charlie smirked and gestured to the chair across from him. Eri sat down in the wooden chair, which creaked as she put her weight down.

"You'd be amazed how easy it is to remain anonymous if you smoke," he said, "people tend to look away out of disgust or fear that they will offend the smoker."

"How long were you watching us?" she asked with suspicion.

Charlie tapped his cigarette on the side of the ashtray. "I walked in when you two started playing darts. I have to say, I'm quite impressed. You and your tall sister would give Francis a run for his money, and he's the best dart player I've ever seen."

Eri's eyes narrowed, intently watching Charlie's mannerisms and movements. "So what are you doing here, exactly? I don't know you well, but my guess would be that it's no coincidence that you came to the exact dive as Ash and me…"

Charlie took another long drag from his cigarette, the smoke once again exiting and entering his mouth with a hiss. He stamped out the ember inside the ashtray as he slowly released the smoke out of his nose. He never looked at her, only looking down at the ashtray. Eri's stomach tightened as the silence grew between them. Charlie was either deliberately remaining quiet or was deep in thought. Once the ember was fully extinguished, he let the butt fall in place inside the ashtray. He slowly leaned back into the leather bench, the leather squealing against his metal arm, and he looked at her with a barely distinguishable grin.

"You said 'I don't know' when I asked you what else was different on the shuttle. Did you not notice anything else, or did you honestly not know?"

"Huh?" Eri asked in confusion.

"Not off to a good start if you need me to repeat the question," he said flatly.

"I just wasn't expecting it," she replied defensively.

"So did you honestly not know, or did you simply not notice anything else?"

She thought for a moment, going over the details in her mind again. There was nothing out of the ordinary that would suggest that there was something else different about the Dart. Charlie gently rested his face on his cybernetic hand as her eyes darted back and forth, trying to recall every detail of the ship. She reverted her eyes back to his, the deep blue irises now clouded by the smoke.

"There was nothing else changed about the shuttle," she said finally. As far as she knew, nothing else had changed about *Fire Arrow* from the original version of the Dart. She nervously took a swig of her mixer and waited for his reply.

"How confident—"

"Extremely," she squeaked.

Charlie nodded slowly with approval. "Your drinks are on me," he said as he stood up. "Tell the tall one to meet me at Andy's Gun Range tomorrow at eight."

"Wait," Eri pleaded, "does this mean I got the job?"

Charlie smirked slightly. "Let me ask you," he began, "do you want this job because you seek the fairy tale adventures that freighters peddle to get recruits or is it because you want to work on the ship's drive core?"

"I've been a certified maintainer for two years now," Eri replied, "and all I've ever been able to do on ship drives—which are what I've always wanted to work on—was winterize some rich asshole's vacation yacht while he spends the winter in nice beach towns like Athens. I want this job because this is the first real opportunity to not only work on the very thing that I want to work on…but to prove that I was born to work on them."

"And who exactly are you trying to prove this to," he asked flatly, "yourself or someone else?"

"I…no one ever believed that I was cut-out for this kind of work. The only one who believed in me was my dad and…well, you know how that turned out."

"You haven't answered my question, Erina," Charlie remarked in a slightly annoyed tone.

"To *everyone* who said I couldn't," she indignantly replied.

Charlie returned to his seat, lit a cigarette, and signaled to the waiter that he wanted another drink. He took a long drag as the puff of smoke from lighting the cigarette lingered over the table, above his left hand. Eri sat patiently, thinking about all the people who told her that she wouldn't be a good maintainer and that she should instead pursue getting a degree from a university.

"And you can just call me Eri," she added.

"I'm not deaf," he retorted with annoyance, "I heard you say it the first time. It's not my problem that your parents used your full name when they were upset with you and it makes you feel uncomfortable when others say your full name."

The longer Eri spoke with Charlie, the more she realized how well he could read people. His assessment was incredibly accurate, albeit a little harsh. Charlie puffed on his cigarette.

"Are you doing it purposefully to make me uncomfortable?" she asked.

Charlie shifted slightly and tapped the cigarette on the side of the ashtray.

"No I'm doing it to stall because the lady next to us won't stop eavesdropping," he answered as he looked to his right. The woman in the table next to them choked on her drink and coughed uncontrollably. Eri used all of her willpower not to laugh.

"Yeah, yeah, great," he told the woman with an annoyed tone, "either call an ambulance because you're choking or fuck off, lady." The patron gathered her belongings while still coughing on her drink and scurried away.

"How did you know?" Eri asked.

"Just a skill I've learned," he said as he distantly scratched his metal hand.

*Why would he scratch the prosthetic?*

"Do you know exactly what kind of work you will be getting into?" he asked, changing the subject.

"Moving cargo can't be that intricate," she stated with a shrug.

"Hmm," he replied as he took another drag from the cigarette, "so you have no clue then."

"Is there something I *should* know?"

"The life of a freighter—an independent one at that—can be extremely dangerous and difficult." The waiter returned with a beer for Charlie, which he quickly sipped.

"People take commercial flights from one planet to the next typically only once or twice a year, so all they've ever experienced is a smooth and boring flight. When you're out there in hyperspace lanes frequently, especially out here in the Frontier Systems, there's always a chance that you'll run into pirate gangs. There's a reason why Francis and I are sparing no expense with the ship's shields and armaments—well, relatively.

"Pirate gangs are not as prominent as some people want you to believe though, but there is always a chance. There's also a chance that we may have to take a job that asks us to take cargo directly through pirate territory, which would be a major issue. Unlikely, but still a clear and present possibility."

Charlie took another drag of his cigarette and sipped from his beer before exhaling through his mouth. "The biggest danger that we can—and will—face is the more realistic scenario of a less than reputable recipient who would rather try to get the cargo without paying. Gunfights may be the result. Now, it's my job to ensure that it happens as little as possible, but it *is* an eventuality. On the other hand, there may be times too when there simply isn't any work for us, and we'll have to do side jobs to keep the ship flying or just to stave off boredom. When you work as an independent freighter, it can be feast or famine."

He took another drag and sip of his beer, letting his words marinate in Eri's mind for a moment, and to allow her to fully process.

"Look, you're a bright-eyed and optimistic woman who has a lot to prove, but don't think for a second that this is just some ordinary job. Even if what I said deters you from it, I would rather you be mentally prepared and well-forewarned before ever accepting the position. I want someone who would be willing to work for at least a year or two and knows exactly what they are getting into."

Eri nodded slowly, watching Charlie's cigarette butt smolder in the ashtray as she thought deeply about the prospect of her new life. "This job has the capability to be life altering—for better or worse—so don't make your decision just yet. Sleep on it. If you still want it, let Francis know tomorrow."

Charlie stood back up, leaving half of a beer. Eri couldn't help but standing and offering her hand. He looked at her hand and then up at her eyes, which shone with determination. He grasped her hand and she realized that she'd offered her right hand reflexively, so he'd reciprocated with his cold, metallic one.

"Remember, your drinks are on me and tell the tall one to meet me at Andy's tomorrow at eight in the morning."

Eri nodded and softly thanked Charlie. He removed his hand and walked over to the bartender, exchanged a few words, gave him cash, and left.

Eri arrived home shortly before midnight, butterflies still in her stomach as she contemplated Charlie's words. He had offered her the job, but the dangers he'd mentioned gave her pause. Sure, she may now be able to finally work on ships, but was the danger and a constant life on the move worth it?

Ash was watching a movie on the couch when Eri walked through the front door. She placed the keys on the counter where Ash always left them and sighed deeply. Ash eyed her curiously.

"What's with ya?" she asked.

Eri grinned. "You'll never believe who I ran into at the bar."

"Who?"

"Charlie."

Ash's head tilted. "Really…"

"Yes…and he wants you to meet him at Andy's tomorrow morning at eight," Eri stated as she leaned in. Ash looked away and chuckled in disbelief. She turned back to Eri, waiting for more information. "Well, his exact words were 'Tell the tall one to meet me,'" she said, trying to impersonate Charlie's deeper, monotone voice.

"He called me 'the tall one?'" Ash asked with annoyance as Eri joined her on the couch. "What a dick…"

"After you left, I saw him in the smoking section in a dark corner like some movie spy waiting for his informant to arrive. He offered me the job."

"That's great, Eri!" Ash exclaimed with pride. "Did ya accept?"

"Well, that's the thing," Eri replied apprehensively, "he talked to me about the dangers and how hard things may get. He said the same thing you did about pirates though: the danger is there, but not likely. The main thing he wanted me to understand was that there would always be the potential for a gunfight if a cargo exchange went south."

Ash nodded. "Yeah, the people that are supposed to get the cargo may not wanna pay, or some local gang may know about the cargo and want it for themselves. There's always that possibility. You'll be the one keepin' the engine in workin' order, though, so you'll be fine," Ash reassured her.

Eri looked down at her hands. "He told me to sleep on it, but I don't know if I'll ever get this opportunity again."

"If you want it, go for it," Ash replied. "You've wanted to work on ships ever since ya started the training program. I want to go along with ya, but I gotta prove myself first."

"You'll do great," Eri reassured her with a smile. "You always have proven the men wrong. You're strong, fast, and smart."

"I don't know about the 'smart' part, but thanks."

"I'm going to bed though." Eri yawned. "Have a good night, and let me know how things go tomorrow morning at the gun range."

"Yeah, definitely," Ash replied confidently, "I'm just going to finish this movie before I go to bed."

# Chapter 3

Ash woke up on the couch in a panic. She forgot to set her alarm. Eri was still fast asleep and enjoying her day off, sleeping late. Ash quickly opened her tool and saw the time. It was 7:43, and it took fifteen minutes to get to Andy's Gun Range from their apartment.

*Fuck.*

Ash quickly changed her clothes and got her holster affixed to her leg. She shimmied her boots onto her feet as she made her way outside and got in the truck. As she darted away from the apartment, she looked at the truck's clock. 7:52.

*FUCK!*

Her morning's bad luck only got worse. Every traffic light was red on her way to the gun range. She pulled into the parking lot at 8:09, already ten minutes late, and that was before she got signed in, signed waivers, and bought extra ammunition. She walked outside to the reserved range lane at 8:21. Charlie had already shot a few downrange; casings were littered on the table and ground in their lane.

*...fuck...*

She approached the lane as Charlie intently looked down his rifle sight, his breathing slow and deliberate, finger lightly resting on the trigger. Charlie had dressed in full armor, minus the helmet. From the look of it, she knew it was incredibly expensive and advanced, military-grade or better. Either way, it was better armor than she ever wore, even when she was in the Frontier Militia. When she was within just a few arms' lengths, Charlie fired. He looked up from his sight and pulled back the bolt, letting the casing fly out of the breach, then pressed down on the safety switch.

"You're late," he said as he adjusted the top knob on his sight.

"I'm sorry," she began shakily, "I forgot to—"

"I don't need your fucking excuses, Tall Hands," he said as he got up and faced her, "you want to be on my ship as part of the security team and you can't even be bothered to wake up early enough."

*"Tall Hands?" Is he makin' fun of my height?*

"Look, I'm sorry, it won't—"

"*Ever* fucking happen again," he growled as he interrupted her, his finger pointing at her face. "Let me ask you: why would I ever consider allowing you on my ship after showing up to the range like this?"

Ash looked down in disgrace. He was absolutely right. If there was any other way to have a worst first impression, she wouldn't know. "If you don't wanna hire me, I understand."

Charlie got into Ash's face so close that she could smell his shitty cigarette breath. "I asked you a fucking question…now answer the question, god damnit," he growled.

Ash stiffly stood there with Charlie's face directly in front of hers. If he was any closer, their noses would touch. She finally looked into Charlie's eyes. His pupils were shrunk like a predatory animal watching its prey.

"Ya should only consider me based on my performance, and my performance so far has been shit," she muttered. "I would like to prove myself with my range skills to at least gain enough of your approval to make up for being late."

"Fucking Christ," he grumbled with disgust as he finally backed away, "you couldn't have answered that more like a corporate PR rep. Did your PAO teach you that before you started driving a money truck?"

"No," she answered sheepishly.

"You know," he began with a scoff, "I figured you all wrong. I thought for sure you were going to be the overcompensating woman with a chip on her shoulder who would be here an hour before I arrived and so fucking uptight and hell-bent on proving your worth that you'd be insufferable. Yet, here I am, *absolutely pissed* that you would show up twenty-two minutes late like a fucking stoner showing up for their dead-end job.

"You were in the militia, but you weren't ever in combat, which means by all calculations you have *everything* to prove, and you've already started off on the wrong foot! Fuck, you're so deep in the cellar already, you might as well write your own fucking epitaph. Do me a favor and either walk away now and fulfill your destiny as being nothing more than a rent-a-cop or step up to this bench and make a hit on that steel. But I warn you: if you miss that fucking steel, you will *never* work for me, not even as a temporary gun-for-hire. I would hire a quadriplegic before I hire you."

Ash was numb. She'd served in the militia for four years, but her ass had never been chewed down to the bone. Charlie's words felt like daggers going straight for her heart and ego. He knew exactly what to say and how to say it to get under her skin. He did have her figured out, the only difference was she was so excited the night before that she forgot to set her alarm for 6:00. She *would* have been the exact kind of woman that he predicted.

If there was anything that she wanted, it was to prove to men like Charlie that she could keep up with them and be just as good of a soldier as them. Francis had mentioned to her that Charlie was a hard-ass and a war veteran, and she really wanted to prove to him that she deserved to be part of his security team.

*Maybe I am just destined to be a security guard…*

"I'm fucking waiting, Tall Hands," he barked, "are you going to hit steel or not?"

*Quit it with the Tall Hands shit, asshole…*

Ash took a deep breath and regained her composure. It was now or never. She slowly approached the bench with the rifle and sat behind it. She shouldered the rifle with her eye affixed to the crosshairs. Her breathing slowed as she composed herself, trying to block out everything Charlie had said. She slowly pushed the bolt forward and locked it in. The steel target looked far, and she knew she needed to adjust for distance. She closed her eyes and felt the light easterly breeze, then placed the crosshairs just above the silhouette's left shoulder. She let her breathing create a rhythm with the rifle, slowly rising and falling until she rested her finger on the trigger.

*Fuck...safety.*

Ash pressed the safety off and once again allowed her breathing to create upward and downward motions. She held her breath and squeezed the trigger with her fingertip. The trigger clicked and the bullet fired much sooner than she expected—it practically surprised her. The trigger was so light that it more than likely required only the absolute bare minimum of squeeze allowed.

The time between firing the shot and confirmation of a hit felt like an eternity. She never let her eye wander from the sight. After what felt like ages, a small puff of dust erupted from the target's right abdomen. She finally realized that she had yet to breathe again. Instead of a gentle sigh of relief, she quickly gasped for air as the sound of the bullet hitting the steel finally reached her ears.

"Well, you hit the steel," Charlie said behind his spotter's scope, unimpressed, "but I know by your shitty breathing that it was half luck. Breathe like a fucking human being and shoot again."

Seven grueling hours and hundreds of rounds later, Charlie finally ended the range session. Ash's shoulder throbbed from shooting the large caliber round so many times. She'd lost count, but Charlie had pushed the brass casings into the dirt in front of the table over a dozen times. The massive pile must have been *far* into the hundreds.

She slowly got up from her chair, dehydrated, exhausted, and stiff. She weakly looked at Charlie. He gazed into her eyes for a moment, then reached for one of his pouches. He unhooked the pouch and pulled out a cold pack and some elastic bandage. He squeezed the pack until the pouch inside burst and started the endothermic process. Without saying anything, he put the pack inside her shirt on the shoulder and wrapped the bandage to hold it in place.

Charlie looked at her again. "Well, Tall Hands," he began as he readjusted the cold pack, "you're not completely useless. I'm going to pack things up, get out of this armor, and then I'll take you home."

"I can drive home, it's okay," Ash replied weakly.

"Here's another lesson then, Tall Hands," Charlie said as he grabbed the rifle's barrel with his prosthetic hand. The barrel was incredibly hot from all the shots. Even with his armor providing some protection from the heat, it would have still burned his skin if he hadn't had a metal arm. A perk of having no nerve endings or skin. She had only seen one other prosthetic arm before, and it was much simpler than his. His arm looked custom. "Doing everything you can to prove that you can hang with the men will only lead to self-destruction.

"There's nothing wrong with admitting when you are hurt," he continued as he grabbed a spare bag, "and there's nothing wrong with understanding your limits and being humble with your abilities. No one likes a show-off and no soldier worth their salt ever wants to share a foxhole with someone who's got a chip on their shoulder. If you want to prove yourself to me, then shut the fuck up and learn to follow orders instead of letting your fragile ego get in the way."

Charlie stared her down as he turned to walk back inside, Ash in-tow.

"Stay right fucking there and I'll be out in ten," he said as he dropped the rifle bag and ammo bag at her feet and headed into the men's locker room with a third. He returned ten minutes later, just as he predicted, wearing street clothes. He grabbed the rifle bag as Ash reached for the ammo bag. Charlie slapped her hand out of the way and grabbed the last bag. "What the fuck did I just say, Tall Hands? You have a memory problem?"

Ash looked away and meekly replied, "No."

Charlie lazily threw all of his bags into the truck bed and headed toward the driver's door. He opened to find Ash sitting in the passenger seat.

"At least you have ears, Tall Hands," he said with a hint of sarcasm.

*What's his fucken deal with callin' me that?*

Charlie adjusted the seat and mirrors and started the truck's power cell. He lowered the top as he pulled out of the parking lot, Ash quietly groaning with frustration.

*Why won't anyone just enjoy the fucken AC?*

Charlie didn't say a word the rest of the drive back to Ash's apartment. It wasn't until they arrived that she realized she never gave him directions to her house.

"How do ya know where I live?" she asked.

Charlie stared at her in disbelief. "Are you serious right now?"

Ash thought for a second. Why would he know her address and why does it seem like it would be obvious that he knows their address?

*The application. The job application has my address on it...*

"Never mind," she said as she got out.

"I'm going to drop my equipment off at the ship and I'll return your truck." Ash nodded quietly and turned toward her apartment. "Hey!" She turned back to look at him. "Don't be late next time," he said as he drove off.

*Can't believe that asshole gave me a second chance. Why'd he gimme a second chance?*

Ash dragged her feet and held the cold pack to her shoulder as she made her way to the front door. She weakly knocked and waited, her eyes now getting heavy despite it being in the middle of the afternoon. Eri slowly opened the door and examined Ash.

"You look like shit," Eri said with surprise.

"I don't wanna talk about it," Ash replied as she moved past her sister and crashed onto the couch. She grunted loudly as she fell on the cushions.

"Wait…have you been shooting with Charlie the *entire day*?" Eri queried in disbelief.

"Practically blew out my fucken shoulder doin' it," Ash grumbled.

Eri pulled the now warm pack away from Ash's shoulder. The bruise was so large and dark, Eri probably would've believed Ash if she told her that she had been clipped by a car.

"I'll get you some ice," Eri said as she went into the apartment's small kitchen. She returned shortly with a bag of ice wrapped in a thin towel and handed it to Ash. She hissed as the heavier ice rested on the dark contusion made by the rifle's recoil. They both sat in silence for a moment while the bag of ice did its work.

"I almost fucked everythin' up," Ash finally admitted, "I think the bruise was Charlie's way of punishin' me."

"What do you mean?" Eri asked quizzically.

"I was twenty fucken minutes late this morning. I fell asleep on the couch last night and forgot to set my alarm."

"Damn!" Eri exclaimed. "And he let you stay?"

"Yeah…"

"He must really like you if he let that go. Francis came over with my contract earlier today and said it's really hard to immediately impress Charlie."

"Well, at least one of us was able to impress him." Ash groaned as she sat up on the couch. "So ya decided to take the job?"

"Yeah," Eri replied happily, "I don't care if there's danger, boredom, or the occasional periods where everyone is broke. I want to work on ships. The sightseeing and adventure are just perks."

"I'm happy for ya," Ash said with a smile. "How much are they paying ya?"

"Five percent of all earnings."

"Please tell me ya asked for more…" Ash asked in disappointment.

"That's my pay after all living expenses. I'll have my own room, they pay for all the food, and they will pay for any parts, tools, and whatever else I need," Eri replied.

"So if you wanna new wardrobe, they'll pay for it?"

"Basically. I have to be reasonable with my requests, but the money I take in is just extra money for myself."

"Well damn, that ain't bad at all…" Ash concluded.

"Francis also said that we may make bonuses and we'll be able to request shore leave up to two months out of the year."

"So if I just wanted off the ship for two whole months, they'd be okay with that?"

"I think so…" Eri replied with a shrug.

Ash sat quietly after hearing the terms of her sister's contract. She hoped that she would receive a similar contract. She turned on the monitor and sighed heavily as she scrolled through shows she wanted to watch. After a long while of indecision, she started watching something; however, her exhaustion essentially turned the show into background noise as her mind drifted into nothingness.

# Chapter 4

Eri quietly cooked a simple dinner for them while her sister zoned out on the couch. She was watching some sort of buddy cop series that she had recently started watching to keep her mind off of her most recent breakup with her boyfriend.

Eri grabbed the saltshaker and watched her tall sister lazily put a numbing ointment that helped with bruising on her shoulder. She smirked as she watched Ash continue to rub the topical ointment on her shoulder, enamored with whatever was happening on the monitor. She seasoned their dinner, and as she grabbed the pot's handle to adjust it on the burner, a sudden knock came to the door.

Ash gasped loudly in fright. The gasp, not the knock, caused Eri to jump, and she dropped the pan. It landed on the linoleum floor and spilled all the hot contents with a loud clang.

"God damnit, Ash," Eri exclaimed as she grabbed a towel, "you scared the *shit* out of me! Go answer the door while I clean this up…"

"Sorry," Ash apologized sheepishly as she opened the door.

"May we come in?" Francis asked. Eri couldn't see him because she was cleaning the mess on the floor, but she recognized the captain's voice.

Before Ash could answer, boots clunked onto the apartment's linoleum floor. More than likely, it was Charlie skipping pleasantries and making his way inside past Ash.

"Good to see you keep this shithole clean, Tall Hands," Charlie said.

Eri snickered upon hearing Charlie give his backhanded compliment. He already had a nickname for Ash, and Eri was thankful that Charlie had yet to find a nickname that would get under her skin. Eri honestly never knew what unhinged, brash, or abrasive thing Charlie would say next.

"Anyways," Francis began, "Ashley, Charlie was quite impressed with your moxie today and wanted to also offer ya a contract."

"Thankfully, using an alarm can easily remedy laziness," Charlie retorted with disdain as he walked into the kitchen. He noticed Eri doing her best to clean up all the food that had spilled all over the floor. She saw Charlie slowly scan the cabinetry, look at a drawer, and open it. Inside, he pulled out a clean dish towel and handed it to her without saying a word.

"How did you—"

"Don't even bother," Francis said before Eri could ask her question, "he'll be able to give your entire life story and predict your habits based on the cleanliness of your room and where certain items are stored in the kitchen."

"Bullshit," Eri replied as she put both dirty towels on the counter. "You probably just thought of the most natural spot for dish towels in a kitchen setup like this."

Charlie folded his arms. "You put the dish towels as a central location between the sink and the stove because you have a tendency to spill, slosh, or drop items on the stove, but you still want people to believe that you leave your dish towels near the cleaning space like a normal person, so you keep them as far away as you can from the stove without making the location a complete inconvenience. You keep your eating utensils in the drawer adjacent to the fridge because you enjoy late-night snacks. You also prefer pots to be stored to the left of the stove and pans on the right because your favorite burner for the pots is the back left and your favorite burner for the pans is the front right."

Eri's mouth gaped. How could Charlie possibly know that she loved late-night sweets and snacks?

"It's been a long time since I've seen Eri speechless," Ash said with a giggle.

"You going to sign the fucking contract or not, Tall Hands?" Charlie asked without looking away from Eri. Ash quickly began signing the different sections of the contract.

Francis shook his head with a smile. "Charlie's skills of deduction are always a great party trick to get easy money from people." Ash handed the contract back to Francis, who reviewed it. "I'm assumin' ya signed the contract quickly 'cause Eri brought ya up to speed on the pay and benefits."

"Yup," Ash said with a smile.

"Eri doesn't get hazard pay," Charlie said as he finally averted his gaze from the still-shocked Eri, "you do, Tall Hands."

"Well…how much more is that?" Ash asked sheepishly.

Charlie rolled his eyes and sighed, then began making his way back to the door. "Do you two want to celebrate your new employment with food and drinks on us? Eri ruined your dinner anyway by spilling it on the floor."

"Ash scared me and made me spill it," Eri muttered defensively.

"Yes, or no?" Charlie asked in the doorway.

"I'll never turn down free food and booze," Ash replied.

"Then get in the car and we'll take you there," Charlie barked as he made his way to his and his cousin's car.

The four arrived at High Ton a short time later. They entered the dart-themed bar and Ash pointed over to a table that they could all use. Charlie ignored her and made his way over to a booth on the far side of the bar in the smoking section. Francis just followed him as if he knew that Charlie would choose that spot.

They all sat down, Charlie against the wall and angled to face the door with Francis taking the spot next to him. Eri sat across from Charlie and Ash across from Francis. Eri noticed that Charlie seemed to intently watch the door, his eyes slightly narrowed.

"Like Charlie said, food and drinks are on us tonight to celebrate *Silver Bow*'s two newest crew members," Francis said with a smile.

"You're calling her *Silver Bow*?" Eri asked, her eyes shining with excitement.

"We're leavin' the ship mostly unpainted, and it was only fittin' 'cause the shuttle's name is *Fire Arrow,*" the dark-haired captain replied.

"I like it," Eri replied with a grin, "it has a certain…poetry to her name."

Eri noticed that Charlie briefly glanced at her when she spoke. She couldn't tell if it was a glance of approval or annoyance though. His expression remained neutral as he watched the door. The server came by and returned with all their drinks. Francis had a whiskey mixer, Ash and Eri had sweet and fruity mixers, and Charlie had a beer.

As the women and Francis exchanged stories, Charlie remained focused on the entrance, occasionally retorting with a few monotone words or correcting Francis on certain details of an encounter without ever averting his watchful stare. Charlie only looked away from the door a few times before finally looking at the food that he had ordered. As soon as he finished eating, he returned to watching the door. Eri could feel something was off. There must have been a reason why he was so focused on the entrance.

After getting their food, Charlie remained silent with only a grunt or two directed at Francis whenever the tall man nudged him with his elbow, trying to include him in the conversation. Halfway into a conversation about Ash and Francis comparing their skills in darts, Eri's focus lapsed completely. She stared at Charlie and wondered why he had remained so distant from the conversation and why he continuously watched the front of the bar.

"Tell me who wins," Charlie said in a mildly bored tone. His sudden break in the silence snapped her out of her trance. Ash apparently had challenged Francis to darts. Despite his focus, Charlie had obviously paid attention to the conversation, observing quietly.

Now that Francis and Ash had split from them, Eri finally had her chance to privately ask Charlie how he had figured out the location of everything in her kitchen, especially how he knew about her love of midnight snacks. Since he had accurately guessed where the dish towels were, she wanted to know how he came to that conclusion.

She was too shy to ask it earlier when the four of them were together and eating because she had no idea what kind of brutally blunt things he would say that would embarrass her. She had a feeling that he had already figured her out if he was able to pinpoint everything in the kitchen. The last thing she needed was something that Ash could hold over her head. She could handle whatever visceral assessment he had in a private setting, but she wouldn't let anyone else hear it.

"Well, now that they're gone—"

"You want to go up to the bar top?" Charlie asked as if he'd heard nothing from her. He finally dropped his focus on the door and looked at Eri.

"Uh…sure," she replied, taken aback by his abrupt question.

Charlie got up from the booth and patiently waited for Eri to get out. Once she stood up, he held his right arm out, gesturing to her to lead the way. Eri made her way through the crowd to the bar top. They sat down in the stools with their drinks, Charlie rotating his glass cyclically, balancing it with the centripetal force and a fingertip on his left hand as he raised his prosthetic to summon the bartender. He ordered another beer and turned to her.

"You want to know how I figured out your kitchen setup," he concluded as the bartender sat his new beer onto the coaster.

"Yes, actually."

"You waited for them to leave because you wanted the conversation to be more private?" he asked, waiting for her to confirm.

"Yeah," she responded shyly, "so, how did you figure it out?"

Charlie snorted and smirked as he grabbed his new beer and sipped it. "The power of deduction is nothing more than a learned skill," he began as he once again sipped his beer and scanned the room. "Take that guy over there," he said as he gestured with his beer toward a man sitting at the bar six seats away. "I can tell you right now that he is currently dealing with massive debts and more than likely divorced."

Eri looked at the man. Nothing out of the ordinary would indicate anything that Charlie had concluded. How could he possibly know that?

"So how do you know that?"

"Look closer," he stressed as he leaned in to keep the conversation private, "you'll notice that his tool is showing multiple notifications, probably missed calls from debt collectors. He constantly fiddles with his left ring finger, which probably means that he's been recently divorced and is reflexively trying to turn or fix the position of the now nonexistent ring. If he isn't divorced, then he's trying to fiddle with a ring he sold recently to pay debts. His hair is well-kept, but his shirt has small holes in the seams, which indicates that he's trying to appear financially stable but can't afford to replace a shirt, which is why he's buying drinks often associated with wealthy people but uses well alcohol instead of branded products.

"If you look closely at his fingernails, you'll notice that, although well-groomed, they have dirt underneath them, which indicates he's stressed and probably doesn't shower nearly as often as he used to—an indicator of depression.

"Between conversations with people, his demeanor will change as if his face muscles strain to maintain a smile. Many are too afraid or embarrassed to admit their financial struggles and instead put on a mask of happiness. You can spot the fake smile because most genuine smiles draw up the face over the cheekbones and slightly obscure the eyes, but his lips simply turn up."

Eri began to focus more on the man and noticed the small details that Charlie illuminated to her.

"Deduction is simply a learned skill," he repeated as he leaned back in his chair and swigged some of his beer. "Try it for yourself," he said as he scanned the bar again. "What can you tell me about that woman across from you? Don't just look *at* her, quietly observe and categorize the minute details, think about why they are there. Some are more obvious than others."

Eri looked at the woman sitting across the bar from her. A woman, probably in her late-forties, maybe early-fifties. Nothing seemed out of the ordinary at first glance. She knew that she needed to look at more than the surface. She needed to see the finer details.

Her hair was thin and heavily colored with bleaching agents and anti-gray coloring. She wore heavy makeup in an attempt to hide her age, but the loose skin on her neck and the very apparent wrinkles on her hands betrayed her attempts to look younger. She held a mixer known for a heavy amount of alcohol, one that she drank in large gulps. She cackled at a joke made by her friend next to her, showing teeth that had clearly been repaired extensively. The biting surfaces of her teeth were blue and translucent, an indication of enamel loss. The teeth were heavily whitened, but the parts of the teeth closest to the gums showed a small halo of deep yellow.

Her muscles were practically nonexistent and hung off her bony frame. Her wrists were especially bony and protruded far beyond her forearms. She wore what appeared to be an expensive necklace, but it was mostly hidden under her blouse. She had been in bad parts of town and was wary of someone trying to rob her. The woman lit up a cigarette and took another large gulp of her drink. Finally, Eri saw the hand holding the glass tremble slightly, an indication of nerve damage.

Eri looked back at Charlie, who was patiently waiting for her conclusion. She looked into his deep blue eyes obscured by the glow of the overhead lights. She smirked slightly. "She is a recovering drug addict."

For the first time, she saw Charlie smile fully. "You're a natural," he concluded as he took a swig of his beer. Ash cheered from behind them. The dart board showed that she won by fifty points. "She's going to lose her money to Francis," he said with a chuckle.

"She just beat him by fifty points," Eri replied in her sister's defense.

"He let her win," he said plainly, "he's now about to ask her to play again, this time for money. He'll let her win again, the second time by an even bigger margin. He'll then increase the stakes—double or triple the amount—and he'll beat her summarily. He and I used to hustle people for money back on Venture."

Eri snickered as she realized Ash's confidence in darts would be her downfall. The two quietly sat at the bar sipping their drinks for a while. No conversation, just drinking as they both scanned the bar. Eri closely observed other people, trying to make her newfound skill useful. At one point, Eri noticed Charlie itching his prosthetic hand.

"So, back to the original subject," she said as she signaled the bartender for another drink, "I can understand now how you'd figure out where the dish towels were since I had sloshed a little of the food onto the stove, but how in the hell could you possibly figure out that I like late-night snacks or which burners I prefer to cook on?"

"It's actually simpler that you think," he started confidently with a swig, "you see, I—"

"Hey," the bartender said to Charlie, "courier dropped off a message for you."

The bartender handed Charlie a folded piece of paper. He opened it away from Eri and immediately crushed the paper in his hand. He quickly tossed the paper into a trashcan under the bar and got up from his seat.

"I'll be right back," he said, his demeanor serious again. Eri watched him as he walked with purpose out of the bar.

# Chapter 5

"So, what's your story, Francis?" Ash inquired as they collected their darts off the board. "Ya may have some fun stories, but ya haven't really talked about yourself."

"What'd'ya wanna know?" he asked apprehensively.

Ash rolled her bruised shoulder. She had put on some topical ointment to reduce the pain before they left for the bar, but it was still stiff. She hoped it wouldn't impact her performance after challenging Francis in darts.

"Well, I remember yesterday that Charlie mentioned ya lost your hearin' in the war. Let's start with that."

"Are ya gonna start, or should I?" he asked, pointing at the board.

"Oh, well, I'll start." Ash focused as she stood up to the line to throw, then paused. "Just doin' 501, right?"

"Yeah," he answered. She lined up her shot again. "I joined the revolution right after it started. Was in the Third Light Infantry Division at the beginnin'."

Ash threw her three during his explanation. "Low ton," she said proudly after she finished.

"Not a bad start," he replied as he lined up.

"So ya fought in all four years of the war?" She rolled her shoulder again to try to loosen it.

Francis nodded as he threw his first dart. "Started in Third LID, then was selected to go into heavy assault school. Became heavy assault infantry after that."

"Seventy-five, not bad," she complimented. Her first round was almost double his points at 140. "So ya saw a lotta action durin' the revolution. Where all did ya fight?"

She lined up and looked at him. He was looking away toward an empty corner of the bar.

"Francis?" she asked with concern.

"Sorry. Was in both battles of Kusa, both battles of New Tibet, both battles of Ankara."

"Shit. I had a friend who was in heavy assault infantry. He was KIA in the Second Battle of Kusa."

"A lot of HAIs were killed in that battle, a lot of 'em green," he said distantly.

She could see bad memories pop up in his mind as his smile slowly faded. As heavy assault infantry in the war, she knew that he would have been in some of the worst fighting. She had heard stories about the retaking of New Tibet, Ankara, and Kusa, and all three of them required horrific urban combat. The kind of combat that was at close range and visceral.

To make matters worse, she heard that New Tibet was a battle that took twice as long because the Independent Frontier Systems Alliance military told its citizens to leave before a certain day, but the message was intercepted by the Federal Navy, which allowed the Feddies to prepare.

The liberation of Ankara was worse because the IFSA military decided not to warn anyone, and civilians were killed by both sides as they were caught in the crossfire. The IFSA brass decided to warn the citizens to leave before a certain date, so when the Federal Marines concentrated the day before, the IFSA Navy attacked the Feddies, and leveled most of the city from orbit to take as many Feddie marines as possible. The Indie fleet shot at the city indiscriminately, hoping that there weren't many civilians left, but many civilians refused to leave. Both the Feddie marines and the remaining civilians suffered a lot of casualties.

"Y'all want shots?" a waitress asked. Both of them pulled away from what they were thinking and looked at her.

"Yeah, dressed shot of Juan Diego for me with a Jumper for a chaser," Francis replied.

"Ya got Korzeck?" Ash inquired. The waitress confirmed. "Shot of that and come back five minutes after that for another Cornucopia."

The waitress left, and Ash saw Francis's smile reappear as he stepped up the dart board. "Got another low ton I see. Nice goin' on that."

"Thanks," she replied happily. "So, Charlie's your cousin. Got any other family?"

"Charlie's got a brother that still lives in the Federation. Their parents are in prison for life. Treason and war crimes, apparently. Charlie says they were patsies. My dad passed away about three months ago. Momma died in a car accident when I was eleven."

"I'm sorry to hear that about your folks. My parents are both gone as well."

He stopped his throw for his third dart. "How'd they go?"

"Mom died during the revolution from a drug overdose. Dad was with Eri's mom and they were killed when they were being robbed in their own house."

"Shit," he said distantly but empathetically. "So did your mom and dad divorce and then he had Eri with her mom or somethin'?"

"Nah, had an affair when I was nine and then ditched us when Eri's mom got pregnant with her. Never met her until after Dad was murdered."

"That's terrible," he said. "A child should always have their father."

He looked distantly at the floor, sighed, then went back to playing darts. He threw his last and hit a double bull.

"Whew," he said, "gotta make shots like that if I'm gonna beat ya."

"Damn right," Ash replied confidently.

"Got your shots," the waitress said happily as she set them down on the table near them.

They both walked over and grabbed their shots. He held his at about chest height so she wouldn't have to reach so far to toast with him. Even for her, he was tall. She preferred men taller than her, and his dapper yet wholesome and down-to-earth looks definitely made her look at him.

"To new adventures," he said.

She slowly clinked the shot glass against his and they threw the shots back. Both smacked their lips happily, and he sucked on the lime with approval.

"Tequila guy, huh?" she asked.

"Yeah, but I like it dressed. Charlie is a fucken psycho that just takes it straight."

Ash looked for them at the table, but they weren't there.

"Where'd they go?"

"Bar," Francis answered with a flick of his chin.

Charlie was sitting close to Eri and saying something secretive while very subtly pointing at a guy at the bar. He looked like a businessman of some sort, and Eri was nodding her head with understanding. Ash wondered what they could be talking about.

"Ten shen he's tryin' to teach her his little party trick. Any time anyone shows any interest, he tries teachin' 'em, but they never get it."

"So it's not just natural skill?" she asked.

"Nah. Told me that someone taught him."

"Huh," she said distantly. She went back up to the line after sipping her Cornucopia and threw a dart. Triple twenty.

"So what was it like growin' up on Yongsan?" he asked her.

"Didn't see much of it," she answered as she threw her second. Eighteen. "Mom couldn't hold a job after Dad left because she was always high on somethin', and a couple times the only thing I had to eat was what was offered at lunch that day in school." Twenty.

"Ninety-Eight. Almost a low ton. You're kickin' my ass right now."

Ash walked back from the board with her darts haughtily. "Only need one fifty-seven to win."

"Yeah, and I got a long way to go," he said as he stepped up to the line.

Ash decided to take her chance. "So besides your cousins and your aunt and uncle bein' in prison, do ya have any more family?"

"My mother's side don't talk to me no more. They didn't really like Dad. I'm uh…also separated from my wife and son."

"Oh," she said with surprise. "Ya don't have a ring."

He lowered his neck collar a little and showed a simple chain to a necklace. "Wear it around my neck."

"Why?"

He retrieved his darts and the holographic screen indicated that he made a low ton. "We're still married and shit, just separated and estranged. I've tried to get things back together, but she don't answer back."

"Sounds complicated," she said as she stepped up to the line.

"Another shot?" the waitress asked.

"Yeah, fuck it," Francis asked as he pointed to Ash.

"Fuck it," she replied with a shrug.

"Alright, I'll get your shots."

"So did she leave ya and just never say why?" she asked as she threw her first. Double bull. One hundred and seven left.

"Nah, it's my fault. Said she'd come back whenever I got my shit back together. When I did, I sent her a message and told her I was ready to get back together. That's when I found out that she's living with another guy. Said she's conflicted and hasn't decided whether to come back or not."

"So why haven't ya divorced her?" Bull. Eighty-two left.

"I guess 'cause I still love her, and I don't want my son growin' up without a father figure in his life."

Bull. Fifty-seven left. She just needed a triple nineteen to win.

"Shit, wish my dad had that kinda dedication to me." She went back to the table and finished her Cornucopia just in time for her shot and another. They toasted again before he threw his darts. Both took a hard drink from their chasers.

"Can we talk about somethin' else?" he asked as he stepped up to the line.

"Yeah, sorry," she apologized. "Just curious is all."

She'd lied. She had hoped he was single and wanted to know the situation to see if she had a way in. She could use the rebound after her last boyfriend, even if it was just something casual. He was tall and handsome after all.

*Kinda good that it's this way though. Would be really awkward on the ship if things didn't work out...*

She silently watched him make another low ton. He was only fifty points away.

She walked up to the line as he drank some of his beer and watched her silently. She took precise aim and hit the triple nineteen. She hollered with glee as she ran up to the board and took her dart.

"Alright, shithead," he said with a grumble. "Now that I'm warmed up, how 'bout we put some money on it?"

She sauntered over to her drink and stood close to him. "How 'bout a hundred shen since I'm also warmed up and my shoulder ain't botherin' me?"

"Ya got the money?"

"Not on me, but there's an ATM here that I won't need."

"Then show me whatcha got, chickenshit."

Ash was ready now. She sauntered up to the line, got a triple twenty, a double bull, and barely missed the triple twenty for a single twenty.

"Damn. A high ton."

"Damn right," she said confidently.

"So I'm assumin' that since ya didn't really know your dad that ya didn't know Eri until his funeral?"

"I knew of her, but nah, met her after the funeral. Wasn't gonna pay my respects or nothin'."

"Shit," he exclaimed as he missed the triple twenty three times.

"Close, but no cigar for ya," she replied as they changed places.

"Yeah, yeah."

"So what made y'all decide to go into the freight business?" she asked casually as she threw her darts.

"After Dad died, I decided to sell the company. I worked for Dad, but I just didn't like warehouse stuff. All we did was charge people for storage and have orders delivered. I wanted to see more of the galaxy than just the places where I fought in the war."

"Another high ton," she said with a smug shrug.

Francis finished his beer and waved the waitress over for another shot and beer. He threw his three while they waited, and he only got a low ton. He was significantly behind. She threw hers and got a low ton. She was only one round away.

"So what about ya?" he asked as they were handed their shots. "Besides Eri, ya got anyone else in your family?"

She shook her head. "Got dumped just a couple of weeks ago too. Shithead decided that apparently one woman wasn't enough for him."

He threw another low ton. She had a significant lead now.

"Well, if ya were still with him, would ya have even considered this job?" he asked as he walked back from the board.

"Dunno. Probably not, actually." She aimed carefully and hit the double twenty and the three to win the game. "Pay up."

"Alright, alright," he said as he produced a one hundred shen bill.

"I'm going to go see how they're doin' at the bar," she said as she flicked her head.

"Hold on, hold on," Francis said quickly. He produced three hundred shen. "Triple or nothin' on the next game. If I win, these are yours. If ya win, ya gimme that hundred and another two hundred."

Ash smiled deviously. "Fine. You're on."

# Chapter 6

"Hey, sorry, miss," the bartender said to Eri, "we're backed up with orders. I'll try to get yours done soon." Eri gestured silently to him that she understood and that she was not upset with the wait. The bar was much more crowded than usual, even for a Friday night.

Ash rushed over to Eri and hugged her, clearly quite a few drinks into her night. "I don't know what Charlie was talkin' about, Francis ain't *that* good at darts."

"So you're winning?" Eri asked.

"Yeah. I've beat him twice now and I'm about to take his money again," she replied with confidence. "I beat him pretty good the first time, and I just crushed him this time."

Eri remembered Charlie's words and couldn't help but smirk. Even when the man wasn't looking directly at something, he noticed.

"Where's Charlie?" her tall sister asked.

"Oh, he got a letter and he stepped out for a moment," Eri replied.

"Okay," Ash said with a shrug as she took three large gulps of her drink and slammed it down on the bar top. "I'm gonna go kick Francis's ass."

"Good luck," Eri wished in a sly tone as Ash walked back towards the captain and the dart board.

"Excuse me," a man said as he stood next to Charlie's stool, "I couldn't help but notice that your drink was empty, can I get you a refill?"

Eri knew what he was offering. He was taller than the average man and clearly lifted weights often. For a moment she imagined being held inside his strong arms, then quickly snapped out of the daydream to look at the rest of his features.

His smile was toothy and disingenuous, but it seemed to Eri that it was out of the awkward situation of approaching a woman for the first time. He was well-groomed and wore musky cologne. His fingernails were clean, perhaps even manicured. He clearly went out to the bar to find single women and cared deeply about his appearance, likely to the point of vanity. He was handsome with a sharp jaw and had generally strong, masculine features. He at least passed the first step to getting her contact ID—now it was a matter of charisma.

"Sure," she said with her typical fake smile, "I'm having a Hyperlane. The bartender is already making it for me though."

"Well that's okay," he replied as he tried to get the bartender's attention, "I'll be more than happy to pay for it for a few minutes of your time. Perhaps I'll get more…"

He indicated to the bartender that he was going to pay for her drink as he began mixing the various liquids into the glass. The bartender nodded, then slid the drink to the man once it was finished.

"I'm Eri," she said with an outstretched hand.

"Donnovan," he replied as he gently shook her hand, "you can call me Don." He handed her the drink and she sipped it. She grimaced slightly from the taste; the bartender had overpoured. It was not a big deal; her drinks were already paid for and she could sleep on the flight out the next morning to Athens. She took another large swig.

"So what about Hyperlanes do you like so much?" he asked, stumbling through small talk.

"It's the fruit syrup," she replied as she took another swig. "I'm a sucker for *sweet things*," she said deviously to offer a rather obvious hint to Don.

Eri pulled the glass up to her lips again to show the handsome man her appreciation for the drink. He was awkwardly cute to Eri, someone who tried to project confidence but ultimately stumbled when in front of a woman.

"So how long are you staying here?" he asked as he fought to regain his composure.

"What do you mean?"

"How long are you staying here in Corinth?" he reiterated. "A cute girl like you wouldn't be living in this shithole voluntarily."

Eri couldn't understand how Don thought that was a compliment. She sat there with a raised eyebrow, glaring at him for his terrible attempt to compliment her.

"And why not? Corinth is a town full of hard-working people. Are you telling me that a beautiful woman can only live in a big city, or are you suggesting that a beautiful woman couldn't possibly work with her hands?" she asked him with disdain.

"Well, no," he said, "I'm just saying that a mining town like this is probably the last place that I'd expect a woman of your—"

A black metal arm reached between them and grabbed a beer off the bar top, "Just quit now, kid, while you're only halfway to digging your own grave," Charlie said with a snicker.

"Who the hell are you?" Don asked angrily.

"Look, if you couldn't already tell, your compliment had the exact opposite effect that you wanted. She works as a maintainer, which means she works with her hands and appreciates the blue collar culture here. Perhaps you should try practicing your lines next time before you walk over to a woman and embarrass yourself."

Don looked back at Eri, who looked away from him. His demeanor changed completely. He quietly looked down in defeat.

"Yeah, yeah, you're sad," Charlie said impatiently. "Go sulk somewhere other than in front of my seat, cowboy." Eri pressed her lips together as she tried to hold back a laugh. Don slowly walked away from them.

"That conversation went downhill so fast," Eri murmured. "It's a shame, he was really handsome."

"A man of his age is incredibly inexperienced, which makes him awkward and stupid," he replied as he sipped his beer. "Take it from someone who was his age nine years ago."

"Wait," Eri blurted, "how old are you?"

"Twenty-eight," he replied.

Eri's brow furrowed. "He's not nineteen…"

"I saw him beg and bribe the guy checking IDs at the front door earlier," Charlie said with a smirk, "you're five years, seven months, and twelve days older than him."

"You never miss a thing, do you?"

"Nope," he said with a smack of his lips. He signaled to the bartender as he pulled a cigarette up to his mouth and lit it. For a moment, Charlie looked upset as he exhaled his smoke. The look almost immediately disappeared as he turned to her. "So, Francis told me earlier that you're going to Athens tomorrow for a wedding."

"Yeah, my friend from high school," she answered as the bartender placed a shot in front of both her and Charlie. She glanced back at him. He gestured toward the shot for her to take as he reached for his. "What are we drinking to?" she asked.

"How about a toast to two people who aren't afraid of getting dirty, but still too cute for this town?" Charlie proposed jokingly. Eri giggled and raised her glass in approval. They toasted and downed the shot. Eri licked her lips, savoring the last remnants of the whiskey.

She put the empty shot glass next to his on the bar top and paused. "Alright," she said with annoyance, "how did you figure out that I liked whiskey?"

Charlie grunted with approval. "Let's just say it was a good guess," he said as he took a drag of his cigarette. "But anyways, what I was going to say was that I also have to go to Athens tomorrow to take care of a few things. I can take you in the *Fire Arrow* instead of whatever way you were getting there."

"You're going to fly your Dart for six hours?" she asked.

"Six hours?" he repeated in confusion. "A low orbit flight only takes about ninety minutes."

"Oh!" she exclaimed with realization. "Sure, that would give me plenty of time to get ready for the wedding instead of rushing as soon as I got off the plane from a six hour atmo flight."

"Great, I'll—"

"Yeah, yeah, yeah," Ash said angrily to Francis as they stepped up next to Eri and Charlie at the bar, "ya played me good, but I'm only buying ya a shot 'cause I'm a woman of my word, not because ya deserve it, asshole."

"Did he beat you in darts?" Charlie asked sarcastically. "I am *truly* shocked."

"Yeah, but he won't trick me next time, and my shoulder pain won't distract me so much," Ash replied as she ordered two shots.

Charlie tried to continue what he was saying to Eri, but Ash interrupted as soon as noise left his mouth.

"So what've ya two been talkin' about?" she asked with slurred speech. Francis grabbed the two shots from the bartender and distributed one to Ash. They clinked their shot glasses together and drank the liquor.

"I should probably head back," Ash said with a very quiet belch, "I got work in the morning and gotta put my two weeks in. Catch y'all later."

Ash made her way to the door, her motor functions clearly beginning to fail on her from all the alcohol. Francis stood there awkwardly staring at his beer. Visibly annoyed, Charlie grabbed his cousin's shirt and forcibly pulled him in. Eri watched anxiously as Charlie growled something quietly in Francis's ear. He nodded and handed Charlie his beer and left. Eri curiously watched Francis leave.

"What was that all about?" she asked.

Charlie glared at Francis as he left the bar, taking one last drag of his cigarette before stamping it out with anger. He took a deep breath to calm himself and looked back at Eri. "Sorry," he began, "I just told him to accompany her to make sure she got home safely. I'll take you back to your apartment in the car."

"You know, for someone who is *not* the ship's captain, you sure seem to be the most responsible out of the crew so far."

Charlie nodded in agreement as he poured the rest of Francis's beer into his glass. He sighed deeply. "Anyways—third time's a charm—I will pick you up outside your apartment at eight thirty and we'll leave by nine."

Eri sipped from her drink and sat it down on the bar top. "That sounds great. It'll give me plenty of time to get ready. I really appreciate it."

"It's no problem at all," he said as he drank some of the beer.

Eri looked at the time on her tool as she drank the last of her mixer. "I should probably head home too. It's getting late and I'm pretty sure that whiskey shot will put me over the edge."

"Okay," Charlie replied, "I'll pay the tab and I'll take you home."

She quietly watched Charlie pay the large bill that the four of them had managed to balloon out of control. Charlie was the cheapest with his beers and the two whiskey shots, Eri not much higher than him with her mixers, but Francis and Ash each had two hundred shen tabs. Charlie grumbled something about shots under his breath as he counted the cash. When he paid the bartender, he gestured to Eri to lead the way. They walked out silently and scanned the parking lot.

"Those stupid, drunk motherfuckers!" Charlie exclaimed with rage. "They took the car…"

Eri groaned in both frustration and embarrassment. Within one day, Ash had managed to anger Charlie twice, and she felt no sympathy for whatever he would do to reprimand her. Charlie breathed sharply through his nose in frustration and defeat.

"C'mon," Charlie said softly, "I'll walk you home."

"It's alright, I can make my way back," she replied with a dismissive wave.

"I'm sure you can, but this is Corinth we're talking about," he argued.

"It's not *that* bad of a town."

"I'm not letting you walk home alone at night, not while you're part of the crew."

She could see that Charlie was being deathly serious, so she caved and started walking.

The two of them quietly walked on the sidewalk side by side toward Eri's apartment. Charlie had both hands in his pockets and was looking down at the concrete beneath their feet. Something was on his mind. After a couple of blocks, Eri finally spoke up.

"Is something wrong?" she asked. "Well, besides the two drunk people driving home alone…"

Charlie didn't say anything and just kept walking, slumped over slightly and looking down at the pavement.

"Hello? Charlie?"

"Hmm?" he asked as if pulled out of a stupor.

"I asked if something is wrong," she reiterated.

"Oh, uh…no," he said quietly, "nothing you need to be concerned about."

"You're not one to open up, are you?" she asked as they passed under a streetlamp.

"Just got some other things on my mind," he replied.

"That's not it," she concluded, "there's something bothering you."

"Maybe I shouldn't have taught you how to look at the finer details…" he grumbled.

"It's too late now," she replied with a shrug. "So why don't you tell me what's on your mind? We have a ways to walk and I'm terrible at small talk."

Charlie finally looked up and out into the darkness to his left. "Like I said, nothing you need to be concerned about."

"Alright," she conceded with a soft smile, "but if something's bothering you, you can always talk to me."

He looked at her as they walked under another streetlamp. "Why do you care so much?" he asked. "Hell, you barely know me…" His tone was not filled with frustration, but genuine curiosity. His expression had softened slightly, but Eri could see that he was still guarded.

"Well," she began, "I know what it's like to suffer alone. Before Ash and I connected, I was by myself after my mom and dad died, and I struggled for a long time. I just don't want anyone else to feel like that, especially if we're going to be in such close proximity on the ship."

Charlie looked forward, their footsteps and the insects droning in the distance the only things breaking the silence. "How did your parents die?" he asked softly, trying to redirect the subject.

Eri didn't respond immediately. They walked silently as she watched her feet move underneath her. "They were murdered. The cops said it was a robbery gone bad. I was away in my last year of maintainer school."

"I'm sorry for your loss," he said reverently, "grief is always the hardest when you lose someone that you love."

"You say that like it comes from experience," she concluded as she looked at him.

Charlie's eyes narrowed as he looked forward. "Nothing dramatic like that," he clarified, "but I've lost a lot of people close to me. I haven't seen any of my close family in three years and…" He choked on his words, then pursed his lips in frustration and breathed sharply through his nose. "Well, anyways…"

They continued on the sidewalk silently. Charlie never finished what he wanted to say. Eri could tell that it was a sore subject.

"Well," Eri managed to say to break the silence, "if you do ever want to talk about it, you can talk to me. Whatever it is, I won't judge." Charlie scoffed. "I'm serious!"

"Look, I appreciate the gesture, honestly, but I know if I ever talked about it, you would judge me. It's why I never talk about it."

"You'll never know unless you do," she replied with a shrug, "but if you're not ready, then I won't pry and I'm sure we'll have plenty of time on the ship to talk about our lives and history to pass the time between jobs. Ash though…she's nosy."

"Thank you for dropping it."

"I do have one question before we drop it," she interjected. The stony first officer glanced at her with a raised eyebrow. She looked at him and her confidence wavered. "I…uh…if I ever…never mind."

Charlie's eyes narrowed, but a smirk appeared on his face. He pushed his breath through his nose with a quick hiss.

"If you're wondering if I would listen if you ever had a problem, I would, though I don't know if I would be the best person to talk to."

"How did you know what I was going to say? More of your learned skill that you haven't taught me yet?" she asked.

Charlie chuckled once. "You can learn a lot from tone, eye movement, and body language, but that's something you have to learn on your own."

Eri hummed with curiosity. "So…why aren't you a good person to talk to?"

"I think you're smart enough to know why," he replied plainly.

"There's nothing wrong with being cynical or blunt, if that's what you mean," she remarked. "It just means that you have a different perspective and are willing to be honest. It might be a perspective I need."

"And why would someone like you need a dose of cynicism? What kind of issue would require such a cudgel?"

Eri shrugged. "You never know," she replied, "sometimes it's better to hear a hard truth."

"Or to confide in someone other than your sister," he concluded.

"Well…I…"

"Relax," he reassured her, "I'm not asking you now, just making observations aloud."

Eri calmed, but she wondered if Charlie had already figured it out. His expression was blank, but she couldn't tell if it was because he was simply maintaining his serious demeanor or if he knew and he was hiding it.

"No, I don't know," he said as if he could read her thoughts.

"It's honestly scary how well you can read people," she told him.

Charlie snickered. "If it bothers you, I'll keep it under control around you."

"You can do that?" Charlie nodded.

"I can," he said confidently. "And when you get to a certain point, I'll teach you to control it as well."

"But why would I want to control it?" she asked.

"Some things are best left alone and in someone's head. One day, you may learn a secret that you don't want to know or should have never known."

"True…" she affirmed. "Can I ask you one last question?" He looked at her and waited. "Why were you watching the entrance earlier? You were really focused on the door."

"Besides the obvious that I'm just people watching, there's quite a lot of reasons. I'm the security chief, so I need to be the one always watching for potential threats. It's also a habit I picked up from the war. A lot of veterans of wars do the same, actually."

"Francis said you served during the Isolde Revolution, but he didn't really say anything else about it."

"That's because I told him to keep his mouth shut. It's not his business to talk about my experiences during the war."

"That bad?" she asked.

"Yes."

Eri should have figured. With only one arm and a face full of scars, he obviously had a rough time and didn't like talking about it.

The two wordlessly turned the corner and began navigating the labyrinth of roads for the prefab apartment complex. They turned on the street to see the car in front of the apartment. Charlie growled as he strode up to the front door, and banged on it as he tried to control his breathing. Ash opened the door as Eri finally caught up with Charlie.

"Where's Francis?" Charlie asked with frustration.

"We're jus' havin' a night cap," Ash said defensively as Charlie pushed passed her.

"Francis," Charlie snarled through his teeth, "put the drink down, go outside, and wait for me in the car." Francis groaned in frustration but did as commanded. "You two are acting like teenagers. Eri, talk to your sister before I have to. Here, have her give you all of her measurements on this before she goes to sleep, and then bring it with you tomorrow morning. I'm going to deal with the *captain*."

Charlie stomped out of the apartment. Eri shook her head at her older half sister as she held out the piece of paper ready for Ash's measurements. Charlie closed the door firmly, but not enough to slam it shut.

"What were you two thinking?" Eri asked. "Who drove the car?"

"Francis," Ash answered defensively, "but I'm not tha' drunk. Besides, he said he was fine ta drive."

"So because he said he was fine, you just went along with it? You both were going drink for drink and he didn't look any better than you. You, once again, left me at the bar to walk home." Eri heard the other car finally turn on and leave the area.

"You've made it home plenny of times on yer own," Ash argued as she swayed slightly.

"Yes, because you always *leave me!*" she yelled with a scowl. "I've only known Charlie for a little over a day and yet he at least made sure I got home safely! All you ever do when you go to the bar is *abandon* me! You were the one that wanted to stick together, but every time when we should, you suddenly forget what a reasonable, responsible adult does!"

"I'm sorry, alright?" Ash snapped. "I just wa'ned to talk to Francis about a couple a things in private. To be honest, I don' even know why I tried to get on this ship with ya. I was *fine* livin' in a 'partment an' bein' a normal person, but as soon as you wan'ed this job, I've been pulled inna bein' part of this whole thing. What makes me sick is 'at I was happy for ya and I *wan'ed* to follow along. But then Charlie showed me that I'm not as good as I think I am and it keeps makin' me wonder if he's only hirin' me 'cause he's hirin' ya and feels sorry for me."

Tears filled Ash's eyes, but she quickly wiped them and sniffled to regain her composure. "Ya got the job effor'lesie and I'm trynna do everythin' I can to show tha' I belong and somehow fuckin' up ev'ry step of the way. Ya were always be'er than me and all I see is yer mother when ya succeed. Yer mom was always prettier, smarter, and more skilled than mine and that's why Dad left me and my mom! I jus' feel like at every turn, I'm draggin' ya down and I keep resentin' ya for it."

Ash fell into the chair and stared blankly at the floor. "I just wanna know that I got this job 'cause of me and not ya. I wanna stop resentin' ya for somethin' ya didn' do, but all I ever see is yer mom. I wa'ned to reconnec' 'cause ya and I are all that's lef' of our family, but I feel like I'm useless and tha' I didn' earn my place on the ship. I don' wanna be pitied, I wanna be respected…"

Eri silently went over to Ash and hugged her. "Charlie wouldn't hire you if he didn't think you were a good fit," she reassured her sister.

"How ya know tha'?" she asked Eri.

"If there's one thing I know about him, it's that he can read people like a book. He saw something in you that you probably don't understand yet. Just give it time and let him explain to you why you belong."

"Alrigh'," Ash said as she conceded to her sister, "but I may st'll ask Francis why they hired me."

"Do what you think is best, Ash," Eri advised, "now help me get all your measurements."

# Chapter 7

Charlie awoke suddenly in the hospital. He had been intubated and immediately reached up with both hands to pull the tubes out, but only his left arm complied. He slowly pulled the lines out of his larynx and esophagus, gagging and retching as he removed them. The straining made his eyes water as spit filled his mouth. He swallowed his saliva to help keep whatever was in his stomach down.

He looked up at the ceiling and took a few deep breaths to compose himself. His entire right side was throbbing with pain and he could feel meters of gauze on his body underneath dozens of bandages. The right side of his face and his neck was also heavily bandaged. Where before his entire side hurt as one massive unit with only a few places hurting slightly more than the rest, he could now feel each individual wound throbbing and radiating pain to the next wound.

He tried lifting his right arm again, but it still did not respond. He felt a tingling itch on the top of his right hand, and he used his left hand to itch, but nothing was there. He finally looked down to see where his arm was, but it was completely gone. He stared silently at the empty space in utter disbelief. He couldn't draw his eyes away from the void where his arm once was.

"Nurse!" he cried out in terror. "Nurse!"

A few moments later, a man ran into the room wearing nurse's scrubs. "Sir? Is everything alright?" he asked with concern.

Charlie still stared at his right side. "Where the fuck is my arm?"

"The doctors had to amputate it," the nurse said calmly with his hands up in a piss poor attempt to calm him. "Just take it easy, alright? You've been through a lot."

Charlie suddenly felt a flash of heat. He was feverish.

"Where am I?" he asked.

"Yongsan Fifth Ward Hospital," the nurse said as he approached Charlie. "Please tell me that you didn't remove your tubes yourself."

"Why did they take my arm?" Charlie asked angrily. "What gives you people the right—"

"Sir, please calm down," the nurse pleaded. "The doctors can explain everything."

"Then get the fucking doctors!" The nurse backed away in fear, but didn't move. "Are you deaf? Get the doctors, now!"

The nurse finally scurried out of the room and Charlie trembled with rage. It was then that he realized he had a catheter in him, which was uncomfortable.

*Why would they just take my arm like that? Was the damage really that bad?*

A doctor came into the room with the nurse and quickly looked at Charlie's vitals.

"Hmm, still feverish," the doctor said. "I'm sorry you had to wake up like you did, sir, but we didn't know when you would come out of your coma."

"Coma?" Charlie asked.

"Yes," the doctor said as he put his stethoscope over Charlie's left lung. "Breathe in for me. I need to hear your lung."

Charlie complied, but he ground his molars with anger.

"Why did you take my arm?" he asked after a couple of breaths.

"Unfortunately," the doctor began as he pulled the stethoscope away, "the damage was simply too much. The sheer amount of shrapnel wounds and all of the contaminants in your open wounds were too much for us to heal with ordinary medicine. Entire chunks were taken out of your arm. When we finally cleared all the mud and dirt, half of your radius was visible, and no amount of treatment could have healed you without weeks of SCR. We realized that you had Garner's disorder when you became feverish within twelve hours of the therapy. We had to put you in a chemically induced coma to help your body heal. Once we realized you had GD, we had no choice but to amputate."

"You took it without my consent," Charlie snarled.

"You weren't in a position to consent," the doctor rebuked. "You were in a coma and if we waited too long, your arm would have become infected, gangrenous, and necrotic. I'm sorry we had to amputate, but it was for the best."

Charlie's breathing slowed, but he was still furious. They had taken the arm all the way up to the shoulder. There was nothing left. He began to feel ill, and not because of the fever from his autoimmune disorder, but because he realized in that moment that he would never be the same person again. He would never be whole.

"How long have I been out?" he asked as he calmed.

"Almost six days," the doctor replied. "We honestly didn't expect you to wake from your coma for another couple of days at least."

"So what…I get a prosthetic because of my Garner's?"

"Unfortunately," he replied, "though you should be thankful we were even able to keep you alive. Between the SCR and your blood transfusion, I'm surprised your body didn't start attacking itself or put you into a permanent coma. Before all of that, we had to resuscitate you three times on the operating table."

Charlie looked at the opposite wall as the doctor examined his shrapnel wounds.

*I died three times…*

"Who brought me in?" Charlie asked as the doctor signaled to the nurse to help rebandage him.

"A woman that claimed you knocked on her door and collapsed when she opened it."

"I barely remember that. I lost consciousness after I fell onto her floor. What's her name?"

"We don't know," he replied as the nurse began rebandaging him from head to hip. "She admitted you anonymously. Wouldn't give her name at all and simply said that she didn't want to be part of whatever happened."

"I wish she had given it," Charlie said, "I'd like to thank her."

"I guess she just wanted her privacy," the doctor replied. "Some people help others anonymously because they don't want the praise or recognition."

"How long do I have to stay here?" Charlie asked.

"We'd like to do some tests now that you are conscious, but I'd like to wait at least until your fever is gone and your body isn't attacking the blood transfusion and SCR before I even start those tests."

Charlie sighed with defeat and frustration.

"Look," the doctor said while the nurse continued to change bandages and gauze, "you still have a long road to recovery. Just be patient."

"And how long will that involve a catheter?" Charlie asked with annoyance.

The doctor let out a breath of levity. "I'll have another nurse remove it while he changes your bandages, but take it easy getting up and out of the bed. Losing a limb causes all sorts of balance issues and you'll find yourself trying to use it. Think consciously about using *only* your left arm."

"That'll be difficult considering I'm right-handed," Charlie retorted.

"Nevertheless, use only your left hand for everything and try to remind yourself that you don't have a right arm right now."

For two days, Charlie was waited on by nurses. He had never felt so helpless, so useless. He fell three times from forgetting that his arm didn't exist when he tried to grasp something or tried to shift his weight on his right side. His fever was almost gone, but his immune system had attacked the blood transfusion, which meant he was low on blood. The doctors couldn't do anything about that though, and Charlie could only let things take their course. His two cracked ribs on his right side screamed at him whenever he took deep breaths.

The first day was full of paperwork and questions about his health history. He must have signed his name seven times with his left hand, and the signature was practically unreadable. In the early afternoon, two police officers visited him and asked questions, but Charlie consistently invoked his right to silence, and they left with a minimal police report for him to sign.

One of the nurses tried talking to him, but he remained silent. She tried to make small talk and help Charlie feel comfortable, but he was distraught by the events that had unfolded and their consequences. How could he ever explain to anyone what he had experienced? Who could he truly talk to that could even remotely understand? Who in their life had ever been shot in the back by their betrothed? How many could say that their own flesh and blood, their brother, tried to kill them?

He had replayed the events in his mind and could not understand why Tristan would try to kill him. The only theory that he could even muster involved Charlie confessing about his defection to IFSA after the Isolde Massacre, but that theory didn't hold up under scrutiny. If he was so upset that he wanted to kill him, he had dozens of chances over the course of a week while they flew to Yongsan in FTL.

And how could Christie, the love of his life, simply throw everything away like that? How could she shoot him in the back if she loved him? The reason she was so aloof on the trip to Yongsan made a lot more sense with the knowledge that she'd been planning to betray him. But why spend all night with him the night before she shot him? Did she have second thoughts? His mind never stopped trying to fill gaps. Regardless of how many theories developed, he knew there was more to it—something that would explain all of it and fill in the voids of information.

For the first time in over three years, Charlie sobbed until he fell asleep. The shock had worn off, and his grief and pain fell on him like a mudslide. He hadn't cried since September 16, 3191 in the waning months of the Isolde Revolution, just two months to the day before the Armistice of Osaka was signed. Both times, he had lost a woman that he loved.

In the early morning of the second full day, Charlie awoke from a nightmare and was so confused that he fought one of the nurses. It took three people to get him back in the bed and restrained. The nightmare had felt so real, and he was visited later by a psychiatrist to discuss options for trauma therapies. Charlie never said a word to the shrink, and after about an hour of trying, the psychiatrist defeatedly left him a bunch of pamphlets to look at. Once he was finally unrestrained in the late afternoon, he threw all of the trauma therapy pamphlets in the garbage.

Charlie didn't know what to do. He had already made plans with Christie and had committed himself to all of those plans and contingencies. What would he do now? Where would he go? His life had been starting to take shape, but with one bullet and one grenade, everything had collapsed.

On the third day, Charlie's fever broke. His bandages were replaced once again, and the doctors tested his blood, urine, stool, and imaged practically every particle of his body. By this point, Charlie had finally accepted his lost arm and was more cognizant of it. He no longer fell over, but his heart had still not replaced all of the blood in his body, and he still required assistance from time to time because of his lightheadedness.

That evening, Charlie was finally able to call his uncle, Frank, and his cousin, Francis. He needed to explain to them what had happened. Before then, the nurses and doctors hadn't realized that Charlie had no way of interacting with the tool that was implanted in his left wrist and thought he had already made calls.

Venture was three FTL days away, and he knew he would have to send a video message and wait hours before he would hear back from them. He asked the nurse to help him record and send. He watched the record timer count down as he prepared himself.

"Hey, Frank," Charlie began with a sigh. "I'm on Yongsan and I could use your help. I'm in the hospital right now. I uh…I lost my arm, my home, and Christie's gone with…"

Charlie just realized that Cicero was on the ship when they left. He worried about his dog and what would become of him.

"Christie's left with the dog. I'm still recovering, so you'll have some time before I need your help. Let me know when you're on the way or if you're too busy to stop by. If so, I'll just take a flight to Venture. Bye."

The nurse turned off the recording and helped him send the message to his uncle.

"Thank you," Charlie said meekly. "I know I haven't been a good patient the past few days…"

The auburn-headed woman smiled softly at him. She was the nurse that had tried to speak to him the first day. He had completely ignored her then, and apologized now for his rudeness. From what Charlie could tell, they were about the same age.

"It's alright," she reassured him. "Anyone in your condition would be distraught. To be honest, you're probably handling it better than most."

Charlie looked at her and gazed into her green eyes, which looked at him with understanding and pity.

*Pity…*

"Can…can you please tell the nurse I attacked yesterday morning that I'm sorry?" he asked sheepishly. "I wasn't in a good headspace when I woke up."

"Water under the bridge," she said dismissively with a smile. "You'd be surprised what happens here in the ICU. She was more startled than anything. Don't think anyone would have expected you to leap up from the bed so quickly."

Charlie looked away with mild shame. She may have been reassuring with her words, but he wasn't fully convinced.

"What's your name?" he asked quietly.

"Anabel," she answered.

"Anabel," Charlie echoed.

There was a silence between them for a moment, but the nurse waited patiently.

"Can I ask you something, Anabel?" he finally inquired.

"Of course," she replied.

"Have you worked with many amputees?"

She pursed her lips. "Because of SCR treatments being so common nowadays, you're only my second," she said.

"Do you know if the pains and itches go away?" he muttered.

"I don't, no," she answered somberly.

There was another silence, but Anabel once again waited patiently for him to say something. He looked at the far wall distantly as he pushed his jaw forward, fighting against his emotions. He bit his bottom lip to hold back his tears.

"Will you stay with me for a while?" he pleaded quietly.

"I have to do my rounds, but I'll stay with you after," she answered gently. "Deal?"

Charlie nodded, still biting his lower lip.

Anabel returned sometime later and sat on his left side. Charlie's head turned to her and he used all of his will to smile, but his frown barely shifted. It felt permanently in place. Anabel smiled softly, her freckles stretching on her rosy cheeks.

"I haven't seen a ginger since Hexham," he said awkwardly, his Feddie accent slightly showing itself in his speech.

"You're from Hexham?" she asked quietly.

"Yeah," he answered, "but it's been seven years since I lived there. I enlisted in the Federal Navy just weeks after the Isolde Parliament declared independence. I visited about three years ago to get all my things after the armistice. Haven't been back since."

"Are you a Feddie?" she asked. Charlie hesitated for a moment.

"I was, but the Isolde Massacre changed that."

"You were a defector?"

Charlie nodded. "Betrayed my country at nineteen. The revolution started two weeks before I graduated high school."

"Then you and I are only a year apart in age. I had just turned seventeen and finished my third year of high school."

Charlie's frown managed to turn into a smile slightly, but only for a moment.

"Did you see a lot of action in the war?" she asked.

"No," he answered plainly.

"My brother was in the revolution," she said somberly. "He was five years older than me. He died in the First Battle of Kusa."

"I'm sorry for your loss," he replied. "My cousin fought in both battles of Kusa—for the rebels…er…revolutionaries."

"He must have seen a lot of terrible things if he fought in both…" she concluded.

Charlie nodded. "He's never been the same. Some wounds never heal."

Silence fell between them for a moment, Charlie snorting with the realization that his last sentence was incredibly ironic given that he'd never get his arm back.

Anabel looked at him quizzically. Charlie flicked his head at his right side. "Some wounds never heal," he reiterated. "Kind of forgot about why I was in the hospital for a second there."

The nurse tried not to laugh at his self-deprecation, so she pursed her lips and smiled.

"It's alright to laugh," he reassured her. "The irony is not lost on me."

"Well you're coping with it a lot better than I would," she complimented.

Charlie gazed at her for a moment in silence. She returned the gaze and gently held his left hand.

"You're stronger than most of the patients I've worked with," she said softly. "I hope you find some peace when this is all over."

He didn't know why, but those words sent him over the edge. His face crumpled and he fought back tears as he looked away.

"Oh, I'm sorry," she apologized as she stood up, "I didn't mean to upset you."

Anabel wrapped her arms around him as he started to sob. He barely knew the woman, but her wishes for him to find peace shattered him. He had already experienced so much in his life, and this woman he barely knew had expressed something that no one had ever said to him. Until that moment, he didn't even know that he needed to hear it.

*Peace...*

Peace seemed like such an unobtainable thing. He wondered if he would ever find it after what happened, but when she wrapped her arms around him, he felt it. Peace.

Her touch was so gentle that even her tight squeeze somehow didn't hurt his healing cuts and gashes. He hadn't been truly touched by anyone in days, and even though his fiancée had betrayed him, he longed for her touch, her warmth, her soothing voice. Anabel gave him all three, and he clung to them for the time she held him gently. Her warm embrace gave him a solace he hadn't known that he needed.

On the fourth day, Charlie had an unexpected visitor. He was expecting the police to come back and ask him questions again, hoping that he would be more willing to help. He didn't expect a man in a suit with a stern and stony expression to walk through the door. The man gazed at Charlie, and Charlie looked at him quizzically, not knowing who he was.

The man in the suit walked over to the windows and closed all the shades. He breathed loudly and intently through his nose as if disappointed, which confused Charlie. He closed the door and pulled out a tablet, placing it next to Charlie where his arm would normally rest. He pressed an icon on the screen and left the item on the bed.

"Hello, Charlie," the man said calmly. "How are you feeling?"

"Should I know you?" Charlie asked with a raised eyebrow.

"You know me," the man answered as he put one hand in a pants pocket while the other revealed credentials from his breast pocket, "though we never met face-to-face."

Charlie leaned forward in the hospital bed and saw an ID card for the Independent Systems Secret Service, IS3. Charlie tilted his head and narrowed his eyes. There were only a few that he knew in IS3 from his work in the war.

"AX-3," the man said. "Axe."

"Axe…" Charlie said with realization. "I would shake your hand, but…"

Axe extended his left hand and Charlie slowly and apprehensively shook it.

"What are you doing here?" Charlie asked.

"I came here to check up on you," he answered. "The agency heard what happened, but we are officially on a gag order and forbidden to talk to you."

"Yet here you stand," Charlie remarked.

"Indeed," Axe supplied.

The two locked eyes for a moment. Charlie could see on the agent's face that it was no coincidence he was visiting him. What kind of information did IS3 have about the incident? Why would IS3 care about the incident other than checking up on an old contact from three years ago?

*It can't be…they knew about the attack not because they were watching me, but someone else…*

"You're about to tell me some terrifying news…aren't you?" he asked.

Axe grabbed the chair next to the bed and sat down next to Charlie. "At least you're still as sharp as ever," he complimented. "After seeing you in person—all things considered—it's clear why you were chosen to lead Blue Team in the war."

"Because the obvious choice was the current director's sister and no one wanted accusations of nepotism," Charlie said flatly.

"You humble only yourself, Charlie," Axe retorted. "It's clear that you were chosen for a reason, and your insight was one of them."

"Get to the point, Axe," Charlie demanded.

Axe pushed out a breath in amusement. "We know about the attack because we have been keeping tabs on you, and when the Pit Vipers suddenly disappeared, we feared the worst."

"Completely?" Charlie asked.

"A couple of analysts believe they went into Federation space, and after the revelation we had today, it's almost certain that theory holds water."

"And what's this sudden revelation?" Charlie asked.

"As I said, we've been watching you since you immigrated after the war. You first joined the Bounty Hunter's Guild under Master Jeong's wing, and we were satisfied for a while…but then you joined the Pit Vipers. For a long time, we tried our best to infiltrate the merc group and plant someone inside, but all of our efforts were stifled. Were you aware that the leader of the group was operating under a pseudonym?"

"Of course I was," Charlie retorted, "It was to keep the government off our backs. What does this have—"

"We didn't know that until this morning. As far as we were concerned, Ali Hayed was a former bounty hunter turned merc like you, but when we saw that it was Tristan…"

"Why is Tristan important?" Charlie asked with a shaky voice.

Axe's green eyes locked with Charlie's blue orbs. He could see Axe's hesitation was because his next words would be devastating. Charlie's heart raced and his breathing began to intensify.

"Axe…why is Tristan important?" he asked again.

"Well, he's not the only one," he started as he checked behind his shoulder. "Your supposed fiancée, Christie Kendrick."

"Out with it, god damnit," Charlie commanded.

"Them, and five others were all field agents from the Federal Intelligence Agency."

Charlie's eyes widened as his mouth gaped.

*FIA agents? Why? What were they up to? Why would Christie…*

Charlie came to a realization in that moment. Christie was not just some woman who started working admin three months after he started working for Tristan. She was chosen to seduce him because he kept stifling Tristan and all of his plans early on.

When Charlie and Tristan first started taking jobs, he raised his concerns with innocent casualties, the choices of targets, the people that hired them, the missions themselves. They must have argued every day for three months. Where Charlie wanted to have a more honorable merc crew like the Steel Battalion, Tristan wanted a merc group that was feared like the Jaguars. It wasn't until Christie came along that their arguments really stopped, and Charlie started to embrace being feared by both mercs and civilians. Christie had often advised him whenever he confided in her, and it was now all visible and brought into focus.

She never loved him. Everything was a *lie*. She was sent to work for the merc group as his handler and to manipulate him.

Charlie breathed heavily as the news struck him like a sledgehammer on an anvil. His mind raced as his eyes danced around in his thoughts. How many times did things seem strange or fell into place too easily? He thought that maybe he and Christie simply connected, but with the knowledge that she was an FIA agent working with Tristan, he knew that it was all a sham.

He didn't know what was worse: knowing that he'd fallen for such a deception, or that it went as far as it did without him ever realizing it. Zoreah would be ashamed. She taught him everything he knew about deduction, and every time he had his doubts or suspicions, they were always quashed by Christie's words, kisses, or sex. He should have listened to his instincts more; he should have seen it sooner. He was so blinded by Christie's beauty, grace, and supposed love that he never looked at the fine details. Had he remained vigilant, he would have noticed long ago.

"That…that explains almost everything," Charlie realized aloud. He turned his head to Axe, who was sitting there patiently, letting his words sink in.

"I'm sorry to be the one to tell you this," Axe finally said, "but you deserved to know."

"What if your bosses find out?" Charlie asked with concern.

"They won't. I'm on assignment here, and as far as anyone knows, I'm getting a physical done, which is in twenty minutes."

"Clever," Charlie complimented him. "Thank you for letting me know…even if it was bad news…"

"It was information that I knew you needed to help understand everything, so I'm glad to help. More than likely, if the director would put aside an old grudge, he'd recruit you into the agency."

"I'll never join an agency," Charlie said. "Your agency is the reason why the public doesn't know the name of the woman that won us the war and buried her behind black ink."

"I know you and the director hate each other over the same person, but you're going to need us for protection. Once Tristan and his bosses find out you're still alive, they're going to come back and finish the job."

"Let them," Charlie spat, "I'll be ready this time. If there's *one* thing I'm good at with my left hand, it's shooting."

Axe sighed. Charlie could see that Axe had been hoping he'd be willing to join.

"So if the director ever proposes such a stupid thing, tell him to eat a bag of dicks."

"Charlie…"

"No," he said resolutely.

Axe inhaled intently to calm himself. "We need you."

"Don't care," Charlie spat. "You all needed Blue Team, and the only op you all ever approved for rescue was for the director's sister, so fuck you. I had to kill my friends just to keep the mission going while you left us to rot while and took all the credit for the intel in the war. If you don't know what's wrong with that, then you and I will never see eye to eye."

"I'm well aware of everything that happened, Charlie. I just wanted you to have the chance to join. With your condition, the section chiefs would pressure the director to at least offer protection if not an analyst position."

"If all you're going to do for the next twenty minutes is try to recruit me, then save your energy and get out after you open all the blinds."

"Have it your way, Charlie," he said as he stood up, "but now is your best chance. Now is not the time for you and the director to rehash a three-year grudge."

Charlie looked away from him. "Thanks for the information, Axe," he said as cordially as possible.

"One day, you two just need to fight it out to see who's right," he replied as he walked out.

"You forgot the blinds, asshole," Charlie reminded him, but Axe closed the door.

After having dinner, Charlie received a message on his tool. It was more than likely Frank's response. Instead of asking for a nurse right away to help him, he waited for one to come into his room. The information that Axe had disclosed made all of the events unfold in his mind with much greater clarity, and so many different things from over the past year with Christie held new meaning to him. He needed the spare time to come to grips with everything, though he was still a long way from fully healing from the betrayal, both physically and mentally.

He stared at the ceiling as he realized just how different everything was to him now. Moments that were once remembered with nostalgia were now sifted with a fine-tooth comb, every detail examined thoroughly for signs that pointed to Christie and Tristan being FIA agents. The missions they had accepted also held new meaning, and it became clear that the Federation was definitely trying to disrupt the peace in the border regions. Why, he didn't know for sure, but whatever the reason was to cause such chaos, he'd been an unwitting actor and partly responsible.

He wouldn't be able to contact Axe again, but he knew how to contact IS3's Counter-Intelligence Department and let them know they needed to focus their efforts on the border planets if they hadn't already taken interest there. The Pit Vipers had scattered and disappeared, which meant that by now, they were already in Federation space. The mercs that weren't FIA agents had probably already joined other mercenary groups if they weren't dead. Intelligence agencies weren't known for their mercy when it came to witnesses.

"Good evening," a familiar voice said.

Charlie finally pulled himself away from his memories and saw Anabel standing there in her scrubs with her auburn hair in a ponytail. She smiled as she pulled Charlie's chart from the end of the hospital bed and recorded his vitals.

"You seem to be doing much better compared to yesterday," she remarked as she put the papers back in the holder. "You'll be out of here in no time."

"That's good to hear," Charlie replied.

Anabel noticed the flashing light on his tool on the left wrist. "You have a message," she announced to him.

"Yeah, I was hoping you could help me when you're done with your rounds."

Anabel smiled, the freckles on her face once again stretching with the skin on her face. "You sure you don't want to see it now?"

"No," Charlie said with a dismissive wave, "Go do your work. I've already waited two hours, what's another thirty or so minutes?"

"You know, it's my job to help the patients," she reminded him. "You don't have to feel like a burden for asking for help. It's our job after all."

Charlie snorted. "I'm fine. If I *needed* help, I would have asked two hours ago."

"Very well," the nurse said. "I'll see you in a half hour or so."

As soon as Anabel left to finish her rounds, Charlie's thoughts once again turned to his memories as he tried to see the patterns. After what felt like only a few short minutes, Anabel returned.

"Back already?" he asked with confusion.

Anabel's eyebrow raised with equal confusion. "I've been gone for an hour and a half dealing with a patient…"

Charlie looked at the clock in the room. The nurse was right. It was long past since she said she would return.

"Huh…must have been lost in my own thoughts," he muttered.

Anabel snickered. "Must have. I thought for sure I'd come back and you'd be angry with how long you waited."

Charlie chuckled. "Never. You've got a job to do, and I wouldn't hold it against you."

"Let's see what your message was," she said as she approached the left side of his bed and gently touched the protruding implant in his wrist to wake the tool.

"I need to make custom gestures when I'm out of here," Charlie noted.

Anabel got to the menu and was ready to select the message. "Ready?" she asked. Charlie nodded affirmatively. She selected the message and flipped the holographic screen toward him so he could see the video message.

"Charlie," Frank began in his thick Indie accent, "what kinda shit did ya get into? I'm on my way to the spaceport right now with Francis to come get ya—and don't think for a minute I wouldn't help ya or come see ya, son. Your cousin and I will be there in about three days, so make sure ya get all the hookers and coke out of your room when I get there."

Anabel laughed at Frank's joke. Charlie smirked.

"We'll talk more face-to-face, son. See ya soon."

"Your uncle sounds like a sweet man," Anabel said as she put the tool back to sleep.

"How he's related to my mother, I'll never know," Charlie replied.

"What do you mean?" she asked.

"Ah," Charlie said as he waved his hand dismissively, "you don't want to hear about that kind of shit."

"I owe you for making you wait so long," she said as she looked into his eyes and gently grasped his forearm.

"My parent's lack of affection isn't something *I* really want to talk about," he clarified.

"Were they neglectful?" she asked.

"Not in the traditional sense," Charlie answered, "they just…were never loving. I always had a roof, food, and I was never left wanting. They just never really hugged, kissed, or said much of anything. Conversations with them were more…"

Charlie stopped and looked at Anabel with narrowed eyes.

"How do you do that?" he asked.

"Do what?" she asked.

"Get me to open up like that," he explained. "I've haven't talked about my parents since I was a kid."

She pulled away from her gentle grasp on Charlie's arm.

*It's the touch…*

"Did they teach you that in nursing school or is it just a natural talent?" he asked.

Anabel smiled. "Bit of both."

Charlie looked away and smiled in spite of himself. Charlie considered her touch and how she was able to manipulate him to talk.

*Not manipulate…coerce? Encourage.*

Before his thoughts lingered for too long, he looked back at Anabel, who patiently waited for him to say something again.

*Encourage is definitely the word. She waits patiently for me to speak so the conversation doesn't feel forced. She practically uses the same tactics that Zoreah taught me. The same mechanisms that human intelligence interrogators use, but in a much gentler way.*

"Thank you for last night," Charlie finally said. "Your words…they meant more than you may understand."

Once again, the nurse smiled brightly. "Happy to help."

"Well, you don't have to linger here, though I appreciate the conversation."

"I know," she replied, "but the rest of the ICU right now are just people who were in accidents of some kind. Work-related injuries, car crashes, things like that. You're the only one in the ward right now that's really *hurting*, and you need more attention and care than the rest."

"I'm fine," he argued.

"Maybe, but last night proved otherwise," she rebutted.

Charlie looked away with embarrassment. "I…was just caught off guard."

"Sure you were," she said with an unconvinced tone as she grasped his forearm again. "The toughest and meanest men that come through those doors are always the ones that cry the hardest when someone shows them the smallest bits of compassion."

Charlie continued looking away. She gripped a little tighter to get his attention. He finally turned his head and looked at her.

"No shame in that, Charlie," she said in a soothing tone. "Just means you're human like everyone else."

# Chapter 8

Eri awoke the next morning to her alarm. She quickly changed her clothes and packed her dress for the wedding, along with a cardigan. Athens was in Magna Graecia's northern hemisphere and experienced winter while Corinth experienced summer in the southern hemisphere. Athens was close enough to the tropics that its winter was mild, but she knew that coming from the oppressive Corinthian summer would still make the mild Athenian weather cold to her. She looked at the time on her tool. Still enough time to spare to make coffee.

As she sipped her coffee, a knock came at the door. Eri walked to the door and opened it. Charlie was there, the car running out in the street. She quickly grabbed her bag and followed him out to the car. She meticulously laid her bag flat on the back seat and sat down in the front passenger seat. Charlie got into the driver's seat and silently put the car in gear.

"I wanted to thank you for taking me to Athens," Eri said, "it made things a lot easier today."

Charlie glanced at her, then returned his gaze to the road. "Like I said, it's no problem. I had things to do in Athens anyways. I just pushed my plans up a few days."

Charlie's blank expression meant that whatever was on his mind the night before remained entrenched. Even for him, he was quieter and more serious than the past two days. They continued onward, both sipping their coffees as they finally made it to *Silver Bow*'s site. Outside were a bunch of workers, and Francis tiredly directing them to certain parts of the ship.

"Did you two hire contractors?" she asked.

"We're too far behind schedule. We'd rather pay for help than spend another month or two than we planned. With a bunch of hired help, things like the interior can be finished so we don't have a drive core and shield generator just sitting out in the elements for weeks before we are able to install them."

Charlie diverted around all the workers and parked close to *Fire Arrow*. They got out and he quickly grabbed her bag out of the back. He carried it into the Dart and hung it from a shelf near the back. Eri followed closely and quietly observed. Charlie also had a bag on the shelves, but he was already dressed for the Athenian winter with pants, a button-up shirt, and a duster. What could be in the bag?

While he got things ready for takeoff, Eri glanced around the cramped cabin, looking at the minute details of the interior. There was only a bunk for one. The Dart was designed by the manufacturer for four people to travel in a tight space, but it appeared that Charlie had completely removed all but one of the bunks to create extra space. Where the other set of bunks were supposed to be, Charlie had made a bank of six jumper seats below a set of cabinets. He had already converted *Fire Arrow* into some sort of charter craft, probably for single-day flights. Next to the singular bed was a locker that used biometrics to open. Whatever was in there, he didn't want anyone to access it.

On an empty space of the wall next to the locker was the ship's name and a picture of a flaming arrow was painted beneath it. The cockpit remained relatively the same, but a few modules had been rigged to the empty spaces on the main console, more than likely the upgraded and added systems.

"Did you paint the arrow and name yourself?" she asked.

"Hmm? Oh, no," he replied with a chuckle, "Francis painted that."

"He's pretty talented," she concluded.

"He is, actually," he agreed as the drive core started with a high-pitched squeal and rhythmic hum. "If not for the revolution, he'd probably be an artist."

"So why didn't he become an artist after the war?"

Charlie turned his head slightly and looked out the window. He then returned his gaze to the console in front of him and started booting up systems. "That's probably a question for you to ask him," he replied in a soft but monotone voice, "it's not my place to say." Charlie then pressed a sequence of buttons on the console to his right. A screen above him turned on and displayed "*COR-TC.*"

"Corinth Traffic Control, this is Foxtrot Alpha Nine-Three-One-Three, requesting permission and instruction for low orbit flight path to Athens Spaceport, over."

"Foxtrot Alpha Nine-Three-One-Three, this is COR-TC, do you have a reserved hangar at ATH-SP, over?"

"Negative, COR-TC, we would like to reserve a hangar now, if possible, over."

"Roger Nine-Three-One-Three, stand by, over."

Charlie started pressing switches and buttons. The engines came to life and droned loudly. A high-pitched hiss joined the orchestra of machines as the vertical takeoff and landing system prepared to do its work.

"Foxtrot Alpha Nine-Three-One-Three, this is COR-TC, we are sending you vector and altitude orders for low orbit flight to ATH-SP. You will travel by two-seven-nine at fifty kay. You will land in hangar fifty-one, how copy?"

"Hangar fifty-one, roger. Foxtrot Alpha Nine-Three-One-Three will launch in thirty seconds, two souls aboard, how copy?"

"Good copy, Nine-Three-One-Three, over and out."

Charlie turned to her from his pilot's seat. "Strap yourself into one of the jumper seats. We're taking off."

Eri quickly sat down and buckled the four-point harness as the rear ramp closed. Charlie then pushed forward on a stick and *Fire Arrow* lifted with the VTOL. The ship lifted vertically until Charlie began to push forward on another stick, causing the engines to whir louder than before. The windscreen's HUD showed his designated flight path as he slowly increased engine power and cut off the VTOL. They cruised for a time as they passed over Corinth's main street and meager spaceport. She watched the monitor as one of the approaching rectangles on the HUD flashed yellow.

"What does that mean?" she asked.

"That's where I'm in much looser speed restrictions," he replied as he gripped the engine throttle. "Hold on tight, we're going to accelerate fast."

As soon as they "passed through" the yellow rectangle on the HUD, Charlie pushed the throttle forward. The engines roared as the ship accelerated. Even though *Fire Arrow* clearly had inertial dampeners, Eri still managed to feel the acceleration. Charlie was going as fast as he was allowed. After some slight course corrections, Charlie turned on the autopilot. Multiple screens displayed "*AP Cruise*" as he pressed a button and the pilot's seat pulled back and turned him around. He got up from the seat as Eri struggled with the four-point harness.

Charlie popped the harness buckle with the side of his prosthetic hand. "That buckle was always finnicky," he said as he woke-up his tool and began typing something.

"Thanks," Eri said as she got up from the jumper seat. "How long have you been flying *Fire Arrow*?"

"Just a little over two years," he said as he pressed a button on the projected screen and caused it to close.

Eri nodded and slowly approached the cockpit area of the ship. The large window, which was an iconic staple of the Dart's design, allowed her to have a mostly unhindered view of the planet from low orbit. Seeing a planet so clearly from fifty kilometers was an incredible view. Awestruck, she simply stood there and watched the planet move past as the engines hummed at cruising thrust.

"This is one of my favorite things about the Dart," he said, "the window allows for the pilot—and passengers—to truly enjoy seeing the galaxy."

"I've never taken a low orbit flight," Eri admitted, "but it by far has the best view."

"I completely agree," Charlie replied, "you can still see the details of the planet while also enjoying the uninhibited vastness of space."

She turned around to see Charlie standing idle with his hands behind his back, gazing out into the darkness. His body language and face showed a deep reverence...and peace.

"You really enjoy this, don't you?" Eri asked softly.

Charlie snapped out of his state and looked at her for a moment. "When you've had a life like mine, moments of peace are rare. You try to enjoy them while you can."

Eri did not know what to say to that. She hadn't expected such a personal yet vague response. When Francis had her sign the contract, he'd mentioned that Charlie fought in the war—she did not know which side—but their experiences seemed wildly different from each other. Francis was a grunt that fought on the front lines, but Charlie showed no indication that he'd done the same, and avoided talking about the war altogether. Charlie clearly was a capable fighter and leader since he oversaw security and Ash's training, so he must have fought as well, but not on the horrific battlefields that took so many of Francis's friends. Charlie's history with the war seemed more personal, more intimate.

"You alright?" Charlie asked.

"Huh?" she muttered as she found herself back in the ship. "Sorry, was just thinking about what you said…"

"What were you thinking about?" he asked.

"It's just the way you talk about the revolution," she explained. "Well, I guess how you *don't* talk about it. It's clear that it gave you *many* scars, but it's not the same way that Francis talks about it. It feels…I don't know how to explain it…"

"Well, if you were referring to the arm, I didn't lose it in the war," he said as he sat down on the bunk, "I lost it because of the war."

"I don't understand," she said.

"It's hard to explain, and I'm not ready to talk about that subject with you. I got out of the war without any major physical injuries, but all of this is because of what I did in the war."

"What could you have possibly done that caused you to lose your arm?" she asked in bewilderment.

"I just told you that I didn't want to talk about it," he reiterated.

It was clear that the arm was a very sensitive subject with him, and not because he lost it, but *why* and *how* he lost it. She wasn't going to try to pry it out of him, though. He'd said that he wasn't ready to talk about it, which meant he might one day.

An awkward silence dwelled in the cabin as the ship continued on its course. Eri sat in one of the jumper seats as Charlie looked at his feet on the bunk. She realized that she had brought back bad memories. She wanted to apologize, but she remained silent.

"So, I wanted to talk to you about something," she said finally, "but I want to make sure that you tell me the truth and won't change the subject or avoid answering altogether." Charlie slowly looked up and silently waited for the question. "Promise me," she demanded.

Charlie sighed and nodded his head slowly. "I promise. What's the question?"

"Ash thinks that you only offered her a job because you offered me a job."

Charlie snorted. "No."

"Then why did you offer her the position?"

Charlie stood up, grabbed his coffee off the pilot's console, and took a large gulp. "There are certain aspects that I'm looking for in the person that has to fight alongside me. I'm not looking for the most talented or decorated. I'm looking for someone that is moldable and willing to put effort into doing what is necessary. Combat skill comes not with sheer talent, but training and experience. We may be one day significantly outnumbered by some scumbags willing to shoot at us for cargo, and I need to know that the person next to me put enough effort into their training that they will be able to do their job without a second thought.

"Ash is someone who may be hardheaded, but it only affects her when it has to do with her ego and reputation, which is fixable. I would not have hired someone who already had years of training and believed that they knew better than me. What I need is someone who will trust my tactics and plans. Ash is confident, but she knows—at least now—that she still has much to learn. That's the kind of person that I wanted in a recruit: someone to mentor. If I wanted a mercenary, I would have just hired a mercenary.

"Lastly, Ash has a personal stake in her job. She obviously cares deeply about you, being her sister and all. Someone with a personal stake in keeping others safe will always try a little harder than someone just earning a paycheck. That little bit of effort can be the difference between life and death. Ash has a lot to learn, but she's probably the best candidate I could have gotten. The next month or so *will* be the hardest of Ash's life, but she will emerge as a skilled fighter, intelligent tactician, efficient soldier, and a good leader."

"Is that what your mentor said to you?" Eri asked.

"No," he replied quietly, "I learned almost everything I know through failure."

"Did you not have a mentor?"

Charlie looked back at the floor and breathed deeply. "I was never given much of a chance to be mentored. Many people train and prepare for leadership, but many, if not more, are thrust into it out of necessity. One of the few things Francis and I have in common when it comes to the revolution."

Eri pondered on what Charlie had said about Ash. It was good to know that Ash was wrong about Charlie's decision. He said that the next month would be the hardest of her life, which meant every day would probably be spent training with him, and judging by his physique, Ash would be even more fit than she was in the militia.

"I just remembered," Charlie finally realized, "do you have Ash's measurements?"

"Oh, yeah," Eri said as she pulled the piece of paper out of her pants. He examined the paper, looking away in thought twice before placing it in his duster's breast pocket.

"That actually brings me to a different subject," Charlie said. Eri noticed that Charlie became uneasy and awkward—a first since she had met him. "I just want you to know that you shouldn't look too much into it because I know how it will probably look and seem when I say it, but..." He paused for a moment. It was clear that he was uneasy about what he wanted to say. His nervousness was alien. "But I will be spending a large sum of cash buying Ash armor since she will be working with me. I...I thought it only fair that I return the favor and also spend a large amount of cash on you."

Eri was intrigued. She raised an eyebrow waiting to receive all of the context.

"Again," he said with an uneasy chuckle, "this could be construed in many different ways, and I only ask that you don't look too deeply into it."

"I never thought I would ever ask you to get to the point, yet here I am…"

"Look, I'm just trying to offer a kind gesture for the sake of fairness and to avoid being accused of favoritism."

"And I would love to finally know what this supposedly kind gesture is," Eri replied impatiently.

Charlie sighed, clearly flustered. He turned around and placed his left thumb on the locker's biometric scanner, a whirring sound indicating that it had unlocked. He reached inside and removed an envelope before closing and locking it again, then turned around and held the envelope out toward her. "This is money for you to spend on yourself," he said as she opened the envelope, revealing a literal stack of cash. "I have a friend in Athens that specializes in makeovers and helping men and women to look their best for special occasions. If she likes you—and I think she will—she can get your hair styled, your makeup professionally done, and a new dress if you want. She's not cheap, so hopefully that will be enough."

The sight of a stack of cash wrapped in bank paper made Eri freeze in the jumper seat. Charlie just casually handed her ten thousand shen for essentially a makeover. Her mouth agape, she looked up at him. He cleared his throat, trying to fight against his nervousness.

"I…I don't know what to say," she muttered in disbelief.

"Like I said, don't look too much into it," he reiterated as he rubbed the back of his head. "I'm not saying that you're ugly and need a makeover or that I'm trying to win you over by flaunting money or anything like that. I'm just going to spend a lot of my funds on Ash's armor and—for the sake of fairness—you should be able to treat yourself and feel good at your friend's wedding at my expense. You already have all the tools you need at the moment, and since Ash's armor will be permanently hers—even if she quits or is fired—you should be able to have something that would also be considered a luxury."

Eri couldn't help but look at the cash again, her eyes blinking slowly in shock. "That's…very thoughtful of you, actually," she replied with a smile, "but you do not need to spend this kind of money on me just because Ash needs expensive equipment."

"I insist," he said in his usual serious demeanor, "you should enjoy your friend's wedding and you may miss out on quite a few because of our work. Besides, I'm still spending less on you than Ash," he admitted.

"I'm kind of curious if Francis knows about this, or if he put you up to this…"

Charlie averted her gaze and shook his head. "No, this is all my idea."

"I…I've never had a makeover," she realized. "This is really sweet, Charlie, thank you." Charlie smirked, still avoiding her gaze.

"Well, it's the best I can do," he replied, "and anything left over is for you to keep and use as you see fit." Charlie reached into his coat pocket and revealed a business card. "That's Michelle's card. Go see her as soon as we land so you can be done in time for the wedding."

Eri grabbed her bag and placed the cash and business card within. Butterflies grew in her stomach as she anticipated the morning's activities.

"I've got a long day ahead of me," Charlie began as he opened the locker again, "I'm going to leave you as soon as we land so I have enough time to do everything. Are you going to be okay by yourself?"

"Yeah, I should be…fine…" She almost forgot what to say as she saw him reveal a handgun, pulled back on the slide to show a chambered round, and holstered it. "Athens is a pretty safe town, at least in all the places that *I'm* going to."

"That's good," he replied as he pulled out another envelope, one much thicker than the one he handed Eri, and stuffed it into one of his breast pockets, "but if you need anything, you have my contact ID." Charlie revealed a large knife in a sheath and stuffed it in his waistband opposite his pistol. "Call if its urgent, message if otherwise." Charlie produced four pistol magazines and attached them to his belt.

"Is there something I should know about?" Eri asked nervously.

"Just preparing for the worst," he replied casually.

"Does the worst involve a gunfight and stabbing and then bribing the police afterward?"

Charlie closed the locker with a chuckle and fixed his clothes to completely conceal all of the weapons and cash. He turned around and looked at her for the first time since he had offered her the stack of cash. "I'm the head of security, which means I deal with the…less savory kind of clientele on Francis's behalf. As freighters, we can't be too picky with our clients, and sometimes that means dealing with individuals who will be even more armed that I am right now. I prefer to be less brazen with my weapons, so I have to be more prepared than they are, which means carrying more than one magazine of ammunition and a knife in case I'm disarmed or run out of ammunition."

"So what's all the cash for?"

Charlie chuckled again. "I told you that I was spending a lot on Ash."

"Oh…"

Charlie put on a pair of gloves and woke his tool to examine the time. With a satisfied nod, he sat down in the pilot's seat. The chair turned around and pulled him up to the console, where he flipped a switch and the screens began to show information again. The HUD showed the rectangles that gave his flight path. Far ahead, a red rectangle slowly approached. He pressed a few switches and the screen above his head displayed "*ATH-SP*."

"ATH-SP, this is Foxtrot Alpha Nine-Three-One-Three on approach to hangar fifty-one. Requesting approach vector, velocity, and timing, over."

"FA Nine-Three-One-Three, ATH-SP, do not deviate from current course vector and reduce velocity to five hundred at first checkpoint and then to one fifty at second checkpoint, over."

"Roger, ATH-SP, Foxtrot Alpha Nine-Three-One-Three maintaining course vector and reducing velocity to five hundred. Out."

Charlie reduced thrust to zero and activated the retro thrusters, quickly reducing their speed from thousands of kilometers per hour to five hundred. Once he hit the correct speed, he returned the engines to thrust and began to follow the designated flight path.

"Strap in again," he commanded.

Eri quietly sat in a jumper seat and buckled the harness, watching the ship fly through the clouds to reveal the city of Athens. She missed seeing the quaint but dense skyline of the city after being gone for a year.

Charlie gracefully flew the ship to their reserved hangar and softly landed. He then flipped multiple switches and the hum of the engine and drive core went quiet. The chair pulled back and turned around again. He left his seat as Eri unbuckled herself out of the harness.

Eri pulled a cardigan out of her bag, readying herself for the thirty-degree difference in temperature. Charlie pressed a button on the console and the back ramp opened. The two exited the ship as a dockworker jogged up to meet them. As soon as Eri cleared the ramp, Charlie jumped off it to one side and pressed the button to close it. The dockworker stopped in front of Charlie as the ramp clanked shut and the first officer pressed a combination of numbers on the pad to lock the entire ship. The dockworker handed him a tablet and a stylus. He signed on the tablet three times and handed the man two hundred shen.

The two made their way to the hangar's exit. The cool breeze hit their faces as they walked together silently. The spaceport had a lot of traffic moving in and out and the constant noise of VTOLs and engines created a symphony that Eri had not heard since her days living in Athens or Yongsan. They reached an automatic conveyer that took them to the exit for taxis, buses, private transport, and such. Eri clutched her bag with both happiness and anxiety. She could go get the dress of her dreams, get her hair styled, and have a professional do her makeup for the wedding, but she was carrying *so much cash*.

Eri finally broke the silence between them. "I just realized…I don't think I ever got your contact in my tool."

"Francis should have given it to you yesterday," he replied matter-of-factly.

"Okay," she said as she woke up the tool and scrolled through her contacts. "No, sorry, it's not there." Charlie woke his tool, went through a few screens, then swiped the holographic image toward her. The screen transferred from one tool to the other. She quickly read the contact info before closing it. "Charlie…*Menillo*? What kind of name is Menillo?"

"Italian, I think," he said with a shrug.

"Well it's a pleasure to finally meet you, Charlie Menillo," she said with a sarcastic grin.

"Don't push it or I'll take the money back," he said dryly.

"You're such a buzzkill," she replied playfully as she turned away from him.

Eri separated from Charlie right outside the spaceport to find herself a bite to eat. She hadn't eaten anything since the night before, and she figured that now would be the perfect time to eat before the reception. Once she scarfed down some of the local street food, she called Michelle's number on the business card that Charlie gave her. After a few rings, she heard a very bubbly woman answer the phone.

"Draper and McKinney, how may I direct your call?"

"Michelle Draper, please."

"May I ask who's calling?"

"My name is Eri Bezek, Charlie Menillo recommended her."

"Of course, hon, I'll connect you now."

For a few minutes Eri anxiously waited while she heard hold music play through her earpiece. She tapped her foot to help alleviate her impatience as the music continued to drone. Suddenly, the music stopped.

"Michelle Draper," a woman said with a flat tone.

"Uh, yes, hi," Eri responded nervously, "Charlie Menillo recommended me to you about getting a dress, hair style, and makeup for a wedding?" There was silence on the other line. Eri checked to make sure she hadn't accidentally hit the mute button. "Hello?"

"Who are you and how do you know Chuck?"
*Chuck?*
"I'm Eri Bezek, I work for him."

Another long silence. "Come meet me at my office—address is on the business card he gave you," she said with her flat tone before hanging up.

That was probably the most awkward phone conversation Eri had ever had with someone. She looked at the card and read the address. She would need a taxi. She ran to the corner and waited to find a taxi in service and hailed it down. The cab drove for fifteen minutes until they reached the financial district, then stopped in front of Draper and McKinney. She'd lived in Athens for a year and she had never heard of the place. She walked inside where she was greeted by the same bubbly woman who answered the phone earlier.

"Hi, hon, how may I help you?" she asked with a smile.

"Michelle Draper asked for me to meet her in her office; I'm Eri Bezek," she said awkwardly.

"Oh yes," she said as she gestured toward a door, "she's waiting for you."

Eri thanked her and made her way to the office. She knocked and slowly opened the door, peering in to make sure she wasn't interrupting anything. She leaned in a little farther to see a middle-aged woman sitting behind the desk. She wore a business casual outfit—a white cardigan draped over a navy blue pencil skirt and a simple top that complimented her runner's figure. Her curly blond hair seemed to naturally rest at the perfect length. In sum, Michelle was a gorgeous woman with style who could get the affection and attention of most men half her age. She was practically a fashion model in terms of her appearance.

"Stand right here, girl," she said with authority.

Eri awkwardly stood across from her. She scanned her and stood up. She walked all around Eri, looking up and down as she went. Michelle then went back to her chair and gestured for Eri to take a seat.

"Well at least this time he sent a woman," she grumbled as she pulled out a piece of paper and began furiously writing notes. Eri's leg shook with nervousness. "Stop shaking your leg, girl," she commanded.

"Sorry," she said sheepishly.

Michelle finished her notes with a flourish of her fountain pen and set it down. "So you work for Chuck?"

"Yes, ma'am."

"Oh god, please don't call me 'ma'am,'" she replied with disgust, "Michelle, please."

"Okay, Michelle," Eri managed to say.

Michelle gazed at her and smirked. "He's never talked about me, has he?"

"I didn't know who you were until forty-five minutes ago," she admitted.

Michelle cackled with laughter. "Typical Chuck. Keeping all his best assets and confidants close to his chest." She leaned back in her chair and crossed her legs. "I help Chuck from time to time when he or a crew member of his needs a makeover, a custom tux, or what have you. How is his brother and that cute girl, Christie?"

"I didn't know he had a brother," Eri confessed, "and I don't know any Christie. Sorry I can't be any more help."

"You must be brand new to the ship, aren't you?" she asked.

"Yeah."

"No matter. So whose wedding are you going to? Did Chuck finally tie the knot?"

*Tie the knot? What is she talking about? Is he…engaged?*

"No, it's my friend's wedding down at the Starian. I had a dress already picked out, but Charlie insisted that I see you."

"Chuck may dress like a bum most of the time," Michelle said as she got up, "but he has *great* taste. I don't know who is paying, but if you are, I want you to know that my services come with a price that is steep but fair for the level of quality that I provide."

"Charlie is paying, and I have the cash on me."

"Excellent. Let's get started."

# Chapter 9

Charlie watched Eri leave for a small street vendor as soon as they exited the spaceport. He thought about the last time he ate, and realized it was the day before at the bar. He could use some food. He woke his tool and sent out a message asking the contact to meet him at Santoku. It was a ten-minute walk, but he could use the fresh, brisk air to help clear his head. He made his way through the crowded sidewalk, reflexively dodging people as he went.

It had only been a few weeks since he was last in Athens, but it felt like much longer. So much had happened to him and Francis since then. As he waited at a crosswalk, his thoughts began to dwell on Eri, wondering if Michelle would like her enough to take her as a client and how she would look once Michelle worked her magic.

*If I have time, I should also give Michelle a visit for a suit...never know when I may need to talk to a wealthy client...*

"Move it," an impatient man said behind him.

Charlie looked up and noticed that he was able to cross. He made his way to the other side of the street and walked down a few more blocks until he reached Santoku. He walked inside and sat down at a table facing the front door. The waiter came by and took his drink order while he waited for his lunch partner. The waiter quickly returned with a carafe of sake and a glass of water. The waiter silently poured his sake into the small cup and left. He was drinking the sake when he noticed a familiar face enter through the doorway. The man made his way to Charlie and sat down.

"Well, well," the man began with a sly smile, "if it isn't my favorite customer. How ya been, Charlie?"

Charlie scanned the restaurant. Nothing out of the ordinary. "I'm doing just fine, Sven." The waiter returned with a glass of water and Charlie silently waited for the waiter to leave. "I've got some merchandise I'd like to purchase and have it fit to spec."

"Sounds fun," Sven replied, "getting yourself another set of armor?"

"Yes, but not for me," Charlie replied as he sipped the sake again, "it's for a crew member. Tall woman with great shooting skills."

"You got her measurements?" he asked as he reached across the table with an open hand.

Charlie pulled the paper out of his pocket and handed it to him. Sven quickly read the paper and put it in his coat. He laughed with a wheeze. "So basically you, if you were a woman," Sven concluded.

"Practically," Charlie admitted, "she's almost exactly my height."

"Oh I bet she's got a great set of thick thighs," Sven said dreamily as he re-examined the measurements, "Oh, yeah…she's got thighs that I'd love to choke me."

"Focus. I want the armor and the generator, just like my set."

"You got the money?" Sven asked seriously. Charlie handed him the envelope under the table. Sven discreetly looked inside to confirm the thirty thousand shen. He looked at Charlie and nodded. He then quickly put the envelope in his coat's breast pocket. "I'll have it ready in three to four weeks."

"You got my number, just send me a message when it's ready," Charlie said as Sven stood up with a grunt. "Aren't you going to stay and have lunch with your favorite customer?"

"I already ate. Enjoy your lunch." With that, Sven left the restaurant. The waiter returned and took Charlie's order after being informed that he would be dining solo.

Charlie walked out of Santoku with his hunger satiated. He was patiently waiting to hail a taxi when he noticed a familiar marking on the building across the street. He looked around and made his way to the sprayed graffiti. He closely examined the marking. It was pointing at the nearest garbage bin, where he found a small piece of paper attached to the side with tape. He pulled the paper off the bin.

*"Kushik Memorial Park, noon,"* was all that was written on the paper.

*Axe...*

Charlie looked at the time. Noon was an hour away. He could do the other errand in the meantime. He hailed a cab and quickly instructed the driver where to go. Twenty minutes later, the cab pulled up to a nightclub called Sinister on the edge of the city near an industrial park. The name was far more appropriate than most understood. He waited for the taxi to leave the area before he moved from his spot in the parking lot. He approached the front door, sighed, and knocked hard on the door. The door opened swiftly to reveal a tall and burly man standing in front of Charlie. The man signaled Charlie to enter.

"You know the drill," the sizeable man said. Charlie spread his legs and stretched his arms out. The large man frisked him and removed the pistol from its holster. Charlie remained silent as the man removed the magazine and the round out of the chamber and laid the pistol on a small table next to the door. The burly man then removed the knife from Charlie's belt and gestured at a man sitting in a booth on the far side of the closed night club. "He's good, boss."

Charlie walked over to the large booth in the VIP section with three men. In the middle sat a man wearing a dress shirt and tie. The dress shirt's sleeves were rolled up above his elbows, the topmost button was unfastened, and the tie sat loose around his neck. On either side of him sat two extremely serious guards with their hands on their concealed weapons. Charlie calmly sat across from them.

"Jessik," Charlie greeted the man in the middle, "you know how much I don't like it when one of your messengers contact me at the bar in Corinth. What do you need?"

"No 'how are you' or 'good to see you?' Not even a calm 'go fuck yourself?'" Jessik asked in annoyance.

"I've got shit to do, Jessik," Charlie replied. "What do you want?"

"Well fuck me for trying to establish some fuckin' decorum, doggie," Jessik spat. "I'm just trying to ease you into the job with some light and cordial conversation." Charlie simply stared at Jessik, showing his boredom. "I've got a job for you, dog, and it'll pay well." He looked around, trying to find something. "Where the fuck are the matches?"

"I got one right here, boss," the goon on the right said as he pulled out a matchbook.

Jessik revealed a cigar from his jacket, cut the tip off, and lit it with a match. He let out a large puff of smoke in Charlie's direction, ensuring that the smoke would directly hit his face. Charlie didn't flinch, cough, or even blink. He wanted Jessik to know that he wasn't in the mood to play games. "So fuckin' serious," he said in a mocking tone, "loosen up, buddy, eh?"

"What's the job?" Charlie asked as he lit a cigarette. "It's obviously important if you sent a guy to the bar last night just to tell me to see you, so out with it."

Jessik puffed again on his cigar. "One of my guys seriously fucked up. He got pulled over by a cop and he fuckin' killed the bastard, all to avoid a simple drug charge."

"How is this my problem, Jessik?" Charlie asked.

"I'm fuckin' getting there, shithead," Jessik replied. "Where was I? Oh, yes. So, my guys aren't allowed to kill cops. We keep the peace by letting them get their minor drug arrests and in return, we don't start a war and kill them. My guy has upset the delicate balance, and now the cops will certainly start shit with me and my guys unless I give them a peace offering, you follow?"

"I get it, Jessik: you don't bother them, and they don't bother you. I'm still waiting on why this is my problem."

"It's not your problem, but you're gonna be the *solution,* dog. The dumb fuck who shot the cop is now a cop killer, which means there's a big bounty on his head, and you're gonna help me deliver him to the cops as a peace offering. He's got a twenty-five grand bounty on him, dead or alive. You're gonna find him, put one of those nice bullets you got in that busted pistol you got over there on the table into his brain, and then you're gonna collect on the bounty. I'll tell you where he's at to make this the easiest bounty you've ever collected, *but I get half.* Finder's fee and all that shit. Deal?"

Charlie stamped out his cigarette in the ashtray in front of him and stood up. Jessik slid a business card with writing on the back across the table, which Charlie clutched and put into this coat pocket. He made his way back to the front door and collected his pistol and knife, the doorman keeping his own pistol ready.

"Do it sooner, rather than later, my little Pit Bull," Jessik added. "I want that peace offering before the cops make my life hell."

Charlie waved his hand dismissively but in affirmation as he walked out of Sinister. He never liked working with a mob boss like Jessik, but he was a means to an end, and mob bosses like him never let go of assets like Charlie. He looked at the time on his tool and could see that he would arrive at the park just in time. He walked ten blocks and found an empty park bench. He looked around to see if he could find Axe, but he was obviously hiding, waiting for his signal. Charlie lit another cigarette and waited. Just as he was about to put out the cigarette, he heard footsteps in the grass behind him. A man with a bag sat down next to him and looked out at the families enjoying the park.

"Axe," Charlie greeted.

"How've you been, Charlie?" he asked in return.

"You have something for me?"

The man opened his bag and revealed three folders full of papers. Axe glanced inside each one, grabbed the second one, and handed it to Charlie. He read the contents inside the folder and looked at Axe, who was glancing at him through the side of his eye.

"He's leading a section now?" Charlie asked in shock, still reading.

"The promotion was official two weeks ago," Axe replied. "He's more ambitious than we thought."

"He's more ambitious than *you* thought," Charlie corrected as he continued looking through the contents of the folder.

"Regardless," Axe said, "this makes things far more difficult for you."

"I understand the implications of him being a section head," Charlie whispered angrily, "it means he can start creating and approving ops—"

"Which means he'll start coming after you with impunity. You know how much Tristan hates you and everything you did for the revolution—everything you stand for. If he can kill or capture you—make an example of you—he'll start doing much more than what he's allowed."

"He'll start trying to find ways to restart the war," Charlie concluded.

"A lot of powerful people in the Federation already believe that the war shouldn't have ended the way it did. They want to restart the damn thing and take back all the systems they lost. They'll use Tristan to make that happen."

"If that were to happen, is IFSA ready to fight?" Charlie asked.

Axe sighed. Charlie could see his fear and uncertainty with that question. IFSA was just starting to recover from its revolution for independence from the Federation almost six years after the armistice. If war came again, the planets in Frontier space would certainly be crippled. The economy was just starting to actually turn upward and recover.

One thing that helped the rebels win the Isolde Revolution was their willingness to fight against the draftees of the Federal Navy, but volunteer manpower in a war could only go so far. Without industry, a large army would only be a mass of meat to catch enemy ordnance.

Axe shook his head, clearly not confident that IFSA was ready for another devastating war.

Charlie closed the folder and returned it to Axe, who immediately hid it back in his bag. Axe then handed him another folder. Charlie quickly scanned the pages within. "Still nothing on her?" he asked for confirmation.

Axe shook his head. "She's ghosted. More than likely, she either assumed a new identity, or we're looking for her assumed identity."

"She'll turn up eventually," Charlie said with conviction, "I know it."

Axe exchanged folders with Charlie again. He read the contents inside and remained still. He closed the folder and silently returned it to Axe.

"How long has Johan been on this assignment?" Charlie asked quietly.

"A little over six months now," Axe replied. "I know that he was on Blue Team and you kept in contact with him in the years proceeding it. I just thought you should know considering how close you two were."

"I hope he's alright…"

"Communication blackouts can be caused by a multitude of things," Axe responded to comfort him, "he could just be lying low for the moment."

"Or he could be dead," Charlie said pessimistically.

"True, but more than likely alive and just lying low."

"What was he doing prior to his radio silence?" Charlie asked.

"I can't tell you that," Axe replied.

"C'mon, Axe," Charlie pleaded quietly, "you let me know about that, but not the op he's working? You know I have contacts outside of IS3 circles. Let me put feelers out there and see if he's okay."

"If I let you try to figure that out, IS3 will know that I gave you the information. They keep tabs on you as much as the FIA." Charlie quietly growled in frustration. "Look, Charlie, I'm helping you out because you deserve to know some of these things, but I can't just leak ops files for your peace of mind. If you want to know everything, you need to join IS3."

"I'm not joining that country club," Charlie sneered with contempt, "both you and the FIA are nothing more than politicians that operate in the shadows instead of the cameras. I won't do it, and I won't become part of an organization that will force me to kill my friends all for the sake of a bullshit notion like 'the greater good' or for the sake of OPSEC. I did enough for the Frontier Systems and I sure as shit have sacrificed enough."

Charlie could barely contain his anger. Even with all the news Axe just gave him, he was still trying to recruit Charlie into the IS3. Axe knew how much Charlie resented intelligence agencies and spies during and after the war, how ambition within the ranks of the agencies caused unnecessary death and destruction, how intelligence agencies often worked outside the law without restrictions, oversight, or accountability. Charlie breathed sharply through his nostrils, doing what he could to mitigate his rage.

"Charlie," Axe said calmly, "I know you hate everything that IS3 does and what they have done, but if you ever want protection from Tristan and to help Johan, you're going to need to join IS3. The director told you as much."

Charlie's hands shook as he lit a cigarette in both fear and rage. Johan, one of three people in Charlie's team that survived the war, was probably in trouble or dead. Worse still, Tristan now had the power to reach out and touch him. He was now truly in danger—him and his crew. He figured that the bureaucracy within the FIA would at least have given him another year or two, but Tristan was hard at work, singularly focused on making an example of Charlie. What if killing Johan was Tristan's first act as section chief? What if Tristan knew about Johan all along?

"I'm not joining IS3," Charlie said finally, "take your proposal to someone who's as naïve as I was…"

"Charlie," Axe began calmly, "things are different now. We can *and will* offer protection, but you know too much. The director will force you to join IS3 before we ever give you, your family, and your friends protection."

"Yeah," Charlie scoffed, "don't want to protect a former or potential asset, only one that you have…we're done here."

Charlie quickly got up from the bench and walked away before Axe had a chance to refute or rebut him. He took a long drag of his cigarette as he left the park. Once he was out of Axe's sight, Charlie woke his tool and drafted a message to Francis. It was simple, and definitely would get the point across.

Charlie: T made section chief.

Charlie had walked for a block when the realization of everything hit him in a wave. He couldn't hold his composure any longer. His hands trembled uncontrollably, his breathing labored, his vision narrowed, his mind raced, and sweat began to erupt from his skin.

He quickly turned into an alleyway and leaned against the wall. He began to hyperventilate as the city noises quieted to a low drone in his ears. He felt and heard his heartrate skyrocket in his temples, the pumping becoming louder and louder. His eyes danced around the wall in front of him as he fruitlessly tried to slow his breathing and calm down. Sweat poured down his brow, the heat of his body flashing high like a fever. He dropped his coat on the ground as he dropped down, his feet tucked up against his rear. His hands continued to tremble as he clutched his head with them, the sweat on his scalp seeping onto his fingers and palms. The walls felt like they were closing in on him.

He suddenly smelled blood, gunpowder, and wheat grain. The concrete alleyway morphed into the abandoned warehouse from three years ago, and his left chest felt tight and heavy. His left shoulder blade burned with pain. He couldn't hear anything except for distant gunfire and the loud shriek of tinnitus. He pulled himself up from the ground, but the bullet wound in his left lung was causing the sack around it to fill up with air and blood. He could feel the pressure growing and crushing his left lung more and more.

"We got to get out of here!" he heard a woman shout in the distance.

"This will finish it," a distant man's voice said with confidence as Charlie heard the thud of a grenade land on the pile of grain next to him.

A hand touched his right shoulder, whipping his mind back into reality.

"Sir," the man next to him said, "you alright?"

He managed to slow his breathing after what seemed to be an eternity. A couple knelt next to him. He finally could see their faces, the details, their concern; they were no longer silhouettes.

"You alright, sir?" the woman asked.

Charlie blinked. He hadn't experienced a flashback in over a year.

*I thought I was over this...*

"Looked like you had a bit of a panic attack," the man said, "do you need an ambulance?"

Charlie closed his eyes and breathed deeply. He reopened them. "No," he said shakily, "I'm fine." He gathered himself and stood up. The man grabbed the coat that Charlie had sat on and handed it to him. "Thank you," Charlie said humbly, "but I'll be fine."

The couple nodded slowly and walked away. Charlie gripped his coat and leaned against the wall, his eyes looking up at the afternoon sky. He steadied his breathing as cold sweat fell down his face and neck. After another few minutes of steadying himself, he gritted his teeth and forcefully regained his focus.

Charlie got back to the sidewalk and joined the crowd. He pulled out the business card that Jessik gave him and read the address. The cop killer's apartment was on the far side of town. Charlie hailed a cab and sat down in the back seat.

He woke his tool and saw that he had an unread message. He tapped on the notification and saw that it was from Michelle.

Michelle: Chuck, darling, when are you going to come back and let me design a new suit for you? I like Erina, I can see why you sent her to me. She's a darling and a stunning beauty waiting to be seen.

Charlie smirked and composed a reply.

Charlie: I thought you'd like her. She's a certified maintainer. Probably spent more time in coveralls in the past few years than dresses her entire life. Send me a picture when you're done.

After a block in the back of the taxi, Charlie woke his tool again and sent Eri a message.

Charlie: Glad to hear Michelle likes you. Let me know if you need anything or if you need me to come get you. Go easy on the liquor.

After spending twenty-five minutes in a cab, Charlie arrived at the cop killer's apartment. He lived in a dingy complex that clearly had seen better days. The siding on the walls showed signs of mildew and mold from rain. Dogs barked aggressively from the windows of some apartments as a police siren wailed in the distance.

He rechecked the business card for the apartment number and slowly approached the apartment door, looking around to see if anyone was watching as he pulled out a small tablet from his inside breast pocket. Charlie pressed a few buttons on the screen to initiate a hack. The lock beeped after a few moments, and he made his way into the apartment, quickly closing the door to make sure no one saw him. He then put the tablet to sleep and placed it back in his breast pocket.

The dingy apartment reeked of stale cigarettes, so he lit one himself, knowing it wouldn't make a difference. He slowly examined the apartment for clues about the cop killer, but it seemed more like a halfway house than the man's apartment.

*Jessik sent him here to lie low, or that's at least what he thinks.*

Charlie sat down at the table in the breakfast nook and finished his cigarette, making sure to put the butt in his coat pocket to leave no evidence. His tool showed a notification on his wrist and he shook his hand back and forth lazily to open it with his custom gesture. The message came from Michelle and it was a picture of Eri, as requested.

Charlie couldn't believe his eyes. Eri had been transformed. Her hair was freshly styled, and she wore a dress with a low neckline and straps that gracefully rested on her upper arms. The bottom of the dress was asymmetrical with the front higher than the back, which accentuated her legs. Her hazel eyes were perfectly elevated by dark eyeliner and subtle eye shadow the same color as her dress. Her face glowed with a genuine, joyous smile. Somehow, Michelle and her team had made Eri into a woman that not even Charlie had imagined.

He took a drag of his cigarette and forwarded the picture to Ash and Francis.

Francis: Wow!

Ash: Holy shit! When did she get a dress like that?

Charlie noticed the time on his tool. It was 1:15 in the afternoon and he wondered how long he would need to wait. He made a fist and flicked his hand down like a head quickly nodding, and his tool went back to sleep. He finished his cigarette and put it in his pocket after he extinguished it, just like the one before.

He retrieved his sidearm from its holster and double-checked that he had a round in the chamber, waiting for the fool to arrive. The afternoon sun began to drop lower in the sky. Two cigarettes later, Charlie heard footsteps in front of the door. He woke his tool to look at the time.

*Two thirty...the wedding started half an hour ago.*

With his custom gesture, the tool went back to sleep. He quickly got up and hid in the kitchenette behind a wall. He heard the door beep with approval and the man walked inside. He heard the familiar hiss of someone smoking and the subsequent tapping of a cigarette in a full ashtray. The man groaned as he stumbled into the living room and dropped onto the couch with a thud. Charlie slowly and silently pulled his sidearm out of its holster and steeled himself.

"Don't move," Charlie calmly commanded as he pointed his gun at the man. He was leaning around the corner to minimize how much of his body was visible. Without hesitation, the man shrieked in fear and jumped through the glass window next to the door.

*Fuck.*

Charlie gave chase as the cop killer ran for his life. He followed him through the parking lot and behind the complex that ran near public rail. The cop killer jumped over a fence and onto the lower area with the rail tracks. Charlie continued to follow, but the cop killer was fast and losing him.

The cop killer turned around the corner of a large barn-like structure that Charlie could cut through to reduce the gap. Charlie emerged on the other side of the barn to see that he had significantly narrowed the margin between him and the target.

"The more you make me run," Charlie yelled between breaths, "the more I'll make you suffer, asshole!"

The cop killer showed no sign of hesitation and continued sprinting as fast as he could. Charlie's athleticism allowed him to continue running, but the cop killer proved to be too fast for him. The gap widened again as they dashed through the rail yard's support structures: fuel depots, cargo warehouses, and maintenance bays.

The cop killer doubled back as he turned a corner, but Charlie wasn't fooled. He knew to continuously check all angles to ensure he maintained sight on him. After the double-back gambit failed, the cop killer finally revealed a hidden pistol from his waistband and fired a couple of shots behind him, but his inexperience with shooting on the move meant that nothing even got close to Charlie.

The cop killer reached the end of a rail car, trying to use it as cover. He then leaned out from behind the car and took aim. Charlie slid on the gravel and took one precise shot. The bullet landed true and flew right through the cop killer's forehead and out the back of his skull. A spray of pink mist flew from behind his head and his body instantly fell lifelessly and unceremoniously to the ground.

Shooting people was not like what civilians saw in movies or on shows. When shot in the right spot, humans simply turned into objects affected by gravity. Their eyes didn't roll into the backs of their heads, body parts didn't jolt at the impact of the bullet, and there wasn't a long hesitation before the villain finally realized they were shot.

Charlie approached cautiously with his pistol still trained on the cop killer. You never knew what kind of strange or unusual thing could happen. He could somehow still be alive or his destroyed brain may send signals to his nerves, causing him to violently spasm. The body remained still, and Charlie robotically holstered his weapon.

He called the police, gave them his information and bounty hunting credentials to legitimize the killing, and then explained to them that he found the cop killer and had to kill him. He waited patiently by the body as the police arrived on scene. As soon as he caught sight of a police officer, Charlie put his hands on the back of his head with his fingers interlocked and peacefully surrendered.

The officers examined the body, searched Charlie, and after reviewing his credentials and finding them legitimate, took his statement as a police report. He then rode in one of the police vehicles back to the station to receive his bounty. While he waited for the cash of twenty-five thousand shen to be counted, he checked the time on his tool.

    *Three thirty. The reception should be starting in thirty minutes.*

# Chapter 10

Francis quietly observed the contractors doing their work as the foreman, Jayce, talked with him. There were three crews currently working. The first was working on restoring the interior to the bridge, the second on the living section, and the third on the cargo bay. Metal walls were being sandblasted or simply removed, flooring panels replaced, and wiring and lighting set up for when the drive core was installed.

"So the bridge crew all said that it shouldn't take long at all. Mostly just rust removal until ya get to the avionics, navigation, and whatnot. When they're done with restoring that, they'll start working on the ducting for all the wires. Our drone showed that most of the ducting was still in good shape, mostly just a few places here and there that need to be replaced. After that, they'll move to the galley."

"Do ya think they'll be done with the bridge and ductin' by tomorrow?" Francis asked. "I got the appliances for the galley coming in two days."

"If nothing goes awry, yeah," Jayce answered.

"Good to hear," he replied. "I'll have the laundry machines comin' in same day. Will the livin' section crew be able to finish by then?"

"Probably not. Because those rooms were perfect spots for animals, there's a lot more work to do there. To be honest, the bridge crew will be done with the galley before the living section. I'll have them move to laundry after that."

"Alright," Francis said distantly.

"And have ya decided what ya wanted to do with that storage closet between laundry and the galley?"

"Yeah. I'm gonna make it into a brig. First officer has a bounty huntin' license, so he may need a way to transport bounties and such."

"Ya didn't tell me ya were gettin' contractors," Ash said from behind them.

Francis turned around and saw Ash with her arms crossed at the bottom of the ramp. She had a ponytail poking out of a plain cap, and with the sun being high, the bill cast a shadow over her face. Even with the shadow, Francis could still see her green eyes clearly.

Charlie had admitted to him after he took her out shooting that he was mesmerized by her green eyes when they met. Francis could hardly argue with that. They were very pretty and complimented her blond hair and fair skin well. She wasn't as lightly skinned as her younger half sister, but she was definitely lighter in complexion than Charlie.

"I thought ya had work," Francis said with confusion.

"I *did*, then the shitheads just let me go and told me to pound sand about a two week notice."

"That's pretty shitty of them." He turned to Jayce. "Anythin' else we need to talk about?"

"Nah, ya go ahead and talk with your crewmate. I'll just be directing all the hands."

"Thanks, Jayce," he said as Ash started walking up the ramp.

"Well, ya picked a helluva day to get laid off," he said as she joined him in the partially restored cargo bay. "Contractors started work today. First thing they did was replace the stairs on each side of the cargo bay."

"Kinda odd shape for stairs," she remarked as she looked at them.

"Yeah, well, ya can't really find any stairs that originally went on the AG-53 anymore, so we just had them made by hand. Instead of the steep stairs like they used to have, Charlie and I agreed to have these long stairs with a landin' over in the far corners like this. Better to have shallower stairs that are easy to climb or drag someone up. Also allows us hide all the gym equipment underneath without gettin' in the way of the main hold."

"What kinda gym equipment y'all gettin'?"

"Free weights, bench, squat rack, basically the same kinda shit you'd see at a little mom-'n-pop place."

She nodded distantly. "Well, since I ain't got nothin' to do today, I could always help ya with the restorin'."

"Nah, just take the day off," he said with a dismissive wave. "Wasn't plannin' on gettin' any help today anyway."

"Are ya able to pull away from the work, or do ya need to stay here?"

"Jayce, the foreman, can take care of everythin' while I'm out. Whatcha need?"

She looked away with unease.

"Well, I could actually use your help findin' me a gun. Charlie said he'd reimburse me for any pistol under a thousand shen, but I don't know a whole lot about guns. Just know how to shoot them. I could use some advice."

Francis smirked. She wanted his advice as someone who'd fought through the entire revolution and had much more experience with guns. What she didn't understand was that the kind of gun she wanted was not the kind of gun he used. For the majority of his time, he either had a shotgun or an automatic carbine rifle. He barely fired his sidearm until the Second Battle of Kusa, when he got desperately low on ammunition.

"Just get somethin' that feels comfortable and good in your hands and feels good to shoot. Lot of gun ranges offer rentals for ya to try. Maybe that should be your first place to go instead of the store."

She looked down with disappointment. "I just dunno where to start. I could use a lot of help, Francis, and I don't wanna make an ass of myself in front of Charlie again."

"He said ya were a damn good shot, what could ya possibly be so worried about?"

"Well, I'm not all that expperienced or knowledgeable with pistols," she admitted. "Shot one maybe a few times in the militia. I just...I just could use some help."

Francis was caught off guard by Ash's lack of confidence. She'd seemed so confident and competent the past two days, and yet now he saw a vulnerability that he never expected from her. She seemed like a different woman. Soft, delicate, unsure. Her hat hung low and covered most of her face. He sighed quietly, trying to not show his own unease at being around guns again, but she clearly needed and wanted his help.

"Alright. I'll let Jayce know and we can go get lunch while we're out and about."

She looked up at him sheepishly with her jade green eyes. "Thanks, Francis."

After a quick lunch, the two went to Andy's Gun Range for Ash to try out various models. Francis suggested for her to use a nine millimeter since it was a cheap and common form of caliber for a pistol. Nine was also good for carrying capacity, and if she had to use a pistol on armored targets, it wouldn't matter much if it was nine millimeter or something else. With the exception of Charlie's gigantic revolver that he called Darling, nothing could penetrate armor without a lot of bullets breaking it. At that rate, it would be easier just to shoot between plates.

He walked with her out to the range while she carried a basket full of different pistols and boxes of ammunition. As they walked up to their designated range, Francis's stomach turned, his chest tightened, a chill up his spine all the way to his neck, and he felt a strange twinge in his feet. The sound of gunshots didn't scare him, though the constant firing did bring him back to his days in the war when his squad or platoon would continuously fire potshots at an entrenched enemy.

Ash put all the pistols on her table, and Francis decided that helping her load ammunition into a magazine wasn't the same as breaking his promise. He grabbed a box of ammo and started putting the bullets into the magazines to help expedite the process. She glanced at him wordlessly as he quickly loaded the magazines, thinking of all the quiet moments in the various battles of the Isolde Revolution between shooting at Feddies where he loaded bullets into magazines, cleaned weapons, or talked with the wounded, telling most of them that help would arrive soon to keep their spirits up as they slowly died.

Before he knew it, he was done with loading the magazines and shook the thoughts of the war out of his head, then wordlessly stepped back and waited for Ash. She shot at a pistol target ten meters away, and even though she was hitting the target, her groupings were pretty bad.

After watching her expend the second magazine, he sighed and walked up to her at the lane as she loaded the third pistol with a magazine.

"Alright, stop," he said with a tinge of frustration. "I can definitely tell you're inexperienced with pistols."

Ash's shoulders slumped as she lowered the pistol. Her face was despondent.

"Assume the stance again," he commanded. "Stand like you're gonna shoot."

She readied herself with her finger off the trigger and the safety still on. He pushed the gun down and started adjusting her body. He twisted her a little, made her stand wider at the feet, and had her lean forward slightly.

He then pushed up on her left hand to lift the pistol up to her eye. He took her left hand and had it cover the right fingers instead of holding the bottom of the handgrip like a saucer and a teacup. She looked at him while he adjusted her hands, and he glanced at her. As soon as his eyes locked with hers, she looked downrange.

"That's how ya stand and hold a pistol," he told her. She looked back at him and smirked slightly.

"Thanks, Francis," she said quietly. He couldn't hear her between his hearing loss and the ear protection, but he could read her lips.

"Go ahead and shoot now," he told her.

She started shooting the pistol, and her groupings improved immediately. He smirked as he watched and nodded with approval. She shot the other three pistols after that. She put four back into the basket and he helped load the magazine for one while she did the other.

"Can't decide which I like better," she explained. "Gonna shoot them again and figure it out."

He nodded as he finished and sat the magazine on the table. She fired both magazines at the target, and Francis could see that she was still conflicted, so he walked back up to the bench and helped load another magazine.

"I honestly can't decide, Francis," she grumbled. "I want your opinion."

"Both are good pistols," he replied as he placed the magazine down.

She held the pistol out to him, her hand safely holding the slide and barrel. He put his hands up and took a step back.

"No, I want your opinion," she reiterated.

"I know, but I don't touch guns no more," he replied.

She furrowed her brow and pulled her head back slightly. "Ya don't?"

"No," he replied as he shifted and shuffled uneasily. "Made a promise I wouldn't."

"Why?" she asked curiously.

"That's…that's a long story," he said as he looked away. He felt Ash gingerly touch his shoulder. He looked at her and he saw a softness on her face.

"Then let's talk about it tonight over a few drinks," she replied. "No judgments either. Besides, I need to regain my honor in darts."

He chuckled. "Best of luck to ya on that."

"My shoulder feels better, shithead. I won't be holdin' back no more."

"Uh-huh," he said with a smug grin as he put his hands on his hips.

She shook her head. "Alright, well, I'll just make a decision on my own, then."

After another two magazines each, she chose the Akashi Armory pistol called the Lancer. He had heard of them, but Charlie could probably explain every detail and quirk about the gun.

The Lancer wasn't much different than Charlie's Spencer & Singh TSR, the pistol that he had on him when he was almost killed by a grenade. The pistol had been damaged by shrapnel, and he only patched the damage with metal without bluing or paint to let the former gashes stand out. He said he wanted Tristan and Christie to know that the pistol saved his life from shrapnel that would have hit his femoral artery.

They went up to the counter and Ash purchased the pistol along with a couple of spare magazines, a thigh and outer waistband holster, and a small red dot sight. They returned to Ash's truck and drove back to the ship by the middle of the afternoon. The contractors were still hard at work, and Francis immediately went to check on the workers' progress.

Ash left in her truck and went back to her apartment while Francis supervised all the work and pitched in every now and then. By the time the contractors were ending for the day, Ash returned in her truck.

She stepped out wearing brown Western-style boots, tan pants, and a moss green sleeveless mock neck top. The top perfectly complimented her jade green eyes and blond hair, making both pop. The lack of sleeves and tighter pants helped accentuate her more muscular physique. Her hair was in a low ponytail, which somehow made her face softer and more feminine. She sauntered over to the cargo ramp with her sunglasses on.

Francis couldn't help but look. He was surprised that he was attracted to a muscular woman, but he found his eyes wandering.

"Hey there," she said as she got to the bottom of the cargo ramp. "Ya ready to go to the bar and get some grub?"

"Shit," he said as he rubbed the sweat off his brow. "I'll need to shower and change first. It gets hot inside *Bow* when she sits in the Corinth sun for a spell."

"Alright," she said. "Just wanna meet me at Akhmed's in about an hour?"

"Uh, yeah, sure," he replied. He was too distracted by her looks to tell her that he had no way of showering because *Fire Arrow* was in Athens and that was how he and Charlie showered. He simply watched her walk away as he tried to think of places to shower.

After going to the spaceport in his and Charlie's car with a change of clothes and all of his toiletries, Francis went back into town to Akhmed's, a small little dive bar on the border with the seedier part of town. He walked in and found Ash sitting with a vodka and soda. He walked over to her with a smile and a wave and sat down.

He wore a simple button-up shirt with pants and shoes. Nothing fancy, just enough to say that he'd dressed up a little to match her.

"Hey there," she said with a smirk. "I just got here about five minutes ago, so good timin' on your part."

"Good to hear. Have ya heard anythin' from Eri?"

"Knowin' her, she's enjoyin' the good life with some free whiskey. Dunno how she likes that shit. Never liked it."

"It's definitely a love or hate kinda thing with most people," he replied with a shrug.

"Have ya heard anythin' else from Charlie besides Eri in her dress?"

"No," he lied. Charlie had messaged him before he sent the picture of Eri—while they were at the shooting range, in fact. He'd let him know that his psycho brother in the FIA had made section chief. Ash didn't need to know that, though.

"Ya with me?" she asked with a raised eyebrow.

Francis snapped out of it. "Yeah, fine. Sorry, just wonderin' what those two are up to."

"So who else is gonna join the crew?"

"Well, I want a ship's doctor so we don't have to rely on hospitals planetside so much. I wanna make sure that if someone gets sick or hurt while we're in FTL or if someone gets hurt durin' a cargo exchange, we still have a way to help them and not just hope they'll be okay until we get somewhere else."

She sipped her vodka soda as the waitress came by and he ordered an Old Fashioned.

"Anyone else?"

"Kinda want one more sec officer if we can, someone who's more experienced than ya, no offense."

"None taken," she said as she sipped again. "Don't need two people for Charlie to train."

"Did he tell ya why he wanted someone to mentor?" he asked. She shook her head. "He wants someone to replace him as first officer. He doesn't want to be a freighter for more than a year or two, so he's trainin' his replacement. That means ya will be first officer in a year or so. Hope ya can handle the responsibility."

She shrugged. "I'll do my best. Does it come with better pay?"

"Yeah, ten percent plus hazard pay and bonuses and shit."

"Not a bad deal."

"Yeah, but it's a lot more responsibility, and you'll understand when the time comes."

The waitress returned with his Old Fashioned, and he sipped it. Not too bad for a divey place like Akhmed's.

"So," Ash said uncomfortably, "ya gonna tell me why ya don't touch guns at all anymore?"

Francis sighed through his nose. "Look, I want ya to know that I'm only tellin' ya because you're a security officer and because ya were so understandin' about the whole thing."

"Just tryin' to understand ya is all," she replied plainly.

He looked at the table and sipped his Old Fashioned. "Alright…well…"

There was a brief silence. Francis always had to fight against himself to talk about shit like the war, but his therapist helped him do a few exercises that will allow him to open up. He knew that opening up was the right thing to do. It helps him heal and to be honest with himself.

"Look, if you're uncomfortable talkin' about it…"

"No, no. Just…it takes a lot of effort to talk about it."

"If it takes effort, Francis, then don't worry about it. Ya can tell me whenever you're more comfortable."

"That's the problem though," he said as he sipped his drink, "if I don't just fucken say it, then I ain't gonna ever say it. Just…gimme a sec…"

Ash looked at him with curious but sympathetic eyes. She could clearly tell it was a very sensitive and sore subject with him.

He was glad that she understood, but it didn't make it any easier to open up. All he wanted to do was just drop the subject, drink more, and go to sleep. He gulped and cleared his throat.

He looked at her, and she looked somber. Just seeing her face made him want to push her away and just drop the subject altogether. He didn't want to bring down the mood and he didn't want to be a burden for someone else.

It took focus and fighting through the tightness in his chest to finally say something.

"The war…I was…I was really gung-ho and all for fightin' for the revolution," he began. Every time he was able to start talking about it, it always felt like he was running downhill, sheer momentum and physics pushing him along. "The Second Battles of Ankara and Kusa made me really change my perspective.

"In Ankara, we were combin' through all the bodies for intel after we took a key buildin' that was vital for the main troops to push forward. That's when I realized that…I killed basically a kid. I was twenty-five, almost twenty-six then, and I killed a kid that must've been drafted the fuckin' day he turned eighteen. He was only eighteen years, three months old. Just some fuckin' kid told to fight to preserve the Federation.

"It fucked me up. Even Charlie by then was just about to turn twenty-two. Less than a year left in the war. Then in Kusa, while desperately defendin' a position, I killed…"

He looked down and took a large swig of his drink, letting the bite and sting of it push him through.

"I killed a fucken married couple. They were nineteen. Either high school sweethearts or kids that connected in basic. I took a family away, and that crushed me. I never shed a tear over a dead Feddie until that day."

"Is that when ya decided?"

He shook his head. "Nah. By then, I already had survivor's guilt. When I found out about the married couple, I had lost eighty-two men under my command by then. My CO even called me 'Charon.' It's the guy from Greek and Roman myth from Earth that took people across a river of lost souls to the underworld. Afterlife."

"That's a pretty shitty thing to call ya," she said sullenly.

"People used to say that if they were ever suicidal, they just had to join my platoon. My CO even said if I hit a hundred by the end of the war, he'd buy me twenty-year-old scotch."

Ash listened intently and quietly, but he could see in her beautiful green eyes that she was empathetic.

"When I came back home…everyone called me a fucken hero. Never felt like one. All the terrible shit I saw and did…"

He finished his Old Fashioned as Ash finished her vodka soda. She gestured to the waitress that they'd want another.

"My guilt and all that made me push people away, and Maria was one of the casualties. I said terrible shit to her just to push her away. I started drinkin', a *lot*. When Maria left with my son Trey, I…"

"Ya were suicidal…" she said distantly.

He nodded as he chewed on the inside of his lower lip to keep tears away.

"If it hadn't been for Charlie…I might've. Promised him that I'd never hold a gun again, and I don't want to. I killed enough people with guns. Don't need to kill no more, don't wanna kill people no more. Just don't want the temptation, ya know?"

The waitress gave them each a drink.

"I feel kinda bad now, jokin' and callin' ya a hero last night when we were eatin'."

He waved his hand dismissively. "Nah. Never held it against ya. I know ya were just as much teasin' as ya were bein' serious. Not a lotta people know my story, so I try not to judge 'em for sayin' shit like that."

"Well, I'm sorry for kinda cornerin' ya like that."

"Nah, it's fine," he replied. "It…it get's easier each time I talk about it with someone. Just don't like talkin' about it unless I know they can at least understand. Ya were in the militia, so ya know what we signed up for, even if ya never saw combat."

"I've always felt guilty about it, but after hearin' that shit…kinda glad now that I just stayed in Yongsan and protected the new Parliament buildin'."

"Good, 'cause ya shouldn't feel any guilt," he said. "Don't feel like ya were a coward or nothin'. Ya had a job to do, and ya did it. I had a job to do, and I wouldn't wish it on anyone." She nodded distantly. "Look, I know I'm gonna sound like a pussy for sayin' it, but…I could really use a hug right now."

Ash smirked and shuffled from her chair to his. She gave him a hug, and he felt better. That was one thing he truly missed about Maria. She was always so willing to give hugs and show affection. He no longer had access to that after she left with Trey.

"Thanks," he said quietly.

"Least I could do after makin' ya dig up that shit," she replied quietly in his ear.

"Ya needed to know. Ain't mad."

"Alright," she said as she released him. "Let's get the mood back up and play some darts."

Francis smiled softly and nodded. His warm smile turned to a smug grin. "Wanna play for money?"

"Ain't fallin' for that shit again, asshole."

# Chapter 11

Eri sat down in a barber's chair as Michelle stood at the back of the room, letting her chosen hair stylist do her magic with Eri. The hair stylist touched and examined Eri's wavy hair and asked her if she had any requests with the length of her hair, if she wanted bangs, or if she would allow her to have creative freedom.

Eri felt nervous. She didn't know what would be best. Charlie had obviously sent her to Michelle for a reason, so Michelle would probably offer advice. She breathed through her nose deliberately and looked at herself in the mirror. The original plan was letting her wavy hair dry and fall naturally, but now that she had options, she couldn't think of a style that she wanted. She looked at Michelle, who stood with her arms folded, through the mirror.

"I'm going to trust your judgement, Michelle," she said anxiously.

"Completely?" she asked with a raised eyebrow. Eri nodded. "You are with the bride, but not in the wedding party, correct? What are the colors for the bridesmaids, again?"

"Lilac with white."

"Very well. Remove one centimeter, add layers, a three centimeter streak of mulberry, and flat iron waves. We want her hair to look lush and bouncy as she walks."

Eri immediately regretted giving her consent. *A dark red streak?* Why would that ever look good with her brown waves?

"Alright," Michelle said to the hairdresser, "I'll let you do your thing while I find the perfect dress to match."

Eri watched nervously as the woman readied her scissors, a razor, and many other pieces of hair cutting equipment. She signaled Eri to go to the sink so she could wash her hair. The hair stylist did not say much through the process, but when she spoke, it was always words of encouragement, particularly about how beautiful Eri would look when everything came together. Whenever Eri asked nervously about a decision, her only response was, "Trust the process, my dear."

She watched her hair slowly transform into a work of art. She never knew that her hair could look that way with her waves. By the time she left the chair, her apprehension had melted away to love and appreciation. She must have thanked the hair stylist over a dozen times. Before Eri left the room, the woman reminded her that she was beautiful and that she had loved working on her hair.

With a blushing face and an endless smile, Eri followed Michelle into the next room to try on dresses. In front of her were three dresses of different styles, all in the same mulberry color as the streak of hair near the front left side of her face. Michelle said nothing as Eri found herself drawn to the one in the middle. She slowly approached as she examined it.

"The fold-over Bardot midi dress?" Michelle asked.

Eri turned around and nodded. Michelle gestured to her to try it on. There were a few alterations needed, but it still fit very well on her. She looked at herself in the mirrors and couldn't believe her eyes. Someone else was looking back at her. Whoever she was, she was stunning.

After the alterations were complete, she was given heels and sent on her way to the makeup artist. The young man looked at her and thoroughly complimented her. Everything felt like a dream as the changes to her appearance all coalesced.

"You have beautiful fair skin that I only want to elevate," he said as he began applying the makeup. "The main thing I want to really accentuate are those beautiful hazel eyes of yours. They are like golden orbs with just an ever so slight addition of green."

While the makeup artist worked, they talked about Michelle and how picky she was with her clientele. She always enjoyed seeing people that were only ordinary to the untrained eye. Her greatest talent was being able to accurately see the end result before the client ever could. She hired the makeup artist because of his and Michelle's shared sensibilities and personal history. He wouldn't explain what kind of history they shared, but their bond seemed strong and heartwarming.

Once the makeup was finished, Eri did everything she could not to cry and smear the artist's work. The makeup artist led her back into the dressing room where Michelle, the tailors, and the hairdresser waited for her. As she entered, the group all doted on her and complimented her.

She asked to hug everyone that had worked on her, and they all obliged with smiles. She finally leaned in to hug Michelle, but the woman pushed her away and simply said, "No hugs, dear," in her flat tone. They exchanged a handshake, whereafter Michelle led her to the office, charged her for the services, and took her outside to a limousine waiting for her.

When they reached the limo, Michelle stopped Eri for a moment. "Chuck sent me a message while you were getting your makeup done. He hopes you enjoyed yourself and that you have a wonderful evening."

"Thanks, Michelle," Eri said with a smile.

"Chuck may have a very thorny and rough exterior, but he has a sweet and delicate center. Send him my love, won't you?"

Eri chuckled. "Sure."

Twenty minutes later, the limousine arrived in front of the hotel where the wedding would be held. The driver got out of his seat and opened the door for Eri with an outstretched hand to assist her. She gently gripped the driver's hand and got out of the limo with a smile, then opened her bag.

"I've never been in a limo before, so I don't know how much I owe you," she said as she started sifting through the cash. The driver simply put his hand over the bag to stop her.

"You already paid me when you paid Miss Draper, but I appreciate you thinking about me. You're her client because you're one of us," he said with a wink.

Eri closed her bag, awkwardly nodded once to him, and started making her way inside. She walked into the events room with plenty of time before the ceremony started. Many people on both sides of the wedding party chatted casually with each other. She could hear laughter and whispers melt into a drone as she tried to keep herself composed. Today was perfect already in her eyes.

Eri woke her tool and noticed she had three messages.

Ash: Hope you're having fun! See you tonight?

Charlie: Glad to hear Michelle likes you. Let me know if you need anything or if you need me to come get you. Go easy on the liquor.

Francis: Just saw a pic of you in your dress. You look great! Enjoy your night and don't let Charlie give you a hard time.

Seeing the messages from her new crewmates made her smile. She barely knew them, and yet they were supportive and kind. The past two days had been so eventful. She didn't know if Francis and Charlie were trying to ensure she stayed around or if they both genuinely always treated their crew this well, but either way, she felt appreciative.

She looked up from her tool and noticed two men from the groom's party quickly avert their eyes from her.

*How long have they been looking at me?*

She narrowed her eyes and watched them like a raptor. One of them turned his eyes back in her direction and immediately looked away. A man had not looked at her that way in a long while, aside from the moron from last night, Don. It made her feel feminine again. Although she truly enjoyed working as a certified maintainer, she was definitely in a male-dominated field.

In many ways, she was just one of the boys while working. The men often treated her the same as any other; the only difference was their friendly roasts often involved her gender. She didn't mind though. She could dish out as much as her male counterparts.

She may have loved her job, but it often made her feel invisible. The stares and glances created a smile on her face that she couldn't contain. Her cheeks felt warm with joy as she gathered more and more attention as the guests piled in. A few of the men even did double-takes as they passed her.

After a brief wait, the groomsmen and bridesmaids began their procession. Two of the bridesmaids, Shu-yen and Jessica, who Eri despised, noticed her and showed visible shock…and jealousy.

Her joyous smile shifted to a devious one as she relished the moment. She rose with the crowd out of their seats as the bride began her procession. Huang looked absolutely gorgeous in her wedding dress.

The wedding ceremony was beautiful. Eri watched with a ceaseless grin as she watched Huang cry tears of joy multiple times. It was the kind of wedding young girls dreamed of. When the guests were dismissed to go toward the reception venue, Eri pushed against the crowd to finally say hello to Huang after not seeing her in person for over a year. Huang squealed with glee as Eri approached.

"You look so pretty, Eri!" Huang said with a smile. "Thank you so much for coming."

"Well, look at *you*! You're practically glowing in that dress!"

"Oh, I'm so glad you like the dress. One of the hardest decisions of my life."

Eri beamed. "Congratulations to you both. I can't explain how happy I am for you."

Huang hugged her friend tightly. A man interrupted them as he cleared his throat. "Excuse me, miss, but the photographer is going to take pictures of the wedding party now."

Eri nervously brushed her hands on her dress. "Okay, sorry," she said as she looked at Huang. "I'll see you at the reception."

Eri quickly left the Starian and made her way to the reception venue, the Athens Historical Society ballroom, at the end of the block. The wedding colors alternated across the tables, a sea of lilac and white, like flowers emerging from snow. She searched the names at the seats and found her spot at a table far from the wedding party. She frowned as she realized she was probably placed there because her attendance was so uncertain for so long.

Guests slowly filled the ballroom and took their seats, conversing with each other. Eri sat in her assigned position, clutching her bag nervously and sipping on a whiskey sour as she was joined by strangers. The table had an empty seat next to her which simply said *"Erina Bezek Guest."* Huang had been kind enough to leave a seat for her plus one, but she didn't have one. Everyone at her table seemed to know each other, and all of them ignored her.

She applauded and cheered when the wedding party arrived, but after that brief moment of happiness, Eri once again found herself invisible at her table. She received her food and ate it gloomily, but her isolation from Huang and the two bridesmaids that she actually liked, Elga and Miani, ruined her appetite.

After eating, she went to go talk to the three women that she knew, but they were surrounded by doting guests. She quietly moved to the bar and ordered another whiskey sour. She drank and watched from a distance, trying not to interrupt or interfere. As soon there was a pause when she could approach and catch up with her friends, the best man and maid of honor began their speeches. As the speeches began, she ordered another whiskey sour.

She quietly and solemnly sat back in her seat at the table, the speeches turning into a low drone as her confidence wavered Huang danced with her handsome father, and her new husband, Keshik, danced with his mother.

They cut the wedding cake, and Huang happily got cake stuffed in her face. The two seemed so happy. After cake, the reception got livelier with dancing, and she finally noticed an opening to go talk to her friends. She approached them and the other bridesmaids as they cackled about something. Huang hugged Eri again.

"You still look so gorgeous, Eri!" she exclaimed.

"I *love* your dress," Elga added.

Miani said nothing to her, but continued to speak with the other two bridesmaids, Shu-yen and Jessica.

"Thanks," Eri said with a smile. "You look really good in lilac, Elga."

"Stop," she said playfully, "so what have you been up to? I haven't seen you in a year!"

"I've just been working a lot down in Corinth as a maintainer. I actually just accepted a new position as a full-time ship's maintainer."

"Well that's great!" Elga replied happily. "I'm glad you found your calling."

"So, are you just working on a ship with a bunch of guys?" Jessica asked with disgust.

"No, my sister Ash is also working on the ship."

Huang became distracted by guests speaking with her and congratulating her. Jessica took her moment while Huang couldn't hear. "Is she a pick-me girl too?"

Eri gritted her teeth. If she wasn't in such a nice dress, she would have punched Jessica.

"Don't be a bitch, Jess," Elga said in Eri's defense.

"Oh please, Elga, she knows I'm joking," Jessica said with a smug face. "So who gave you that dress?"

"Oh, no, I picked this out myself," Eri replied with a sneer.

"And how much does it cost to *rent*?"

"I wouldn't know, Jessica, I bought it," Eri growled, "but I know that girdle of yours probably cost a few hundred."

"Shut up, Eri, you know she suffered from an eating disorder," Shu-yen spat in Jessica's defense.

"Hey, hey," Huang interjected as she intervened, "I don't want anyone fighting at my wedding, got it? This is *my* night and I don't want my friends at each other's throats the entire time."

Eri took a sip of her whiskey sour. Her cheeks started to feel flushed as the alcohol ran its course. "Sorry, Huang," Eri said. The other girls remained quiet.

"Holy shit, who is *that* talking to your parents, Huang?" Jessica asked. Eri turned around and saw a man wearing a charcoal gray suit speaking with her friend's parents. It was then she noticed a familiar set of scars on the right side of his head.

*Charlie?*

Eri quickly walked over as they shook hands and parted ways. As she approached, she could hear him say, "We can iron out the details once that time gets closer." Charlie turned to his right and smirked as Eri approached. "Sorry I'm late," he said casually.

"Charlie? What are you doing in a suit?" she whispered loudly.

"Well, Michelle told me that dark gray is a good winter color as a wedding guest and if it accompanied this tie, it would match your dress."

"No, I mean what are you doing *here*?" she reiterated.

"Relax," he said as he leaned in, "I did a little research and discovered that your friend's parents *and* in-laws are both potential clients."

Eri began fuming. "You crashed the reception to get jobs?" she whispered loudly again, "I can't believe you! I can't...I can't believe you're wearing a suit..."

"I'll take that as a compliment somewhere along the lines of 'you clean up nicely,'" he responded as he took a sip of whiskey. He quickly examined her from head to toe. "Might I add that you do as well. I guess we both *are* too cute for Corinth."

Eri slowly shook her head. "You know, if I was having a better time, I'd be a *lot* more mad at you right now."

"I could tell that you weren't having as good of a time as you were hoping. I could practically hear the hissing from across the room," Charlie remarked. "Who's the bitch?"

"Ugh, Jessica," she groaned. "She's never liked me since we were sophomores in high school, all because I 'stole her man' out from under her. The guy just didn't like her."

"Well it looks like she misunderstood our relationship and she's trying to reciprocate all these years later," he pointed out wryly.

"Aren't you going to introduce us to your handsome friend, Eri?" Shu-yen asked as the bridesmaids all gathered around. "He is just your friend, right? There's no way you two are going out..."

Eri cleared her throat. She became extremely nervous, not because her friends may have misunderstood them, but because she had no idea what unhinged and harshly truthful thing would come out of Charlie's mouth. He could alienate her from what few friends she had at the wedding already.

"Well, this is, um..." she muttered nervously.

Charlie extended his right hand for a handshake, exposing the prosthetic clearly to them. "Charlie Menillo," he said as he gently grasped Shu-yen's hand and moved to the other bridesmaids. "And yes, we're just friends. I work on the ship with her."

"A cybernetic hand," Jessica noted with a seductive voice, "how mysterious. I've always liked a man with some scars that tell stories."

"Well thanks for that," Charlie said with fake enthusiasm. Eri could feel the conversation was about to take a turn.

"So since you're not taken, why don't you dance with me and tell me how you got your scars," Jessica said coyly, "That is…if you can handle me."

Charlie snickered mockingly.

"And what is so funny?" Jessica asked.

"Oh, nothing—"

*Oh, God, here it comes…*

"It's just the only women who have ever asked me if I could 'handle them' were the ones who were passed around by all the boys in high school and yet have no skill to show for all that experience in the bedroom."

Jessica gasped while the other bridesmaids gaped in horror. Charlie had somehow pinpointed Jessica's entire promiscuous life in high school. Charlie did not move, he simply stared Jessica down with condescending disdain. Jessica scoffed and stomped away, Shu-yen following.

"Holy shit," Elga said with a laugh, "that was *brutal!* I don't think I've ever seen Jessica get insulted so quickly and accurately. I already love your friend, Eri."

Eri said nothing, only held her face in her hand and shook her head.

Miani finally spoke up for the first time that night. "What do you do for work on the ship, Charlie?"

"Oh, I'm just a hired hand who loads and off-loads the cargo," he lied.

"So what do you even offer that's valued?" she asked flatly with a raised eyebrow.

"Miani," Eri pleaded.

"No, no, it's alright," Charlie replied softly with his hand up. He took a sip of his whiskey. "Let me guess, you have an undergraduate degree…I'm going to say in marketing."

"What of it?" she asked in annoyance.

"Well, considering how little you've spoken, the way you've silently sneered with disgust at Eri since I arrived, and the way you worded your question, I'd conclude that you believe that you are somehow better than the both of us. The problem is this—"

"Charlie—" Eri cautiously advised him.

"—you only feel like your degree somehow makes you better because you have nothing else to show for your life. You've never done anything of value and subsequently can value yourself by only one metric: where you sit in your corporation's ladder, which is why you've abandoned all hope of proving yourself through merit—"

"*Charlie…*" Eri's voice got angrier.

"I think you get the point," he said as his stare pierced into Miani's soul. Elga looked away in shock, trying to maintain her composure. Eri breathed with focus, doing what she could to not to react to his remarks.

"Fuck you, asshole," Miani murmured as she stormed away.

"Ah," Charlie exclaimed with sarcastic relief, "now we actually have an interesting group of people."

"You and I are going to have a very long talk on the ride back to Corinth," Eri growled, her fingers pinching the bridge of her nose in frustration.

"In the meantime," Charlie said as he held his hand out to Elga, "I'd like to get to know your friend a little more. Would you like to dance, Elga?"

"Sure! But I don't know if I could handle what you have to say about me," she exclaimed with a cackle.

Eri finished her whiskey sour and immediately went over to the bartender and got another. She was glad that Charlie had been able to put the three women in their place, but a wedding reception was not the time. He had embarrassed her.

Eri took a swig of her drink and watched Elga and Charlie converse as they did Huang's family's traditional dance. They inherited the dance from their ancestors when they left Earth before Precipice became the seat of human power in the Milky Way about three centuries ago. The people who left Earth to colonize alien worlds over the past seven hundred years often kept some of their traditions. Dance and food was the most common.

Eri watched them and smiled, knowing that at least Elga appreciated Charlie's brutal honesty too. Eri would never admit that to Charlie though. She knew it would more than likely embolden him.

Eri was really starting to feel the alcohol. She already had five drinks and was working on her sixth, and the reception had only been about an hour and a half. Her face felt tingly as she observed her friend dancing with the first officer, still sipping. The two suddenly walked out of the crowd of dancers and headed toward a door, away from the main entrance. Confused, she started to follow. Her feet felt heavy as she walked around the dance floor. She opened the door and peered out. Both of them were conversing cordially on a balcony and smoking cigarettes.

"Elga!" Eri gasped. "When did you start smoking?"

Her friend chuckled as she exhaled. "It's my first," she said with a giggle, "he offered."

Eri glared at Charlie. He didn't look at her as he took a drag from his cigarette. "You are a bad influence," she said.

"Only at parties," he said with a devious grin. Eri only shook her head.

"Well, I should get back in," Elga said to break the silence, "I'm sure the girls are waiting for me. Thanks for the dance, Charlie, it was fun."

"What about the cigarette?" he asked as she tossed it over the side of the balcony.

"Not for me," she replied with a grimace.

"You know," Eri said as she sipped the last bit of her sixth whiskey sour, "I was at first mad you came, but I'm glad you did."

"Why?" Charlie asked with a chuckle.

Eri instinctively clutched Charlie's arm for stability, both of her arms wrapping around his still intact one. "Besides Elga and Huang, I was really lonely," she admitted. Charlie remained still and allowed Eri to hang on him. "It really hit me today how much things have changed with both me and my friends since high school. They all went to college and got their degrees while I went into maintainer school."

Charlie carefully dropped his cigarette and stomped it out while Eri continued to cling onto him. "Real friends like Elga stay around no matter what. She doesn't care about you having a blue collar job and is actually quite happy for you."

Eri finally let go and looked up at Charlie. "She is?" she asked.

"Yeah, she and I talked about it while we danced."

Eri tried to sip her whiskey sour and realized that she had already finished it. "Welp, time to get another," she giggled. Charlie smirked and shook his head.

He opened the door for her as she walked with purpose to the bar again, getting her seventh whiskey sour. They stood together near the bar and silently watched the guests and wedding party dance on the ballroom floor. Eri tipsily rested her head on Charlie's shoulder, taking sips from her glass. Charlie remained still, but she could tell that he felt awkward and uncomfortable despite allowing her to rest her head on his shoulder. She obliged by pulling away.

"Sorry," she apologized as she caressed her glass.

"Shy people are always more touchy-feely when they get drunk," he replied. "I expected it from you."

"I'm not drunk *yet*," she argued.

"Well, there's still a lot of time between now and the end of the reception," he said. "Are you going to be alright?"

"Yeah," she said as she finished another whiskey sour.

"You better pump the brakes if you want to be able to walk," he advised.

Eri sighed with frustration. "I know my limits."

The music slowed to a romantic ballad. Eri sighed deeply with longing as the lights lowered. "I love this song," she admitted.

Charlie groaned and lifted his left hand up in front of her. "I got the hint…"

Eri straightened herself and looked up at him. "Hmm?"

"I may be an asshole, but I can tell when a woman wants to dance to a certain song."

Eri pulled back slightly. "Oh, no, you don't have to—"

"I'm already offering, now either dance with me or don't," Charlie demanded. "Either way, this will probably be your *only* chance because it's a special occasion. You just can't tell anybody. I have a reputation to maintain."

Eri looked down with a soft smile. She sat her empty glass on a nearby table and softly held Charlie's hand. He gently grasped her hand, led her to the dance floor, found a spot, and stood still, waiting for her to go forward and face him. She stepped in front of him, his deep blue eyes affixed to hers. She gently placed her hand into his palm and rested her left arm on the front of his shoulder. He reached behind her and placed his right hand in the middle of her back.

The music played as Charlie began to slowly move his feet. Eri smiled softly as she followed him. They silently danced for a while until Eri couldn't help but look down; his piercing eyes had not averted away from hers even once. It was the first time that Eri felt that Charlie's focus was completely in the moment, rather than only partially focusing while scanning and studying the room.

"Thank you for everything tonight…*Chuck*."

Charlie scoffed and looked away, "Oh god…"

"Don't like your nickname?" she asked.

"No," he said sharply. Eri giggled at his annoyance. "I'm not a cut of steak…"

"Well at least I know how to get on your nerves," she said.

"You call me Chuck again and I'll kick you off the ship myself," he replied jokingly.

Eri's giggle turned into a laugh. Charlie was charming when he was less serious. She pulled herself closer. In her whiskey-induced state, she felt compelled to rest her head near his collarbone. She looked up at him again.

"Seriously though," she said tenderly, "thank you. You made my night." Another notification appeared on Eri's tool, but she ignored it.

The two danced silently again, Charlie's movements less deliberate and stiff. The whiskey once again told her to place her head on Charlie's shoulder. She was already close enough that it wouldn't matter all that much. She ignored the thought and simply remained close and looked at him.

Charlie stopped looking at her when she got closer, but near the end of the song, he turned his head to look at her. The whiskey was no longer telling her to rest her head on his shoulder, but she felt a tightness in her chest when he looked at her. She couldn't tell if it was because of how close their faces were or if it was something else. Once the music changed, she pulled back away from him and smiled.

Charlie lowered his hands to his sides. "Are you going to stay here a little longer?"

"Yeah," she replied as she looked over at Huang and Elga, "I can't leave them just yet. Still got a lot of catching up to do."

Charlie nodded. "Alright then. I'm going back to the ship and changing. Enjoy the reception."

"You can stay if you want," she blurted out.

"Thanks, but I still have some things to do and I've already gotten the Mings as a potential client," he replied as he put his hand on her shoulder. "Go enjoy yourself." Eri smiled as Charlie swaggered away with his right hand in his pocket, his gaze once again dancing around the room.

Eri joined Elga and Huang, who were reminiscing about something. "Yeah, and then you just sat there and said, 'I thought you had it.'" The two then cackled with delight, Huang snorting as she did whenever something truly tickled her.

"What are you two crones cackling about?" Eri said playfully.

"Hey, so is that guy *actually* your friend?" Huang asked.

"Yeah, well kinda," she answered, "we've only known each other for a few days."

"Didn't look like it from here," Elga said as she revealed a picture of the two dancing.

"Look," Eri said defensively, "he's just a guy that I work with and he's…he's a hard-headed asshole who has a soft side. Besides, I think he likes my sister anyway…in his own 'mean because I like you' kind of way."

"Uh-huh," Elga replied, unconvinced.

"So, why did he come to the reception for only forty-five minutes wearing an expensive suit, if he is only a friend? Why come at all?" Huang asked as she peered at Eri.

"He was trying to get your parents as a client," she argued.

Elga thought for a moment. "I think I know what will solve this little debate. Did he know about your little makeover?"

Eri's brow furrowed. "Well yeah," she replied, "he was the one who referred me to the woman that did it. He thought I should look nice for the wedding…"

Elga and Huang exchanged glances at each other. "Honey," Elga began, "he didn't come to get a client—he came to see *you*."

"And trying to get my parents as a client was probably just an added bonus," Huang added.

"It's *not* like that!" Eri reiterated angrily. "I know him enough to know that he came here first and foremost to get a new client. He even told me as much."

Elga and Huang sipped their drink, clearly unconvinced.

"I would like that picture though," Eri said devilishly, "I can probably use it for some casual blackmail." Elga chuckled as she sent the picture to Eri. "You don't understand," Eri began, "he's always super-serious and I know that he'd hate it if I outed his softer side to the other crew members."

The three women talked and laughed for two hours, sharing about each other's lives and occupations. Before Eri knew it, she had many more whiskey sours. She missed the bouquet toss at the end of the reception because of how drunk she was. The floor felt like it was shifting under her feet to the point that she needed to take off her heels just to ensure she didn't fall. She joined the rest of the guests who left at the formal end to the reception, her bag and shoes clutched in her hands as she finished one last drink. She hailed a cab and went back to the spaceport. As she sat in the back, she looked at her tool for the time. Her vision blurred and showed double as she glared at the screen. She focused with all that she could and noticed that it was half past eight. She managed to compose and send a message to Charlie.

Eri: Omw back ti th spacepirt sys.

Eri drunkenly flipped through the pictures from the night when she paused on the picture that Elga had sent her. Her eyes glazed over as she swayed slightly in her seat.

*He didn't come to get a client—he came to see* you.

*Relax. I did a little research and discovered that your friend's parents and in-laws are both potential clients.*

*So, why did he come to the reception for only forty-five minutes wearing an expensive suit, if he was only a friend? Why come at all?*

*When you've had a life like mine, moments of peace are rare. You try to enjoy them while you can.*

*So whose wedding are you going to? Did Chuck finally tie the knot?*

Eri sighed and shook her head

*He's already with someone. It was just dancing between friends. But who is Christie? Why hasn't Charlie or Francis mentioned her?*

Before she could dwell on it any further, the cab stopped outside the spaceport. She paid and tipped the driver and got out, feet still bare and legs wobbly. She stumbled to hangar fifty-one. *Fire Arrow* was already running and ready to fly. She trudged up the back ramp and used the interior wall for support. She saw Charlie glance over his shoulder.

"Hurry up, Little Fawn," he commanded jokingly, "I only have two more minutes to launch."

Eri stumbled to the jumper seat and struggled with the harness as the rear ramp closed automatically. Charlie quickly got out of the pilot seat and assisted her. He returned to the pilot's chair and lifted off. Despite the inertial dampeners, Eri could still feel the ship lurch upward with the VTOL, which made her feel slightly nauseous. She was resting her head on the panel behind her when she realized what he'd said.

"Wait…what'd ya call me?" she asked.

Charlie chuckled slightly. "You looked like a newborn deer with how much your legs buckled underneath you," he said as they approached the checkpoint for faster speeds. "Seems like you drank more than you could handle."

"I'm not *that* drunk," she answered with a slur, "I'm jus' really buzzed's all."

"And I'm the mayor of Corinth," he joked as he pushed the engine throttle forward to accelerate. The engines roared again as the atmosphere slowly dissipated in front of the pilot's viewport.

"I'm not drunk, I'm jus' really buzzed n'kay?"

Charlie put the ship on autopilot and got out of the seat. Eri struggled again with the harness, but before Charlie could help her, she remembered how he unbuckled it earlier. She slapped the central buckle and the restraints fell limp, slowly returning to their original position.

"See?" she said proudly as she gestured at the harness, "I wouldn't've been able to do that if I was drunk."

"Okay, you're not drunk," he answered condescendingly as he opened the locker.

"Ya took no time gettin' out of that suit," she remarked.

Charlie removed his weapons and placed them back in the locker. "The people I needed to see would have asked questions, and I don't like exposing what I do when I'm not doing work for them." He pulled an envelope out of his breast pocket, placing it on the small shelves inside the locker along with his spare pistol magazines. He closed the locker and it whirred as it locked once again. "Did you have fun at the reception?" he asked genuinely as he gazed out through the main window.

"I did," she replied. Charlie stood there in the clothes he'd worn that morning with his hands clasped behind his back, silently observing his surroundings like a sentinel.

"Michelle's secretary returned the clothes that you left in her office," he remarked as he stood motionless.

"Oh shi'…" she whispered as she realized that she never took her casual clothes with her to the reception. She had been so focused on her new look that it completely escaped her mind.

"You're not the first to do it and you certainly won't be the last," he pointed out with understanding.

"Speakin' of Michelle," Eri mentioned as she stood up, "Who's Christie?"

Charlie swiftly turned his head and glanced over his left shoulder. "How do you know that name?" he demanded.

His sudden change in mood startled her. She had not expected that kind of reaction. "Michelle asked me about 'er," she nervously replied, "should I not ask about the other person she mentioned?".

"You should not," he growled as he turned back to the window.

"I'm sorry," she shakily replied, "I didn' know it was a touchy subject. I won' mention it again…"

Charlie sighed. "I shouldn't be angry with you," he admitted, "let's just never speak of those two again."

*Did the brother seduce her away from him?* Her mind raced for explanations for his sudden rage.

"I hope you enjoyed today," he said after a long silence. "We probably won't have a moment of peace like that for a while."

"I did," she replied, happy that the subject changed. "Thanks again."

Charlie didn't respond and looked out silently. Eri still wanted a drink. She wanted to keep her buzz going. She thought carefully for a moment, thinking about where Charlie would hide some alcohol on the ship if it wasn't in the locker. Perhaps he would keep it close to him, like his personal history.

She got up and knelt down next to the bunk, grasped the handle to the drawer beneath the bed, quietly opened it, and found a bottle of whiskey with a few collapsible cups inside. The bottle had already been opened and was half consumed. She turned the bottle around and read the label.

*Dry Dredge Number Five. Good choice…*

She wriggled the cork to open the bottle. She strained until it finally gave way, noisily popping as she removed it from the bottle's neck. Charlie slowly turned around and saw her pouring two glasses. He silently stared at her as she recorked the bottle, stood up, and extended a cup toward him.

"I figured you'd only allow me to do it if I poured you one as well," she concluded innocently.

Charlie shook his head and slowly grasped the cup. "It seems my little lesson paid in dividends for you," he remarked.

"It was jus' a lucky guess," she replied with a shrug.

"No," he retorted plainly, "you genuinely thought about it. You made a proper deduction about me." Eri looked at her cup shyly. She could hear a faint amount of pride in his voice.

"I had a good teacher," she said humbly as she sipped on her whiskey. The oaky alcohol tingled on her tongue and slid easily down her throat with minimal discomfort. Smooth and flavorful. She savored another sip when she noticed Charlie had his cup extended toward her. He still faced toward the window, only his arm reaching back. She peered in the cup and noticed that it was empty. He was silently asking for another. She removed the cork again and poured him equal to two shots of the whiskey. As soon as he heard her stop pouring, he brought the cup back in front of his body.

Eri swayed slightly as she continued to sip her whiskey in silence. Charlie managed to finish two before she had finished her first. The tension in the ship's cabin grew as Charlie remained still and reclusive. She put her cup and the bottle back in the drawer and moved toward the back, where she saw her casual clothes on a shelf. She grabbed them and moved to the small module that housed the toilet, shower, and sink.

"I'm going to shower and change," she announced meekly. Charlie simply turned his head slightly and nodded once before returning his gaze out to the void in front of him. Eri shimmied into the module and pressed two buttons, which caused the toilet and sink to retract into the wall. She closed and locked the door, placing her casual clothes inside a compartment. Eri then slowly disrobed, using the walls to maintain balance, then carefully folded the dress and placed it in a compartment away from the splashing water. She turned on the water and simply stood there for a moment.

The warm water drizzled onto her face and chest, refreshing her. She leaned her head back to let the water soak her hair, but quickly had to return upright as the room began to spin on her.

*Okay, maybe I am drunk...*

With her newly realized state of drunkenness, she deliberately bathed as quickly as possible before the rest of the alcohol hit her. She turned off the water and grabbed two towels out of a compartment. She wrapped her hair and dried herself with as much focus as she could. Bending over or lifting her feet caused dizziness.

She emerged from the module wearing her street clothes with damp hair that she blotted and rubbed with her towel to dry faster. She noticed that the bottle had been removed from the drawer once again and was on the console in front of Charlie, who still stood next to the pilot's seat. He gently swirled the whiskey in his cup, gazing at it solemnly.

Eri removed her dress from the module and placed it on the shelves where her casual clothes once lay. She then stumbled over to the bunk and sat down, enjoying the more comfortable bed over the rigid jumper seat. While Charlie upended his glass to finish the last drops, she took a deep breath as the alcohol began to hit her like a train. Her eyes felt heavy as she became more relaxed and drunk.

"Sorry about earlier," Charlie said softly, "it's just a very sore subject with me…"

Eri looked at him and started seeing double again. "Nah, 's fine," she said with a slur.

Charlie glanced over his shoulder at her. "That last little bit of whiskey did you in, did it?"

"Room's startin' to spin," she admitted, "I think I'll be n'kay 's long as I don' move that mush."

Charlie chuckled as he collapsed his cup and corked the bottle. He walked over to the bunk, knelt down, and grasped the handle on the drawer. Eri sluggishly lifted her leg out of the way. He gently placed the bottle and cup back inside the drawer and closed it.

"How mush longer 'fore we land?" she asked.

"Fifteen minutes," he responded as he stood up.

"Can I jus' sleep on the ship?" she asked weakly. "I dunno if I c'n make it back."

Charlie hesitated for a moment and breathed deliberately through his nose. "Alright," he finally replied.

"Thanks," she said happily. Charlie sighed and got back in the pilot's seat. Eri lay down on the bunk. "Do I hafta get back in a jumper seat an' buckle up?"

Charlie turned the chair back around and looked at her for a moment. "I have a feeling it would be best if you stayed on that bunk," he concluded, "I'll just make a slower landing."

"Hmm," she hummed with approval.

Charlie turned on retro thrusters earlier to smoothen his deceleration. When they crossed into the speed restrictions checkpoint, he once again looked at Eri, who seemed to be drifting into sleep. He placed the comms headset on his head and relayed information for descent and approach for Corinth Traffic Control as quietly as he could. He then came toward *Silver Bow* slowly and took his time landing the craft so it wouldn't jostle the sleepy maintainer.

Charlie got up from the pilot's seat and began making his way to his bags near the back ramp. He would need to use the side airlock to leave quietly enough for her; however, as soon as he was next to her, she grasped his pant leg.

"Stay wiff me…please," she pleaded, "I've ne'er had a good night drunk. I jus' need someone here to make sure I'm n'kay…"

Charlie sighed heavily. He knew that staying with her would help her feel safe and subsequently more compliant about sleeping the alcohol off, but staying with her also meant that he would not be sleeping in a bed that night. He'd already had a long day. What if the panic attack earlier was a precursor to his nightmares returning? If he had a nightmare, he would more than likely wake her up, which would only lead to more questions. He didn't want her to ask any more questions. Hell, he didn't even want to *think* about Christie and Tristan.

Moreover, his thoughts were torn between admitting to her and Ash about his past or keeping it hidden. If he told them, they could be prepared for Tristan inevitably making a move to capture or kill Charlie and the rest of the crew; however, telling them that his mere presence put them in danger was a surefire way to get them to leave the ship. He would then need to recruit again and put the entire business on hold for an indefinite amount of time.

If he didn't tell them, they would remain on the ship, the business would start on schedule, but their lives would be in danger and he eventually would have to tell them anyway. Tristan making his move was only a matter of time, not probability. His brother was driven by hatred and a singular focus on wiping Charlie from existence.

"Please?" Eri begged in her stupor.

He sighed heavily again. "Alright," he conceded. She weakly thanked him as he sat down on the floor in front of the bunk. His mind raced for a time while the drunk maintainer slumbered behind him. He turned and looked at her after a while of remaining still and noticed that she had fallen asleep on top of the sheets.

The Corinth nights were cold because of its climate, but there was no way of pulling the sheets back over her without waking her. He quietly stood up, removed his duster, and gently laid it over her. Reflexively, she hummed as the warmth embraced her. She clutched onto the coat, rolling over to get more comfortable, tucking her legs up into her chest to put her body completely underneath it. He looked over at the shelves and noticed her new dress folded up haphazardly on one of them. He quietly walked over and hung it on his coat hanger to avoid wrinkles or creases, then stared at the dress for a moment. If Tristan came sooner rather than later, this would probably be a memento of her last peaceful night. A chill crawled up Charlie's spine as he thought of the terrifying notion of being hunted by Tristan and his FIA goons and the implications of such a thing.

Charlie closed his eyes and breathed deeply, trying to calm himself down. He returned to his restful crewmate and once again sat on the floor. He remained still as he deliberately breathed to slow his heart rate. After a long time, he too fell asleep.

# Chapter 12

Charlie sat in the hospital bed as he read a book. Two evenings before, he'd asked Anabel if there were any books available for patients to read. When she had confirmed that there was an entire library for patients to utilize, Charlie immediately asked her for a recommendation.

"Oh, you probably wouldn't want to read what I like," she said with unusual shyness.

"Why not?" he asked.

"Well…" she began as she started to blush, "I like…*romance* novels."

Charlie snickered. "Smut isn't really my thing," he teased.

Shortly after their conversation, Charlie asked to go see the library, but he was forbidden as an ICU patient. He instead had to look at a list and request it from her. After he read the list, he asked for *The Picture of Dorian Gray*, a classic novel he had yet to read. The novel was small enough that he could finish it by the time Francis and his father Frank would arrive at the hospital.

He was only about fifty pages from finishing the book when a familiar face popped into the room through the doorway. Anabel's freckled face smiled as she rapped on the doorframe to catch his attention. He held his place with a finger and looked up.

"I thought you were night shift," he said curiously.

"I'm on day shift for the next two weeks," she replied, "that's why you didn't see me yesterday. Had my rest day."

"Well, I don't need anything at the moment, but thank you," he said courteously.

"Oh, no, I came to let you know that your uncle and cousin are here to visit. They're signing in right now. You definitely didn't get your height from their side of the family."

Charlie glared at her. "Thanks," he said with annoyance, making her giggle.

"Right in here, gentlemen," she said as she looked down the hallway. "I'll check in with you after lunch," she informed him with a wink.

Frank and Francis walked into Charlie's room, their eyes immediately darting to his right side, where his arm no longer existed. Charlie's mood had improved over the past week, but seeing their pained faces made him feel downtrodden.

"Hey, son," Frank said quietly, "how're ya feelin'?"

Frank and Francis were both incredibly tall, but Frank's age showed with his more rounded features compared to his thirty-year-old son, who was still built like a tall runner. Frank's ever-present bushy mustache, accompanied with stubble, complemented his olive-skinned face. Francis in many ways was simply a younger version of his father, minus his new beard. Just a year ago, Francis had only sported a small goatee, but he had now manicured his facial hair to a short beard. It suited him.

"Lighter," Charlie said sarcastically.

Francis chuckled quietly and shook his head. He clearly had not expected Charlie's jest. The two took the visitor's chairs on each side of the hospital bed and sat. Even sitting in the low and deep chairs, their tall frames still managed to tower over him. Frank put his hand gently on Charlie's right shoulder.

"So what happened to ya, son?" Frank asked quietly. Since the end of the Isolde Revolution, Charlie's uncle had always referred to him as "son." Frank knew that his sister, Charlie's mother, was hardly the kind of person to show any sort of love or affection, and that her husband would be just as cold and distant. He had taken it upon himself to be the father figure that Charlie never had.

"I told Tristan that I had defected in the war," Charlie said distantly. "Six days later, Christie shot me in the back and Tristan threw a grenade to finish me off. That's my theory, anyway. Only thing that seems to line up."

"He would kill his own flesh and blood like that?" Francis asked with disgust. "And why would Christie shoot ya! Ya two were supposed to get married in a few days!"

Charlie looked at Frank and pointed his chin at the door, his uncle complying and shutting it shortly after. As Frank sat back down in his chair, Charlie looked over at Francis.

"A friend from IS3 told me that they were both FIA agents."

"What?" they both asked in shock.

Charlie looked down. "Yeah…try being engaged to one…"

"I told ya joinin' that crew with Tristan was—"

"Dad. He don't need to hear ya tell him 'I told ya so.' I'm sure he's heard ya say it plenty of times in his head since it happened."

"Right, sorry, son."

Charlie sat there for a moment. "They probably thought I was dead, but I survived and walked probably ten klicks to civilization. Managed to get someone to help me and I woke up here a week ago."

"You're a tough sonofabitch, Charlie," Francis said as he lightly punched his cousin's left shoulder. "If anyone could've survived that, ya could."

"How much longer are they keeping ya here?" Frank asked.

"Doctors haven't given me a definite answer," Charlie answered. "One told me this morning that I'll be out of here in a few days, but the other doctor yesterday said I could be here for almost a month."

"Well, if they're keeping ya here a month, I might as well start looking for a prosthetic for ya."

"I've already started looking, but I appreciate the gesture."

"Then just tell me what ya want and I'll pay for it," Frank retorted quickly.

"I could never—"

"It don't matter what ya want or what ya'd do. Not like ya can say no to me. Probably ain't got enough shen in your accounts anyway."

Charlie looked to his cousin for help, but he shook his head, refusing to be part of the argument. Charlie glared at him, then let out a quiet sigh through his nose. "Fine, but you have to let me repay you."

"Shit, if Francis said that to me every time I paid for somethin' he didn't want me to buy, he'd need a damn mortgage! You're family, Charlie. No payin' back nothing."

Charlie managed a smirk and slowly nodded.

"Maybe we should wait for the doctor to give a more definite release time before we start gettin' this kind of thing done," Francis proposed. "Don't need to stay here no longer than needed."

"Yeah," Charlie replied, "I'll ask the doctor when he visits tomorrow morning. I'm supposed to get results for all my labs and radiology as well."

"We'll definitely get a better idea when they're gonna let ya leave once they get those test results. We'll get out of your hair, son. Keep restin' up and gettin' better. Plannin' is for tomorrow."

Charlie slowly nodded. Francis got up from his seat as soon as Frank stood. Francis then grasped his cousin's shoulder. He looked up at Francis with solemn eyes.

"Ya keep fightin' like ya always have, Charlie," he said resolutely. "When we get back to Venture, we'll help ya get back on your feet. Right, Dad?"

"Absolutely," Frank answered with a nod. "You're family, and not just 'cause you're my sister's son. Ya and Francis are more brothers than Tristan was with ya anyhow."

"Thanks," Charlie said as he looked into the middle distance. The two men walked out quietly and left him in the room alone. Though he appreciated them trying to cheer him up and feel welcome in their family and home, it only made him think about Tristan's betrayal.

*Why did you do it, Tristan? I know you're a patriot, but trying to kill me seems too far. Was I the target all along or was it because the FIA won't leave witnesses?*

The thought of Tristan being so quick to kill him forced his molars together. They creaked as he clenched and grinded them.

In that moment, something swelled inside him. His breathing became more deliberate as he sat up straight in the hospital bed. His face flushed with heat as he felt his cracked ribs ache and throb in pain as he took the deepest breaths he'd ever taken. His one fist clenched with such force that his fingernails drew blood in his palm.

Rage. Pure rage.

He stood up in his hospital gown and paced, trying to expend the energy that he had built up over the course of a week in a bed. He could barely contain himself. He may have been somber, depressed, and downtrodden for the past week, but when Francis put it so plainly as Tristan's willingness to "kill his own flesh and blood," his anger boiled to the surface.

Charlie had so much rage that he rushed to the bathroom to splash water on his face and calm himself again. He turned on the cold water and reflexively reached with both hands, but when only one arm appeared, he froze. The water ran as he slowly looked up to the small mirror in the bathroom. Since the attack, he hadn't looked at himself.

He had used the bathroom many times since he was hospitalized, but he never looked up at the mirror. He didn't know why. Perhaps it was simply his sadness that kept his head low, perhaps it was the fear of what he would see. His wild, rage-filled eyes stared back at him in the mirror, his pupils were tiny in the water closet's mirror light shining into his eyes, making them look animalistic.

In front of him was a man, but it wasn't *him*. He had seen himself in the mirror for twenty-five years, and never once was this figure looking back at him. Bandages covered the entire right side of his face. The right side of his head had been shaved to allow the doctors and nurses to see and operate on his wounds. The bandages had been replaced twice since he regained consciousness, but finally seeing the sheer number of them and how much they covered his face and neck made him understand the extent of the damage the grenade did to his body. He hadn't touched his right ear, but he noticed a visible chunk had been removed by a piece of shrapnel. It looked like a cartoon character's ear, the edges forming a perfect V-shape with sharp, distinguished lines.

He reached across his body with his left hand and began removing the bandages, one by one. His breathing slowed as he saw all of the different sutures keeping his wounds closed. He turned his head slowly and noticed that there were even cuts behind his ear. His neck was mostly spared because of his hand and arm taking the brunt of the shrapnel, but he had two stitched wounds there too.

Charlie could feel the other bandages on his chest and abdomen calling to him. He gripped the collar of his hospital gown and pulled it with force, making the buttons pop and snap away. He removed all of his bandages and gazed at the sight. His chest and abdomen were just as bad, if not worse, than his face.

He looked at his naked body in the mirror, his left hand no longer clutching the hospital gown. His eyes moved from his hips and up to his ribs, the multiple wounds all revealed for him to see. Cuts of various lengths and in random directions littered his entire right side. He turned slightly and saw that most of his cuts were, naturally, closer to his back since the grenade exploded when he was prone and on his stomach, clawing for life as his left chest roared in a fiery pain.

His eyes continued upward until, finally, his eyes met with his amputation. The skin had been pulled and stretched over the area just above his armpit. One massive seam had been made and was stitched the entire length, the edges of the skin still inflamed and pink, making the cut look like puckered lips. His breath trembled at the sight of his dressed surgery wound.

*All of this...for what? Why did I deserve this?*

A single tear fell down Charlie's face as he continued to stare at the amputation. The rage returned. He couldn't stand the sight of himself. He looked hideous, monstrous. The thought of being so permanently disfigured made him clench his fist again, drawing more blood from his palm. He let out a roar of agony and furor as loud as a tempest in the ocean or a hurricane smashing against a coast.

He punched the mirror with all of his strength. The entire apparatus bent, forcing silvered glass to shatter and fall. The bent container for the mirror pulled away from its meager anchors on the wall, and it crashed onto the sink before finally ending on the floor with a thunderous bang. Glass was dispersed throughout his knuckles. They cried out to him with a terrible pain as they bled, but he simply punched the wall. The glass cut deeper into his skin, and two of his fingers broke.

He didn't care. The rage eclipsed the pain in his hand. He continued to scream and howl with hatred as he punched the wall again and again, streaks of blood now painting the once pristine tiles that lived in the darkness behind the mirror. He could hear people speaking to him, but he understood none of it. The sounds were distant. He shouted as he swung again, breaking a third bone in his hand.

He felt two auto-injectors strike into his muscles on his left neck and shoulder, and he instantly felt dizzy and woozy. His legs gave out from underneath him, and he instinctively tried to brace himself with his right hand, but he simply slammed into the wall. One of the sutured wounds on his face slapped against the wall and shrieked at him as he fell to the floor. Before he fell unconscious, he realized that he had slipped on a broken piece of glass and a shard had entered the arch of his left foot.

Charlie awoke in the hospital bed, Anabel writing down Charlie's vitals onto his chart. He groaned with grogginess. The nurse's eyes flicked to him as he squinted in the light and tried to look at her. His vision was foggy and he felt exhausted. His left arm and legs had been restrained, and he pulled at them in a futile attempt to break from his fetters.

"Won't work," she said as she glared at him.

"How long was I out?" he asked weakly.

"You've been sedated for the past eighteen hours," she said with a monotone voice as she closed the folder with his charts. She marched over to the end of the bed and placed the papers in their container, then walked out of the room without saying anything else.

"Wait," he pleaded.

She never acknowledged him and continued on to the next patient. He knew that she was furious with him for destroying the mirror in the bathroom in his blind rage. He lay there with heavy eyelids, an IV slowly dripping sedatives into his veins. He had one outburst already and attacked a nurse when he awoke from a nightmare, but his second had forced the hospital staff to sedate him on top of using the restraints.

The IV hydrated him, which meant that he now needed to urinate after being under for eighteen hours. He did not have a catheter, which meant he needed to get up to use the bathroom, or in the very least have a nurse let him use a bed pan. He was bound tightly, which meant he couldn't use the call button.

"Nurse!" he weakly shouted for aid. No one came. He tried calling for a nurse again, but his pleas fell on deaf ears. Another nurse walked by his room some time later and he called out to her, but she continued on as if she didn't hear him.

"Can I please get a nurse!" he shouted from his room. Once again, no one came. He attempted to get a nurse's attention a few more times and even called out to the doctor, but no one acknowledged him. His bladder began to hurt as he continued to wait, still calling for a nurse or doctor to help, but all of them seemed to be actively ignoring him.

After a long while, a man walked into the room with a pad of paper and a pen. He wore a tweed jacket with plain pants and an unassuming shirt. He quietly sat down next to Charlie as he writhed in the bed, doing what he could to save his dignity and relieve himself in the toilet.

"Thank you," he said with relief, "I need to piss so fucking bad and no one will help me out of the restraints."

"You have been put into the restraints because of the damage you caused to yourself and the bathroom during a psychotic episode," the man said officiously as he adjusted his glasses.

"Please," he pleaded, "I'm about to fucking burst over here. Just let me take a fucking piss already."

"I am the Fifth Ward Hospital's psychologist and I am here to evaluate you," he continued as if Charlie had said nothing.

"I don't give a shit!" he shouted angrily. "I *need* to piss. Do you understand? Why won't anyone help me?"

"I'll be more than happy to get your nurse if you just answer a few questions for me," he once again retorted officiously.

"Whatever! Just let me up!" he screamed.

"Sir, I'm going to have to ask you to calm down," he said with a bored tone.

"I'll fucking calm down when I can take a piss!"

"Sir, if you can't calm down, I can't help you."

"What the *fuck* do you want?!"

Charlie groaned as he felt shooting pains in his abdomen. He couldn't hold his urine for much longer.

"I just wanted to make sure that you aren't thinking about hurting yourself or others," he said in a monotone.

"If you don't let me out of this *fucking* bed to let me *finally* piss, I *will* start hurting you," he threatened.

"Sir, I don't take threats lightly," he said as he stood up with annoyance.

"Just let me piss and I'll answer your fucking questions!"

The man did not say a word and walked out of the room. Charlie groaned again with pain. He remained there and tried calling out for help again, but still no one came. At last, the inevitable happened. His entire groin burned as all of the urine forced itself out. The whole bed was wet, warm, and stank of his piss. With the restraints, he was unable to move and simply lay in the soiled bed, seething with rage. He remained still and glared at the wall, fuming from his indignity.

He heard footsteps near his door and saw his uncle and cousin standing next to the door with a nurse.

"Just remember, he had a manic episode last night and you cannot get within arm's reach of him."

"Well of course he's manic!" Frank said in Charlie's defense. "Two people he loved tried to kill him almost two weeks ago! Wouldn't ya be manic too?"

"Sir, he could be a danger to himself or others, and we just want to evaluate him," she replied.

"Y'all are so cold that ya can't even empathize with a man who's hurtin' and lost an arm? Did y'all ever ask him if he was alright, or did y'all just treat him like a damn violent prisoner?"

"Dad," Francis interrupted as he gestured toward Charlie, who was still in the soiled and soaked hospital bed. Frank looked over and walked into the room.

"Sorry you had to hear that, son," Frank apologized. "What the hell's that smell?"

Charlie looked away in shame. "They wouldn't let me out of the bed and I don't have a catheter or bed pan."

"What?" Frank asked in anger. "Nurse!"

The woman they'd spoken with just a moment before returned.

"Why are ya makin' my cousin piss the bed and not lettin' him up to go to the bathroom!" Francis demanded.

"I don't know what you're talking about, sir," she replied.

"Then ya come in here and smell what he's talkin' about," Frank growled.

The nurse entered, and Charlie did whatever he could to contain his anger. The nurse walked over and looked under the sheets. No bed pan, no catheter.

"Sir, I am *so* sorry," she apologized weakly, "we were told not to interact with you until you were evaluated by the psychologist."

"Get me his doctor, the chief nurse, and that pissant shrink," Frank demanded. "Right. Fucken. Now."

Charlie remained in his soiled hospital bed, restrained and visibly angry, as Frank berated Charlie's doctor, the chief nurse, and the officious and bureaucratic psychologist outside his room. Francis watched him sit there in his restraints, still lying in his indignity.

"Dad, enough," Francis commanded. "Charlie's still just lyin' in his own piss while ya chew 'em out."

Frank stopped and looked at his son. He seemed to realize that while he was telling the three how he felt, Charlie was still languishing in urine-soaked sheets. The chief nurse immediately summoned a nurse walking by and told her to help the patient, but Frank immediately demanded that the chief take responsibility and do it herself. The older, plump woman ground her molars, but she wisely bit her tongue and did as he demanded.

The ham-fisted woman walked into the room and began undoing Charlie's restraints. He got out of the bed and glared at the woman the entire time. He had called to her at least twice during the whole ordeal when she passed by his room. Charlie stood there in his hospital gown as the chief nurse grabbed all of the bedding to be discarded and exchanged.

"What the hell is going on here?" a voice said outside the room.

"It's alright, we're handling it," the doctor said.

Charlie's eyes flicked to the sound of the commotion, and there, five hours later, was Anabel. His jaw clenched.

"I hope you're trying to get a spot at the comedy club if ya think what you've done to my nephew would be considered 'handling it.' And *you*. Ain't ya his nurse? Where'd ya go? He needed ya to help him out of the restraints so he could relieve himself in the toilet, and I come in here to smell him wallowing in all of it in the bed."

"What?" Anabel asked in horror. "Did none of the other nurses help him?"

"The chief nurse specifically told everyone that only you were allowed to interact with him until the psychologist evaluated him," the doctor answered defensively.

"Yes, but I had a personal emergency! I told her that someone needed to take my place and help him while I was out!"

"Well apparently ain't a one got the memo," Frank replied with a sneer.

Charlie stood there motionless, still watching the crowd outside his room while the chief nurse quietly licked her wounds as she left with his soiled bedding. He could see Anabel was seething with anger, but he felt no sympathy for her. She was the first to ignore his pleas.

Some more hospital staff came and introduced themselves to Frank and Francis, who were both standing tall with crossed arms and intimidating stares. Apparently, the administration had heard about the incident and were now in damage-control mode. They profusely apologized to Frank and Francis, but they didn't want to hear it.

"Y'all should be apologizin' to the man in there," Francis replied indignantly.

Charlie didn't care to hear their false apologies. They had treated him like a dangerous animal. They had every right to restrain him and fear for his mental state because of his outburst, but he had practically begged for help, but everyone had coldly ignored him. He remained still and listless as the administrators apologized to him.

"Can I finally have a bath and change of clothes now?" Charlie asked.

"Yes, yes, of course. Whatever you need," one of the administrators groveled. "Ma'am, can you help him?"

Anabel started walking into the room.

"Not her, at least not right now," Charlie said.

She stiffened at his words and looked down.

"We'll find another nurse to help you for the rest of the day, sir."

The male nurse from the first day helped to clean Charlie and gave him a fresh gown. The restraints had been removed in exchange for him not having another outburst. By then, it was the middle of the afternoon, and he had yet to be visited by the doctor with all of his results.

He sat in the fresh bedding silently and looked to the middle distance, still fuming at his treatment by the staff. The blow would have been softened—and avoided altogether—if Anabel had not ignored him. He lay numbly as Frank ranted for a couple of hours, doing what he could to show support for his nephew. Charlie barely listened to a single iota uttered from his uncle's lips.

The doctor finally came in just before dinner with a thick folder. After looking at nothing for hours, Charlie's eyes finally fixated on the man. It was the doctor who told him that he might be in the hospital for a month, but he knew more than likely him being the one to bring the news had nothing to do with his prediction and everything to do with the other doctor being the one that had ignored him and was subsequently berated by Frank.

"Mr. Menillo," the doctor said as amicably as possible while still sounding distant and cold. "I have all of your test results, and thankfully most of them are good."

"And the bad ones?" Charlie asked plainly.

The doctor sighed and closed the folder. "You have significant head trauma, and it may cause permanent brain damage."

"How bad are we talking, Doc?" he asked.

"Hard to say at this stage because you're finally starting to drain all the blood from your cerebral hemorrhage. You would need to come back in a few months for additional imaging."

"Head trauma can cause mood swings," Charlie thought aloud.

"Correct," the doctor coldly confirmed, "So if you feel like you may have another episode like you did yesterday, let one of the nurses know and they'll give you some sedatives to help."

"So how long until I'm out of here, Doc?"

"We're going to keep you under observation for one more week, mostly to ensure that you don't have any more hemorrhaging and subsequent seizures from it. You only had one while you were in your chemically induced coma, but we're just taking every precaution given your Garner's disorder."

Charlie nodded his head. "Thanks for the information, Doc."

"Of course," he said as he swiftly walked out of the room.

"I'll see you two tomorrow," Charlie said to his uncle and cousin.

"Ya sure?" Frank asked with concern.

"Yeah."

The two tall men departed and left Charlie alone in his room. He remained still and contemplated the possibility of brain damage, but besides him not having an arm, everything felt normal in terms of motor function and memory, so he was hopeful. The burst of rage the day before may have been caused by the head trauma, but he didn't know for sure. The rage was real and natural in his state. Who wouldn't feel like him if they were in his situation? The fact that he had managed to keep it in for so long was a miracle in his eyes.

Someone rapped on the doorframe, and his eyes flicked to it. Anabel was standing there with apologetic eyes. It was around dinnertime, so he figured she was just announcing herself before she came in with the bland hospital food. She instead held up a bag of food from a local restaurant. Charlie knew that she was trying to bribe him to accept her apology. He simply watched her to see how she would act.

"I figured you could use something better to eat," she explained sheepishly.

He didn't respond and only looked at her. Her will wavered at his gaze and she looked down.

"I'm sorry," she began, "I was angry with you and wanted to go finish my rounds before I talked to you. When I was about halfway done, I got a call saying that my father was in the Second Ward Hospital. I went over there to see him, and I guess the chief didn't assign someone else to you. They were under strict orders not to interact with you until you were evaluated by the psychologist, so all of them thought that you weren't their problem."

She looked at him with a soft expression, her eyes pleading with him to accept her apology. He stared at her with a scowl for a while, then finally spoke.

"Are you going to bring it in here or are you just going to let it get cold?" he asked. Anabel smirked and walked in, closing the door behind her.

She sat down next to him, pulled items out of the bag, and placed a couple in front of him. He shifted to sit up straight as she removed items for herself.

"I figured you'd want something that didn't require utensils, so I got you a sandwich with some fries," she explained quietly as she revealed a salad for her to eat.

"If your father is in the hospital, why are you here with me?" he asked.

"Dad's fine, just a broken leg from a car crash," she explained. "He's already asleep and I still have a couple hours left before my shift is over."

Charlie grabbed the box with the sandwich and placed it in his lap. He silently ate his sandwich as Anabel awkwardly ate her salad.

"I saw myself yesterday," Charlie said after he finished his food. "Don't know how you don't stare every time you come in here."

Anabel pulled her head up from her food and looked at him somberly.

"No one warned me what I would look like," he said.

"I thought you would have already looked at yourself," Anabel replied. "Is that why you broke the mirror?"

Charlie glanced at his bandaged hand. "Yeah…"

"What did you see that made you break the mirror?" she asked.

"Someone else," he replied.

The nurse's eyes looked back down at her salad. "You'll look much better when everything is healed and closed. After a year or two, you'll just have a lot of scars."

"Not that," he clarified softly as she ate more of her salad.

She looked up at him and chewed with a raised eyebrow. "Then what?"

He slowly turned his head and looked into her green eyes. He then looked at the far wall and returned his gaze to the middle distance.

"A monster."

# Chapter 13

Eri awoke groggily to the sound of a thud. She realized that Charlie's coat was on her, keeping her warm in *Fire Arrow*'s cool, unheated cabin. She drowsily groaned and slowly closed her eyes again, readjusting underneath the duster, too lazy and somnolent to get under the covers. It was wrapped around her tightly enough that she could smell a mixture of leather and cigarettes. Her eyes closed, and she returned to her peaceful slumber. Another thud woke her. She slowly opened her eyes again and noticed a hand clutching the floor.

She lifted her body up, her right elbow balancing her weight as she rubbed her face with her left hand, and blinked. As her vision came into focus, she finally noticed Charlie's labored breathing. She lifted herself higher and leaned over the bed. *Silver Bow*'s first officer was prone on the floor, his cybernetic arm limp off to his side, his left arm outstretched and desperately clutching at the floor. His shirt and hair were drenched in sweat.

"Charlie?" she quietly called to him with concern. His state remained. He was having an intense nightmare, it seemed.

The man jolted awake with a frightened yell and scooted his way to the opposite wall in terror. His intense breathing wheezed and approached hyperventilation. The dim light of dawn leaked into the ship's cabin, a small beam of the purple and blue sky striking him in the face. His eyes danced across the room as he fully regained consciousness.

Eri sat on the bed, frightened and confused. She had the duster wrapped around herself in the front, holding it like a protective shield. Her eyes were affixed to his terrified face. Cold sweat dripped from his brow, chin, and nose as his breathing slowed. Finally realizing where he was, Charlie slowly pulled his head back and rested it against the airlock door.

Eri saw his breathing slow, but it continued to tremble. She had seen men scared before, but Charlie's expression had exhibited pure terror. His moment of vulnerability made her feel extremely uncomfortable, uneasy…and unsafe. Whatever it was, the confident, blunt, and rarely lighthearted crewmate had withered away and revealed a broken and hysterical man.

It was almost as if he had been replaced by a body double. To her, the man in front of her was not Charlie, but someone else that just looked like him. Color slowly returned to his face and he regained himself. He closed his eyes and took a long, slow breath. His breath hissed as it entered his nose forcefully and whooshed as it exited his mouth.

Charlie looked down, his mind still reeling from the nightmare. Eri slowly got off the bed, her head pounding from her hangover. She blocked the headache as she gently lowered herself in front of him. Charlie sat placidly like a mannequin, his breathing almost normal again. A drop of sweat fell from his nose and slapped onto the floor, increasing the size of the pool between his legs. His knees hid part of his face, but the hands gripping his knees trembled. His blue eyes remained still and listless as they gazed at the floor in front of him.

Eri felt compelled to do something. She slowly reached out to hold his hand to comfort and console him, but as soon as her fingertips brushed his hand, it robotically recoiled.

"Go back to sleep," he muttered.

Eri rubbed her head; the hangover could no longer be ignored. There was no way she was going to go back to sleep with her head pounding like that. She sat the duster down on the floor next to Charlie, who still had not moved, went back to the drawer underneath the bunk, grabbed the collapsible cups, washed them out in the sink, then filled them with water.

Groaning, she sat down next to him against the airlock door and voraciously drank the water, trying to get rid of the hangover. She gasped once she'd finished her cup with one chug, then sat the other cup down next to the trembling man, but he didn't move. She got up and refilled her cup, chugging it once more, gasping again with satisfaction before filling it a third time and finally returning to her seat next to him.

"Charlie, you're really scaring me," she admitted quietly.

"Fine," he muttered.

"No you're not," she replied. "You're drenched in—"

"I said 'I'm fine,' god damnit," he snarled.

Eri sat there and looked intently at him. He had managed to calm down, but his demeanor had only changed from terror to rage. What could have possibly happened in his dream that would affect him like that? Was it a war flashback?

The sweat faded from his face and neck and his hands no longer trembled, but his gaze remained affixed to the floor in front of him. Eri remained by Charlie's side, hoping that she could help him fully calm down. The sun rose and a beam of sunlight hit Charlie's face. As if the sun had activated something, he leaned his head back, closed his eyes, and breathed deeply.

He slowly opened his eyes. The sun hitting his face completely altered his demeanor. It was as if his terrified state had simply waited for the sun. He returned to his serious self and quickly consumed the water, then rose to his feet with purpose and lowered the ramp. Glad, but ultimately confused, Eri got up and followed him.

"Uh…Charlie?" she asked as she tried to keep up with his determined pace.

Charlie suddenly stopped and turned around. "Nothing happened in there, do you understand?" he commanded.

"I just want to make sure you're alright," she replied.

Charlie's seriousness wavered for a moment as he looked away. He quickly returned to looking at her. "I'm fine now, but we will never speak of what happened." He turned back around and marched into *Silver Bow*'s cargo bay. Driven by her curiosity, she followed and watched from a distance. Francis joined the two, happily walking through the maze of crates used as a staging area as Charlie removed a panel from the cargo bay's flooring. He reached inside and removed two blue vests and dropped them on the floor with a metallic thud.

"Well, well," Francis said jovially, "glad ya two are back, did ya have fun?"

"Uh, yeah," Eri replied nervously, "We got back late last night, but I was so drunk that I just slept on the bed in *Fire Arrow*." Charlie returned the floor panel to its proper place, dropping it with a loud bang.

"So where did Charlie sleep if ya took his bed?"

"I'm sorry, what?"

"Where did Charlie sleep if ya slept in his bed?" Francis reiterated.

"Oh…I didn't know that's where he slept," Eri admitted as Charlie walked down the ramp with the thick vests in each hand and a large bag on his back.

"Yeah," Francis said in a distracted voice, "hey, Charlie, we need to talk about that message ya sent me yesterday."

"Later," Charlie demanded as he walked away. "Tell Ash to meet me in the north junkyard. Her training begins as soon as she arrives."

Francis stood there, befuddled with Charlie's behavior. "I don't think I've ever seen him this motivated in the morning…"

"Is that what he is? Motivated?"

"Maybe 'determined' would be a better word…so where did he sleep?"

"On the floor. I was pretty drunk last night," she admitted sheepishly. "So what is on the renovation agenda today?"

"Livin' quarters, mostly," Francis replied with a smirk,

"Sounds like fun," she said. "What do you need me to do?"

"Ya can drive a loader mech, right?" he asked.

"Sure can!"

"Then you'll be moving materials in the mech pretty much all day."

Eri may have been able to hide it, but Charlie's newfound determination frightened her slightly. She knew whatever happened in his dream had forced him to focus with rage. What scared her more than anything was how quiet he was while enraged.

Ash arrived in her truck and emerged with four coffees in a drink carrier. "Hey there! How was the weddin' and reception?"

"Good, though my head isn't enjoying what I did so much this morning." Eri tried to block out what happened in *Fire Arrow*, but the image of Charlie's terrified face and abrupt rage remained. He'd offered subtle hints before that his life had been hard since the war, but his expression had showed a deep sense of fear and guilt that she didn't fully understand.

"Hangover is never fun to deal with," Ash said as she handed Eri a coffee. "It's got vanilla and milk, just like how ya always make it." She then grabbed a cup and handed it to Francis.

"Charlie is over in the junkyard to the north," Francis said as he received his coffee. "He wants ya to meet him out there immediately to start your security trainin'."

"Awesome, sounds fun," she said confidently.

"Ya won't be so glad once ya get there," Francis warned her. "It's the most determined I've seen him in years." He looked at Eri and then back at Ash. "He's gonna wear your ass out."

"I was one of the best at PT in my unit with the militia, I ain't worried," she replied arrogantly.

"I don't think ya understand, Ash," Francis began, "we both met up shortly after the war when I was in my absolute prime and Charlie ran circles around me. That man probably trains harder than commandos because he was average or below average in athletics— at best—before he joined the military. He had a lot to prove to his drill instructors in basic, and by the end, he *impressed* them." Ash's smile melted off her face and revealed fearful dread. "Ya better hurry. He's impatient when he's motivated."

Ash sighed heavily and slowly trudged with the coffee over to the junkyard. Eri looked at Francis with a curious look.

"Are you serious about Charlie?"

"Oh, yeah," he replied. "Just wait until ya see them later. He'll be winded and a little tired. Ash'll probably be throwin' up."

Ash walked toward the junkyard with the two remaining coffees. She navigated through the piles of scrap, looking around for Charlie. She continued onward, calling his name to find him. With no responses, she continued deeper into the scrapyard. She looked left, right, and back, trying to find him. At one intersection of scrap piles, she glanced right and saw Charlie fiddling with some sort of thick vest. It looked a lot like an armored plate carrier, but the thickness was too uniform throughout.

"Good, there you are," he said as he grabbed a vest off the ground. "Your training starts today, Tall Hands." He handed her the vest before she was able to place the coffees on the ground, causing them to fall and spill in the dirt. When she had a firm grip, he let it drop. The vest was surprisingly heavy, and it hit the ground with a thud.

"How fucken heavy is this thing?" she asked as she lifted it off the ground.

"Twenty-five kilograms," he replied. "This will help you get used to the weight of your equipment when it is ready. In the meantime, we will be running with these to help train your leg muscles with weighted training." Ash put the vest on clumsily. The weight made her top heavy. "Anyone can become a runner with enough training, but weighted runs are the only way to create the strength and endurance you'll need to be a menace on the battlefield."

Ash moved around in the vest. It felt loose. Charlie inspected her vest and began adjusting straps and clips. Finally, the vest was snug—too snug.

"This is a little tight," she complained.

"It's going to be that tight because that is how well your armor will fit your body. It's form fitting, which is why I asked for your measurements two nights ago when you and my stupid cousin drove drunk." Ash glanced down at her feet in embarrassment. "Now, are you ready to start your training?" Ash simply nodded in reply. "Good. One more thing: no coffee or any other form of caffeine during our training. You and I will both be staying away from all coffee in the morning. Coffee is a privilege, and you need to be able to do things without using it as a crutch to wake up or get pep in your step." Ash groaned at the idea of going without coffee for at least a couple of weeks. "Let's go, Tall Hands."

Throughout the rest of the morning, Charlie and Ash appeared and disappeared around *Silver Bow*. Eri was engrossed in her work with the mech loader and hardly noticed the two. It wasn't until lunchtime when she emerged from the mech did she finally see her sister and the resolute first officer. The contract workers had already left the site and would return in an hour and a half. Francis had ordered food to be delivered and waited on a crate with his second coffee in his hand. Eri walked over to the ship's captain sipping on a cup of water with added electrolytes to cure her hangover.

Eri then heard two sets of footsteps and distant words. Around the corner of the ship, the two in training emerged, Charlie leading an exhausted Ash. Charlie was even sweatier than he was when he woke from his nightmare that morning, but not by much. He came to a stop, winded, encouraging Ash to sprint the last fifty meters.

Ash seemed to gather every last bit of strength and sprinted toward him. Eri glanced at the captain, and Francis watched with a blank expression. Ash finally reached Charlie, then collapsed. Francis jumped off the crate in concern, but Charlie extended his hand towards his cousin, signaling him to stay still. Short of breath, Charlie ran over to Ash, who wheezed and groaned on the ground, her legs spasming with exhaustion.

"No, don't lie down," Charlie commanded as he grabbed the strap on the back of the vest, "Stand up, Tall Hands." She struggled to get to her feet, but her legs seemed inoperable. Charlie lifted her up with only his left arm and a forceful exhale. Ash stumbled with exhaustion and leaned against the hot mech.

"Nope," he said as he grabbed the front of her vest and pulled her away from the mech. "You stand up. Walk around if you need to. Your legs will still work if you walk, but if you stay idle, that's when you get in trouble and your muscles give out."

He gently pushed her from behind the vest to keep moving as she struggled to catch her breath, sweat dripping constantly from her fingertips, nose, chin, ears, and brows. The vest and shirt were soaked in her sweat. Francis grabbed a water bottle and approached the two, but Charlie again signaled to him to stay away. Ash weakly pleaded for water between wheezes.

"Not yet," he replied flatly, "five minutes of cooldown, remember?" She meekly nodded her head.

Eri watched as Charlie walked with her in circles for five minutes as she gasped for air, keeping her focused and calming her. "Breathe…just breathe," he reassured her calmly, "you're done. You did good." Charlie extended his hand toward Francis, who walked over with the water bottle. Charlie set it down on the mech's seat.

"Alright, Tall Hands, let's get this vest off you." Ash weakly stood still, her beathing less labored, but still winded. He gently and calmly unbuckled the vest and helped pull it over her head. She grunted and groaned in pain as he removed it. He gently sat it down next to Eri and removed his own with only a quick grunt, placing it next to Ash's vest. He handed Ash the water bottle but gripped it tightly when she tried to take it from him.

"Remember, small sips."

Ash voraciously gulped twice in her desperation for water and immediately vomited.

"I told you *small* sips, Tall Hands. Drink slower, deliberately, and in *small* sips."

Eri watched silently as Ash used all of her willpower not to completely chug the water. By this point, Charlie was calm. The level of fitness between them was such a massive margin. How would Charlie ever help her shrink the gap?

He put his arm around Ash proudly and said, "What you just did—pushing yourself beyond your limits…is why I hired you." Eri looked over as Ash quietly nodded, showing that she heard and understood him. She couldn't help but smile with pride at her sister after hearing Charlie's kind and motivating words.

"That's enough physical training for today. After lunch, we're going to do some shooting drills with your new Lancer."

Eri looked at the sweaty vests against the crates. She looked over at Francis, who exchanged a look with her, but she couldn't quite understand what he was trying to say. She looked at them again, then gripped the strap attached to Ash's vest. She tried to lift with one hand, but it was really heavy. She needed two hands to lift it. "Damn! How much does this weigh?" she asked them.

"Twenty-five kilos," Ash muttered as she used her shirt to wipe sweat from her brow.

"You both wore twenty-five kilogram vests and ran in them?" Eri asked in amazement.

"She did," Charlie said as he sipped some water, "mine's forty kilos."

"Bullshit," Ash asserted, "There ain't no way ya wore a forty-kilo vest, outpaced me, and are as calm as ya are now."

"I told ya he would wear your ass out," Francis replied. "We only have two weighted vests: a twenty-five and a forty kilo vest. Charlie probably didn't want ya to think his trainin' was unfair so he wore a vest with ya and just suffered through the heavier one."

Charlie waved his hand. "It's only been a month since I've run with it, so it wasn't that bad."

Ash stared at his vest with amazement.

"Don't beat yourself up about it, Tall Hands," Charlie reassured her, "It took me years and *many* injuries to get to this level. You just need to get used to the twenty-five kilo vest. Your armor will weigh twenty kilos and your weapons and ammunition will be another five. All I'm doing is just preparing for when shit really hits the fan."

Francis leaned in toward Eri and whispered in her ear, "Now here comes the history lesson, courtesy of our first officer."

"The sad part is that back in the twenty-first century on Earth, militaries regularly asked their troops to run and fight with fifty kilos of equipment or more on their bodies. We're the lucky ones with modern armor and lighter ammunition."

Francis gave a joking smirk at Eri as he walked to meet the food delivery car.

"How do you know about that?" Eri asked.

Charlie finally looked at Eri after doting over his protégé. "Read about it in a Navy field manual."

Francis returned with the food for the four of them and they all sat down around crates and ate as a crew. Ash and Francis did most of the talking during lunch. Charlie sat quietly, as usual, but he didn't eat his lunch with the same vigor and speed as he usually did. Eri glanced over at him as Francis told a story about a man that worked for his dad before the war and all of the funny pranks he'd pulled on management.

Charlie was statuesque as he held his food, staring listlessly at *Silver Bow.* His eyes were slightly widened, as if he was sleepy and was drawing them open more to keep himself awake. He remained still for a while as Francis and Ash continued to converse. He suddenly blinked deliberately, returned to reality, and resumed eating his lunch.

"Are you done eating?" Charlie asked as he turned his head to Ash. She nodded at him. "Go home, shower, and change. I'll meet you at the apartment in thirty minutes."

Ash tried to get up, but her legs were obviously sore. Francis stood and helped her with an outstretched hand. She wished Eri goodbye, jogged stiffly to her truck, and left. Shortly after, Charlie finished his food, got up, and started moving to *Fire Arrow.* Eri put her food down on the crate and ran after him.

"Charlie?" she asked as she caught up to him.

"What do you need, Eri?" he asked as he continued to *Fire Arrow*.

"Can you stop for a second? I want to talk to you."

"About what?"

Frustrated, Eri got in front of him and blocked his path. Charlie looked annoyed as he stood with folded arms. "I want to talk about what happened just now at lunch because I'm pretty sure it has to do with what happened this morning."

"There's nothing to talk about," he said as he tried to walk around her.

She blocked his path once again, pushing against his chest. "Yes, there is!" she exclaimed. "Look, you don't have to tell me what happened in your nightmare or what caused you to look like you saw your own death, but you *need* to talk to *someone* about it."

"What would you know?" he growled as he tried going around her again.

She stopped him for a third time. "I know that—whatever you're going through—you need to talk to someone because it's *clearly* trauma related."

"Not another word about that," he barked quietly as he pointed his finger in her face. "If you bring it up again, I'll fire you myself." Eri stiffened at the threat. "It's none of your business, nor your concern, understand?"

Eri looked away, fuming with anger. "Fine," she muttered as she held back her rage. She stormed back to the mech loader and jumped into the seat. "Your cousin is a hardheaded asshole, Francis!" she shouted as the cage lowered in front of her.

"Ya ain't telling me nothin' I don't already know, Eri," Francis replied jokingly.

# Chapter 14

For a week, the crew fell into a routine. Each day Eri would move things onto the ship for the contractors to place and assemble as necessary, Ash and Charlie would train all day, and Francis would happily supervise. Charlie's training was exhausting to say the least, and Ash found herself slamming her face into her pillow on the bed every night, groaning with lament. She understood why Charlie was training her hard, but she felt like she needed a break. She wouldn't show weakness around the first officer though. She knew that Charlie would chastise her. She wanted to prove herself, and she would shut up and keep fighting through all the training.

It was the second day in a row that Charlie had been teaching her how to properly clear interior rooms. She was trained a little on room clearing in the militia, but Charlie's instruction had a lot of depth and context that she sorely needed to fully understand.

Despite Charlie being a prick at least fifty percent of the time, she still saw someone who understood how a leader should behave. He took the time to ensure that she understood his instructions and the information that he gave her. Even if he used that shitty nickname of his or angrily repeated himself, he was still patient with her. He wanted her to fully understand his teaching.

Charlie had made a little box in the dirt by dragging the heel of his boot to demarcate the walls and entrance into the floor. She stood there with an unloaded rifle near the "entrance."

"Alright, Tall Hands. You're in position one. What do you do?"

Ash waved her non-firing hand to tell Charlie to take the other side of the door. He moved as instructed, and she counted down with her fingers. When she hit zero, she pushed into the "room." Charlie followed her inside the room skillfully and robotically, then moved to his position. He clearly had a lot of training with how smooth and mechanical his movements were.

"Clear," Charlie said.

"Clear," Ash responded.

While Ash relaxed, Charlie turned around and smirked as his cousin approached.

"How's it going, Francis?" he asked, "Come to offer some advice on urban warfare and show us your own skills?"

"Nah, nothin' like that," the captain replied with a humble wave of his hand.

"That's a shame," Charlie lamented, "but I understand."

"We finally found our ship's medic," Francis said with his toothy grin. Ash looked at the tall captain with a smirk. The man seemed to be in even better spirits than normal. Knowing his history, she was glad to see him genuinely happy.

"Excellent," Charlie replied, "when do we get to meet them?"

"He'll be here at lunchtime," Francis said as he handed him a tablet, "that's all the info he provided in the application."

"Kai Ishida," Charlie read aloud, "I'll do some research before he gets here. Go and help the captain with whatever he needs, Tall Hands."

Ash silently followed Francis around the ship where Eri was sitting idle and bored in the mech loader. "Eri, come down a sec," Francis gently commanded. The maintainer hopped out of the mech and dusted off her hands as she approached. "We've got an applicant for the ship's medic. All four of us'll meet him when he arrives at lunch. Charlie will have final say, of course, but I also want your opinions about him. You're part of the crew now and I would rather run this ship a little more democratically than Charlie wants."

"I don't know anything about medicine, but I'm sure I can come up with some questions between now and lunch," Eri replied with a shrug.

"Great," Francis said as he clasped his hands together, "in the meantime, go ahead and move those boxes full of books to Charlie's quarters."

Ash raised an eyebrow. "That's gotta be around fifty books or so," she said with surprise. "Charlie don't seem like a reader."

"As of right now, no," Francis replied, "but once we have a lot of spare time between jobs or on watch, he'll always have a book in his hands, and all of them borin'."

"Do you just want us to bring them up there or do you want us to put them on the shelves as well?" Eri asked as she pulled a book out of one of the boxes and read the title.

"Oh, just take them up there. Charlie would burst a damn blood vessel if ya tried to organize his books for him."

Eri and Ash hauled the heavy boxes of books up to Charlie's room, and the shelves that she and Ash moved the day before suddenly made a lot more sense. All of the rooms for the crew had a few shelves for books or knick-knacks, but the captain's quarters and the first officer's quarters had been customized. Francis' quarters, which was actually smaller than Charlie's and was originally the first officer's quarters, was devoid of shelves, only cabinets and drawers. Charlie's was supposed to be the captain's quarters, so it was larger and had enough room for the dozens of shelves that he would be utilizing for his library.

They spent twenty minutes moving the heavy book boxes up the stairs towards the living section. Each of them took five trips and stacked the boxes next to the executive desk in the middle of the room. Once they had moved all the boxes, they walked down the cargo ramp and saw Charlie and Francis having a discussion. Charlie had the tablet that Francis gave him earlier and seemed to be showing him something on the screen. He jabbed repeatedly at the screen, apparently trying to make a point. The two women joined them.

"Ash, can ya tell the workers to finish the day early?" Francis asked kindly, "We have some unexpected business that we need to take care of after meetin' with the doc."

Ash nodded.

"We can't hear your head rattle, Tall Hands," Charlie barked without looking at her.

"Yes, sir," she responded robotically. She quickly made her way back into *Silver Bow*.

"Charlie," Francis pleaded, "she don't need to call me 'sir' or nothin' like that."

"I know she doesn't," he said as he glanced at him through the side of his eye, "but she and everyone else will give you the respect your station requires." Charlie's side-glance showed that he was not going to back down, no matter what Francis said in return. Francis sighed in frustration. "The same goes for you too, Eri," Charlie clarified.

"Aye aye," Eri replied with a smile.

"Don't be a smart ass," Charlie grunted. "We don't need to run the ship like we're in the military, but you will address Francis by his title or rank frequently. I don't care if you call him by his name every now and then, but you should reflexively call him 'Captain' or 'sir,' understood?" Eri nodded, avoiding the first officer's gaze. Charlie's seriousness came with authority and demanded cooperation. He clearly would not yield on the subject and wanted the crew to understand that Francis was in command of *Silver Bow*.

"Ya done?" Francis asked with an annoyed tone.

"With *that* subject, yes," Charlie replied as he once again held the tablet up. "My main concern is that he's only worked in Athens for the past six years, and in a part of town that consists mostly of rich and out-of-touch people. He only worked as a field physician for two years in the war, and from what I see, it was a pretty cushy position."

"Well, let's ask him about his experience more when he arrives," Francis said as he waved his hand.

"Of course, Captain," Charlie replied as he put away the tablet. Francis glared at his cousin when Ash joined them. As the contractors began to leave, a taxi arrived next to all of the workers' trucks.

"That must be our man," Francis concluded.

Charlie quietly hummed with apprehension. A man emerged from the taxi and walked up to the construction site.

"I suppose I am at the right place," he said when he was halfway between his starting point and the crew. "The directions you gave were rather vague."

"Can't even handle a short moment of silence," Charlie remarked quietly. "I have an inkling suspicion that he'll have a hard time shutting the fuck up."

Ash snickered, but quickly recomposed herself as the man approached. Eri shook her head.

"Hello," he said as he extended his hand toward Francis, "you must be the captain. Kai Ishida."

"Welcome," Francis said with a smile. "This is the crew so far. Certified Maintainer Erina Bezek—"

"Eri," she corrected as she shook Kai's hand.

"Security Specialist Ashley Erikson—"

"Ash," she clarified as she grasped Kai's hand.

"And First Officer Charlie Menillo—"

"Let me guess, Chuck?" Kai asked with a smile as he extended his hand.

Charlie stood motionless, staring deep into Kai's brown eyes. The three could feel the tension between the two. Eri knew how much Charlie hated the name Chuck, and it took everything in her not to laugh at Charlie's indignation.

"Just Charlie," he finally replied as he extended his prosthetic.

"Oh!" Kai exclaimed as he noticed the prosthetic. "I have not seen a Heltech in *years*. May I?" Kai didn't wait for a response and immediately began to inspect the cybernetic arm. "Zinc carbide?" he asked as he turned the arm to inspect the elbow mechanism.

"Still haven't shook my hand, Doc," Charlie noted irritably.

"Oh, yes, apologies," he stammered as he once again extended his hand. Charlie slowly grasped Kai's hand and let go, his blank expression still conveying annoyance as he held out the arm for further investigation. "Do you know the model number?"

"Doesn't have one anymore," he replied plainly. "The arm was custom made from multiple models."

"Ah," he said with exuberance, "that explains why I could not determine the model. What kind of shoulder joint?"

Charlie, unamused, glanced at Francis, who smirked and removed the arm from the connection point in his shoulder.

"Hmm, the servos look custom," the doctor keenly remarked. Eri had no idea that a doctor could be as interested in the same things as her. She had never seen Charlie's arm off, and she noticed that the ball joint for his shoulder and the hub to connect his arm was all custom. She could see streaks of grease inside.

"Built by hand," Charlie replied with his own smirk. "The stock Heltech connections wouldn't move fast enough for my liking. SCR stifled any new developments on cybernetic prosthetics, so I had to go custom."

"When was the last time you had those servos serviced?" Kai asked as he leaned in closer to the connection. He was thinking the same as Eri. The streaks of grease showed a need for maintenance.

"About four months ago," he replied, "around the same time you lost your medical license."

Kai suddenly froze, looked up at Charlie, and slowly pulled away. Francis grunted as he returned the cybernetic arm back into its socket. Eri could hear the servos inside the shoulder hub whir, which meant the arm needed maintenance. She shouldn't be able to hear them at all.

"Yes, well, you have certainly done your homework," Kai replied with a shudder.

"Enough to know that the only reason you lost your license instead of getting an interview with the news is because you exposed a politically connected billionaire as an abuser," Charlie replied plainly. "The main question I have for you is this: will you be able to procure medical supplies without any trouble?"

"Of course," he replied excitedly, "if there is anything *extremely* controlled, I may have difficulties, but I have plenty of colleagues throughout the Independent Systems that would be more than willing to assist me. Many agree with your assessment."

Charlie glanced again at Francis and nodded once. He silently turned around, hands clasped behind his back, and walked into *Silver Bow*. Kai looked around with confusion.

Francis silently looked at the two women. Ash smirked and shrugged. Eri nodded eagerly. "If I were to offer ya a position, Kai," Francis began, "would ya be willin' to help design and build the medical bay?"

"Absolutely," he replied warmly as he extended his hand, "I would relish in the freedom of designing my own medical bay."

"Be warned, Kai, you're gonna be limited with supplies and equipment. You'll practically be workin' like a field doctor in the military."

"I will be right at home then," Kai retorted keenly, "I worked as a field surgeon in the last two years of war."

"I know," Francis replied.

"Oh, well..."

"Welcome to *Silver Bow*, Kai," Eri said with a smile.

While Francis showed Kai around the ship, Eri finished moving the supplies for the next day's activities into the cargo bay with the loader mech. When she finished, she sighed with relief as she jumped out and went up to the galley to get some water. The contractors had left a cooler with ice to keep bottled water cool since the ship did not have life support. She walked up the strangely configured starboard staircase into the living section when she heard a thunk coming from Charlie's quarters. She slowly looked around the corner and saw Charlie organizing his books. The shelves were already filled about halfway.

"So how many books do you have?" Eri asked from the doorway. Charlie turned quickly to face her. She realized that he had been so engrossed in the moment that he didn't even hear her footsteps approaching. "Oh, sorry. Didn't mean to scare you."

"No," he said softly, "just lost in my own thoughts." Eri nodded. Charlie's demeanor and attitude had softened over the past week, enough for her to notice. "I have one hundred and seven books. I've read only eighty-eight of them, though," he admitted.

"Oh, *only* eighty-eight?" she asked sarcastically, as if unimpressed.

Charlie snorted, "You'll have a lot of time on your hands as a freighter. Most of these I read the last time I worked on a ship. Before then, I never read much."

"So the boredom is what got you into reading?"

"Yes and no…a crewmate suggested a few to help me pass the time. She was the one that got me hooked—she was very well-read," he said with conflicted smile, "and much of these were once hers."

Eri silently observed Charlie's expression as he looked at the books with pained nostalgia.

"So Christie got you into reading," she deduced.

Charlie slowly turned his head and looked at her through the side of his eye. His face turned from bittersweet to pensive. He turned his view back to the books and breathed sharply through his nose.

"Yeah…" he said finally with a longing sigh.

He had already mentioned before that he didn't want to talk about her, and his demeanor had shifted the two times she mentioned the enigmatic woman. The two had a history, more than likely a bad breakup. Eri could tell that despite everything, Charlie still had some feelings for the woman deep down.

"You two were engaged…" she blurted the moment she realized. She found herself discovering more and more about Charlie through the very skill he had taught her. It was like an entirely new world to her. It felt godly to be able to understand people so well with ease.

Just a few days before, she had noticed that Ash seemed to be very fond of Francis and seemed to be very gentle around him, which was unusual. Ash wasn't a brute by any means, but she had never seen her sister be that gentle with any of her previous boyfriends.

"I'm sorry, I shouldn't pry like that," Eri admitted before Charlie could respond.

"You're a good student," he replied proudly, "to be honest, I never thought you would get to this level this quickly. I think you are experiencing the same thing I did when I first began to grasp the skill."

"What is that?" she asked.

"Addiction," he replied. "Now you can't help but do it, and when you notice that fine detail, it makes you feel…powerful…and you only want to learn more."

Charlie understood and felt the same way as she did. It made Eri smile knowing that it wasn't just her.

"Let's drop the subject though," he urged.

"Okay…sorry."

Charlie continued to unpack his books and place them in various spots on the shelves. Eri began reading the titles of the books. She found one book that was worn and heavily used. She slowly removed it from the shelf and read the title out loud.

"*The Inferno* by Dant—"

"Dante Alighieri," Charlie replied as he revealed two more books, "Dante's *Inferno* is a political piece from the Medieval period that expresses his concerns with men serving themselves in the name of God and righteousness. An interesting read if you know who he's talking about, otherwise you'll spend more time reading and learning about the people he criticizes than you will reading the book. I've only read it once."

*If he had only read it once, then its wear most likely came from Christie. It must have been one of her favorites.*

"Here's one of my personal favorites of the classics," he said as he produced a book.

The corners of the soft book cover revealed the inner layers of paper, which meant it had been moved and read multiple times. The soft spine had large creases throughout. The paper was yellowed, more than likely from Charlie's cigarette smoke, and some brown spots from coffee stains were speckled throughout.

"*The Count of Monte Cristo* by Alexandre—"

"Dumas," he interrupted, "I know it looks like 'dumbass' but it's pronounced Doo-mah. I also have the d'Artagnan romances next to it."

She looked at the other books by Dumas and noticed that they too were also worn, but not nearly to the extent as *The Count of Monte Cristo*.

"Why do you like this one so much?" she asked.

"It's a great story about hope, revenge, and loss."

"Let me guess, you like the revenge plot the most?" she asked with a smirk. The first officer grunted a chuckle as he removed a few more books from a box and began to place them on the shelves.

"No, actually," he replied, "though it is one of the best revenge stories of all time, I like it because it reminds me that anyone can have a happy ending."

"You also relate to the main character," she concluded.

Charlie stopped and turned to her. "I think we need to have a rule about reading each other until I teach you how to control it," he said plainly.

"I'll tell you what," she began as she put her hands on her hips, "I'll stop if you tell me how you figured out that I liked midnight snacks."

He smirked as he put the book away, "Alright, fair enough. When I—"

"Charlie, get down here!" Francis commanded from the cargo bay.

Charlie looked at her. "Stay here."

# Chapter 15

Charlie quickly left the room and joined Kai and Ash, who stood outside the ship in shock, while Francis looked down at his feet with shame. Six cars had pulled up and dozens of men emerged holding weapons of various types and calibers. It was Jessik with a large crew of his goons. Charlie stepped up next to Francis, who looked at him solemnly.

"That's why you had the contractors leave," Charlie realized. His stomach turned as he wondered why Jessik came with so many men.

"Charlie, my mangy little attack dog, how are you?" Jessik asked jovially. Ash looked at Francis for answers, but he wouldn't look at her.

"I have a very bad feeling about this," Kai remarked quietly.

"What do you want, Jessik?" Charlie asked as he approached Jessik with twelve men while the other twelve stayed next to the vehicles.

"The fuckin' manners on this guy," Jessik complained to the man on his left as he revealed a cigar and lit it. "I came here to check in on my investment and to meet your new crew members. Thought that seemed obvious."

"That won't be necessary, Jessik," Charlie replied, "we're on schedule to finish in two weeks and we'll start helping you move product as soon as she's ready."

"I will fuckin' tell you what is and is not necessary, dog," Jessik shouted angrily, "Now get the fuckin' crew gathered and bring them to me *now*."

"C'mon, let's go," Francis said to Kai and Ash meekly, "we don't want to anger him."

"Who the fuck is that?" Jessik growled at Charlie as he pointed toward the ship. Charlie turned around and looked to see where he was pointing, hoping it wasn't Eri.

"Is that the grease monkey? Get down here, girl!" Eri joined the crew outside, standing behind Charlie. "Come over here off to the side so I can see you." Eri quietly complied and stood next to Charlie. "Excellent. What a cute little crew, eh?"

Charlie was the only person among the crew that dared hold their gaze on Jessik. Everyone else looked away. "What do you want, Jessik?" Charlie asked.

"I got a job for you, doggie," Jessik replied as slowly paced in front of the crew and looked at them. "There's a gang—the Sun Scorpions—here in town that think they can invade my territory. I want you to kill their leader and show them who runs Magna Graecia. This is *my* planet, not theirs. They exist because I allow it. Think ya can explain that to them?"

Charlie's jaw clenched with rage. "Consider it done, but it'll cost you ten grand."

"Oh, you must be under the illusion that because I gave you half of that bounty a while back that suddenly I will pay you for your services," he said condescendingly, "you do this to help settle some of your lanky cousin's debts."

"So you're calling in one of your three favors then?" Charlie clarified.

"Why the fuck would I call in a favor just to have some shit stain killed?" he asked furiously. "This is to help settle some of Francis's debts."

"I already paid ya, Jessik, I don't owe ya nothing," Francis spat. One of the guards immediately pistol whipped him on the head. He fell to one knee, and a small gash appeared on his forehead. Francis groaned in pain as blood oozed from his cut.

"Listen here, ya little fuck," he snarled with indignation as he got in Francis face with his cigar, "just because you don't owe any more of your *father's* debts, doesn't mean you don't have debts of your own, and these debts aren't monetary in nature, understand? I settled your father's debts because I'm a merciful piece of shit, but now you owe me because of that mercy. Charlie being my little Pit Bull here in Corinth is a good start."

Francis looked at Charlie with fear and regret as he slowly stood. Charlie returned a blank expression. He wasn't going to show his fear. Jessik continued to examine the crew and went to Eri. He took a long puff of his cigar as Eri looked down at the ground.

"Look at me, girl," Jessik said authoritatively. Eri breathed in slowly as she looked up at him. "Ah," he said as he leaned back and looked at the guard closest to him, "she's a cutie." He reached towards her and gently caressed her cheek. Charlie could see her fear as she stiffened. "You should come work—"

Charlie moved like a blur and gripped Jessik's wrist with his right hand. "Don't touch the crew," he slowly and deliberately commanded. The guards all began to point their guns at Charlie as Jessik gritted his teeth from the pain.

"Let him go, now!" one guard cried, pointing his barrel at Charlie's left temple.

"I'll do your job, but you don't touch the crew," Charlie growled as he slowly released his grip. Jessik yanked his arm away and rubbed his wrist to ease the pain.

"You will do the job," he spat, "but now you'll only have two days to get it done…alone. Francis, why don't you tell your crew to go into the cargo bay? Me and my boys need to have a word with your first mate."

"Jessik, please," Francis pleaded.

"If you don't take your motherfuckin' crew back up to your shitty fuckin' ship, I'm going to extend our little conversation to all of ya, and then I'll have my men take turns on the women." Charlie reflexively stood in front of Eri. "What? You fuckin' her or somethin'? That why you're so protective?"

"Eri, let's go," Francis demanded. Eri slowly complied and followed Francis and the rest of the crew back into the cargo bay. Her hands trembled. Charlie remained still in front of Jessik and showed only rage.

"Hold him," Jessik commanded two guards. They immediately complied and forcefully held Charlie. "You see, my little Pit Bull," he began as he took a puff of his cigar and signaled more guards to approach, "just like any other mangy dog, sometimes you gotta establish some discipline." He pointed down, and the guards forced Charlie to his knees. "Give him a lesson in manners, but don't kill him," he commanded the guards. "He's still got a job to do."

The guards began punching and kicking Charlie all over his head and torso. He grunted in pain as each strike hit him. One of the guards tore his shirt off and kicked him hard in the ribs, causing Charlie to howl in pain. The beating continued for a while until Charlie stopped making noises when he was hit.

"Alright stand him up," Jessik commanded as the sun began to set. The guards lifted him up by his armpits. He barely stood, his knees buckling. Blood slowly poured from his mouth, and he knew that his left eye was going to shut from how much it hurt and the pressure that he felt in his eyelid. Jessik produced a knife and started talking to him quietly. If he knew that he wouldn't be beaten again, Charlie would have spit blood in the mafia don's face.

"My final parting gift to you, dog," Jessik said quietly, "The next time you touch me or threaten me, I'm going to rape your little girlfriend over there until I start chafing. Then, I'm gonna jam this knife right up her pussy and elongate her little greasy cunt all the way up to her mouth and pry her open…in front of you." With those final words, Jessik slowly pushed the knife into Charlie's left torso, just below the ribs. Charlie cried out through his bloodied teeth as the mobster slowly pulled the knife out. Blood dripped onto the dirt beneath him as he tried to remain quiet.

"Motherfucker," Ash snarled quietly as she stood up from the crate in the cargo bay.

"No, Ash, please," Francis begged, "you'll only make it worse."

"Let's see how good your skills are, Doctor," Jessik mockingly shouted as the men adjourned to their vehicles.

"Charlie!" Ash cried out as she tried to run to him. Francis stood in front of her with raised hands.

"Wait! Wait!" Francis pleaded. "It's a trap. Wait until they all leave."

"So we're just supposed to sit here and let him bleed in the dirt?" Ash shouted.

Francis could only produce one quiet word as he looked down.

"Please…"

"Ya *fucking coward*," Ash growled through her teeth.

Francis's lower lip quivered as tears emerged in his eyes.

"They are gone, Francis," Kai announced.

"C'mon, Doc," Ash demanded.

Eri remained seated on the crate next to the ashamed captain; neither could move. Ash and Kai raced over to Charlie, who weakly held his stab wound with his left hand.

"Charlie? Charlie, we're here," Ash said shakily, "We're gonna get ya patched up, okay? Doc, help me turn him over."

The two cooperated and lifted the weak, bloodied man. Because he collapsed onto the dirt, all of the blood on his face and body was caked with dirt. Ash instructed Kai to go toward *Fire Arrow*, since there wasn't anything for them to lay Charlie on, nor any way to keep him out of the elements. The two huffed and puffed as they carried him to the smaller ship and placed Charlie on the bed.

"Get the power on so I can have some light," Kai demanded. "I will get my kit." The unlicensed doctor then ran towards *Silver Bow* as Ash struggled to find the right switches to get the power running.

"Main start toggle to idle," Charlie said weakly, "press ignition, then aux power."

Ash did as directed and the drive core hummed to life. She then looked around and saw a small control panel next to the washroom module. She pressed the cabin lights button and the interior lit up. Charlie shifted to get himself comfortable with a grunt, but Ash gently pushed down on his shoulders to keep him in the same position.

"Stay still, Charlie," she pleaded, "Kai will be back soon to patch ya up."

"Are they gone?" he asked. "Is everyone safe?"

Ash stood straight in shock. After everything that Jessik and his men did to Charlie, his only concern was the safety of the crew. She wouldn't be able to think about anything else if she was stabbed.

Kai ran up the ramp with a large bag on his back. He dropped the pack on the floor next to the bunk as Charlie's stab wound continued to bleed down his side and onto the bunk. He produced absorbent cloth and handed it to Ash.

"Ashley," he began as he rummaged through his bag, "I need you to put that bandage over the stab wound and put pressure on it. It will hurt, but it will slow the bleeding."

Ash followed Kai's instructions and pressed down on the bandage. Charlie winced in pain, revealing a mouth full of blood. Kai then removed a small plastic kit from the pack and opened it.

"No," Charlie said weakly as he tried to grab Kai's hand.

"Hey, it's okay," Ash reassured him, "Kai will take care of ya."

"No," he said again, "Garner's disorder. No SCR."

Kai looked up at him and sighed. "So you have to heal the old way?" Charlie weakly nodded as his swollen left eye closed from the pressure of the blood pooling in his eye socket. Kai then grabbed a cold pack and popped the inner container to start the cooling reaction. He placed it in Charlie's prosthetic hand and pushed the fingers inward to let him grip it. "Make yourself useful and put that cold pack on your eye."

Charlie grunted with a chuckle as he passed the cold pack to his left hand and placed it on his swollen eye.

"Well, since SCR does not work on you," Kai began as he continued to remove items from his pack, "I'm going to have to start you on an IV of fluids and anti-inflammatories to reduce the swelling and bruising. Do you have any allergies that I need to be aware of?" Charlie slowly shook his head. "First, I will get that stab wound patched." Kai removed a canister and a package with a sterile flexible tube. He removed the packaging for the tube and placed it on the top of the canister. "Do you know what this is?" he asked. Charlie slowly nodded. "Then you know how much it will hurt. Do you need to bite down on something?"

"Just get it over with," he weakly said with a mouthful of blood.

"As you wish," Kai replied, "Ashley, go ahead and remove that bandage, fold it over, and let Charlie spit the blood out of his mouth. After that, get some water and a cup—or whatever he can spit on or into—to clean his mouth." Ash removed the bandage and held it to the side of Charlie's head, who turned and spit foamy blood. The blood dribbled off his lips and Ash simply stood there, letting it slowly fall onto the bandage.

"Ashley, wipe his face," Kai said with annoyance. Ash slowly wiped Charlie's mouth, the bandage now heavily soaked in blood. She dropped it on the floor in the washroom as she searched for a cup in the cabinets. "Sorry for kneeling on your arm, Charlie. Are you ready?" The first officer nodded.

While Ash searched for the cup, she could hear Kai using the canister. With a sloshy whoosh, the foam was shot through the tube and into Charlie's wound. She knew how painful that shit was, and she didn't envy him in that moment.

Kai produced a small metal box from his kit as Ash finally returned from the washroom with two cups, one empty and one with water. She held the water cup up to Charlie's lips, and he sipped from it. He swished the water around his mouth and then spit into the empty cup with watery blood and repeated the process until there was no more water. The doctor removed a syringe from the kit and stabbed the needle into a small container's lid, drawing out a clear liquid.

"Local anesthetic so I can stitch you up without hurting you too much," he said to Charlie as he began poking the skin around the wound and slightly depressing the plunger. Kai then quickly made four stitches and closed the wound as Ash poured the bloody water down the sink's drain. Kai dressed it with gauze and a thin adhesive bandage.

The three heard footsteps on the back ramp. Eri slowly ascended the ramp, her left hand grasping her right arm.

"Is he going to be okay?" she asked quietly.

Kai smiled calmly. "He will be fine, Erina," he replied, "he just needs some rest and medicine."

Ash could see on Eri's face that she was very shaken from the whole ordeal.

"Hey," Ash said to get her sister's attention, "ya look a little shaken up. Ya okay?"

Eri nodded as she looked at the first officer on the bunk, his body bruised and bloodied. She remained at the top of the ramp just inside the ship's cabin, silently watching as Kai started an IV drip and pushed anti-inflammatories and painkillers into the tube with a syringe.

"How are you feeling?" Kai asked.

"Better," Charlie murmured, "I think I have a cracked rib or two though."

Kai pressed on Charlie's ribs until he hissed and winced with pain. The remaining ribs were normal. "Well thankfully it is only one rib," Kai explained. "Ribs heal on their own, though because of your GD, it will take six weeks instead of six days to fully heal. I'm sure you will take my advice and do as little exercise as possible and not completely ignore it and make the healing process take longer."

"Of course," Charlie replied sarcastically.

"Well that is all I can really do for you," Kai said as he removed his gloves and began to clean up his workspace. "I will come back in three hours once your bag is empty. Now you just need plenty of rest. Will you need sleep aids?"

"Probably."

Kai produced a small bottle and shook out two tablets. "Melatonin. These can just dissolve on your tongue. I'll give you some stronger stuff to get you to fall asleep; the melatonin will keep you asleep."

Charlie placed the tabs in his mouth as Kai once again used a syringe and pushed more medicine into the IV.

"Kai," Eri asked sheepishly, "I can disconnect the IV bag if you show me, that way you don't have to come back in three hours."

Kai smiled and led Eri through the process of disconnecting the drip and bag from Charlie's IV. After he was satisfied that she knew the steps, he grabbed his bag and left the ship.

"Are ya sure you're okay, Squirt?" Ash asked her little sister.

She nodded slowly, her eyes still on Charlie. "I'm fine now. You go ahead and get the blood off your clothes."

Ash looked down and noticed that a good amount of Charlie's blood was on her shirt. "Yeah, alright. Send me a message if ya need anythin'."

Eri walked over and silently looked at Charlie, who looked back at her. Ash could tell that Eri felt obligated to help him after he had protected her, and he seemed glad that she was untouched. The way they both looked at each other, she wondered if either had any sort of feelings for each other or if Charlie was just doing his job and Eri was just thankful for it.

She pulled herself away and left *Fire Arrow*. She then made her way to *Silver Bow*'s cargo bay. The closer she got to the cargo bay, the harder she stomped. She was furious with Francis.

Charlie had finally been stabilized and Eri, not Francis, was the one staying by his side that night. Francis had stood by and let his subordinate take a beating from half a dozen men and then get stabbed. She couldn't believe his inaction before, during, and after the attack. When she helped Kai carry Charlie over to *Fire Arrow*, she saw Francis sitting pathetically on a crate, and the image filled her with rage.

"Ya fuckin' coward!" she yelled as she turned the corner. Francis had not moved since the encounter, and Kai was placing a couple of butterfly bandages on his forehead where he was pistol whipped. "Ya haven't even moved from that spot," she spat. "Your first officer—your cousin—took a beatin' for ya because ya did *nothin'*. How can ya live with yourself and just sit there while the two of us patched him up!"

Francis sat listless as Kai removed his gloves.

"I'm talkin' to ya!" she shouted as she grabbed his shirt. "Say something, god damnit. I know ya ain't touchin' guns no more, but ya coulda done *somethin'*."

"There's nothin' I could've done," he replied meekly, avoiding her eyes.

"There's *always* something ya could do," she argued. "Ya said a couple days ago that we *all* have a responsibility to look after each other, but you're the only one who ain't done nothin'!" She let go of the shirt with a slight shove. "I was ready for a fight, why weren't ya? Just cause ya don't carry guns no more, don't mean ya can't help or fight."

Kai slowly left the area without drawing attention from Ash or Francis. "Ya know why, god damnit," he replied with a shudder. The two stared at each other, Ash's eyes blazing with rage as Francis's eyes pleaded with sorrow.

"I don't care if you've become some monk who refuses to have a gun in your hand no more," Ash said angrily. "Ya saw a lotta shit and did a lotta shit and I can respect ya for tryin' to keep the intrusive and dark shit away. What I care about is that ya did nothin', even after that piece of shit left with all his men! Eri right now is sittin' in *Fire Arrow* watchin' over Charlie while ya sit here in the cargo bay sulkin' like a scolded kid.

"It don't matter if all of it or none of it is your fault, ya need to show your appreciation for Charlie protectin' my sister—and maybe all of us—while ya cowered and begged. People don't really care one way or the other about peaceful people, but no one likes *pacifists*. At least peaceful people are still ready to fight when necessary."

"Ya have no clue how much violence I faced," he growled. "I've barely told ya a fraction of the shit I witnessed, the terrible shit I had to do, Ash. I've killed *hundreds*, Ash, lost almost a hundred.

"Ya ain't killed no one and ya ain't ever had to hold someone in your arms and tell them that they'll be alright as the light fades from their eyes, so don't ya act all high and mighty on me! Ya have no idea what it's like to keep all your rage and guilt inside, knowin' that if ya fight, ya turn into the monster that ya fucken hate."

"I don't care if ya fight, Francis. I care that ya didn't help."

Ash shook her head and stormed back down the ramp toward her truck. She got in the truck, slammed the door, and sped off.

Eri stood over the first officer lying still on the bed, his left eye still swollen, but no longer shut. She could see in the light that a blood vessel had ruptured in his left eye, causing the white of it to be red instead. He didn't say anything, only looked up at her.

"Since you watched over me the other night when I was wasted, I thought I could watch over you tonight," she said with a slight smile.

"You don't have to do that," he replied quietly.

"I know," she said as she turned off the cabin lights, raised the back ramp, and sat across from him, "but it's what friends do, right?"

"Friends…" he said distantly.

Charlie smiled slightly and hissed. The cut on his lip reopened. He licked the cut to keep the blood from oozing out. Eri gazed at him in the dim light for a while. He lay on the bunk, his eyes halfway closed with grogginess and weariness.

"Why did you do that?" she finally asked.

"Hmm?" he replied as his eyes opened more.

"Why did you grab Jessik's arm? You knew what he would do to you…"

Charlie snorted. "If I didn't, Francis would have done something," he said sleepily. "He's full of guilt about Jessik, but all of it was because of his father, Frank. He had gambling debts with Jessik, and he died three months ago. Jessik wasn't about to forgive the massive debt, so we sold off his family's company to pay him off, but Jessik was never going to let either of us walk away." Charlie blinked deliberately.

"Before Frank passed, Jessik already had made me one of his assets. Frank had me run drugs for Jessik to help pay off his debts, but he found out that I was ex-military and a mercenary for a year. That's why he calls me Pit Bull. One of his lieutenants said I was his little attack dog, and the name stuck. Sometimes, I just had to beat someone to send a message or as restitution for not paying protection money. Other times…"

"Why didn't you tell me?" she asked.

"I was hoping I'd never have to," he said distantly. "We were trying to finish everything before Jessik got impatient. Francis and I both were hoping you'd never know about it. We were just going to do a few jobs for him while we got the business started."

"So…is he a mob boss or something?" she asked quietly.

He nodded slowly. "Yeah."

"Are you going to kill that gang leader?" she asked shakily.

"I have to," he replied plainly, "if I don't, he'll hurt or kill all of you just to make an example. I won't let that be on my conscience."

"But…you're going to *murder* someone," she argued.

"That someone is the leader of a gang who terrorizes people," he corrected, "and I will *not* let anyone hurt you or anyone else on the crew—whatever it takes, I'll protect…" Charlie dozed off for a moment. He reopened his eyes, but Eri placed her hand on his shoulder. She grabbed his duster off the back of the pilot's seat and gently laid it over him, repaying him in full for the night they came back from Athens.

"Get some sleep," she said softly.

"Hmm," he hummed.

Eri sat in the comfortable pilot's seat and woke her tool to browse through videos and news, keeping vigil over the stoic first officer. She, Ash, and Kai were now all in deep, but she knew that she couldn't just walk away from it. They were stuck, but she hoped that Jessik would at least stay away from her after Charlie had intervened.

She let a video play despite not paying attention to it. All she could hear and see in her mind were the words that Jessik said to Charlie before stabbing him. If he didn't help Jessik, he'd rape and kill her in front of him. The thought made her stomach turn.

After three hours, Eri disconnected the IV bag just as Kai taught her and put it in the trash bin in the washroom. Kai had returned not long after Charlie initially fell asleep and removed his blood soaked pants to get washed and to release any unnecessary tension around his hips if they had been hurt.

Eri had looked away when Kai removed the pants, but he said, "He is still wearing underwear and I could use some help. Now is not the time for modesty, Erina." She'd helped, but only by pulling on the end of his pants near his feet. She would let the doctor touch him near his hips and groin.

The night was beginning to get cold, so she quietly left out of the side airlock. She walked over to *Silver Bow* in the darkness. She turned the corner to walk up the ramp into the cargo bay when a light shined in her eyes. She recoiled and shaded her eyes with her hands.

"Who's there?" a voice asked sternly, "Oh, Eri…" The light lowered from her face. She blinked as she saw Francis standing in the cargo bay with a light. "Sorry. Didn't expect ya to come this way. Is everythin' alright?"

"Yeah, just wanted to get something to keep warm in *Fire Arrow,*" she replied as she walked up the ramp.

"Well, I have an extra cot somewhere, you're welcome to take that," he replied.

"Wait…you and Charlie *both* sleep out here? Do you not have anywhere to stay? I thought for sure you two would have an extended stay room somewhere."

"Nah," Francis said with a wave of his hand, "Charlie didn't want to pay for a room and I slept out in the elements so much during the revolution that it doesn't bother me. Besides, we both wanted to guard the ships at night. *Fire Arrow* is his ship, so he sleeps in the little girl, but I sleep in *Silver Bow.* She's *my* mistress." Eri giggled at Francis's jest. It was good to see him in better spirits. "Listen, if ya need something to keep warm, Charlie's sheets and comforter are in his quarters. I can grab them for ya. The spare cot is in the drive core room."

"Thanks, Captain," she said gratefully.

"Oh! And speaking of the drive core room," he began with a toothy grin, "I got a message earlier that the drive core and shield generator will arrive tomorrow."

"That's exciting!" she exclaimed quietly, "I can't wait."

"Finally she'll have a heart," Francis said happily as he looked around the cargo bay. "She's getting' there…"

"Well, if the drive core is coming soon, I better get that cot out of the engine room."

"Right, I'll get the beddin' for ya."

The two met back at *Fire Arrow* a short time later, Eri with the cot and Francis with bedding. The two quietly got inside through the side airlock and set everything up. Once complete, Francis gazed at the slumbering first officer who had seen better days.

"How's he doin'?" he whispered.

"He hasn't moved at all, didn't even stir when I disconnected the IV," she replied quietly.

"Good," he whispered, "I'm going back to the ship. Sleep well."

The captain silently left *Fire Arrow*. Eri removed her boots and pulled the zipper down her coveralls.

*This is going to be awkward, but there's no way I'll sleep in these coveralls…*

She quietly pulled her coveralls down and discarded them, leaving her in only her bra and shorts. She slid into the sheets and pulled the comforter up to her neck. The bedding was warm and soft. Unlike Charlie's duster, it didn't smell of cigarettes. The bedding instead had a sweet and musky smell, like chocolate and whiskey. She looked across from her and saw Charlie sleeping peacefully despite his injuries.

*I will not let anyone hurt you or anyone else on the crew—whatever it takes…*

The stoic, abrasive, and blunt first officer clearly took his job seriously, but had an internalized duty to protect others. Whatever else he was, Charlie deep down was a selfless, good man. He may not be cordial to strangers, show much emotion, or have patience for the plain and ordinary, but he obviously still felt obligated to help others. In short, he was complicated.

Eri's eyes remained affixed to Charlie's peaceful face as she slowly drifted to sleep.

Ash returned to *Silver Bow* in her truck. She quietly trudged up to the half-built ship when a light blinded her momentarily.

"Oh," Francis said groggily, "I thought ya were someone trying to pick parts."

"Ya sleep on *Silver Bow*?" she asked in confusion, blinking to regain her eyesight.

"Both of ya, I swear," he replied with frustration, "is it so hard to believe that I sleep with my ship and protect my investment?"

"I just figured ya would have stayed in a hotel until life support was working," she commented.

"What do ya need?" he asked as he turned off the light and sat down on his cot.

"I had a couple of drinks and cooled off," she stated, "and I wanted to come by and check up on Charlie before I went to bed. Was going to send ya an apology on your tool after."

"It's fine, Ash," he said with a wave of his hand, "I know ya didn't mean it."

"It don't make it right though," she replied. "I can't even imagine what ya saw and experienced as a heavy assault troop, and here I was, someone who never fired a gun at anythin' other than a steel target, criticizin' ya for making the right decision. We were outnumbered and outgunned. If I tried to pick a fight, we might've all been killed."

"What's done is done, Ash," he stated calmly, "no use beatin' yourself up for being in the moment and worryin' about your mentor. I know ya felt helpless and that ya felt cowardly as ya watched Charlie get hurt, but he knew what he was doin'. He gambled that Jessik wouldn't do nothin' to him because he wanted Charlie to do a job. He bet on black and hit red, and he don't regret it. Besides, he's the kind of martyr that will keep Jessik's attention away from all of us. There's nothin' ya can do that will change his mind.

"And…you're right too, Ash. There *is* a difference between peaceful people and pacifists. My problem is that I've been such a monster that I don't…I don't want to hurt *no one* ever again. I've killed so many fathers, husbands, sons, mothers, wives, and daughters…I just don't want to take nothin' else from the galaxy. He may be haunted by his decisions, but Charlie…at least he saved lives at certain parts of his life…"

"Maybe," Ash replied quietly, "but whether or not ya become a pacifist, Charlie and I will always be there to protect ya, Eri, and Kai. If ya don't want to take lives anymore, I understand and respect that."

"Thank ya, Ash. That means more than ya know…"

Ash looked at him pensively in the darkness as the insects continued to make noise outside in the junkyard.

"I know ya probably don't want to hear me talkin' about it, but I hope Maria sees how much ya changed over these past four years. Ya don't deserve to be alone like this, Francis."

He looked at her. "Thank ya, Ash."

# Chapter 16

Charlie walked in a desert, the sand loose underfoot. The sandy void stretched on for eternity in every direction until he noticed a small glint in the distance. He robotically started moving towards the object. He felt as though he was being controlled remotely, only able to look around as he was forced to trudge towards the anomaly.

"It has to be you," Zoreah said softly.

"I'm sorry," Christie rasped.

He slowly approached what appeared to be a red crate partially buried in the sand.

"Don't leave me for the FIA…a dignified death," Zoreah said again.

"Being a merc requires you to be infamous," Christie said flatly.

Charlie stopped in front of the red crate, wind rushing behind him and causing the small particles of silica to fly off the surface of the desert. He stared at the crate for an unknown amount of time. Finally, he heard a woman whimper in pain and breathe assiduously. He walked around the crate to find a woman sitting up against it. She looked at Charlie with desperation visible on her bloody face. Both of her femurs were broken, the bones stuck out of the skin and through her prison uniform.

"Leave me," she demanded softly, "they'll capture you too."

"No!" Charlie cried out as he wrapped his arms underneath the woman's armpits. He began to drag her, her legs completely limp. "I'm not leaving you behind this time!" His right heel slapped against a rock, causing them to fall over. The woman lay lifeless. He pulled her up and held her face with his hand. "Zoreah? Zoreah, wake up!" Her body slowly turned to sand, the particles flying away in the wind. He grasped the ground where she once was, looking at the sand, then stood up, desperately trying to believe that she wasn't gone. He cupped his hands around his mouth and cried, "Zoreah! Where are you!"

Charlie's chest and back felt hot. He fell to the ground as the bullet exited under his armpit, grazing his left tricep. He slowly lifted his head. The crate was not far away from him, the paint slowly chipping away in the sandstorm. Zoreah had somehow returned to the box, still bloody with broken femurs sticking out of her prison uniform. He reached out to her with his right arm.

"Zoreah," he weakly muttered.

"This'll finish him…" Tristan growled.

A grenade landed near him, but Charlie couldn't move. He only stared at the grenade in terror. The metal orb exploded. His right arm was now gone and he was bleeding everywhere. He groaned in pain as he pulled himself forward toward Zoreah with his left arm.

Suddenly, a knee pressed down on his back atop the bullet's entry point. A set of hands pressed down on the back of his head and neck and began to suffocate him. Two more hands gripped him at the tops of his shoulders and pressed him down into the sand with greater strength. Charlie could feel his lungs burn as they consumed less and less oxygen. He clawed with his left arm and tried pushing himself up with all his might, screaming in defiance with one last effort.

Eri was startled awake by the sound of a loud gasp. Instinctively, she threw the sheets and comforter off her and saw Charlie holding his chest with his right hand, once again drenched in sweat, and panting heavily. Eri suddenly remembered that she only had her bra on, and quickly covered herself with the comforter. While one hand kept the blanket over her body, she reached with the other and gently placed it on Charlie's sweat-soaked shoulder.

"Hey, you're okay," she reassured him softly. Charlie turned his head and looked at her with wide eyes, still panting. "Are you still having nightmares?" she asked quietly.

Charlie's breathing slowed. He looked down at himself. "Sorry if I scared you."

"It's alright, I'm just worried about you," she replied as she removed her hand and wiped the sweat off with the comforter. "How often do you have these nightmares?" Charlie didn't respond. He got up from the bunk and wearily stumbled over to the washroom, using the walls for stability. "Easy! You need to stay still or you'll rip your stitches!" she pleaded.

Charlie still refused to respond. The washroom light turned on and then the sink. She heard him splash his face with water for a short period and emerged with a cotton ball in his right hand. He shimmied between the bed and the cot and sat on the edge with a pained groan. Eri sat there, still holding the comforter up with her hand as Charlie began peeling at the medical tape that held down the IV stent in his elbow.

"You should probably leave that alone—oh my god!"

Charlie removed the tape, placed the cotton ball at the point the stent entered his arm, and gently began to pull it out. He then tossed the needle onto the main console and pressed down on the cotton ball.

Eri hated needles and held herself with both arms as she recoiled and shivered in disgust. "I can't believe you just fucking did that," she said with a shudder.

"It's not that bad if you know what you're doing," he replied. He looked up and seemed to notice that although the comforter covered her front, her side and back were exposed. "Are…are you naked in my sheets?"

Eri shifted to hide her back, her face flushed. "I'm not naked, I just didn't have a shirt to wear and the coveralls are too itchy to sleep in. Besides, you don't have any pants, so we're even."

Charlie looked down and realized that he was only in his underwear. "When and why did you all take off my pants?"

"They had a lot of blood on them, so Kai took them to get cleaned," she replied, still cautiously holding up the comforter and blushing.

Charlie removed the cotton ball from its place, inspected it, then threw it near the console. He examined his surroundings and noticed his duster on the bed. He picked it up, but immediately dropped it. He brushed the coat off the bunk, got under the covers, and breathed deeply.

The cabin remained silent for a while as Charlie deliberately closed his eyes to fall back asleep. Eri, however, would not leave her question unanswered.

"How often do you have nightmares?" she asked with concern.

"Almost every night," he replied.

"There are medications that help with that kind of stuff—"

"They don't work well," he interrupted. "I'd rather just deal with the nightmares."

"Have you talked about it with anyone?" she asked softly.

"No. Now go back to sleep."

"Charlie, it's not healthy—"

"I thought you said Ash was the nosy one," he rebuked.

Eri slowly got back under the covers in defeat, but turned her back toward him, staring instead at the jumper seats across from her. *Fire Arrow*'s interior once again fell silent.

Ash awoke the next morning in her apartment. She woke up earlier than usual, so she decided that she was going to get coffee for the crew. She knew that Charlie would be upset about her having coffee, but she figured that everyone else would need it. She took the truck over to a local coffee shop, paid, and headed to the junkyard behind Ray's.

When she arrived, she went up into the cargo bay, but Francis wasn't there. She stood near the cargo ramp and sipped her coffee as she looked at her feet, thinking about everything that happened the night before.

Two things stood out in her mind. The first was Charlie's willingness to take the brunt of that shithead Jessik's anger. The second was Francis. Over the past ten days, she'd had a lot of talks with him, and she was starting to see him in a whole different way.

When they first met, Ash just saw him as a happy-go-lucky kinda guy. A man who had a big smile and a bigger heart. Now that she had really started to understand him, she saw a man who hid behind his smile, a man who wanted nothing more than a simple, normal life.

"Morning," Eri greeted her groggily, "everything alright?"

Ash looked up from her feet and saw her little sister. "Just thinkin' about what happened last night. How's Charlie?"

"Fast asleep," she replied, "The injuries I could see are healing slowly."

"He apparently has Garner's disorder, so it'll take a while to get back to normal."

"Garner's? What's that?"

Ash shrugged. "Dunno. Just know he can't take no SCR. Did ya enjoy your little slumber party?" Ash teased.

"I would have if he hadn't woken up in the middle of the night. He pulled his IV out right in front of me!" Eri shuddered and grimaced with disgust.

"Is he okay?" Ash asked with horror.

"He knew what he was doing apparently," she replied with a shrug. "He didn't bleed out overnight if that's what you're asking. How's Francis?"

"I haven't seen him since last night. He's not in *Silver Bow* on his cot. Did ya know he sleeps in the cargo bay?"

"Yeah, that's how I managed to sleep on a cot instead of the floor. Wait…did you come back or something?"

Ash pursed her lips. "After a couple of drinks, I came back and apologized. He didn't deserve what I said to him. He's…I don't know if you've ever talked to him about what he did in the war, but he saw a lot of terrible shit."

"Charlie mentioned it once, but never elaborated," Eri answered. "He said that it wasn't his place to talk about Francis's service during the revolution and I just never asked."

"He's…he's just seen so much death and *caused* so much death, and I called him a coward for doin' nothin'. He didn't deserve that, and Charlie knew what he was gettin' into. I just felt so helpless doin' nothin' and I directed all that rage at Francis. He's just a gentle man who wants to live a peaceful life."

"'You will never know or understand the sheer volume of monstrous violence that made me this gentle,'" Charlie quoted reverently. They both turned and looked at him.

Charlie leaned against *Silver Bow* weakly. He had a new change of clothes that had clearly been folded for a long time. The creases on his shirt and pants were like stripes. His left eye was heavily blackened and still slightly swollen. His lips were cut, and his cheeks and jaw heavily bruised.

"You should be in bed, resting," Eri pleaded.

"I'm fine," Charlie grunted, "besides, you're going to need me today. The drive core and shield generator are going to be here soon. You'll need someone driving the mech."

Charlie held his left side where Jessik had stabbed him, his breath weak and shallow. There was no way for him to take a full breath with the stab wound and his broken rib. The painkillers that were in his IV the night before were long gone from his system.

"Ash, help me put this jackass back in bed," Eri demanded.

"You touch me, Tall Hands, and I'll personally take off my metal arm and beat you with it," Charlie threatened between his shallow breaths.

"You can hardly stand and you can't even breathe well," Eri argued.

"That's just because the painkillers have worn off, but I'm not going back to bed, damnit," he said feebly.

"Charlie, ya look like shit," Ash agreed as footsteps approached from behind her.

"What are you doing out of bed!" Kai shouted with horror as he joined the women, "You need your rest, especially since you cannot use SCR!" Kai immediately ran to Charlie to try to usher him back to *Fire Arrow*. With unnatural strength, Charlie pushed the doctor away with one arm, causing him to stumble backward.

"I'm *not* going to bed," he hissed through his teeth. "If you want to help, Doc, give me some anti-inflammatories, some pain meds, and check my stitches. Otherwise, stay away."

"You are so ignorant and stubborn!" Eri yelled as she stomped away.

Charlie still held his side and tried to calm his breathing. "What did I say about coffee?" he asked Ash with annoyance.

"Like ya can do anything about it," Ash rebuked fearlessly.

"I'll remember that," he said as he tried to catch his breath.

Kai slowly lifted Charlie's shirt and examined the stitches. "You are still oozing blood a little," he remarked.

"Oh, is that why there's a fresh blood stain on my sheets?" Charlie asked sarcastically.

"It just needs some more gauze and a bandage to let the blood coagulate," he said as he walked back toward his car. "I am going to get my bag."

"You're a grumpy little shit when you're hurt," Ash concluded jokingly. Charlie sneered in response. "Ya *do* need your rest though," she continued seriously, "Jessik wanted ya to kill that gang leader by tomorrow night. Ya need every moment to get better."

Charlie scoffed. "That will be easier than putting in the drive core," he said. "Jessik just wanted to show us who was boss."

Kai quickly returned with his bag and rebandaged the stab wound. He then examined Charlie's other injuries by gently holding his jaw and turning his head.

"That eye is going to swell back again. You need to use a cold pack once every two hours as needed to keep the swelling down. Keep it on the eye for twenty minutes." Kai quickly removed a cold pack from his bag and activated it. He angrily shoved it into Charlie's chest, causing him to grunt with pain. The first officer silently put it over his eye and stood still, waiting for more instructions from the doctor.

"Here are your anti-inflammatories and your pain meds—two tablets of both, every eight hours. If you return to me before tomorrow at the exact same time without two extra tablets, I will know you are abusing them and I will not procure anything more than over-the-counter NSAIDs, understood?"

Charlie nodded as he stood up straight. He quickly took the four tablets and threw them into his mouth. He held out his hand towards Ash.

"What? Nah, get your own coffee," she replied. Charlie angrily re-extended his hand. "Fine," she whined as she handed him the cup.

"You should not have any stimulants like—"

Charlie took a swig of the coffee to wash the tablets down, then returned the cup to its rightful owner. In obvious defiance, Charlie pulled out a cigarette and lit it, staring directly at Kai as he did so.

"I do not even know why I signed that contract," the doctor lamented as he walked away.

Charlie took a long drag from his cigarette and looked at his protégé. "Francis will be here any minute with the engine and shields. He'll need your help today since I'll be useless." Ash nodded quietly, glad that he'd finally backed down. "I'm…I'm going back to *Fire Arrow* for a while."

After a couple of hours, two large trucks arrived carrying the pieces for the drive core and shield generator. Ash smirked as she watched her sister grin from ear to ear. Eri walked down to the trucks to look at the pieces to the drive core. Ash followed behind her with her hands in her pockets.

The workers jumped out of the trucks as her sister approached in her coveralls. Soon, the ratchet straps and tarps were removed. The maintainer quickly climbed onto the truck and closely examined the components.

"You got a pre-buyout E-7?" she asked Francis with glee as he joined Ash. He smiled as he looked at Eri, his hands on his hips. "Wait…so does that mean the shield generator—"

"Bestok D-453," Francis said proudly, "We bought the Bestok the day after ya signed your contract, but it took ages—and a little more money than I wanted to spend—to get a pre-buyout E-7. They're practically sold within minutes of being put on the market."

"With good reason," Eri replied as she gently caressed the back third of the drive core, "I've been told that these are the best drive cores ever made for this size. Did it come with the manual?"

Francis produced a tablet. "Right here."

"Any hard copies? You never know when something catastrophic might happen and you have to do things the old-fashioned way."

"You'd make Charlie swoon if he heard ya say that," Francis said with a laugh, then turned to Ash. "Speaking of which, how's the first officer, Ash?"

"Well, he had to be told by three different people just to get back in bed and rest before he actually did it," Ash responded with an annoyed tone, "Is he always grumpy when he's recoverin' from an injury?"

Francis chuckled. "He don't like being useless, so he's always hurtin' himself tryin' to help. Thank ya for getting him back in bed."

"Kai was the one that actually got him to do it," she quickly replied.

"He'll always listen to Doc," he said venerably.

Eri jumped off the truck, landing with a grunt. She continued to smile as she moved to the other truck with what Ash assumed was the shield generator.

"What's on your mind?" Francis asked.

"I haven't seen her this happy before," she replied with torn emotions, "I'm glad to see that she's finally doing her dream job, but…"

"Ya wondered forever if she would ever be happy after her parents died."

Ash looked at the tall captain and then back at Eri. "Yeah."

"I remember the first time Charlie smiled after everything happened to him," Francis reminisced. "After he lost his arm, I started to think that he would never smile again. The circumstances surroundin' that incident are enough to break anyone, and he took it pretty hard. I think it was almost six months before I saw him smile. If he's been as happy as our little grease monkey is right now, I don't think so."

The two stood there silently together and watched Eri with smiles because of her pure and innocent happiness. After a short while, Ash finally turned back to Francis.

"How *did* he lose the arm? What happened?"

"You're honestly askin' the wrong person," he said. "I only know the footnotes. He's never fully opened up about it nor given me details. I just know that he was betrayed by his fiancée and brother—both of which turned out to be FIA agents. Charlie thinks that it was because he confessed to his *very* patriotic brother—who he didn't know was an FIA agent at the time—that he had defected in the middle of the war and became a double agent for IFSA. His team provided intelligence for IS3."

"Charlie was a Feddie?" she asked with shock. "He's probably the last person I would suspect…"

"That's why he defected," he replied plainly, "he was very quickly disillusioned, especially after Isolde."

"Damn…"

"Don't bring it up though," Francis demanded, "He'd kill me if he found out I told ya. He's not one for lettin' others talk about his past without his permission. He keeps it close to his chest."

Eri ran up and joined them. "What are we waiting for? Let's get these installed!"

"We were just waitin' on ya to give your 'okay' after ya inspected them," Francis replied with a grin. "Ya are the ship's certified maintainer, after all."

For six hours, Eri, Ash, Francis, and Kai, along with the workers, assembled and installed the drive core and shield generator. Eri often interjected and took over certain tasks or refused to allow the workers to do them. The main point of contention was welding the core's frame to the back wall and flooring. One of the workers had started a weld when she immediately commanded him to stop. The weld would be considered passible to most, but Eri refused to allow a weld of that quality. She redid the section with a significantly better weld and continued until they needed her help with installing other components and the shield generator.

The engine and shield generator was now *her* project, and she allowed very few things to happen without her consent and outright refused to let others do certain tasks. If it meant that she needed to stay up late every night working on it, she would.

As the workers all left the site for the day, Eri continued to make her welds. Ash had never seen her so singularly focused and driven before. Working on a ship's engine truly was her dream, and she couldn't be more happy or proud of her sister.

"Hey, Kai," Francis said to the winded and sweaty doctor sitting against the wall of the engine bay, "why don't ya go check up on Charlie and make sure he eats a sandwich."

Kai nodded robotically and stood up. "I did not think my first full workday as this ship's doctor would involve so much manual labor," he lamented.

"Just remember, ya and Charlie get to design and build the medbay," the captain replied, "and then it will be Eri's turn to sweat and toil for your project."

Eri did not even flinch at the mention of her name. She was so focused on her weld that she seemed to have blocked out all sound. Ash sighed as she walked out of the engine bay and into the cargo bay, where a slight breeze rolled inside and cooled her off.

"God, I can't wait until the power is on and we have AC…" she grumbled.

"Not too much longer now," Francis replied quietly as he looked at the inside of the ship with a loving smile. "She's got a heart now…"

"I can't wait until she's finished."

The quiet moment was broken by Kai's rapid footsteps and heavy breathing. He stopped at the bottom of the cargo ramp and gathered himself for a moment.

"Everythin' alright?" Francis asked with apprehension.

Kai looked up at the captain with wide eyes. "He is not in there. I have no idea where he went."

# Chapter 17

Charlie walked back to *Fire Arrow* as the sound of loud trucks rolled up to *Silver Bow*'s construction site. He slowly ascended the ramp, took off his spare boots, sighed heavily, and lay on top of the bunk's bedding, glancing over at his sheets on the cot.

*I'm going to kill Francis. He knew that I'd be pissed if she used my sheets instead of the spares. Any excuse to make me mad...*

With a sigh, he continued resting with the cold pack on his eye. He knew that he needed rest, but he hated feeling useless while everyone else worked hard. He had especially awaited this day more than any other to help install the drive core.

*I hope Eri likes our purchase.*

He stared at the ceiling, trying to slow his pained breathing. He could not determine whether the stab wound or his broken rib was more painful when he breathed. He closed his eyes and tried to wait for the pain meds to finally get into his system. After a long while and no sleep, he opened his eyes and sighed. The cold pack was now warm from his body heat. He quickly threw it toward the console in frustration. He couldn't help but think about the challenge he had to somehow find and kill a gang leader for Jessik. His thoughts drifted until he remembered what the mob boss had told him.

*I'm going to rape your little girlfriend over there until I start chafing. Then, I'm gonna jam this knife right up her pussy and elongate her little greasy cunt all the way up to her mouth and pry her open...in front of you.*

Charlie's fists clenched. He only had one more day to do the job, and he knew that meant it needed to be done that night. If he waited any longer, Jessik would use his procrastination as a reason to continue his harassment of the crew. He wasn't going to give Jessik an excuse to come back.

He winced as he rose, his broken rib still throbbing, even with the painkillers. He could hear banging, clanging, and shouting. The crew and the contractors were hard at work installing the engine. It was his best chance to slip away unnoticed. He put his boots on, picked up his duster off the floor, donned the jacket, then retrieved his pistol, extra magazines, a knife, a sterile and unused syringe, and twenty thousand in cash. He slammed the locker shut and immediately walked out, ensuring that he was surrounded by vehicles, crates, and other forms of concealment so no one would see him.

He strode to the front of the dealership while he used his tool to message for a taxi. Charlie's jaw clenched, and he grinded his teeth from his rage, determination, and pain. The cab arrived shortly after, and he directed the driver to go to one of the seedier bars in the area.

Charlie entered the bar around midday, which meant it was mostly night-shift miners filling the establishment. The music inside boomed and thumped with deep, rhythmic bass of industrial darksynth. His eyes narrowed as he peered around in the dark, windowless bar. He noticed someone who clearly abused stimulants of some kind and approached him.

"Hey, man," Charlie said as if desperate, "who's your supplier? I need some shit and my guy's out."

The man looked around with suspicion. "I don't know whatchu talkin' 'bout," he replied apprehensively.

Charlie pulled out a one hundred shen bill and handed it to him. "I got money, man, my guy's just out of my stuff. Who's your guy?" Charlie looked around like he too was suspicious of anyone seeing the interaction. The addict pocketed the money and produced a paper card with a name and contact ID. Charlie quickly put the paper in his pocket, quietly thanked him, and left the bar.

He walked outside, the heat of the day bearing down on him, but he wouldn't dare remove the duster. His spare clothes from *Fire Arrow* were too formfitting and would reveal his weapons and magazines. He put his earpiece in and lit a cigarette as he called the number.

"Hello?" the young woman on the other side of the call asked. She sounded young.

"Hey, I got your contact from a guy I know at Blackout. My usual guy doesn't have what I need, but maybe you do."

"Whatcha need?"

"Fruit," he said as he took a drag from his cigarette.

There was a long pause on the other end. "I got some," she finally said, "how much you want?"

"I just need three, that should last me. What kinds do you got?'

"I got cherry, apple, and lemon," she replied slyly.

*Cherry. Red combat stims used for hyperfocus. Won't need that right now, but I'll probably need one in the future. Apple. Green combat stims used for strength, speed, and dexterity. Lemon. Yellow combat stims used as an anesthetic that offer some of the effects that Red and Green stims give, but not as strongly. Basically legal PCP for military and law enforcement...and the only shit I can take right now with these meds in my system.*

"I could use two lemons and a cherry.

"You gonna stay at Blackout for a while?"

"Not long, but I can stay for another half hour."

"I'll be there in half an hour. You better have good money."

"I do," he replied.

"Good," she said, "what's your name and what are you wearing?"

"Daniel," he lied, "I'm wearing a brown duster. You can't miss me. I got the metal arm."

"See you soon," she said mischievously as she disconnected.

Charlie finished his cigarette and tossed it in the street. He returned inside and ordered a double vodka on ice. The pain was already starting to return. The alcohol would dull it for a time.

*Every eight hours, my ass...weak fucking pain meds.*

He sat in a booth with his drink and lit another cigarette. The music changed to an extremely aggressive beat and tone. Some of the patrons cheered for the song being played and the woman behind the bar turned up the volume on the speakers. The entire room pulsed with the bass. Charlie closed his eyes and let the beat drone against his ears and felt the compression of air hit his skin.

After thirty minutes of drones, thumps, and electronic sounds, a young woman sat down in the booth with him.

"Hiya, Daniel," she said coyly, "I didn't expect to see someone like *you*. You single?"

"Are you even out of High School yet?" he asked with apprehension.

"Graduated three months ago," she replied devilishly as she leaned in. "If someone hadn't kicked the shit out of you, I'd probably see how you taste, but I'll settle to see what those metal fingers feel like inside me."

"Charming," he said with annoyance, "you got the fruit?" She bit her lip sexually and reached inside her cleavage, revealing three vials, then pushed them back down. "How much?" he asked.

"Normally three hundred per, but since you're a first time customer, it's my policy to—"

Charlie revealed a wad of folded money. It was far more than what she was going to ask for. She greedily reached for the cash, but he quickly pulled it away.

"The extra is for information if you can provide it. Otherwise, your standard price, understood?"

"Nah, you're a cop," she replied as she stood up.

Charlie grabbed her by the wrist and pulled her back in the booth. "I'm not a fucking pig," he said angrily. "I just need to find someone and I promise nothing will ever come back to you."

"Let go of me," she pleaded.

"Look, I know you're not a dealer, you're just a courier for the dealer. No one's going to suspect you and nothing will come to you. I just need to find someone. If you don't know, I'll still buy the fruit." Charlie slowly released her wrist. "Who's the leader of the Sun Scorpions and where can I find them? I know they're the main suppliers and dealers around Corinth, but I don't know where they're at. Point me in the right direction."

"Asher Al-Sajji. All the suppliers come from his house off Eighty-Third and Eleventh Av. I've been there once."

"What does the house look like?" he asked calmly as the music rose in volume and intensity. "Does anyone else live with him? What does he look like?"

"You can't miss it. It's the nicest one on the block and there's always at least two guards out front. He only has a mistress that shows up every now and then. He's a lot like you, but with both arms and his hair and skin are darker."

"Thank you…what's your name?"

"Why the fuck do you care?" she asked angrily.

"Because I want to thank you properly before I hand you this cash."

The young woman looked down and gently pulled her raven black hair behind her ear. "Wei-Lu," she meekly replied.

"Thank you, Wei-Lu," he said with a smirk as he extended the cash toward her. She grasped the money and put it in her waistband, then pulled the vials back out from her cleavage. Clearly embarrassed, she looked away as she handed the vials to him.

"Before you go," he said calmly as he took the vials, "how did a girl like you get into the drug trade?"

"Why do you care?" she asked with a sneer.

"If you don't want to talk about it, that's your business; however, if you are ever in need of *my* services, here's my contact ID."

She glanced back at him as she took the card and he put the vials in his breast pocket. "And what are your services?"

"I offer many, but someone in your line of work and with your looks is bound to be in need of pest control. I can be discreet or very conspicuous, gentle or rough.

"I too have a first-time customer discount, especially for young women who are in way over their head." She quietly looked down at the card and placed it in her waistband. Her sexual persona had faded when she finally realized that he was not a normal customer. Charlie slammed back the rest of his vodka and set the glass down on the table. He rose up and adjusted himself. "A word of advice from someone who *is* in too deep: get out while you still can. You're too pretty and smart to be in this business."

She stood up, her confidence suddenly returning. She leaned in close to his ear so no one could eavesdrop. "You're a killer, aren't you?"

"On occasion," he replied plainly.

"I've never kissed a murderer before. I'll give you the extra money back if you do."

"No thanks," he replied as he gently pushed her away at the shoulders, "but I'll oblige your kink *if* you get out of the business."

"I can't just 'get out,' Daniel, you know that," she replied with frustration.

"You can while you're still new and young, you just need to have a plan. Send me a message if you ever need me."

Charlie walked past her and exited Blackout. The loud music faded as he stepped outside and lit another cigarette. He woke his tool and examined a map of Corinth, found the intersection of Eighty-Third Street and Eleventh Avenue, then walked across the street to a convenience store. Inside, he purchased two bottles of water, a belt, cigarettes, and a bandana. He opened one of the bottles and took two more anti-inflammatories and painkillers.

Charlie made his way towards Eighty-Third and Eleventh, finishing the water bottle along the way. He walked around the block, observing every bit of the area in front, behind, and around Asher Al-Sajji's house. Two guards were posted out front posed as guys just hanging out on the porch while a third stood by the back door with an automatic rifle. Charlie observed the comings and goings of the house through surveillance throughout the day. Things seemed to be standard affair for a small-time drug lord.

He went to the nearest coffee shop and waited until nightfall. By dinnertime, his tool went off with notifications of messages from all the crew members. He simply marked all notifications read. He then silenced the tool and put it to sleep as he silently ate and drank in the coffee shop. He didn't need distractions or notification chimes giving him away when he was supposed to sneak somewhere.

Once night fell, Charlie slowly walked back to the block. As he approached, he noticed that only one guard was out front. The guards had also changed for the night.

*Asher's gone. Must have left earlier. I'll have to wait it out.*

Charlie went to the end of the street where he saw a few prostitutes standing on the corner. He approached them slowly. A man stood near them, either a guard, their pimp, or both. He formulated a plan of action the women started to holler and solicit him.

"How much?" Charlie asked the man.

"Each have their own rates," the pimp replied.

"I have a hotel room, but I'd like for things to be a little more private. Is there a room you can provide?"

"Definitely his first time in Corinth," one of the girls said cheekily.

"From the house next to the nice one with the guards, all the way to this corner are mine for you to use. You see any you like?"

Charlie began to act like a customer and examined the women's bodies, seeing who would be the best fit. He pointed at one woman with his prosthetic.

"You," he said, "ever wondered what one of these felt like?" He let her see his metal hand.

"Depends," she said coyly, "what do you plan on doing with it?"

"I can make it give a small electric shock, just enough to stimulate nerves in ways you've never imagined. What's good about fucking a woman if you can't make her cum first?"

The woman hummed with excitement. "Sounds like a great time. I'll take you to whichever house you choose. It's two hundred an hour, another fifty an hour if I have to be gentle," she said as she examined his bruises.

"How much extra if I want the whole house to myself?"

The woman looked at the pimp, who simply nodded. "An extra hundred an hour."

"Let's go to the one on the end to have some privacy," he said deviously as he walked back toward Asher's house.

*I hope this works...*

The two walked through the unlocked front door next to Asher's place. The entire house was musty with the scent with sweat, sex, and cigarettes. She undid the buttons on her shirt, turned around, and kissed him with a moan.

Charlie gently pushed her away. "Easy, sweet thing," he said as he caressed her abdomen near her navel, "let's go upstairs first."

"Do I need to be gentle with you? I hope the other guy got what he deserved."

"He'll definitely get what's coming to him," he replied.

She softly grabbed his hand and led him upstairs. At the top floor, two doors were open. Charlie firmly but gently directed her toward the room to the right. She turned on the light and turned around, then playfully tugged on his duster and pulled him close for a kiss, brushing off the coat as her tongue gently caressed his. The duster fell to the floor as they continued to kiss deeply and shuffled to the bed. As her heels clicked against the bed, she pulled him down onto it.

It happened so fast that it was one fluid movement. Between standing up and lying on the bed, Charlie had managed to cover her mouth with one hand and bring his pistol up to her throat. He used his weight to keep her from struggling free.

"Don't move and don't make a single sound," he commanded quietly. "You do exactly as I say and no harm will come to you. Blink twice if you understand."

Her breathing was shaky. The poor woman was terrified, but Charlie had no other choice. With tears in her eyes, she deliberately blinked twice. Charlie slowly holstered his pistol, keeping his hand over her mouth, but with much less force.

"I need information and your discretion. If you give me both, I promise it'll be the easiest three grand you've ever made. Can I trust you to be quiet? Blink twice if yes." She responded with two blinks and he slowly removed his hand from her mouth. He stood up slowly.

"What do you want?" she asked in a shaky voice as she sat up on the bed.

"Asher, next door," he said as he closed the door to the room, "is he normally gone this time of night?"

"Yeah," she replied as she scooted herself toward the bed's headboard, covering herself in the process.

"Sorry to scare you, but I had no other choice. I had to improvise and you were the prettiest of the bunch," he said plainly as he picked up the duster and hung it on the doorknob.

"Where's the money?" she asked.

Charlie reached in the hanging coat's breast pocket and flashed the money. "How long until he gets back?"

"About two hours," she replied.

"Is he consistent with his schedule?"

"You could set your clock to it."

"Good, then you need to stay in here for at least two hours. I'll pay you the three grand when I leave."

"Who are you?" she asked with fear.

"Just an attack dog," he replied, "Asher has started encroaching on my employer's territory." The woman sat there, watching Charlie closely. He stopped for a moment and looked at her. "What's your name?"

"Zephyr," she said quietly.

"Your *real* name," he clarified.

"Netsai," she replied meekly.

"Well, Netsai," he began as he sat on the edge of the bed, "get comfortable. It's going to be a long two hours while we wait."

"Are you going to kill Asher?" she asked quietly.

Charlie turned his head and looked at her over his shoulder. "Does my answer determine whether or not you stay quiet?"

She looked away from him. "As long as I get my three grand…"

"Well, it's not actually up to me," he replied. "It's up to him whether or not he dies tonight."

The room went silent, Netsai had pulled her knees up to her face as a defense mechanism. She had yet to rebutton her blouse and her breasts were barely covered by the thin cloth.

"So what's the story with your face?" she asked.

"My employer was displeased with me," he said plainly.

"Who's your employer?"

"That's not how this works," he replied. "Besides, if they ask you for information, you need to give as little as possible."

"If they find out I helped you, they'll kill me."

"It can't be considered aiding me if you did it under duress. Besides, you're the prettiest of the bunch; they'd never kill you."

"You think so?" she asked mischievously. She slid behind him and caressed him with her brown fingers. "You know, there are better ways to pass the time." She bit his ear and reached into his pants.

Charlies eyes closed and he breathed deeply as she gently gripped him. He suddenly snapped out of it and stood up. "I'm not going to fall for that," he said as he turned to her. "The last thing I need is for you to literally catch me with my pants down."

"Your head may be saying no, but your body sure is saying yes," she said as she bit her lip. "Does your arm really shock and stimulate?"

"Wouldn't you like to know," he said as he readjusted himself.

"I would," she said coyly, "you can always tie me up to the bed if you don't trust me." She lay back on the bed, extending her arms toward the ends of the headboard, ensuring that her blouse would open up enough to expose her bare breasts.

Charlie's willpower started to fade as he saw her chest in the lamplight. "I didn't plan ahead," he hinted.

Netsai smiled as she looked at the nightstand, "There are some condoms in the top drawer, rope will be in the one below that."

"You *will* need to be gentle, though," he said as he removed his shirt and revealed his bloodstained bandage and bruises.

"Where could he possibly be?" Ash asked, "He's ain't respondin' to any of my messages."

"Mine neither," Kai added.

"He must have gone out to do the job for Jessik," Eri lamented.

"He was in no condition to do anything," the doctor exclaimed. "He could get seriously hurt. His stitches could rip and he would get an infection if not treated fast enough."

"There's no use worryin' about it now," Francis remarked, "We'll do rotatin' shifts watchin' *Fire Arrow* and *Silver Bow*. He'll return eventually. When ya aren't on watch, Eri, finish the welds. Tomorrow, we need to test the drive core and get everythin' connected if we are gonna stay on schedule."

Eri nodded quietly. She retrieved the welding mask and placed it back on her head. She resumed her welding, but Charlie's disappearance plagued her concentration.

*Are you going to kill that gang leader?*

*I have to.*

Up until that moment, the idea of Charlie killing anyone had never seemed like an actual possibility. He had the capacity, but it never seemed like he would. After everything he said last night and that morning, it was clear that Charlie had killed many people. Whether or not those people were innocent was another story, which frightened her. He'd warned her that working out in space was dangerous business, but the realization that he would kill—not just to protect the crew, but as Jessik's personal assassin—made her stomach turn.

She continued her welds for what seemed to be a short time when Ash told her that it was her turn to watch the ship and wait for Charlie. She waited for a short while, but she knew that unless she continued working on the welds, she would be up all night finishing her welds while other people would be on watch.

Knowing Charlie and how stubborn he was, he would show up on his own time and his own terms. Even if he somehow showed up during her shift, which wasn't likely because it was still early in the evening, he would be too curious about the noise that she would be making with the torch and would find her anyway.

On top of that, she was worried about him, and she knew that worrying about him wouldn't solve anything in that moment. She needed to focus on her welding to keep the ship on schedule. The faster they left Magna Graecia and went to another planet, the faster they would get away from Jessik.

She put down her welding mask, grabbed the torch, and paused. Her hands shook as Jessik's threat to Charlie echoed in her mind. She took a few deep breaths. She needed to do something to keep her mind off of that psychopath.

Eri finally resumed her welding and made her way around the base of the drive core, completing about three-quarters of the base with ease. Her torch stopped suddenly. She lifted the mask and saw that the pressure indicator on the tank read as empty. She threw the mask off in frustration and took off her gloves. She had just gotten into a rhythm and finally had gotten Jessik's threat out of her mind.

She disconnected the hose and rolled the gas tank out of the ship, stopping next to crate with full tanks in the staging area on the hill. She wiped her face as the brisk air began to cool her off. What felt to her as a short period of time now came into focus as multiple hours. She opened the crate as the sound of certain insects let her know that it was late into the night. Eri's shift was almost over and Kai would relieve her just in time for her to finish the last welds. She pulled a new tank out with a grunt and set it upright for her to attach to the dolly.

"I thought you'd be done with the weld by now," Charlie said weakly.

Eri shrieked when she heard him speak in the darkness somewhere near her. The gas canister fell over with a loud thud as Eri placed her hand over her heart.

"God damnit, Charlie!" she shouted angrily. "You scared the shit out of me." She looked around but couldn't see him. "Charlie?"

"I think you should call the doc," she heard him say with a pained moan from the darkness to her left. Wherever he was, he was farther away from *Silver Bow* than she was.

She squinted as she moved toward his voice. "I can't see you, Charlie. Where are you?"

"Left," she heard him weakly mutter.

She turned to her left and saw him sitting against a crate, slumped over in the darkness. He held his side as he took deliberate breaths. His breathing seemed shallow and extremely weak. She ran and knelt next to him, but when she moved his left hand, she felt blood.

"Jesus," she muttered, "you broke the stitches."

"Get the doc," he said. "Anemic…fruits…"

"What? What's wrong?" she stuttered with confusion.

He weakly grabbed her wrist with his left hand, which had been covered in blood. "Fruits…doctor…"

Eri quickly pulled her left sleeve up to her elbow and woke her tool. She called Kai, who answered after a few rings.

"Eri? Is Charlie with you?"

"Yes, Kai, and his stitches have split open. He's bleeding *real* bad and he keeps muttering something about fruit."

"*Fruits?*" he asked angrily, "I'll be there as fast as I can. You need to use a towel and put as much pressure as you can—even if it hurts him—on the opening until I get there or he *will* bleed to death."

"What? Why?" she asked in horror. His stitches tearing open should not have caused that much blood, and Kai even mentioned that Jessik purposefully stabbed Charlie in a spot that would barely threaten his life.

"Just do it, and fast!"

Kai disconnected the call. Eri ran as fast as she could into *Silver Bow* to find towels. She searched everywhere in the cargo bay for a towel, but nothing of use was there, only used and dirty rags. She desperately sprinted over to *Fire Arrow*, where she knew there would be towels. She ran into the washroom and grabbed two. Panting and wheezing, she sprinted back to the spot where she found Charlie. He lay limp on his side, his torso dimly illuminated by the temporary lights that were powered by a power cell in the cargo bay. The light revealed that his shirt had been cut at the top of his abdomen and some sort of cloth was wadded into a large slashing wound to absorb the blood.

"Charlie?" she called out to him. "Charlie can you hear me?" The man did not respond. She put him on his back and pressed down hard onto the wound with the towel. Charlie quietly groaned. "Charlie, if you can hear me, Kai is on the way, just hang on."

# Chapter 18

Charlie put his pants back on as Netsai slowly caught her breath. He walked across the room where he had discarded his knife and pistol where the hooker couldn't reach them. He woke his tool and noticed that it was almost time for Asher to return. With a satisfied moan, Netsai slowly sat herself up, using the ropes tied to the headboard as support.

"God, even though you had to go slow, the stimulation more than made up for it," she said dreamily as Charlie put his shirt back on. "Oh, so serious now," she said sarcastically.

Charlie lit a cigarette and rubbed his right eye.

"Do you think we have enough time for a third go?" she asked as she bit her lip and opened her legs. "Maybe this time you can trust me and let me treat you for your…kindness."

Charlie glanced at her and back at his tool as he walked over to the window that faced Asher's house.

"Not one for pillow talk, huh?" she asked as she closed her legs, still lying on the bed naked.

"Asher will be home any minute," Charlie finally said as he looked out through the blinds.

"It's too bad that you might hafta kill him," she lamented. "He's not so bad."

Charlie went over to his duster and removed a vial full of clear yellow liquid, a belt, and his clean syringe. He sat down on the chair next to the window and finished his cigarette before he wrapped the belt around his left bicep. He tapped his veins with his right fingers to ensure they were fully erect and visible under his skin, pulled the syringe cap off with his teeth, then pierced the top of the vial and removed twenty milliliters with the syringe.

"You just gonna shoot up fruits and ignore me?" Netsai asked angrily.

Charlie put the vial in his pocket and pierced his skin with the needle, injecting himself with the drug. He slowly pushed in the plunger, leaving ten milliliters in the syringe, and immediately started to feel its effects. His head felt light, his heart raced, the pain subsided completely, and he felt stronger. He removed the syringe, took the belt off his arm, placed the cap back on the syringe, and returned them all back to his coat.

"Sorry, Netsai, but I have to leave your beautiful golden brown ass here," he said. He donned the duster, removed three thousand shen from the breast pocket, and placed it in one of her shoes. "You stay quiet for five minutes, then you scream bloody murder. The money is in one of your heels, so no one will see it. The guard next door will come to help you and release you. Just tell him that I tied you up, left out the back door, and stiffed you on the money."

"Fine," she replied.

"How about a parting gift for all your help?" Charlie's right hand reached between her thighs and his cybernetic fingertips gently stimulated her. She quietly moaned with pleasure as he kissed her, her legs and body contorting.

Charlie quickly made his way down the stairs and out the back door of the sex house and into the overgrown back yard. He quietly waited by the side gate, his body tingling with ecstasy from the combat stim. He could feel his heart pounding. He heard Netsai scream for help from the room.

*She's playing her part well...*

The guard from the back door came running around the corner. As soon as he heard the front door to the sex house open, Charlie quickly jumped over the fence, landing in a bush, but the screams muffled the noise. He snuck to the back door and checked the knob.

*Idiots. Left the back door unlocked.*

He gently opened the back door and made his way inside. He could see through the window that the guard out front was concerned and was walking away from the front door out toward the street so he could see the commotion. While he was distracted, Charlie made his way upstairs to an empty room and hid inside.

Charlie quietly closed the door until there was a small crack big enough for him to see out of. About twenty minutes went by, and he heard the front door open and close swiftly. He heard only one set of footsteps walking around the house.

*He's alone. Perfect.*

Wei-Lu's description, though vague, was quite accurate. The cracked door allowed Charlie to see Asher as he ascended the stairs. Asher was only slightly taller than Charlie and built about the same. His skin was browner than Charlie's light olive tone, and his hair was jet black instead of his tri-color brown. He readied his knife and approached the cracked door, waiting for Asher to have his back to him. The drug lord turned the corner and walked away from Charlie. He gently pulled the door open and silently followed.

Asher opened the master bedroom door and turned on the light. He sighed with relief and Charlie pounced. He covered Asher's mouth with his left hand and pressed the knife against the skin on his throat, the point directly next to his carotid artery.

"Move and you're dead, Asher," Charlie whispered, "try to scream, and you're dead. You'll die from blood loss before your incompetent and complacent guards pull you out of the house." Asher stood still and stiffly, the breath through his nose intensified with fear. "We're going to talk because my employer decided to make an incredibly fatal mistake. You and I can either become great allies, or I can kill you and complete the job as expected. I'm going to remove my hand, but if you speak louder than a whisper, your life is forfeit."

Charlie slowly removed his hand from Asher's mouth, but still gripped him firmly to prevent escape.

"Who are you?" he asked with a shaky voice, "What do you want?"

"I'm Jessik's Pit Bull," he replied, "Perhaps you've heard of me."

"Oh god…"

"I already told you, we can be allies. You see, Jessik used to play the game fairly. Any ire or harassment was only ever directed at me, but he got greedy and wanted to try to establish dominance. He threatened my people and used their safety as a weapon against me. I was supposed to kill you tonight and send a message, but I think it's time that Jessik is given a little…*poetic justice*. Wouldn't you agree?"

Asher stiffly stood there, silently waiting.

"Here's what I propose, and you have to decide now. You call up one person, someone you can trust the most. You fake your death tonight with a house fire or explosion, your lieutenant takes over for two weeks and allows Jessik and the other Corinth gangs to take some of your territory, and then I take out Jessik. Once he's dead, you can take as much territory here and in Athens as you please."

"What about the other gangs?" he asked quietly.

"What about them?"

"The Cobras and Rock Solid allied with me. We were planning on making a move against Jessik in a few weeks."

"Move up your plans then," Charlie responded, "but your boys will dismantle the Cobras. I will not allow human traffickers. Sex work is one thing, *forced* sex work is another thing entirely, especially with minors."

"I can't just betray my ally like that. Rock Solid will think I'm going for them next."

"Do what you must, but the Cobras—and Jessik's gang—are finished. You also can't let your allies know that you're still alive until you hear about Jessik's death. Understand?"

"I understand," he replied with a whisper.

"Good," Charlie replied ruthlessly, "now, for this to be believable, I'll have to kill your guards. It's only business."

"I understand," he said solemnly.

"I'll be leaving now. If you make a sound, you'll be the first to die. Watch the news in two weeks. You'll know when to strike."

Charlie quickly and quietly walked downstairs and toward the back door, knife still in hand. He looked out the window next to the door and saw the guard standing sentinel, completely unaware of his presence. He slowly and stealthily opened the door, lunged at the guard, covered his mouth, pulled his head to the left, and stabbed the man in the throat. The dying guard gurgled quietly as he quickly bled out. Charlie gently set him down on the porch.

Like a silent blur, Charlie then crouched behind the front door and peered out the window. Asher still had not made a noise, which meant he had consented fully to Charlie's deal. He could feel himself coming down from the combat stim's high. He did not have much time. He already felt pain all over and decided it was the perfect time to shoot up while he was concealed and the other two guards were unaware. It was more dangerous to fight them while he came down from the high than to simply take more. He would be sluggish and his reaction time would be too slow for a two-on-one fight, even if he had the element of surprise. If Jessik's goons hadn't beaten him, he wouldn't have needed stims in the first place.

His veins were already bulging because of the stimulant, so he simply removed the cap, stuck it in his hand's vein and pushed the plunger. Again, his whole body felt tingly and tight with strength. He put the cap back on the syringe and placed it in his pocket. His hand bled slightly from the syringe piercing his vein, but he ignored it. His heart raced again, and he could feel that the stim was now fully in effect.

Charlie took two deep breaths and shoved the door open. The door hit the guard on the right, dazing him for a moment. The man on the left, however, was ready for a fight. He immediately picked up a machete and slashed before Charlie could close the distance. The machete grazed Charlie's abdomen, cutting him and grazing the stitches from Jessik's knife. The combat stim made time move slower in his mind, and he could feel the very tip of the machete pull and pop each knot on his stitches.

The machete then clanged against brick. With his left hand, Charlie grabbed the assailant's wrist, pulled him inward, and thrust his knife into the man's heart, causing the guard to drop the machete. The other guard had finally sidestepped the door that hit him and was reaching for his pistol. Robotically, but with great speed, Charlie drew his pistol and shot the man twice in the chest and once in the head, pink mist spraying as the man's lifeless body collapsed.

Charlie quickly holstered his pistol and retrieved the knife embedded in the other body. He then retrieved the bandana from his pocket and stuffed it in the cut across his abdomen. Blood was already oozing from the opening. He pulled his shirt down and ran as fast as he could. *Silver Bow* was ten kilometers from the house. He felt the slash on his abdomen bleed as he ran, the stimulant keeping the pain at bay. He avoided major roads and ran through side streets, which made his route turn from ten kilometers to twelve. Charlie knew that he couldn't be admitted to the hospital, so he had to get to *Silver Bow* and have the doc treat him before he bled out.

The worst side effect of yellow stims was that they thinned the blood heavily and made the person anemic. Soldiers, police officers, and others who used the yellow stims were warned to take it with a medication that would help the blood thicken and coagulate before injection of the stim.

He would have preferred the green stim, but it could not be mixed with painkillers and anti-inflammatories. If he had taken the green stim, he would have had a heart attack shortly after making his deal with Asher. If he had taken a red, he would have had a cerebral hemorrhage caused once again by its interaction with painkillers. Yellow was his only option, but he hadn't planned on getting hurt in the process. He now had two bleeding wounds and little time before it was too late.

Charlie's loss of blood made the last kilometer feel like five and in water. The pain from the slash was agonizing, and he groaned loudly to keep the worst of it at bay. By that point, the stim had worn off and his clothes were drenched in his blood. He trudged up to the junkyard where *Silver Bow* sat. There were temporary lights set up in the cargo bay, which illuminated the staging area in front of the cargo bay ramp. He was only about fifteen meters away when he collapsed against a crate.

*This is it…*

He fell on the ground and sat against the crate, his body barely obeying his commands. His shallow breathing was met with the returning sound of insects no longer afraid of his presence. After a quiet moment, he tried to pull himself back up, but the loss of blood made him weak and muddleheaded. He needed to get up, but no matter how hard he tried, he felt practically paralyzed.

A small clang followed by footsteps came from behind him. Someone had descended the cargo ramp. He still had a chance. He pressed against the now blood-soaked bandana, pain searing through his stomach. He could hear a crate opening, a metallic bonging noise, and a thud.

*Eri...she's replacing a gas tank for her welding torch!*

Charlie's mouth opened and he gathered all of his strength. He knew he wouldn't be able to shout because of how weak he felt, so he just had to speak as loudly as he could. He shallowly breathed in, desperate to make his voice loud enough to be heard.

"I thought you'd be done with the welds by now," he managed to say in a normal volume.

Eri said something, but he was beginning to lose consciousness. His vision narrowed and his hearing muffled as the pain subsided. She needed to call Kai right away. He mustered more strength and managed to speak again at a normal volume.

"I think you should call the doc."

He could barely make out her voice, but she eventually came into view, the cargo bay's lights illuminating her from behind.

"Left," he managed to mutter.

Eri turned toward him as his vision began to fail and turn gray. He could no longer see detail, only basic silhouettes and shapes. She said something, but it sounded like she was trying to speak to him underwater. She pushed his hand out of the way and felt his abdomen.

"Get the doc," he managed to say. He needed to explain how dire his situation truly was, but the only words that he could manage to say were "anemic" and "fruits." He could feel himself peacefully drifting away. Blood loss like his was not violent in the end; it felt more like the peaceful slumber you drift into as you weakly climb into bed after a long day of work. Your eyes got heavy, your body comfortable, and your mind slowly turned off.

She pulled up her hand, and he summoned all the energy and strength he had left to grab her wrist. His blood-soaked hand felt numb, but he had just enough consciousness to remember how to close his fist by tightening certain muscles in his forearm and constricting the tendons that connected to the ends of his fingers.

The slightest movements took so much focus and concentration that only great effort could achieve the goal.

"Fruits…doctor…" were the only words he could manage. He felt himself grow colder in his extremities as his body fought for its very survival, pulling all of the blood back into his torso and brain. For a moment, he was lucid as the blood returned to his vital organs. The pain returned as a dull throb. These were the final stages of blood loss, and he knew it. His moment of clarity then turned to faded vision and loss of hearing. Before he lost consciousness, he could see the faint amber glow from Eri's tool turn on and off.

*Good girl…*

He felt himself fall into a peaceful sleep as his limp body slapped against the dirt.

# Chapter 19

"Good," Colonel Monnigan said with folded arms, "again."

Charlie did the movements again. In March of 3194, Charlie had met the commander of the Frontier Commandos by chance, though he always wondered in the back of his mind if it was only under the guise of happenstance rather than a planned meeting through IS3. Since he had fully recovered from his injuries and Frank had bought him a cybernetic prosthetic, two different IS3 agents on two separate occasions had tried to recruit him into the agency, but he refused them flatly each time. Charlie was not interested in the politics of an intelligence agency. He wanted only one thing: to kill Tristan and Christie and exact his vengeance.

Since he first saw his face in the mirror at Yongsan's Fifth Ward Hospital, his only thoughts each day consisted of him getting closer and closer to that goal. By now, the two curs would know that he survived and would be cursing their failure. The FIA didn't leave witnesses, and they would be reprimanded in the very least. That always put a target on his head, but he was ready. If the FIA ever came to kill or capture him, they wouldn't be able to surprise him now.

Once he was discharged from the hospital, every waking moment was fueled by his rage and hatred. Whenever he wasn't working for Frank and his company to repay him for the arm, he was training and learning. While he was a mercenary for the Pit Vipers, he would exercise to maintain his level of fitness and strength, but every day he pushed himself harder and harder to reach beyond his limits. His shooting skills had been more than acceptable for a merc, but he had spent entire weekends practicing in the two months since he had been released. He was already seeing improvement, despite suffering a couple of injuries to push him level of fitness further.

When he met Colonel Monnigan a week ago, all of that training and improvement finally had an outlet, and he had a way to apply his newfound strength, speed, stamina, and skill. He told Charlie that the Frontier Commandos often worked with IS3 to raid and capture FIA agents throughout the Independent Systems, and Charlie took the opportunity and expressed his interest. If anyone knew how to fight the FIA, it was the commandos.

Monnigan thought that he had managed to recruit a commando, but in reality, Charlie only wanted to be trained, then leave. He had no interest in staying in the unit for ten years—which was part of every commando's contract—he just wanted the skills so that he could use them against Tristan and Christie. He had learned enough from his time in the war to see his allies as useful tools.

He managed to get Monnigan to agree to start training him before he made his decision and to ensure that he was worthy of being a commando. Charlie didn't think he would agree, but the colonel strangely accepted his proposal. A useful fool.

"Excellent," Monnigan said with pride, "I can tell that you've been training in your free time."

"Every free moment, sir," Charlie responded.

"Then let's take those movements into practice and see how well you can apply them," he said as he stepped forward. "For this exercise, you need to think about all of the movements and see how they work to defend yourself in an attack."

Charlie readied himself in the stance the colonel taught him. "Ready when you are."

Monnigan pushed forward with a downward hammer fist and Charlie blocked with the first movement. He swung with a haymaker with his right, then his left, and Charlie once again blocked them with the second and third movements, robotically moving to a rhythm. He thought about the fourth movement, but Monnigan changed his attack pattern, forcing Charlie to block his heel kick with the seventh movement.

Despite only having done the movements over and over, the stances and techniques came naturally to him as he blocked each of Monnigan's attacks. Charlie had been lightly trained in hand-to-hand combat when he was in boot camp with the Federal Navy, but the martial art that Monnigan taught him and every other commando was something else entirely. It was fluid but abrupt, sharp but smooth. Monnigan called it *huling labanan*, which meant "last combat" in Tagolog, or hu-la for short.

Monnigan's former second-in-command, Major Jacinto "Jace" Magbanua, had developed hu-la as a mixed martial art for hand-to-hand combat in a world where opponents regularly wore armor that protected parts of the body that older martial arts once exploited. Jace wanted hu-la to be abrupt and brutal, but fine-tuned for the modern battlefield with armored opponents. Most attacks focused on disabling joints while defensive movements would focus on opening the opponent for the crippling attacks. The grappling portion of hu-la took many techniques from jiu jitsu, wrestling, and judo.

The martial art was initially designed to fight against mostly untrained opponents, but during the Isolde Revolution that ended over three years prior, Major Magbanua developed it further to fight against trained opponents after the commandos experienced a defeat at the hands of the Federal Navy's special operations group known as the Longbows, who went through extensive training, including multiple martial arts for hand-to-hand fighting.

Hu-la had three phases of techniques, and the third and most difficult phase was designed to fight Longbows and other highly trained martial fighters. Charlie had only learned the defensive motions against strikes in the first phase, but it was the most important phase.

Hu-la was taught to be practiced as if fighting in actual combat. Punches were never pulled and strikes were at full force. The training needed to be real, and the best way to learn and train the body for such things was to have extreme and full-contact sparring without protective equipment. If a trainee failed a block, they would remember how much it hurt.

"Though your technique still requires some adjustment, you have exceeded my expectations, Menillo," the colonel replied as he finished his test. "The most important thing to remember is that these blocks are also designed to hurt and wear down your opponent, so make sure you strike back and push hard. Keep practicing the defensive motions, but let's move on to the first phase's offensive strikes."

As Venture's late summer suns set, Charlie followed the colonel through the offensive techniques. Once he mastered the strikes, he would move on to the first phase's grapples. After being dismissed for the evening, Charlie returned to Frank's warehouse yard on his motorcycle.

Since being taken in by Frank, Charlie had furnished a spare insulated cargo container as his home. Francis insisted that his cousin live in the second bedroom in his apartment, but Charlie wanted a space of his own to relax, plan, study, read, and sleep. It wasn't until about a month into their arrangement that Frank discovered that his nephew was living in a half-furnished cargo container on his business's property. An overnight security guard had discovered Charlie when he went into the main office to use the toilet late at night. What the guard, Frank, or Francis never knew was that Charlie had woken up from a recurring nightmare that he had been experiencing since he had left the hospital on Yongsan.

Since Charlie had already done so much with the container, Frank simply allowed it. Despite being a strong-willed man, Frank always lived by a rule that people should be given enough leeway to make their own mistakes and learn from them, and he knew that Charlie would eventually want more space, more privacy, and better accommodations, so the container would eventually be emptied.

Charlie opened a container next to his motley yet simple living space and put his motorcycle in it. He closed and locked the container and began working on the new movements. The movements were a great decompression tool for him after a long day, and a good way for him to start his mornings. The movements weren't necessarily relaxing, but doing them over and over put him in a trancelike state that cleared his mind. Since he was attacked, having a clear head seemed harder and harder for him to do, but the motions always helped.

Charlie suddenly stopped his movement and drew his sidearm. He heard footsteps coming toward him. He remained still as they continued to approach, but Charlie knew the cadence of the footsteps. It was Frank.

*What is he doing here so late at night?* Charlie holstered the weapon.

"Charlie?" he heard Frank ask as he walked around the corner of his living quarters. "Oh, there you are."

"What brings you here so late at night, Frank?" he asked with veiled apprehension.

"I need your help, son," the man said seriously to his nephew.

Charlie's eyes narrowed. What could Frank need from him? Was Francis unavailable? Why was his uncle so serious?

"What is it?" Charlie asked.

"I need ya to come with me to Athens on Magna Graecia. It's two days of FTL each way. Wouldn't ask if I didn't need ya."

"What's on Magna Graecia?" Charlie asked with a raised eyebrow.

"I can't really tell ya—at least not yet," Frank said in a low tone. "But before I even ask for your help, I need your word that you'll be discreet and keep it secret."

Charlie's eyes narrowed as he examined Frank's expression in the dim and distant lights of the warehouse. Frank was trying to seem icy in his calmness, but Charlie could tell it was a mask to hold back his fear and desperation.

*What is he afraid of?*

He further examined Frank's body language. He was desperate in many ways and seemed to be rushed for time, but tried to stay calm and appear as if nothing was the matter. Why would he put up the mask if he was so desperate?

*He's embarrassed. Something he doesn't want Francis to know about, but Frank needs help from someone he can trust.*

"Fine," Charlie conceded, "but you tell me now."

Frank's eyes darted to and fro, clearly considering whether he would—or should—accept Charlie's offer. He finally slumped his shoulders in defeat and looked down at his feet.

"I…have some pretty significant gambling debts," he admitted, "and none of them are with reputable people."

"Loan sharks or bookies?" Charlie asked plainly, unfazed by Frank's words. Everyone had a vice, and Charlie wouldn't judge his uncle for having a gambling problem.

"Not a loan shark, per se," Frank clarified, "but a powerful man who lent me the money to pay off my debts with the bookies."

"That's what a loan shark is, Frank," Charlie rebuked.

"Not this one," Frank replied, "he…does a lot more than just that."

Charlie thought for a moment as he tried to decipher his uncle's words. "Fuck, you've borrowed money from a gang leader, haven't you?" he asked.

Frank slowly nodded.

"How much do you owe?" Charlie asked.

"The amount is irrelevant," Frank said with a meek shrug, "what matters is that he's offered to reduce some of my debt in exchange for helping him."

"And you volunteered me?" Charlie asked rhetorically.

Frank nodded.

"You're the only one I can trust that can also fly a ship. I wouldn't ask if there was someone just as qualified."

Charlie sighed with frustration. "Fine, but you owe me, Frank."

"Whatever ya want, son," he responded with his hands up in supplication.

"When do we leave?" he asked plainly.

"As soon as possible."

Charlie nodded. "What did you tell Francis?"

"Simple business trip and I asked ya to help since ya knew the company. Told him to be the boss while I was gone."

Charlie breathed with intent. "I'll get my things."

Charlie and Frank flew to Athens by charter on a freighter with some other people. To pass the time, Charlie continued to practice his motions in a corridor where he wouldn't be bothered—at least that was the plan. After only a short while, the merc in charge of security was standing in the hallway, watching him. Charlie finished the set and stopped.

"Something wrong?" Charlie finally asked the merc.

"Just keeping an eye on you since you're away from everyone else," the merc calmly said.

"Just trying to stay out of people's way," Charlie calmly replied.

"What kind of martial art is that?" he asked.

"You've never heard of it," Charlie said with a dismissive wave.

"Try me."

"No thanks."

The merc stood still and waited, but Charlie did the same.

"You can continue," he said with an outstretched hand. "Just making sure you aren't going anywhere you're not supposed to…"

Charlie sighed with annoyance, but continued. He was eventually able to ignore the merc and went back into his trance.

"There ya are!" Frank said after a while. "I've been trying to find ya."

Charlie stopped and took a deep breath. "What do you need, Frank?" he asked.

"The captain said that lunch would be available soon."

"Not hungry," he simply stated.

"Alright…" Frank said apprehensively as he walked away.

Charlie immediately started his movements, but he was distracted again.

"What happened with your arm?" the merc asked.

Charlie closed his eyes and took another deep breath to keep himself calm.

"I'd figure it's pretty obvious, considering it's metal," he replied sarcastically.

"Well, yeah, but how'd ya lose it?" he asked.

"It was amputated," Charlie said with a hard stare.

"Not one for small talk, huh?"

"No. If you're bored, then go. I'll just be in here."

"Sorry, but orders are orders," he said with a shrug. "Gotta keep an eye on ya."

"Well, you can do it quietly, can't you?"

"If ya think being an asshole will somehow make me leave, you're mistaken, kid."

Charlie's stare hardened further to a scowl. He slowly closed his eyes and breathed intently to calm himself.

*He'll eventually get bored and leave. Just keep going. There will be distractions in a fight.*

Charlie resumed his movements in the corridor, once again returning to his trance state. After a while, he stopped and realized the merc had finally left. He woke his tool and checked the time. Three o'clock UTC. He then moved to the cargo bay where the crew had a gym in a far corner. He did what he could to exercise, but two of the hired guns came into the area and started working out as well.

Someone else exercising next to him wasn't enough to bother him, but he soon got the message that the mercs didn't want him there and kept asking to use the equipment that he was using. He couldn't argue or resist given that he was at the mercy of the freighters. If they disliked him enough, they could always fine him and Frank and force them to pay a steeper price than originally negotiated, so he gave up and left.

He used the community shower and changed just in time for dinner. The crew offered them meager amounts of food, but he wouldn't complain. He would just eat more the next day to make up for his lower caloric intake.

After dinner, Charlie returned to his and Frank's room. He opened one of the many field manuals that Monnigan had told him to read. After an hour, Frank walked into the small room and got into the bunk below him with a pained grunt.

"Don't get old, kid," he told his nephew. "You'll end up like me with joints that're always stiff."

"I'll try not to," Charlie said distantly as he continued reading.

"What're ya readin'?" he asked.

"Nothing you'd care to read," Charlie told him.

"Thanks for coming with me," Frank said meekly.

"You act like I had much of a choice."

"Ya did," he argued.

"Like hell I did," Charlie replied angrily as he slapped the book closed. "You cornered me and told me that you were in trouble and needed my help. Who the hell do you owe money to?"

Frank didn't respond immediately, but Charlie waited. "His name is Jessik Kepov," Frank said slowly.

"Kepov…" Charlie said as he racked his brain, "where have I heard that name before?"

Frank didn't say anything from below on his bunk.

*Jorgie Kepov hired the Pit Vipers once…he was a mafia don! Jessik must be a relative!*

Charlie immediately jumped down from the bunk, his feet slamming on the floor. He turned around and glared at his uncle.

"You owe money to a fucking mafia don?!" Charlie asked furiously. "Why would you *ever* take a loan from a mafia boss? What kind of trouble are you in?"

Frank looked down in shame.

"Answer me, god damnit," Charlie growled.

Frank gulped and cleared his throat. "He got rid of my gamblin' debt with the bookies on Venture," he finally answered. "They were gonna put a lien on my house and business if I didn't pay."

"On both? How much money did you owe?"

Frank's face twisted as he tried to remain composed. Charlie stood over him, his fists clenched with rage. The man would not look at his upset nephew.

"How. Much," Charlie reiterated in a low tone.

"About four hundred grand."

"Fuck, Frank!" Charlie exclaimed. "Did you not think that you had a problem when you hit six digits?"

"Most of it was on one bet," he replied defensively. "It was a sure-shot bet, but everythin' went wrong. If it had been any other day, they woulda won!"

"That doesn't matter, Frank! You shouldn't be gambling that kind of money if you can't afford to pay it back, you fucking idiot!"

Frank shot to his feet. Charlie didn't flinch or budge. He only looked up to meet his uncle's eyes. They stood silently for a moment, their eyes still as they locked wills.

"If you think you can intimidate me, you're mistaken," Charlie said in a surprisingly calm voice. His uncle was a full head taller than him, but between his fitness, his toughness, and his new training, Frank was truly picking the worst opponent on the ship. "You take one swing, and your jaw will be broken in three pieces."

"Ya better watch your words, boy," Frank spat, "because ya live on Venture only 'cause of my generosity and charity. Ya call me stupid again, and I'll kick ya to the streets without sheddin' a tear."

"You're not in a position to make threats, Frank," Charlie replied calmly, "especially weak ones like that. Now get back in your bunk and shut the fuck up."

Frank's eyes finally looked away from Charlie's. The nephew was right, and they both knew it. They also knew that Frank had no one else to rely on.

"So who the fuck is this, Frankie?" the man in the night club booth asked. He was wearing a suit without a tie and smoking a cigar between two women. One was wearing a pencil dress, the other a cocktail dress with leggings.

"This is my nephew, Charlie," Frank replied meekly. He turned to his nephew. "Charlie, this is Jessik Kepov."

"How're ya doing, Charlie-boy?" Jessik asked mockingly. Charlie didn't respond, he just stood and blinked as he waited. The mafia don's eyes then flicked to Frank. "Not much of a talker, huh? That's fine," he said as he stood in the booth, "I prefer my runners to keep their fuckin' mouths shut."

Frank shifted nervously, drawing Charlie's eyes in his direction for a moment. He returned his eyes back to Jessik.

"Runner?" he asked.

"Charlie-boy speaks," the don said sarcastically. He looked at the two women. "Con, Siu, go take your place before the club opens. We need some privacy."

The two women shuffled out of the circular booth on each side. The woman wearing the cocktail dress eyed Charlie as she passed, but only for a moment.

Jessik shuffled out of the booth and walked up to Charlie. The man was barely taller than him, maybe a centimeter or two. He puffed his cigar and ensured that the smoke blew in Charlie's direction. Charlie acted like it didn't bother him.

"You're going to run some coke for me, Charlie-boy. I have a buyer in Vladivostok on Rus. Ya know how to get there?"

"Yeah."

"Good. You go to Vladivostok, deliver the coke, and come back. Simple as that. If you don't do it at the price that I want or in a timely fashion, I'll shoot your dumb fuckin' uncle in the kneecaps after I have my guys beat him to an inch of his life. Understand?"

Charlie swallowed. "I understand."

"I don't think ya do," he said condescendingly. He turned to look at one of his enforcers. "Xi, why don't ya give Charlie-boy here a quick demonstration so he understands."

The large man walked over to Frank, who stiffened. The enforcer punched Frank hard in the stomach and forced him to double over with a grunt. Charlie clenched his jaw as he fought against his instinct to protect Frank.

The enforcer then kicked Frank in his side, forcing him onto the floor. Frank moaned with pain, and the enforcer kicked him in the stomach twice. His uncle writhed as he clutched his stomach.

Jessik finally looked back at Charlie. "Now imagine if six guys were all doin' that at the same time for an hour. Am I clear, Charlie-boy?"

"Yes," he muttered as he grinded his molars.

"Frankie will be my little hostage until you return. Get your detailed orders from Constance over there and get the fuck out of my establishment."

# Chapter 20

Charlie's eyes opened slowly. He was inside *Silver Bow*'s cargo bay on a cot. His clothes had been removed, leaving him once again in only his underwear. Heavy blankets covered his body while his left arm was resting on a crate. On his face rested an oxygen tube blowing the gas slowly into his nostrils, aiding him in the healing process. He felt something warm entering into his arm. He slowly turned his head to the left, where Kai sat with a tube also in his arm, blood running between them. He was giving Charlie a blood transfusion.

"Wait, Garner's…" Charlie weakly muttered.

"I know," Kai replied, "Do you know how lucky you are that I am AM4C and can keep your Garner's at bay for a while? Very few places in the Frontier have my rare blood antigen type. If you had not hired me, you would certainly be dead. Corinth General Hospital does not have any AM4C available in O negative—or any other blood type for that matter."

"How long was I out?" Charlie asked as he could hear banging and clanging in the background.

"Thirteen hours now," Kai said as he stopped the flow from both sides of the tube. "There is one benefit to all of your blood loss though: my blood can receive SCR, so your wounds will heal much faster while my blood flows through your circulatory system." Kai removed the tube from his arm and disconnected Charlie's side, leaving the stent in his hand. He stood up and examined the flow of the IV, then adjusted the drip. "Do *not* get out of bed. I will not let you move until your IV is finished."

"I won't," Charlie reassured the doctor. He realized that Kai wasn't calm and clinical, but irate with him. Charlie wanted to say something, but no words could escape his lips.

"I will inform the captain that you are awake," the doctor stated flatly as he walked away.

The first officer lay on the cot, his senses all returning to him. He did not feel weak, but simply tired. The stem cell regeneration was doing its work and healing him faster than he had ever experienced. To be able to achieve what normally took him days or weeks in mere hours was a privilege he envied. It made him wonder if the doctor could do it again if he was ever badly wounded or injured, but he knew that would be asking a lot of the doctor, and he didn't feel like paying him that much. He had already purchased all the weapons systems.

Challenges were ahead of *Silver Bow*'s crew, and he knew that Tristan making his move was only a matter of time. He needed to create contingencies and plans for that inevitability, but Jessik and his machinations continuously slowed Charlie's progress. He could only hope that Ash would be ready in time to have his back when shit hit the fan.

Charlie heard a set of angry boots slam down on every step behind him on the starboard stairs.

"What the hell were ya thinkin'?" Francis growled.

"Good to see you too, dear cousin," Charlie replied.

"Ya disappear, ignore every message we send ya, then, after we started takin' shifts for the night waiting for ya to come back, Eri finds ya bleedin' up against a crate! And to top it all off, Kai tells me ya shot up combat stims without any proper precautions! Ya almost died last night!"

"Yes," Charlie replied plainly, "and the job is done. Jessik has no excuse to harass the crew anymore."

"Ya think by riskin' your life to kill some gang leader that Jessik'll leave us alone?" Francis retorted. "He will keep comin' after us and keep makin' ya kill to supposedly settle my debts with him. By doin' this so recklessly while you're hurt, he knows that it don't matter how badly hurt ya are…you'll still get the job done as long as he threatens the crew. All he knows now is the proper buttons to push to get ya to do his biddin' without question. You've only made shit worse, Charlie!"

"He would have come back and done what he promised me," Charlie replied solemnly, "I'm not going to let him hurt the crew."

"I would have done what I could to make sure that wouldn't happen and to let ya recover. Now he's coming back today, and he'll probably have another job for ya—after his guys beat the shit out of ya…*again!* Ya think you're helping, but this won't stop until we get off world. All you've done is make this much harder, and now I've got to be the one to talk to Jessik because you're in absolutely no condition to face him again."

"He will stop," Charlie replied, "just let me take care of it, Francis,"

"No!" Francis cried, "I won't let ya—"

"Captain," the first officer pleaded calmly, "I have a plan. You have to trust me."

"And what plan is that?" he asked as the banging and clanging stopped.

"I have it under control," Charlie said, "you need to trust me."

Francis breathed heavily through his nose and his fists clenched, the knuckles on his fingers turning pale and white from the exertion.

"Ya have one chance, but I'll only give it to ya if ya tell me your batshit crazy right now."

Charlie cleared his throat. "If I refuse?"

"Why do ya have to keep it secret?" he asked angrily as he raised his hands in frustration.

"Anything could tip Jessik off. If you don't know, it's less likely he'll figure it out. Please trust me, Francis."

The captain's jaw clenched as the engineering compartment doors opened. He grinded his teeth as Eri marched over to the ailing first officer.

"Fine," he said through his teeth, "but this had better work. If ya fuck it up, you'll only make things worse."

"Charlie," Eri said as she stormed over. Charlie turned his head towards her, he smiled slightly with gratitude, then started to lift himself up on the cot to thank her. She ignored that and hit his left cheek, the bruise from the previous beating throbbing anew with pain from the hard slap. Francis quickly grabbed the maintainer's arms and pulled her away.

"You would have *died* last night if my torch hadn't run out of gas!" she shouted, incensed at his behavior. "You wouldn't return our calls or messages! We had no idea where you were! And then Kai said you were *high* after he spent all night stabilizing you! None of us got any sleep because we were all worried about you and had to help the doctor keep you alive! Do you realize how *lucky* you are!"

Charlie said nothing. He only looked her in the eyes as she ranted and raved at him and thought about Jessik's words. She would never know what the mob boss would have done to her if he hadn't completed his task—at least, what Jessik believed to be completed. The pissant of a mob boss would soon receive his just deserts, and they would be free from him. The daggers from her lips, the scoldings from Francis and Doc, the slash on his abdomen—all of it was worth it in the end, even if he was the only one to truly know what he'd managed to prevent.

"Say something god damnit!" she demanded.

"Thank you," Charlie said quietly.

There was a moment of silence between them, Francis still latched onto Eri's arms as her red face slowly returned to its normal fair coloration and her hazel eyes widened with disbelief. Her breathing slowed and her rage seemed to melt away. Charlie did not move or show any signs of regret, remorse, or anger. Francis slowly released her.

"You saved my life, and you have my gratitude."

Eri took a deep breath and stormed back into the engineering compartment. Francis watched her as she stomped away and then looked back at Charlie, who stared at the floor.

"Whatever your plan is, Charlie, I hope it works," Francis said. He then walked back up the stairs, his footsteps slowly fading from Charlie's ears.

The first officer lay there on the cot as the IV bag slowly drained. The crew members mostly ignored him and continued their work, Kai only occasionally checking on the drip without saying any words. By the middle of the afternoon, the IV had finished its work, and Kai once again checked on his patient. He examined the wounds and noticed them healing well.

"You will recover by tomorrow," he said matter-of-factly. "Your broken rib will still take a week to heal, but the SCR in my blood will help with that. Your slash thankfully was only a flesh wound. If it had gone any deeper, you would not have made it back to *Silver Bow*. Your quick thinking with the rag saved your life, though. Why did you not go to the hospital?"

Charlie sat up, many of his bruises now gone or mostly faded. "If I did, would I have had a better chance?" he asked.

"Maybe," Kai replied, "in the very least they could have prevented you from losing so much blood."

"Then cops would have been involved, Doc. I couldn't risk that."

"Regardless, you are stable, but still weak. At least take it easy until tomorrow. I do not know if your body will attack the SCR in a day or two, so we need to carefully watch your internal temperature. If you get feverish from your immune system fighting back, we might need to take you to a hospital. I do not have the equipment or medications to help you if your GD starts killing you."

Charlie nodded. "Thank you. I'll give you some money as payment."

"I already helped myself to five thousand out of the cash you had on you," he said as he gave the first officer a change of clothes. "It will be adequate for my next trip to the casino. The other ten is soaked in blood, so you might want to wash it before giving it to anyone."

Charlie chuckled quietly. "I know the whole crew is pissed at me, Doc, but I did what I had to do. I won't apologize for that."

Kai removed Charlie's IV and bandaged his elbow. "I know," he replied. "You are a man of action, and a martyr. I met plenty of soldiers like you at field hospitals during the war. You do what you think is right, and that may be honorable, but in the end, you *will* end up pushing many friends away because of your stubbornness. Sometimes, people need to hear you apologize so that they know you at least care about how they felt in the moment.

Regardless of whether you should or should not apologize, some just need to hear it to feel justified in their anger or sadness."

"Wise words, Doc. I'll think about it."

"One hundred shen says you will not. I have yet to meet a martyr who took my advice."

Charlie snorted.

"Do not exert yourself too much today. Even though that slash is now only a scab and your stab wound will be healed by tomorrow, you're still slightly anemic from the combat stimulant. If you get even a small cut or the scabs open, you need to let me know immediately. Understand?"

"As you wish, Doc," he replied. "Can you get Ash? I need to talk to her right away."

Kai nodded and left. The first officer stood up, the wounds and bruises throbbing. He put on his pants and buckled his belt. As he grabbed his shirt, Ash came down the stairs.

"Well look who's back from the brink of death," Ash said happily as she descended the steps. "Glad to see you're already up and movin' around." Charlie put his shirt on and faced Ash. "Kai said ya wanna see me."

"Yeah. First, do we know if Jessik is coming back today like he said he would?"

"I'd assume so. Francis has been on edge and he keeps looking at his tool while we hook up all the systems. Why?"

"I have a job for you, but you can't tell *anyone*. Do you understand?"

"Sure, what is it?"

"Follow me," Charlie commanded. He walked out of the cargo bay and down the ramp. He paused for a second, feeling lightheaded, and blinked slowly as he regained himself. Even though he had a blood transfusion, it was clear he was still reeling from the loss of blood.

"Hey, ya alright?" she asked with concern.

"Yeah," he replied, "just a little dizzy."

"Just take things slow, okay?"

Charlie nodded and continued onward but at a significantly slower pace. The two reached *Fire Arrow* and Charlie closed the ramp behind Ash.

"What's goin' on, Charlie? What's this about?"

The first officer did not answer. He slowly knelt down by the bunk, opened the left drawer, and removed it completely. He then got lower to the floor and peered inside the opening. He reached inside and pressed a button with a loud click. He quickly pulled his arm back as the bunk lifted on the support track, revealing a trunk hidden beneath the bed. He tried to rise to his feet, but the dizziness persisted. He closed his eyes and pushed hard off the floor to stand. Ash noticed his struggle getting up and assisted him.

"Thanks," he said weakly. The trunk and bed stopped moving with a clank, and Charlie pressed his tool against a small bulge extruding from the trunk. Both lit up and as a quick communication between them sounded with a beep, and the trunk's lid unlocked with a loud click. Charlie slowly opened the trunk, revealing a massive cache of weapons, ammunition, and his armor.

"What the fuck…" Ash said slowly in awe.

Charlie reached in and revealed the rifle they fired that first day. He twisted and pulled on the bolt to inspect the chamber. Satisfied that the rifle was clear, he returned the bolt to its locking position and handed it to her. She quietly held the rifle, still clearly confused. He grabbed a box of twenty rounds and handed it to her. He then removed his armor, a large metal pack, a belt with multiple loops, and a shotgun with a box of twenty-four shells. He closed the trunk, locked it, and returned everything back to its original position.

"I need you to take that rifle and ammo to the top of *Silver Bow*'s hull through the top airlock and place it there with a clear shot toward the street at the bottom of the hill with all the crates."

"Charlie, what's this—"

"Just listen. Take the rifle up there like you're setting up for a shot toward the bottom of the hill and leave it there. When Jessik arrives, you immediately get behind that rifle and you keep him in your sights. If I lift my hand and close my fist, you have permission to take the shot. Are you ready to take that kind of shot?"

"Charlie, I don't know about this—"

Charlie forcefully grabbed her shirt by the collar and pulled her close. "Are you ready to take a life if you have to?"

Ash's breath became shaky as her heart rate spiked. She gulped and steeled herself.

"If that's what it takes," she said as she stared into his fiery eyes. "I'm ready."

"Only take the shot if I give you the signal," he said as he slowly released her shirt, "This gambit isn't to kill him, only to get his attention. We're going to show him today that you and I will not allow that piece of shit to hurt any one of us again. No matter what I say or do, you do nothing but keep him in your sights and only pull the trigger *if* I signal you. The situation may be tense, but you must keep your cool. Understand?"

Ash nodded, her face tense as she seemed to realize what Charlie was going to do. He would create a standoff and make Jessik decide how things would conclude.

"Good," he said as he blinked with effort. The dizziness had returned. "Be discreet. Don't let anyone see you, and be ready." Charlie checked his tool for the time. "If I'm right, Jessik will be here in about an hour. Go get set up. I'll be here getting ready."

"Right," she said stoically.

"One last thing," Charlie interjected. "To be a good protector, you must be willing to be a monster. If things go down, and you have to kill Jessik…you use every round you have or until all of the guards are dead. If you run out and there's still men to shoot, you go down the hatch and you protect the crew. Do you understand?"

Ash breathed deeply, her eyes wide but determined. "I understand."

"Go."

# Chapter 21

Ash lowered the ramp and left, heading toward the cargo bay. As she made her way up the cargo ramp, she looked around to see if any of the crew could see her. No one was around. She took her opportunity and quickly ran up the left stairs next to the soon-to-be renovated medical bay and then onto the catwalk that connected the two stairs.

She slung the rifle over her shoulder, stuffed the box of rounds in her pocket, and ascended the ladder to the airlock. She reached the top and pried the door open with her hand. At the top of *Silver Bow*'s hull, she could see all the way to the street, ideal for a sniper's perch. If she needed to, she could warn Charlie when Jessik was coming with a message.

Charlie's instructions were to just set up and then wait for them to arrive, but with her vantage point, she could offer early warning that they could utilize. If Charlie wanted to create a standoff, wouldn't it be better for them to be able to dictate where the standoff occurred?

The first officer said in her training the week before that subordinates should trust their orders from a superior; however, that didn't mean that they needed to follow them to the letter, and a good soldier—or in her case, a good security officer—should adapt based on the situation. She sighed as she considered, then sent Charlie a message.

Ash: I have a good view up here. I'm going to keep watch.

As she found her spot and took the rifle off of her shoulder, she received a reply.

Charlie: If you think that's best. Armor taking a long time to get on. Make sure you have

a good view of the bottom of the hill where you
jump the curb in your truck.

She acknowledged, then quickly typed a warning message to him and saved it as a draft. She felt the breeze hit her as she knelt down next her spot. At the back of the ship by the left engine, she could use the corner as a nest and see most of the staging area full of crates. She extended the bipod and assumed a prone position, then looked through the scope and scanned the area to ensure that she would have a clear shot.

Satisfied, she waited. Her heart continued to race as her stomach filled with butterflies and anxiety. She may have said that she was ready to pull the trigger, but was she truly?

*It's not a matter if you're ready or not. Ya* have *to do it if it comes to that.*

She waited patiently, watching the road that led to the ship from the dealership. She breathed with intent to slow her heart rate and remain calm. A group of clouds emerged and covered the sun. She hadn't seen clouds in months and felt the sweet relief of shade.

The hour she waited felt like an eternity. The shade did not last long, and the sun hit her legs, arms, and part of her neck, warming her to the point of sweat. She continuously wiped her brow above her shooting eye to keep the sweat out, and her shirt slowly became more and more damp. Sitting atop a metal ship meant that things were hotter than normal, but she dared not move. Finally, she saw six cars come from behind the dealership.

*It's him.*

Charlie received Ash's message and he opened it with the built-in interface on his armor.

Ash: Jessik's here.

Charlie stood with a grunt, buckled the bandolier of shotgun shells around his waist, holstered his pistol, and picked up the shotgun. He made a quick call on his tool to the police and hung up after saying that Jessik Kepov was with his enforcers at his location.

He lowered *Fire Arrow*'s back ramp and donned his helmet as he waited. He marched in his armor with purpose toward the spot he wanted to stand to give Ash a clear shot. In his weakened state, his armor felt heavier and more unwieldy than usual. Walking in the armor required significantly more effort than before. He continued on, trying to keep himself from getting lightheaded again by breathing deliberately. Francis walked down the ramp as Charlie walked parallel to him.

"Francis," Charlie commanded, "take Eri and Kai and get deep into the ship. Lock yourselves in the bridge if you have to."

"Charlie, what the fuck are ya up to?" Francis asked when he saw Charlie wearing his armor and holding a shotgun.

"Just do it, now!"

Furious but compliant, Francis ran back up the ramp. Charlie then pressed a button on his helmet and the visor closed, activating a speaker attached to a microphone so others could hear his voice from inside the helmet, then pressed the button to raise the protective armor plate with slits for his eyes.

He walked around the crates and saw Jessik get out of the cars with his guards. He turned on his shield with the button on his chest plate and walked out to meet the mob boss, his shotgun at the low-ready. The guards immediately drew their weapons and pointed them at Charlie, who was still twenty meters from them.

Charlie stood stoic in front of the twenty or so men with drawn guns.

*If things go south, my shields could withstand forty or so pistol rounds before the shield collapsed and the armor took over. The armor is capable of deflecting five or so pistol rounds per plate. They're all unarmored and only three of them have rifles. Hopefully Ash will target them first.*

"Is that you, dog?" Jessik asked.

"I did what you wanted," Charlie replied through the speaker, "Asher Al-Sajji is dead."

"Oh I heard about that little explosion at his house," the still-confident mob boss replied as he pushed his way through his enforcers. The men moved forward along with him. Charlie knew that Jessik, as usual, was testing his limits. Once he moved another two meters toward him, Charlie loudly clicked the safety off his shotgun. Jessik halted immediately and held his hand up to the guards, commanding them to stop moving.

"What's with the armor and getup, dog? You not ready for another lesson in discipline?"

"I'm here to tell you right now: you only get one more job from me, and then we part ways. No more killing or beating. No more touching or threatening my crew. I've got the names and locations of the leaders for the Cobras and Rock Solid. They allied themselves with Asher Al-Sajji and were planning on making a move on you. Give me two weeks and I'll kill both of them. I'll go up to Athens with a quarter million as a parting gift, and we never speak to each other again."

"Your overconfidence in that fancy armor of yours will get you euthanized, dog," Jessik spat. "You don't get to leave, understand? Besides, you fight and you'll die, even with that suit."

"You'll never live to see it," Charlie said. "There's a crosshair in a rifle scope aimed at you right now from the top of the ship. My…*little pup*…is waiting for me to tell her to place one in the middle of your forehead. The back of your skull will hit Xi's face before you even knew a fight broke out."

Jessik grinded his molars in rage, his guards all still aiming their weapons at Charlie.

"If you couldn't tell, this armor is equipped with the strongest personal shield generator on the market and the plates are made of polymerized titanium. It'd take hundreds of bullets or a couple of *incredibly* lucky shots between the plates to kill me.

"I'm offering to finish your little territorial expansion along with a quarter mil as blood money. You can take my generosity, or you can die in the dirt right here, Jessik, but either way, you're not going to come around here ever again.

"You see, you may have been able to tame *me*, but you played the wrong game. I'm much more cooperative when you pay me instead of threatening my crew to force me to do your bidding. When you threaten uninvolved innocents, any willingness I had to work for you is gone, especially when you don't pay me the compensation that I rightfully deserve."

"So, what? You want money? Is that what this is about? Fine, I'll pay you for the job."

"Oh no," Charlie said calmly, "we're *way* beyond that now…"

"Fuck this, and fuck you—"

"You might want to hurry with your decision though," Charlie interrupted. "CPD is on its way…and they know you're here. My guess would be practically half the force in full gear in about three more minutes. I'd suggest taking my generous offer."

Jessik shouted with indelible rage, finally realizing that Charlie was forcing him to accept the deal. "Fine! Two weeks, a quarter mil, and a finished job! Let's go!" Jessik and his men scrambled into the cars and took off as fast as they could. Charlie remained still, shotgun in hand. Once the men could no longer see him, Charlie opened his helmet and fell down to all fours, gasping for air.

After about a minute, Ash rushed down to him, the rifle slung on her back as she knelt beside him and helped him sit upright on the dirt, his armor weighing him down. He turned off his shield and tried to get his helmet off, but couldn't manage it. Ash moved to his other side and pulled back on the latch that connected the helmet to his neck collar. It disconnected with a hiss. Charlie threw the helmet off, sucking in as much air as he could. The winded first officer managed to thank Ash between breaths, but he was close to passing out.

Sirens wailed as police vehicles came to a stop in the street, the officers in full gear getting out with rifles, shotguns, and pistols drawn.

"Show me your hands!" one of the officers commanded.

Ash quickly complied with her hands up. "They're gone! They left about two minutes ago!" she shouted.

Police officers started to tactically advance on the two as they both kept their hands up.

"I called…I'm the one that called in about Jessik Kepov," Charlie managed to say between breaths.

Four officers moved in, their weapons still trained on them. Two officers helped them up while the other two removed their weapons. The officers searched them and lowered their weapons after removing Ash's rifle and Charlie's shotgun and pistol.

"Some fancy armor you got there," a police lieutenant said as he approached. "Were you planning on fighting it out?"

"No," Charlie said as he slumped over.

"Sir, he's really dizzy; he needs to sit down," Ash pleaded.

The lieutenant signaled two officers to help Charlie sit.

"Do you need medical attention, sir?" the lieutenant asked.

Charlie weakly shook his head. "Just dizzy is all…adrenaline and all that."

The officer nodded. "Would you two be willing to give a statement and file a police report?"

"Will it help get that piece of shit mob boss in prison any faster?" Ash asked.

"He's well-connected and well-protected. If he was here and knew that police were coming his way, he's probably already getting on an orbital flight back to Athens."

"Why won't ya guys just arrest him?" Ash asked with frustration. "If ya all know he's a mob boss, just get him."

"It's not that simple and we need a surefire way to keep him off the streets," the lieutenant explained. "He's smart enough to never do any of his dirty work, so we need to have enough evidence to convict him of conspiracy for all the crimes he's committed. I know that doesn't sound right, but mobsters like him skirt the law to stay out of prison. It's up to us to get him convicted without a chance of letting him go free."

"Mob lawyers are paid to find every loophole and mistake the police make when they arrest them so they can either get a mistrial, charges dropped, or a jury who won't convict," Charlie added, "To get him in prison, they have to do everything right and by the book so the mob lawyers have nothing to stand on."

"For a man with such incredible fighting equipment, you sure know a lot about the law," the lieutenant remarked.

Charlie woke his tool with the interface on his armor and showed his certified bounty hunter credentials. The lieutenant snorted.

"You can look up my file. I took down one of Jessik's men a couple weeks ago in Athens. He came back to get restitution for me killing his man. The guy was a cop killer."

"Well we appreciate you hunting him down. Not enough good bounty hunters willing to arrest or kill a mobster's drug runner. If you two don't want to file a report or a statement, my guys will go ahead and leave, but for your safety, I'm going to ask the chief to assign one car to the junkyard. I'm assuming that work in progress is yours?"

"Yes, sir!" Ash responded pridefully. "Her name is *Silver Bow*."

"Nice looking ship. I'll have to stop by once it's all finished and cleaned up."

"I'll let you know when we're finished if ya gimme your card," Ash replied with a sly smile.

The dark skinned officer removed a business card from his tactical vest and wrote something on the back with a pen from his pocket. "My personal number is on the back as well if you can't reach me at my work contact," he said with a grin.

"Heh," Charlie grunted. He knew what the officer was getting at with Ashley.

"Well, anyways," the lieutenant said awkwardly. "We'll head back to the station."

"Sorry we couldn't keep them here long enough," Charlie lied. "I'm sure you would have rather had him stay for a good old-fashioned shootout."

The other officers left and the lieutenant signaled to Ash where their weapons were placed. "I'm sure you looked forward to that more than we did," he replied.

"I'll invoke my right to silence on that inference," Charlie muttered.

With that, the police returned to their vehicles, turned off their lights, and left without incident. Charlie fell backward onto the dirt, chuckling as he did. Ash sighed in relief. The two sat there, enjoying the fact that things had concluded peacefully with both Jessik and the police. Both instances could have turned bad in a hurry. The doctor quickly came to Charlie's side, winded but ready to help.

"Are you alright?" Kai asked.

"Yup, I'm fine," Ash replied sarcastically as she gathered the weapons and removed the rounds.

Kai shook his head. "Can you get up, Charlie?"

"I'm just going to sit here for a little bit, Doc. Ash can help me up in a minute."

"What about your cuts?"

Charlie grunted with amusement, "This armor is so formfitting that it's pressing against them. They won't open up."

"What were you two thinking?" Eri asked as she got close to the group.

"It was all Charlie's idea. I just followed instructions. Not a thought in this noggin'," Ash said cheerfully.

"Funny," Eri deadpanned.

"How's the drive core coming along?" Charlie asked as he looked up at the sky, relieved that he hadn't needed to get into a gunfight.

"Don't change the subject," Eri demanded with a snarl.

"I just wanted Jessik to stay away," Charlie said. "I showed my hand and he thankfully folded."

"Remind me to never play ya in poker," Ash said as she walked away with the weapons.

Charlie chuckled at Ash's remark. "I forced him into a pragmatic solution. I finish his little side project, pay him some money, and we go our separate ways. If he didn't agree to my terms, he would have died right here."

"And what happens when you go to him with the money? What if he wants to hurt or kill you then?"

"We'll cross that bridge when we get to it, Eri," Charlie grumbled, "just let me have this little victory, please."

"Well, I hope you're less shortsighted once we get off world," she said as she angrily walked away.

"I can now see why ya wouldn't tell me your crazy fucken plan," Francis said, "I would've never let ya do it if I knew."

Charlie said nothing. He simply kept looking up at the sky. Everything was working according to his plan. He had made contact with the ball, now it was simply a matter of follow-through. Jessik would stay in Athens at Sinister, where Charlie would make his move and permanently end Jessik's grip on Francis.

"C'mon," Francis said as he grabbed Charlie's arm and pulled him up. Charlie was still dizzy, but with the captain's help, he was able to get to his feet.

"I got him, Captain," Ash said as she returned. "I'll come help ya finish setting up avionics and navigation after I drop him off at *Fire Arrow.*"

Ash put herself under Charlie's arm and helped him to the shuttle. As they passed the cargo ramp, she finally spoke up.

"Ya got brass balls and nerves of steel, ya know that?" she commented with awe. "What ya did…I don't think I ever could have done."

"You're wrong, Tall Hands," he replied. "You would do it for your family as well."

"I dunno about that," she admitted.

"You would," he said proudly. "I know you would."

"Well, at least I didn't have to be a monster today," she jested.

"You will one day," he prophesied, "and you have to be ready to do horrible things for the sake of protecting the crew. Don't ever lose sight of your duty, your responsibility. We must occasionally become monsters to protect them from the horrors of this world."

"You've said that twice today," Ash stated as they got inside *Fire Arrow*, "what's the reason for hammerin' it in my skull?"

Charlie undid the neck collar and unlocked his gloves. "Because when we start hauling who-knows-what across the Frontier, we're the first and last line of defense for *Silver Bow*. Everything I've taught you so far and everything I will teach you over the next two weeks will be the difference between tragedy and victory. Today, your training came through and you probably didn't even know it."

Charlie removed his gloves and put them on the console before slumping into the pilot's seat. The dizziness had returned.

"I taught you to follow orders, and you did so beautifully. I taught you to trust me and my plans, and you did. I also taught you how to adapt to the situation at hand, so you stayed up on top of *Silver Bow.* We worked on your physical fitness to show that you can always go beyond your limits and to get you used to being uncomfortable. You stayed on the hot ship the entire hour we waited for Jessik and I obliged by feigning strength and calm despite being on the edge of collapsing—all just to execute the plan.

"If I had collapsed, I would be dead and you would have had to fight off all the guards. If you had questioned my orders and informed Francis, he might have tried to intervene and would have made the situation worse. If you weren't used to being uncomfortable and going beyond your limits, you might have gotten off the roof to cool yourself off and not spotted Jessik and his gang in time. Training is always about preparing for all situations, planned or unplanned, and how to overcome them. Training is not always about improving your skills and abilities, it's about readying you to be the protector and fighter you *need* to be. What no commando or war hero will tell you is that victory is ninety-five percent mental. The last five is nothing more than sheer talent.

"I'm telling you this because you will stare down some of the most evil and reprehensible people in the galaxy in our journeys. Your training is to not only keep yourself calm and focused when facing these people, but also to help you understand that oftentimes the only way to eliminate a threat is with your training—and ultimately, extreme violence. Some people cannot be bribed, manipulated, intimidated, or reasoned with; some people will only stop when their heart no longer beats. Think about what I said. Take the night off, have a drink, and come back tomorrow, ready to learn more and train to be the nastiest bitch no one will want to fuck with."

Ash collected herself and nodded. She turned around and left *Fire Arrow.* She headed back to *Silver Bow* with purpose, determination, and pride fueling her steps. Charlie smiled as she stepped away. For the first time, he felt like he was actually accomplishing something.

# Chapter 22

Eri returned to engineering and shut the door. With a sigh of relief, she unzipped the top half of her coveralls and pulled them down. The engine room was hot around the end of the day as the metal ship radiated the heat collected from the roof. She wore only her bra under the coveralls because of the heat, which allowed her torso and arms to breathe and remain cool. She picked up the second third of the manual, now printed in paper and placed into massive binders, grabbed the A-frame ladder, and began the step-by-step guide on properly hooking power cables to the core and which ports would be best based on their predicted power draw.

She flipped a page, but she couldn't focus on the manual. Thoughts of Jessik's quiet threat to Charlie two days before and seeing him weakly leaning against a crate with a slashed abdomen remained behind her eyes. She had probed Ash the day before if she heard anything about Jessik's threat before he stabbed Charlie, but Ash said she heard nothing. When her sister asked what Jessik said to Charlie, she simply waved it off and said that she couldn't hear it either.

She couldn't tell Ash what she'd heard Jessik say; if she did, Ash would have probably shot the man in the head without a second thought. Her sister may have never killed anyone, but hearing a threat like that would have probably sent her over the edge. Charlie was the kind of man who kept things secret for Eri's sake, so he'd never mentioned what Jessik said to him either.

She clenched her jaw. The thought of Charlie killing people to save her made her feel helpless. He had mentioned before that he worked for Jessik to keep him away from Frank, and then later Francis, but now he was working for Jessik to keep him away from her.

Eri's stomach turned at the thought of what the heavily scarred first officer did. She had seen glimpses of him being a kind and gentle man with a terrible past, and the thought that she was a part of making him have an even darker past made her chest tighten. She didn't want to be the reason he had to kill, and the man had nearly passed out earlier while threatening a mob boss just to keep him away from her. Whether she wanted to admit it or not, Charlie was the only thing standing in Jessik's way, and she could hear in his voice that he had resigned himself to that. He was going to kill two more gang leaders and pay the mobster a quarter of a million shen just to keep him away.

A quarter million. How much money did Charlie have anyway? Was he taking every last bit of his and Francis's money for the business to do it? Was he using his own money? His life savings? She grabbed the nearest wrench and hurled it at the far wall with frustration, then pinched the bridge of her nose with a defeated sigh.

*Why would he do all of this for me?*

It didn't make sense to her. He may have been friendly with her, but he also kept her at arm's length, and she didn't understand why he had nearly died for her.

She couldn't let her thoughts dwell on him much longer though. The guilt was starting to get to her, and she could feel the kind of tightness in her stomach that she felt whenever she thought about her parents and their murders. She needed to focus on the task at hand.

Blinking deliberately, she started reading the page in the manual that demonstrated how to connect a shield generator and weapons systems. On that page, there were notes for an "overclocked setup" later in the binder. Her brow furled with curiosity.

She stood on the ladder and flipped through the pages until she found the section about overclocking the drive core. She had heard that the E-7 was able to temporarily boost power, but she always read recommendations for the drive core because of its reliability. Even reviews when it was first launched thirty years ago droned on and on about its reliability. The overclock feature was nothing more than a mention most times, something that no one seemed to really care about other than it was a novel feature that required extensive reconfiguration.

Fascinated and intrigued, she began to read the overclock system in the manual and see if it was feasible with *Silver Bow* and all the things Francis and Charlie intended to install. Charlie after all wanted to put in beam cannons, and they likely required a lot of output.

The first officer finally managed to remove his armor and put his street clothes back on. The dizziness had subsided and he felt somewhat normal again. The dizziness disappearing also meant his pain returned. Doc must have used significantly stronger painkillers than the ones he gave him the day before, which was the most likely cause of the dizziness, alongside his lower blood volume. He trudged his way back to *Silver Bow* after placing everything back in *Fire Arrow*'s secret compartment under the bunk, breathing shallowly as his broken rib stabbed him in the chest with pain. Wearing the formfitting armor was not ideal for his rib, but it was necessary.

He began his ascent up the cargo ramp, his lethargy fight against him with every step. At the ramp, he took a second to stop and breathe. Doing simple tasks required so much effort. Sighing, he resumed his walk toward the engine room, but paused at the access door. With some effort, he finally managed to get the door to open, using the door's momentum to open it with one hand as he clung to the doorframe with the other for support. He peered into the room, but he didn't look at the drive core. He gazed at Eri on the ladder. He couldn't help but look at her.

The maintainer was deep in thought, reading a binder on top of the ladder. She was bent over the drive core's top section, her coveralls pulled down to her hips, and was wearing only a bra, which revealed her fair-skinned abdomen and chest, both of which glistened with sweat from the room's heat. Her wavy brown hair had been parted off to one side and pulled behind her right ear, more than likely to help cool her neck. The strip of hair that had been dyed mulberry red two weeks before was in the first stages of fading, but still very visible. Her eyes quickly moved back and forth and her lips twitched, silently mouthing words as she read, a knuckle pressed against her lips.

Charlie managed to look away and cleared his throat to make his presence known as he hung on to the doorframe. Eri snapped out of her focused reading and looked at the doorway and Charlie standing in it, averting his eyes from her.

"Oh shit! Sorry!" she said as she pulled the coveralls up, zipping it to the base of her neck. "It gets so hot in here toward the end of the day and I didn't think anyone would come in," she explained as she descended the ladder. She looked away, clearly mortified that Charlie had once again seen her in her bra.

"It's alright," Charlie said as he finally looked up, "just an unexpected sight when you come to look at the core. Did it fit as well as we thought?"

"Oh yeah, you weren't here for that," she realized sarcastically. Her demeanor suddenly shifted from shy embarrassment to an indignant scowl. "You were too busy getting high."

"I didn't come here for your judgement nor your indignation," he said as he finally stood up straight. "Everything I've done in the past two days was for you and everyone else on this boat."

"So getting high was part of the plan too?"

"First of all," Charlie began as he pointed his finger at her, "what I took was completely legal and is used in combat *regularly*. Francis has probably had over three liters of it put into his system over his lifetime, and I can only count the number of times I've used stims on one hand. Secondly, it was. I had to overpower two men simultaneously and if I hadn't—especially in my state—I would have been dead."

"But you almost died anyway because of the stim and not taking the right precautions," she interjected venomously.

"Fuck you, Eri," Charlie spat angrily, "you've never had to deal with hard choices or having to make split decisions without being able to prepare. Everything can be black and white for you from your lack of life experience, but the galaxy is full of gray, especially out here in the Frontier. You're only mad because you know what I know."

"Oh yeah? And what's that?" she replied indignantly, arms folded.

"That I almost died just to kill a man for a psychopath that takes pleasure in raping and killing women! That you almost had to live with survivor's guilt knowing that I died trying to protect you from one of the most evil people you will ever meet. I did all of that, and yet I barely know you!

"You're mad because you finally realized how naïve you were to believe that the only monsters would be outside the hull and not sleeping two doors down from you. Only now have you finally realized that when shit goes *really* south, you may have to kill as well. You're not mad at me, you're mad at yourself. I'm just the thing that made you realize it."

Silence pierced the hot room as Charlie began to breathe heavily again. The shouting made him lightheaded. He slowly moved to the wall and slid down it to sit on the floor. He controlled his breathing in an effort to stop seeing stars.

"You're mad because you feel guilty, I get it—more than you know. I have enough guilt for both of us, but I take *no* pleasure in killing or hurting people on Jessik's behalf. He's probably one of three people I would actually *enjoy* killing if I had the chance. I've only done horrible things for him to protect Francis and his dad—and now to protect you, Ash, and Kai. You may look at me and be angry or frightened, but at the end of the day I'm the only thing keeping you safe from the likes of him. If that means I have to cover my hands in blood, so be it. But I have a duty, responsibility, and obligation to keep *Silver Bow*'s crew safe.

"Look, I'm sorry that I disappeared on all of you and made you worry. I may have even traumatized you with how much I was bleeding last night. I made bad decisions trying to do what was right, and I'll apologize for *that*, but not for protecting my family and friends.

"I'm a man who's been fucked up by the consequences of his failed decisions, and I won't allow any more of my friends to be hurt because of my actions. I'm sorry that I disappeared for hours and never responded to your messages. I thought that if I ignored them, I could remain focused on the task at hand. I didn't even think that I would later return on the brink of death because I did everything myself, and haphazardly at that. I just…I just didn't want you all to be involved in such nasty work."

Charlie sighed, defeated. He continued to breathe as best as he could to keep the brain fog away. He looked down at the floor in front of him as Eri stood over him. She watched him closely as sweat appeared on his forehead from the heat, silently pondering his words.

Although she may not agree with him killing on Jessik's behalf, he could see that she conceded that it was necessary. She didn't want to admit it, but it was true. He remembered how fearful she was of the mobster and how Jessik had threatened to rape her in front of him. She eventually looked away with shame.

"I'm sorry I slapped you," she finally said. "You didn't deserve that. I was upset that you showed no remorse or regret and I couldn't understand why you wouldn't be affected by it. I don't understand and maybe I never will, but the thought of *killing* someone…

"I may never understand," Eri said after a pause. "Ash told me last night that you're just trying to do what's necessary to protect us. She was the only one who wasn't completely enraged by what you did or how you did it. I thought maybe it was just because you had manipulated her through all her training, but it's clear that she just…*understands*. It made me wonder if she would do the same— and the thought terrified me because I've only ever known her as a sweet, caring, and lighthearted woman.

"I thought that being around you had corrupted her and she had somehow become numb to terrible things. It shattered everything I believed about heroes, about being a good person. I didn't want to believe that good people would also have to do horrible things to protect others. I guess I just never truly understood it until now.

"I was mad because I didn't even consider that working on this ship would lead to days like these or that the very people protecting me would need to be…*violent*. Maybe I was just in denial and believed that somehow everything would be a safe and fun adventure and that your warnings about danger and violence were only to make sure that I was committed. Realizing that made me feel stupid, and I took that self-loathing out on you. I'm sorry."

Silence once again fell between them. The hot air in the room felt like a heavy blanket.

"I'm no saint, Eri—far from it, but I am only trying to keep you safe, and I won't apologize for it. I *am* sorry for making you all worried though."

"I know," she said after a long silence. "I think a lot of my anger is just because I feel helpless…"

"I know," he replied quietly, "I once felt the same as you. The difference is whether or not you're willing to rely on others or be independent in exchange for purity. Are you willing to shoot someone so you don't have to rely on others? Are you ready to watch the light fade from their eyes and realize that they are dying because of you?"

Eri held her arm nervously.

"No," she answered with a trembling voice, "and I think that's what bothers me the most. Who will protect you and Ash if you're both hurt? Would I be willing to shoot back if I had to? Would I even be able to move when we get shot at? I'm worried one day I'll be everyone's last hope and I'll freeze…just like when Jessik showed up."

"There's nothing wrong with freezing. It just means you're human."

Eri looked away as she tried to compose herself. Charlie could sense that there was something deeper that she wanted to talk about, but he knew it wasn't the right time.

"So are we done with our apologies?" Charlie asked before she was able to speak. "I'd rather put this behind us than just spill out all of our guilt."

Eri forced a smirk. He saw her realize that he too felt awkward.

"Fine, let me show you something then," she said as she extended her arm.

Charlie looked up at her and smirked, grasped her arm with his prosthetic and they both struggled to get him up.

"God, you're heavy," she groaned as she pulled him up.

"I would be helping more," he said as he caught his breath, blinking deliberately as he fought his exhaustion, "if I wasn't so weak right now."

Eri quickly left him and ascended the ladder. She grabbed the binder, flipped back a few pages, and descended. She walked over and stood next to him, holding the binder between them so they could both read.

"It's not *The Count of Monte Cristo*, but you may find it interesting," she remarked.

Charlie silently read the pages, and his eyes began to widen with realization. Eri watched his eyes dart back and forth, genuine excitement slowly filling his expression.

"So the E-7 has the ability to increase its output above one hundred percent for a period of time?" he asked as he turned to her. "I've never heard of a drive core do this before."

"It was a feature only on the E-7, and not many people really cared about it," she explained. "People get the E-7 for its reliability, but with all the weapons that you're adding onto the ship, I figured that you and Francis might want to take advantage of this feature."

"I would, but that's something that Francis would have final say on," he replied. He hummed with intrigue. "I wonder what else we could do with the overclock feature…"

"Besides better shields and weapons?" she asked.

"Yeah. We could increase output to the engines and use them for escape. We could bring in extra equipment like massive beacons normally used for larger ships to boost a distress call and use them as a signal jammer. It could allow us to use the extra power to save people who have lost life support on a derelict or…"

Charlie's eyes darted all around as his mind raced.

"Or what?" she asked with anticipation.

"We might be able to do short jumps. There are dead zones near hyperlanes because there is a minimum distance for the ship to accelerate to FTL, right?"

"Sure, but what are you getting at?" she asked.

"What if we could somehow use the increased output as a way to increase the acceleration into FTL? We could shorten the minimum distance, and with modification, we might be able to shorten it so much that dead zones might not exist for us."

Eri looked away, obviously trying to think if there would be any other roadblocks besides the navigation system not being able to chart a course like that. Charlie knew though to do all of that would require tons of modifications, including a prototype inertial dampener that could handle the acceleration and a completely rewritten nav system.

"I would have never thought about that," she said.

"I wouldn't have either if I didn't have to deal with dead zones all the time during the war," Charlie said as he flipped through the pages. "If we only we had this…"

*Naba and Dinesh would be alive. They would been able to avoid that patrol by Svea…*

He snapped himself out of the thought, pursed his lips, and gently pushed the binder towards her. "Well, that's all theoretical anyway. We'd have to do some serious modification and testing." His serious and cold expression once again returned to his face. "The other abilities that the overclocking provides are as equally impressive and exciting though. You should let Francis know when you have the chance."

Charlie wiped the sweat from his forehead. "How much longer until all the essential systems are connected?" he asked.

"It'll be done by tomorrow. Francis said while we finish it, you and Kai will be designing and getting materials for the medical bay."

Charlie gazed at the drive core for a moment. "Well…I should try to get some rest so I can be more useful tomorrow. Good find, Eri. You really should let Francis know. He'll be excited about it." Charlie then walked around her and out the door. He heard her breathe in, but she never spoke. Whatever it was, she was probably too shy or nervous to say it.

Either way, he knew that talking about the previous subject any more wouldn't be productive for either of them.

# Chapter 23

Eri and Ash awoke the next morning and heard rain. The monsoon season was finally starting in Corinth. Every year, the summer was almost three and a half months of cloudless skies followed by two months of heavy rain almost every day. That morning seemed to be the first day of many that would be full of mud, humidity, and flooding.

The two made their way in the rain toward the spot where *Silver Bow* sat in the junkyard. Ash jumped the curb and drove up the muddy hill to get as close to the cargo ramp as possible. The two had already gathered and donned their monsoon season essentials, but they both still didn't like dealing with the rain or the subsequent mud and puddles.

As they came to a stop in the truck, Eri noticed Charlie lying on two crates outside, the rain drenching him and his clothes. Concerned that the first officer had passed out, she jumped out of the truck and ran over to him.

"Charlie?" she shouted through the rhythmic tapping and splattering of heavy rain. "Charlie, are you okay?"

Charlie turned his head and looked at her. He smiled slightly and simply replied with, "Good morning."

"Are you just going to lay out here?" she asked in her bewilderment.

"Yeah," he replied softly. He turned his head back up toward the rain, closed his eyes, and continued to smile.

Ash shrugged as she walked up the ramp. Once she was out of the rain, she removed her raincoat and stomped the mud off her boots. Eri followed, removing her raincoat and stomping the mud off her boots as well, all the while watching Charlie remain motionless but peaceful on the crates.

"He grew up on Hexham," Francis said as he emerged from engineering with three cups of coffee and distributed them. "It rains almost three-quarters of the year there. Any time it rains, he does that."

"Why though?" Eri asked before she sipped her coffee.

"The last time I asked him, he simply said 'it reminds me of the last time I was truly at peace.' He left Hexham to join the war and only went back to get some of his things from his parents' house. He used to tell me how ya could spot the locals from the tourists simply by whether or not they had umbrellas. If they walked in the rain without one, they're a local. Locals always wore waterproof clothes and shoes and never bothered to use umbrellas 'cause they'd never have more than one free hand."

Eri continued to watch him as the water hit his face and body and made rhythmic clanks on the metal hull above her.

"When he worked for my dad, the workers said his only days off were when it rained. On Venture, it don't rain that much, but when it would, Charlie did nothin' all day and just sat in the rain."

Charlie finally sat up and jumped down from the crates, the mud splashing underneath his boots as he landed. He walked up the ramp and sighed heavily, the smile remaining on his face. "You too will miss the rain after we've been on ship for long periods of time." The first officer sloshed over to a crate full of his belongings, retrieved a cigarette, and lit it. He pulled his wet hair back, the cowlick being uncooperative and keeping some of his wet hair standing straight. Charlie then took a long drag of his cigarette and walked back over to the cargo bay's entrance. "You'll find yourself longing for things that were mundane or even annoying once you've become used to the sterile and stale environment of a ship."

He took another long drag from his cigarette and looked out toward the rain.

"You say that you love rain, but you open your
umbrella when it rains.
You say that you love the sun, but you find a
shadowy spot when the sun shines.

You say that you love the wind, but you close your
windows when wind blows.
This is why I am afraid, you say that you love me
too."

"What's that from?" Eri asked. She found the poem quite
beautiful.

"I don't remember exactly, just a poem that I learned in high
school," Charlie said as he inhaled more smoke.

"Don't get him started on Shakespeare," Francis said
jokingly.

"I hardly know Shakespeare," Charlie retorted, "he's too
hard of a read for me."

Eri snickered as she realized that Charlie didn't understand
Francis' sarcasm. Ash snickered as well.

"Where's Doc?" Charlie asked Francis.

"Up in what will be our new medical bay, lookin' around
and plannin'. Ya should go join him." Charlie nodded and left to
join Kai. "As for ya two, we still gotta finish the essential systems
and ensure that everythin' works. Ash, I need ya to especially work
on routin' the cables to life support when it gets here—and
auxiliary. The rain is forecasted to last until lunchtime, and we'll
need to ensure that the systems are ready when the workers arrive to
begin work on water, HVAC, and the galley."

"I wanted to talk to you about something first, Captain," Eri
interjected.

"What about?" the captain asked.

"The drive core. There's a unique feature that I forgot to
mention to you when we first installed it. I showed Charlie and he's
as optimistic as I am about it, but he said that I needed to speak with
you first before I did anything."

"Ominous," he remarked, "does it require additional parts or
work?"

"Not additional parts, but a lot more work," she replied with
a sigh. Ash, not interested in such things, left to do her tasks. "The
E-7 has a feature that allows it to essentially provide more power
output than usual for a period of time. How much extra power it
produces depends on how long the period will last. It can provide up

to two hundred percent output for about thirty minutes. Anywhere in between one hundred and two hundred will be longer than that, but exactly how long is vague and not explicitly provided. I can set it up according to default configuration, but if we do this setup that allows for overclocking the drive core—"

"Do it," Francis commanded.

"I'm going to need help. The setup requires a lot of work—at least one extra set of hands."

"I'll have Charlie help ya when he can. Let's make sure all essential systems are workin' properly and then ya can change the setup."

"Okay then!" she said excitedly.

Eri returned to the engineering bay and worked on getting all the systems connected to the proper ports. She skipped cable management because she would need to disconnect the cables to switch the engine over to the overclock setup. After she was satisfied with the cabling, she waited for Francis and Ash to finish installing the systems. By the late morning, she took a break from reading the guide for the overclock setup and walked out of the engine bay to find Charlie and Kai deliberating over the medical bay's setup with a schematic of the ship. Kai sipped his tea while Charlie lit a cigarette.

"All I'm saying is that there won't be enough room for all the equipment that you want," Charlie argued as he slowly released smoke from his nose.

"Then extend the walls."

"We can't just 'extend the walls' on a ship," Charlie explained. "If you extend the walls, you can cause a snowball effect with the construction and create a design flaw. Where you want to extend the walls here, you will push that wall all the way to the hull and block off the hallway that wraps around the captain's quarters and the medbay.

"You also have to think about the design of the ship. If you make a wall there, you will have to carry the wall to the engine bay to make it sturdy enough for impact or damage, which means you'd have to cut off all of the cabling that is already laid underneath the flooring. You're talking about diverting literally half of the ship's cables so you can put in a CTMRI. If any of us need one of those, we'll be going to a hospital anyway. This is a freight vessel, not a hospital. We need a place to keep people stable, not cure them of cancer."

"A CTMRI is essential for the diagnostic process—"

"Doc, you're not working at Athens General, you're basically working at a field hospital. I'm not going to do it and Francis will agree that what you're asking for is way beyond the scope of the medbay—and technically your abilities to diagnose because you're unlicensed."

"Well the drive core has more than enough output to be able to power something like a CTMRI—"

"You're not helping, Eri—"

"But Charlie is right, Kai. Once you mess with the structure of the ship, you're talking about basically redesigning the entire ship."

"We're doing that already!" Kai shouted.

"There's a big difference between restoration with slight modification and *redesign*, especially once you have to start restructuring compartments and the hull," Eri retorted.

"So we aren't doing it, Doc," Charlie said sternly. "I understand that you're used to certain things being available in a fully equipped hospital, but you need to think about the medbay being more like a field hospital. You'll have plenty of counter space and cabinets to fill up with all the *necessary* medical supplies that you need, but we can't put in something like a CTMRI. You'll have a machine that can do basic imaging of both bone and soft tissue, and I'll look into the budget to see if we'll have enough for the extras you want, but I'm drawing the line at the CTMRI."

Kai sighed defeatedly. "Fine."

Charlie finally looked to Eri and took a drag. "Francis told me he gave you the green light on the overclock setup."

"Yes, but I'm going to need your help doing it. I'm pretty sure you're the only one that will be savvy enough to help."

"I can't, Eri. I have far too much on my plate as it is," he replied. "I'm helping Kai with the medbay, training your sister, getting the armory set up, and overseeing all of the weapon systems."

"We can divert a few workers to help get the medbay completed once you're done helping him design the compartment, and I'm sure Francis can take over the weapons."

"Francis doesn't know a thing about the weapons nor will I let him oversee the armory. That room is *my* baby. You have the drive core, I have the weapons and armory."

"Please, Charlie," Eri pleaded, "if I don't get some help from someone who is knowledgeable enough, then getting the overclock system set up may extend construction for another week."

Charlie looked away and sighed. "I'll talk with Francis, but there may be days where you and I just have to work overnight if things don't go well with the weapons."

"I'm fine with that, if it comes to it."

"Who is that?" Kai asked.

Charlie turned to look out and saw Axe standing patiently out in the rain on the access road with an umbrella.

"Stay here," he said as he extinguished his cigarette in an ashtray. He stood up and walked out into the rain, careful not to slip. As Charlie approached, Axe began walking back toward the dealership, away from prying eyes and ears. Charlie followed at a normal pace, not necessarily trying to catch up to the IS3 agent, simply following until he would stop to talk. Once they had rounded the corner on the road and could no longer be seen by the crewmates, Axe stopped and waited.

"I thought you would be in Athens on assignment, Axe," he said as he got close. "What are you doing here?"

"This couldn't wait. I left Athens immediately." The agent produced a folder from underneath his trench coat, the folder protected from the rain with his umbrella. Charlie opened the folder and read its contents.

"I know you keep tabs on me, Axe, I don't care," Charlie said plainly.

"Keep reading," he simply replied.

Charlie read more papers inside the folder under Axe's umbrella. "Again, I know Tristan is probably watching me with surveillance teams. None of this is news to me."

"Keep reading," he reiterated.

Charlie sighed and turned the page. He read a report stating that Tristan had tried to recruit his parents as FIA confidential informants. "This…this makes no sense," Charlie uttered, "why would Tristan get my parents charged with treason and war crimes only to then try to recruit them as CIs almost two years later?"

"We don't know, that's why I'm asking you, Charlie. The timing also seems too convenient. Your parents were officially placed in prison after their trial nineteen months ago, but only now are they being recruited as CIs? CIs are usually recruited by having crimes wiped away in exchange, not after they have been in prison for almost two years. It seems like a long and drawn-out plan by your brother."

Charlie thought for a moment as the rain slowly reduced in intensity. "You may be right. He may have planned it from the beginning. He just wanted my parents in a place where they couldn't leave. He wanted to keep them in one spot until his day finally came. For what purpose is beyond me. He must know something that we don't."

"Didn't your parents work on Top Secret Feddie projects before the war?"

"Yeah, but they never told me anything, Axe. I was a kid!"

"Do you know if it was for a specific company or if it was a Federal project?"

"Axe, I was a kid back then. I didn't care to learn or know why."

"Charlie, *any* information can point us in the right direction," Axe said with frustration.

"I don't know what information I could possibly give you that would be helpful! I grew up on Hexham my entire childhood and teenage years. Whatever projects they worked on, they were on Hexham. Besides that, I don't know."

"Do you think there might be any connection between this and Johan's disappearance?"

"It didn't cross my mind until you just asked me," Charlie replied. "Is there a connection?"

"The timing just feels too coincidental. Two weeks after your brother becomes section head, Johan doesn't check in while undercover, and two weeks after that Tristan visits your parents and tries to make them CIs? There's no way they aren't connected."

Charlie thought hard about how the two would be connected. "If you'd tell me what Johan was doing, I might know the connection. Other than that, your guess is as good as mine."

"You know I can't tell you, Charlie. Hell, I shouldn't even be talking to you right now. If they found out they could charge me with espionage."

"Then why are you!"

"Because you're a war hero, god damnit," he growled. "Without you and Blue Team, we might have never won the war— or in the very least, it would have extended for years. You matched the Feddies with the lengths they were willing to go, and you ensured that the mission stayed alive, no matter the cost. You, Ade, and Johan understood that more than anyone else in IS3, and you deserve to know. The director may hate your guts because of what you did to his sister, but I know the truth, and that you only did what you had to do."

"I'm not a hero Axe," he said solemnly. "I'm just a survivor."

"You can deal with your guilt on your own time, Charlie. There's one more thing and then I *have* to leave."

Charlie turned the page and read the report of a mysterious death. The analyst who wrote the report concluded that more than likely the death was not natural, but a targeted assassination. "The FIA assassinated Colonel Monnigan?"

"Yes, and again, I believe it's connected with you and Tristan making section chief."

"How? Why?"

"We're working on it, Charlie," Axe said as he took the folder from him and returned it to his trench coat. "We don't know why exactly other than a theory that Tristan is simply sending you a message that he's coming for you, but I have a theory of my own."

"And what's that?"

"I can't prove any of it just yet; call it intuition or a hunch. I think he's trying to kill anyone who has ever helped you. He's not sending a message, he's eliminating your base of support, one by one, until you are alone. Think about it, Charlie. There are a lot of people who have helped you in the past few years. With Monnigan dead, the only person left is Francis. Anyone else who has ever helped you is dead. That's no coincidence."

"If your theory is right and he knows about you, Axe, that puts you in danger."

"I'm aware of the risks, which is why you probably won't hear from me for a while. If you think of anything that can help us understand all of this, you need to contact the main office immediately and speak with Counter-Intel. The longer you sit on information or don't divulge key details, the more likely we won't be able to help you."

"IS3 is already refusing to help me, so what would change?"

"Just because we aren't offering you protection without joining the agency doesn't mean we aren't helping in other ways, Charlie. I got to go. Stay safe."

Before Charlie could say anything more, Axe immediately walked away. Charlie remained in the rain, doing everything he could to figure out what Tristan was up to. After a while, he finally moved back toward *Silver Bow*, his mind racing.

*How are they connected? Why is Tristan killing anyone who has ever helped me? Is he coming for Francis? Is he coming for the crew? Why would he try to recruit Mom and Dad? What could they know that could let them become CIs? Should I tell the crew?*

Before he knew it, he was back in the cargo bay.

"Charlie?" Eri asked with concern.

The first officer looked up from his feet. His hair, fingers, nose, and chin dripped with rainwater.

"So who was that guy? Are you alright?"

"Just an old friend," he responded robotically, "he helps me out from time to time."

"Well, while you were out there talking with him," she began, "I talked with Francis about your busy schedule, and he's going to help with some of your workload so you can help me with the drive core. He wants to talk with you about it when you get a chance."

"Where's Kai?"

"Talking with Francis about the plans for the medbay. They're up on the bridge."

Charlie thanked her and walked up the stairs toward the living quarters. As he passed his room, his chest tightened, and his breathing became rapid and erratic. He gripped his chest and stumbled into his quarters. Sweat began to bead on his skin as his vision narrowed and he began to hear the loud screech of tinnitus. He gripped onto his desk as he felt a burning sensation in his left lung.

Francis went over all the plans about the medbay with Kai while Ash continued to connect components to power cables underneath the flooring in the bridge. He once again tried to convince someone of the necessity of the CTMRI, but Francis wanted nothing of it or the required changes to the medbay to accommodate the large diagnostic machine.

"I don't believe for a minute that Charlie would allow this," Francis said with frustration. "Where is he anyway? I ain't seen him for an hour."

"He might still be outside talking with the strange man that was standing out in the rain."

"What are ya talkin' about?"

"Well, when we were discussing the medbay, I noticed a man wearing a trench coat with an umbrella on the access road. He was just standing there, watching us in the cargo bay. When I mentioned something, Charlie went out there to meet him. They walked away out of sight shortly after."

Francis's stomach turned. Something was up. Was it that IS3 agent that Charlie would contact out in Athens occasionally? "I'll go find him. I'm puttin' my foot down on the expansion, Kai, and I know that Charlie would never approve that. Ya try to go around his head again, and I'll vent ya out the airlock myself when we're underway." Francis quickly marched out of the bridge, through the unfinished galley, and out toward the living quarters. He descended the stairs toward the cargo bay and saw no one. He then walked into the engine room where Eri was organizing her tools.

"Hey, Eri? Have ya seen Charlie?"

"I talked to him about twenty minutes ago," she said with confusion. "He asked where Kai was and I told him that he was with you. He headed toward the bridge right after that."

"He never met me on the bridge," Francis replied. "Kai said there was a guy out on the access road and Charlie talked to him. Do you know what he's talkin' about?"

"Yeah, the guy was just standing there watching us. It was really creepy. When Charlie went out there, the guy walked away, but Charlie didn't seem concerned and followed him out toward the dealership. He came back twenty minutes later, but something was off about him. I can't put my finger on it."

Francis sighed. "Thanks, I'll go look for him."

The captain quickly ascended the stairs that led to the living quarters. He peered into Charlie's room, but didn't see anything. He was thinking of any other place he could be when he realized that he heard someone panting.

"Charlie? Charlie, are ya in here?" he asked as he entered the room cautiously. He slowly walked around the desk and saw the first officer there, sitting on the floor with his knees tucked up and his hands clasping them. He was staring at the built-in bookshelves behind the desk.

"Jesus," he exclaimed as he got down next to him. He gently put his hand on Charlie's shoulder. The first officer gasped and looked at Francis with terror. "Charlie? Do ya need any water from *Fire Arrow*?" he asked slowly, emphasizing *Fire Arrow* to help him realize where he was. Light suddenly came back to Charlie's eyes as he blinked. He seemed to become aware of Francis and his surroundings, looking all around as he slowly came back to the present.

"Francis," he muttered as his breathing calmed.

"Yeah, it's me, Charlie, I'm here," he said with a calming voice. "The rain's about to end outside and the workers'll be here soon to finish the bridge and galley."

Charlie's eyes and hands trembled as he stood up. He took a deep breath and looked at Francis with willful intent. "Right, the rain should be over soon. After lunch I can take Ash out for training while you and Eri test the systems."

Francis gently grasped Charlie's shoulders and maintained eye contact. "Yeah, but after we finish our tests and ya finish Ash's training, ya need to help Eri with the overclock system, remember?"

Charlie took another deep breath and nodded. "God, Francis, I was there again. They're getting worse."

Francis gripped Charlie's shoulders a little harder. "You're right here, with *Silver Bow*, and we'll always be here to help ya." Francis would not waste the opportunity and hugged his cousin. He knew that Charlie was not one to hug people. His parents were the same—Tristan and Charlie both hardly received any affection from their parents. "We'll get through this, Charlie. Did that IS3 agent trigger the flashback?"

Charlie gently pushed away and steeled himself. As if a switch had flipped, Charlie immediately returned to his serious and cold self. "He thinks Tristan is making his move. You remember when I secretly started training to be a commando after your dad took me in?"

"I remember," he answered.

"The man that trained me died four days ago, Francis, and the same way Frank died. A completely sudden and unexplained heart attack with nothing showing up on toxicology. IS3 has ruled it an assassination."

"Ya think Tristan's killin' anyone that's ever helped ya?" he asked.

"My contact believes as much, but most of IS3 either believes that he was just assassinated for his involvement in the war or Tristan was sending me a message that I'm not safe," Charlie replied. "If he's right, that means you and the crew are next. I can't just keep it quiet, Francis; they *need* to know."

"We've already talked about this, Charlie," Francis reminded him.

"I don't care, Francis. They have the right to know about the dangers ahead of them."

"We don't know anythin' for certain, Charlie," Francis whispered. "He's probably too fucken busy with all the ops he's in charge of to do anythin' about ya anymore."

"But what if Tristan comes after me? I'm putting their lives at risk just by being on the ship."

"We can't know for certain, Charlie. If ya tell them now, and they leave, who knows how long we'll be behind schedule and over budget. We can't tell them, not yet at least."

"They deserve to know what they're getting into, Francis," he argued again.

"They do, but now is not the time, 'specially when we are getting' so close to finishin' *Bow* and gettin' away from Jessik. And what if ya tell them, they leave, and nothin' happens? That means it was a giant waste, all for the sake of being honorable.

"Be pragmatic, Charlie. You've already done so much trainin' with Ash and ya said she was probably the best we would ever be able to get without tryin' to scout and recruit a seasoned merc. Still don't think she's the best fit, but that was your call. Eri is also a damn good maintainer. If we lose one, we'll lose both. I can't let ya push them away all for the sake of keepin' yourself guilt-free. We keep movin' forward and we'll cross that bridge *if* we get to it, alright?"

Charlie's eyes raced around the room, slowly went still, then looked up at Francis. "Alright, but if I get ostracized for it, I'm going to blame you publicly. I'm not going to take the fall for this."

"I'm the captain, it was my decision, I'll take full responsibility," he said matter-of-factly.

"You better," Charlie spat.

"Better what?" Ash asked from the doorway. The two of them looked at her, both surprised that someone was at the door.

"Is everythin' hooked up?" Francis asked calmly.

"Yeah, I was just trying to find ya to let you know."

"Good. Go tell Eri and we'll start the systems check shortly."

"Understood, Captain," she said as she left.

"If ya train her to be half as good as ya are, Charlie, we won't need to worry."

"You say that now, Francis, but Tristan *will* make his move and he'll do so methodically and with a meticulous plan. She can't be half as good, she needs to be *just* as good."

The two heard her climb the steps towards Charlie's quarters again. "She's ready when ya are," she reported.

"I'll be on the bridge. Ya and Charlie get lunch. You've got trainin' again."

Ash nodded with excitement and looked to Charlie for guidance.

"I'll meet you back here in an hour and a half," he said. "Get some food and change into clothes you don't mind getting covered in mud. We're going to do some hand-to-hand training today."

Ash smiled deviously and left. Charlie looked back at Francis. "I honestly hope you're right, but I'm not optimistic."

# Chapter 24

"You may have been taught hand-to-hand fighting in the militia, but that style of fighting is only for the most desperate of situations in the hopes that your opponent will not have the proper training to fight back," Charlie said as he donned sparring gloves. "But the real world is much less sterile, fair, or predictable than the rubber mats or flat, grassy fields that you're used to. What kind of training and techniques did they give you?"

"We were taught a little bit of Judo and Jujitsu for grapplin'. For strikin', they taught us Kickboxin' mostly."

"Judo and Jujitsu are good martial arts for grappling, but the kinds of techniques and knowledge that they do *not* teach you are going to be the focus of today's training. We'll also work on developing the proper mindset when facing an enemy while unarmed. Let me see some of your strikes."

"Ya got gloves?" she asked, looking at her knuckles with worry.

"No," Charlie replied, "this is the real world. You won't have time to wrap your hands or get proper gloves on. You need to strike properly without those crutches. Bare-knuckle fighting requires tons of technique because you don't have wraps or gloves to soften the recoil of a punch on your hand. You have to be ready and willing to break your hand or knuckles to subdue an opponent."

Ash took a deep breath. "Here goes…"

Charlie held the gloves up for her to hit and she began making her strikes. The mud made her slip and sink, weakening her attacks. "Hit the gloves, Tall Hands. You're not telling the gloves that they're bad girls who need to be punished, they're the faces of men who are trying to stab you."

Ash tried, but the mud made everything difficult. The mud began to cover her shins and calves halfway up to her knees. The effort needed to plant her feet, move, and swing seemed to double with the mud in the pit that Charlie had cordoned off.

"I can't fucken move without sinkin'," the winded security officer complained.

"Then what should you do about it, Tall Hands?" he asked as he slushed and squished around her, seemingly without any additional effort.

"In a situation like this, grapplin' would be best since ya don't have to rely on just your feet."

"Perhaps, but how many of your learned techniques require you to push off with your feet and heels as leverage?" Charlie then removed the gloves and placed them back in the bag. He assumed a Judo stance and stood in front of her. She approached confidently and grabbed him high on the shoulder, but he quickly made a palm strike to her abdomen. She bent over in pain.

"What the fuck," she groaned after a few coughs.

"A mixture of techniques is always the best idea. Strikes can only do so much damage and grapples have their utility to bring your opponent into an optimal position, but you must learn that real world hand-to-hand fighting is different from a spar. You are a woman and unfortunately will always be at a disadvantage when it comes to strength. It's up to you to understand proper technique and to use your mind to overcome your opponents because most of them will be men ready to kill you, not love tap for points.

"You need to understand when you should strike and when will be the best for a grapple. You went high trying to start a Judo throw by using my weight against me, but a good fighter will see right through that and strike you, just like I did. Unarmed fighting in the real world will be brutal and abrupt, and you should respond just as brutally and fast. You must think about the fastest ways to cripple or beat your opponent because they won't fight fair."

Ash nodded with understanding.

"Now forget all that bullshit you were taught and start doing some drills with me."

"Good," Charlie said, "now do it again, Tall Hands, but this time, faster and as if you are actually trying to disarm me."

Ash anxiously nodded her head. Charlie moved quick with the stabbing motion, and Ash was unable to conduct the drill. The knife subsequently and swiftly jabbed her in the ribs.

"Fuck, that hurts," she complained.

"Now imagine if it was a real knife," Charlie responded. "You would be dead, or at least gravely injured. Getting stabbed in the lung is an easy way to die. Let's do it again, and this time, move quickly."

Ash readied herself as she saw Eri leaning against the cargo ramp and observing from a distance. Charlie seized the opportunity and jabbed his protégé with the fake knife again.

"Shit!" Ash exclaimed again.

"Never get distracted," he said. "The battlefield is full of distraction. When you face an enemy, your focus should only be on them, not Eri standing by the cargo ramp."

*How the fucken hell did he know?*

"Do it again, Tall Hands."

The two stared each other down, and Charlie made his attack. Ash managed to start the technique but her follow-through was weak. Charlie didn't let her finish and broke free.

"God damnit, Tall Hands. I'm not going to feel anything, it's my fucking prosthetic. Strike it!"

"I just don't wanna break it. It looks expensive and—"

"I don't care!" he shouted, "You have to be willing to break both your opponent and yourself! You need to fight with every bit of your body, mind, and soul. You have to be ready to deliver *and* receive pain!"

Charlie turned around and quickly punched the hull as hard as he could with his left hand. Ash clearly heard a pop while the hull clanged loudly. She looked to her sister to see if she saw it happen, and the maintainer stared with wide eyes and her hands over her mouth.

Ash's mentor held up his hand and put it close to her face.

"You can't ever pull your punches or the enemy *will* kill you. You must be willing to break every bone in your hand to survive and achieve victory."

The shock of Charlie willingly breaking his hand caused Ash's body and breathing to tremble. The simple fact that Charlie did not recoil, wince, or even hiss with pain left Ash unable to fully comprehend or process what had happened. Charlie stared the security officer down as he went to the bag on the crate and revealed a long rag that he used to wrap his hand.

The first officer returned, picked up the training knife, and stood ready. Ash calmed herself and blocked out the incredibly insane moment that she just witnessed. She readied herself and watched Charlie closely. He lunged, and Ash moved through the drill. She grabbed the wrist as she stepped back, pulled his arm across his body, and swiftly struck her palm against the prosthetic's elbow. The strike was strong and hurt her hand, but she managed to complete the drill.

"Good," he responded as he examined the elbow, "thankfully, I work as a good training dummy. The elbow automatically hyperextends like that to prevent breaks."

Ash bit her lip, trying not to reveal how much her palm hurt from the strike. Charlie gently grabbed her left wrist with his broken hand and examined her palm.

"Nothing broken, but it'll bruise pretty well," he said calmly. His posture and expression had changed. It was no longer cold and harsh. He seemed wise and fatherly, but strangely regretful.

"Remember what I told you: combat is ninety-five percent mental. In order to beat your opponent, you must be willing to overcome your most base of instincts: trying to avoid pain and injury. I'll get a wooden fence post for you to practice your strikes on. You *must* learn to fight against avoiding pain and instead lean into survival at all costs for both yourself and the people you have been charged to protect."

Charlie, still gently holding her wrist, looked into her eyes. "Look at your sister," he commanded. She slowly complied and looked at the mortified maintainer.

"Whenever you have to lean back on this training, remember her. She's counting on you. *I'm* counting on you. If you're not willing to hurt yourself to protect others, it will haunt you for the rest of your life. Don't..."

Ash looked back at Charlie's dark blue eyes. She could see that whatever he was trying to say was difficult to utter.

"Don't fail like I did."

Ash's jaw clenched at the realization that Charlie only learned this lesson the hard way. His training now had context, perspective. These were not simply things to prepare her for what lied ahead, but instead to teach her all the things that he learned through his previous failures.

"Don't fail like I did," echoed in her mind. She could see his regret, his sorrow, his guilt, and in that moment, she wanted nothing more than to hug him, but she knew that it wouldn't end well. She decided to do the next best thing.

"I won't if ya keep teachin' me," she said softly, "I'll do whatever it takes to make ya proud and to know that ya made the right decision bringin' me onboard."

"I hope so," he said as he released her wrist. "Your training is over for today. Unfortunately, I'm not going to be able to finish your training before we set off in two weeks. Between jobs and during long jumps from planet to planet, we'll continue training. In the meantime, I want you to fight your instincts. I'll get a fence post for you to practice fighting against pain avoidance at the end of each day. Just don't overdo it. Once you feel confident that you can bloody your knuckles in one punch and without hesitation, we'll do some more training."

Ash nodded.

"Now go ask Francis if he needs help with anything and don't forget to keep running in your weighted vest. Hopefully, you'll have your armor before we take off, so you need to be used to the weight."

Eri finally took a breath after what felt like an hour. Watching Charlie willingly break his hand just to make a point shocked her. He never made a sound or telegraphed in his expression that he felt pain. She watched the first officer talking to her sister as he gently held her hand, and she could see that Charlie was teaching Ash some sort of valuable lesson.

Ash looked at Eri, and Charlie was clearly saying something to her sister about protecting the crew. When Ash looked back, Eri noticed Charlie's face showed a kind of sorrow that came from regret and guilt.

After a few more words, Ash quickly ran back into the cargo bay as Charlie stood still, looking disinterested at his now swollen hand. Eri walked over and tried to gently examine it, but Charlie recoiled with a hiss.

"Damnit, Eri!" he shouted. "You know it's broken. Why are you just grabbing it?"

"So *now* you're going to act like it hurts?" she asked in confusion.

"Of course it hurts," he replied. She gently grabbed his forearm and lifted it to look at his hand. He either willingly or unwillingly allowed her to continue her examination. "I broke my hand, why wouldn't it hurt?"

"Then why did you conceal the pain?" she asked as she released him.

"It was to teach her that she *has* to fight through the pain and never show weakness in the face of the enemy. If she can do what I just did, then she'll be tough enough for what is in store for all of us."

"What do you mean?"

"Hey!" Francis yelled from the cargo ramp, "Quit chatting and get back to work! Get started on the overclockin', Eri! Charlie, I need your list of weapons and a layout of the armory before end of day so I can get everythin' ordered!"

"Understood, Captain," Charlie replied loudly as he walked past Eri.

Charlie sat in the cargo bay off to the side with pieces of paper and a pencil. The crate he was using as a table had many discarded wads of paper. The list of the weapons was finished, but the pain in his hand distracted him from designing the armory. He needed to design the armory to not only accommodate all of his and Ash's equipment and weapons, but to also allow for expansion for at least three more. The cousins might need to hire temporary mercenaries on certain jobs, so he needed more room.

The biggest issue he faced was also having enough room to store eight normal suits and thruster packs, but he couldn't find the right configuration. The armory was long and narrow, but he hadn't realized until he made a to-scale schematic that the storage lockers he had in mind would be too big for the thin width of the room.

As he chewed on the pencil with frustration, a bag of ice slowly lowered onto his throbbing, swollen hand. He looked up and to the left to see Eri standing over him.

"How goes the designing?" she asked with her hands behind her back.

"Awful," he lamented as he looked down at his schematic. "There's just not a way to fit everything."

"Take your mind off it for a while," she demanded. "I need your help with the drive core. The best part is that you won't need to use your hand and you can just ice it while you help me."

"Alright," Charlie replied with a shrug as he rose to his feet, holding the bag of ice over his hand. The two walked into the engine room. She waited for him to cross the threshold and closed the door behind him. He walked toward the core, getting a better look at it than the day before. His blue eyes scanned the structure up and down, thinking about its potential with the overclock feature.

"First off," she began nervously with her hands behind her back, "I wanted to set a couple of things straight with you, privately."

Charlie turned around and looked at her. He could hear a mixture of embarrassment, nervousness, and shyness in her voice. The change in behavior intrigued him.

"I, uh…well, I went to the store last night after work." Eri grabbed the zipper to her coveralls and pulled it down. As she undid the zipper, Charlie noticed that she was wearing a tank top.

"I know we're going to get life support soon, so this won't really matter that much, but I just wanted you to know that what happened yesterday won't happen again. We've already had two awkward moments and I don't want to have a third."

Charlie smirked. Her shyness bordered on demure.

"It's in the past," he said with a wave of his hand, "I understand why you did it, especially with how hot the ship can be by the end of the day."

"Yeah, but it was still *really* unprofessional," she admitted, averting her eyes from his as she pulled her arms out of her sleeves. "So this is the worst you'll see."

"Noted," he said with an approving nod, "and the second thing?"

"Huh?"

"What's the second thing?" he asked plainly.

"Oh, yeah," she replied as she awkwardly scratched the back of her head.

"I know we both said our piece yesterday, but—"

"You don't need to say anything else, Eri. We both have some issues we're trying to get through, let's just leave it at that."

"No, I can't," she refused as she composed herself. "You said that you would listen and talk to me if I had an issue."

Charlie sighed. "Go ahead," he conceded.

Eri breathed out slowly. "I was mad at myself because everything that happened over those days made me feel like I was in over my head, which made me feel stupid, which made me mad that you made me feel stupid."

Charlie shifted awkwardly. He just wanted to drop the subject, but he could see that she needed to get something off her chest.

"*But*…I was also mad because I was so scared that things would end up like how things did with my parents, and they almost did." Eri paused, looked down at her feet, and took a deep breath.

"You see, if the torch hadn't run out of gas, I wouldn't have found you while I was getting a replacement tank. I…"

Tears welled up inside her eyes and she quietly began to cry. Charlie had a feeling this would happen. He could tell from the night before that things were much deeper than she'd let on.

He knew what he had to do, but he didn't want to do it. Eri, when she was not angry with someone, was a kind person who wanted to help others. She was the type of person who would want a hug.

Charlie walked up to her and awkwardly tried to hug her, but the ice pack fell off his hand as he wrapped his arms around her shoulders. Eri heard the ice bag fall to the floor and immediately pulled away.

"I'm sorry, here," she said as she grabbed the bag and handed it back to him. She wiped the tears from her eyes and tried to calm herself. "You need to ice that broken hand. I told myself I wouldn't cry and here I am already bawling…"

"Listen, Eri, you don't have to—"

"No, I *need* to say it," she dictated as she sniffled. "I was supposed to watch for your return and I just started welding the drive core's frame to the structure. It never occurred to me that Francis had me stay on watch because he knew you'd come back eventually and possibly hurt. I ignored that and thought only about finishing the welds for the drive core. You're a person, and I stopped worrying about you and got lost in my own project."

"Eri, it's not—"

"My mom always sent me messages and I never once thought there was something wrong. I wanted to pass my certification exam so I just kept studying. Days and days went on before I ever *thought* about them. Eleven days passed between their murder and the day I messaged them. It took another three days for their neighbors—their neighbors, not me—to ask for someone to check on them. They had been dead for two weeks, and only then did I realize how self-absorbed I was. I could have finished the drive core and found you hours after you'd already turned cold—or even worse, someone else could have found you the next morning in the daylight!"

"But it didn't happen. I'm not angry and you shouldn't feel guilty."

"But I do, Charlie," she admitted. "When I saw Kai, Ash, and Francis all fight for your life, I just stood there like an idiot and watched when *I* should have been the one helping Kai."

Tears continued to stream down her face as she tried to catch her breath. Besides her erratic breathing, the room was deathly quiet. Charlie wanted to say a few words, but he could not manage to utter them without sounding like a hypocrite. Charlie knew that she felt guilty, and that she believed she needed to voice her guilt.

His own guilt plagued him every day, but no one, not even Francis, would be able to fully understand the horrific decisions he had to make—how they haunted him in his sleep and every waking hour. He didn't voice his guilt because he would commit espionage if it was with anyone other than a therapist, but he also knew that his story was so insane and depressing that no one would want to hear it.

"You almost died because of my negligence," she finally continued as her lips quivered, "and all I could think in that moment was whether or not they would blame me because I wasn't paying attention. You almost died and I almost let everyone down because I cared more about my work.

"My parents bloated and rotted in their house because I cared more about my career than I did about them. I never got to see them one last time because of how they looked after decomposing for two weeks. They wouldn't even let me identify the bodies. They only allowed me to give them a tissue sample for DNA. I told myself I would never let that happen again, and it almost did…"

Charlie pursed his lips. "You don't need to cry on my behalf," he said quietly, "Don't be guilty. There's nothing wrong with making a mistake—"

"It's not just a *mistake*, Charlie—"

"You had your say, now let me have mine," he replied sternly. "I've made many decisions that I've regretted every day since I made them, so I know how it feels, but what happened is nothing more than a lesson. You still found me and you still saved me. Please, just learn from this and don't drag yourself down into dark places with what ifs when there are plenty of opportunities in the future for any of us to actually fuck up. I accept your apology, but it wasn't necessary, Eri.

"When I sat against that crate, I thought I was going to die because of my own actions and decisions. I would have *never* blamed you, even if I knew that you were welding instead of watching for me. If there's anyone you should apologize to, it's Francis. He gave you a job and you were derelict in that duty. Now, wipe your eyes, take a deep breath, and let's move on. You can cry if someone actually dies because we are already starting to fall behind with our work."

Eri nodded quietly and looked down. Charlie readjusted the ice pack on his hand and waited for Eri's instructions. She wiped her eyes and took a deep breath.

"I'm sorry for just throwing that on you," she said meekly. "I just needed to talk to you about it so you would understand."

"It's alright," Charlie said with a raised hand. "Let's get this work done."

"Right," she said with a smirk. She walked over to her tool bench past him and handed him a binder. "Read the instructions starting with twenty-three dot four."

Charlie nodded as he grabbed the binder with one hand. He quietly read the instructions to himself as Eri climbed the ladder to the top of the drive core.

Charlie looked up at her. "Eri," he said.

She looked at him quizzically.

"If you ever need to talk about it again…"

Eri smiled and Charlie could see the small details in her expression that she was grateful that he offered. "I'll let you know…and I promise I won't get so emotional next time."

Charlie chuckled as he looked at her. She seemed to be at peace.

*I hope you find some peace when this is all over.*

# Chapter 25

The monsoon rains returned again the next morning. Ash got up at her usual time and was getting ready when she realized that Eri was not up yet. She knocked on Eri's door and heard her groan, clearly not wanting to wake up. That was usually a sign that Eri had a long night or didn't sleep well.

Judging by how she went to bed at her typical time, her sister didn't sleep well.

Ash remained persistent until Eri finally admitted that she was up and out of bed, then put on some coffee for her sister while she ate a light breakfast. Before she'd started her training with the stoic and fit first officer, she never ate food in the morning; however, with all the physical training she had done in the past weeks, she had grown accustomed to getting some calories in her system before running with her vest on.

Eri slowly emerged from her room with disheveled hair, rubbing her eyes. She then poured the coffee into her portable mug that had been stained from a year's worth of use, added in her typical vanilla-flavored cream with some sugar, and stirred it lazily.

"Didn't sleep well?" Ash asked while putting her dish in the sink.

"Couldn't sleep," she clarified as she closed the lid on her travel mug.

"Excited to work on the engine doing that overwatch thing?"

"Over*clock*," she corrected, "and yes, I am excited, but that's not what kept me up."

"Then what?" she asked with concern.

"I apologized to Charlie yesterday for being so hateful to him. I started bawling in front of him because all of my guilt about

Mom and Dad boiled up to the top. I know it was really awkward for him."

"So what?" Ash asked.

"I could have handled it better, and to make things worse, he told me not to cry on his account and then *thanked* me, despite almost being the reason he died."

"He wouldn't've ever blamed ya, Eri," she replied.

"I just cornered him like that and I know he probably thinks I'm an emotional wreck. He even asked me to drop it, but I just started talking and couldn't stop."

"I don't see what's the problem, to be honest," Ash said with a shrug as she put on her raincoat.

"It's just embarrassing. We *just* started to be friendly again, then I bawled my eyes out and vomited all my feelings and issues onto him, and I know he didn't want to hear any of it."

"I don't think it's 'cause he didn't *want* to hear any of it," Ash clarified as they walked out to the truck in the rain. "He just knew that ya had some unresolved issues and didn't want ya to feel like ya had to explain yourself, is all."

"I'm glad you didn't see it," Eri said as she got in the truck, her hair dripping from the downpour. "He tried to give me the most awkward hug of my life."

"He voluntarily broke his hand against the ship yesterday," Ash said with a chuckle. "Ya think he's the kind of man that would be good at huggin'?"

Eri looked away and out towards the rain. "He has the *capacity* to be gentle and nice," she said in his defense. "He's just got a lot of unresolved trauma. I'm pretty sure he hugged me to shut me up, but I'd *like* to think it's because he cared."

"He cares a lot, just in his own way."

"You've been around him a lot more than me because of your training," she started, "so you've probably seen a lot more of his softer side than me, but the few times I have…"

"He likes ya, ya know," Ash remarked plainly.

Eri immediately turned to look at Ash with shock.

"Well, he likes ya, but not what you're thinkin'," she clarified. "He respects ya and your work ethic. He asked me one time while we were doin' drills if ya were always so carin' for others or if there was something else. He wasn't surprised when I told him that you're a nice girl who just wants her friends to be happy. He seemed satisfied with that answer."

"Does he think I have a thing for him?" she asked.

"I think it was just to make sure that he was correct with his assessment of ya."

"True," Eri agreed, "he can read people like a book."

"Yeah, and then he started teachin' ya how to do it, and now I can't get away with any lie."

Eri giggled.

Ash pulled the truck up close to *Silver Bow*. Eri saw Charlie near where he was the day before when he broke his hand, using a post driver to slowly hammer down a thick wooden post into the mud as the rain poured on him. His left hand was wrapped expertly.

As Eri got out of the truck and Ash raced up the cargo ramp, she saw Charlie's hand slip and he shook it with pain as it slapped against the metal handle. The thought gave her sympathetic pains and made her wince on his behalf. She went up the cargo ramp with her coffee, now finally awake, and stood next to Francis, who sat there enjoying the morning with a coffee of his own.

"Where does Charlie keep the vests?" Ash inquired. Francis walked away to show her as Eri continued to watch Charlie pound the post into the thick mud, his feet slowly sinking along with the post.

Ash ran out into the rain with her vest on and Charlie stopped her. He said some words, but Eri couldn't hear from the cargo bay. Francis joined her as Ash nodded at Charlie and ran off deeper into the junkyard to continue her physical training.

"Is Kai here yet?" Eri asked.

"I'm sure he'll be fashionably on time as usual," Francis declared, "but I *know* ya girls will never be late, especially after that tongue lashin' Charlie gave Ash the first day."

"She used to be like Kai and always walking in as the time would change to the exact moment she was supposed to be anywhere," Eri remarked, "but now she looks at the clock anxiously and wants to be early everywhere, not just for work."

"Well, havin' a mentor like Charlie will do that to ya."

Charlie's hand slipped again and he cried out an explicative. Eri sighed and went toward the newly finished galley. The cooler was still there, and it was full of ice the day before. Some of it would be melted by now, which would make for a good ice pack. With how loudly Charlie had yelled, more than likely he would need one.

She made her way up the stairs towards the living quarters, past the first officer's room full of books, and into the galley. Eri then grabbed a small bag and dunked it into the cooler. The ice had remained mostly solid overnight, but there was still enough water in there to make the ice pack soft against the broken bone. She carefully closed the bag and turned around. She didn't expect to see Charlie immediately behind her, but there he was, standing and holding his now unwrapped hand gently. She shrieked when she saw him and placed a hand over her heart.

"I think I rebroke it," he said sheepishly. A sheepish Charlie was a first for her. His typical seriousness had disappeared as he winced in pain and it was clear he was disappointed in himself.

Eri gently placed the bag under his hand. He put his metal hand underneath hers to allow her to release it. He winced, then walked over to sit down at the table. He sighed with frustration.

"When is the doc supposed to get here?" he asked begrudgingly.

Eri woke her tool and read the time. "Not for another ten minutes or so," she replied.

"Fuck it, I should just go to the hospital and get this looked at," he said as he stood up.

"No," she said as she pointed her finger at him. "Sit down and wait for Kai and let him decide what you should do."

"Judging by how much pressure there is in that part of my hand, I'd say the bones have actually separated."

"You're not a doctor, so wait for Kai to get here," she demanded.

"Technically, he's not a doctor anymore…"

Eri glared at him. They both looked into each other's eyes, locking their wills. Charlie surprisingly submitted and looked away.

"Fine, I'll wait here."

"You just *had* to feel like you weren't useless," she bemoaned, "now I won't get any help from you for a few hours while you go get your hand fixed. Why couldn't you just wait for your hand to recover before you used the post hammer?"

"Because I'm an insufferable cunt who doesn't like sitting around," he assessed plainly. Eri snickered at his self-degrading comment. She didn't expect him to be in a joking mood after rebreaking his hand.

"Thanks for the ice," he said quietly.

Eri looked at him and saw him press his lips together with gracious shame. "Well, at least I know that I'll have someone who will read me instructions for the next few days so I can focus on my work. It'll save me some time. Would have been better if you were able to do more than that…"

"Sorry," he replied through the side of his mouth.

Eri left Charlie in the galley and went to the cargo bay to wait for Kai. Shortly after, the man walked up the cargo ramp.

"Good morning, Kai," she said kindly, "you may want to go look at our first officer. I think he may have broken his hand."

"I am aware of his broken hand," he said as he shimmied his raincoat off his shoulders, "he wrapped it expertly yesterday."

"No, Kai. I think he broke it *again*."

Kai's happy expression immediately turned sour with disappointment. He looked at Francis, who was shaking his head in shame. "Well, at least your beloved cousin keeps me busy."

Eri had Kai follow her to the galley, where Charlie remained seated with his hand on the bag of ice. Kai approached with an annoyed sigh.

"Alright, Charlie, show me your hand."

Charlie slowly lifted his hand away from the bag of ice. The side of his hand had already bruised and ballooned with swelling. Eri grimaced as she saw it.

"It broke in this direction yesterday, but I think it broke upward while I was using a post driver," he explained as Kai examined it. The doctor clicked his tongue at him.

"You will need to go to a hospital and get it pinned. Hopefully, there's enough SCR still flowing through your veins that will make this an easy fix. Come along, Charlie."

Charlie got up and followed Kai with his head lowered in embarrassment. Eri simply shook her head. As Kai reported to Francis about taking the first officer to the hospital, the captain simply responded with, "God damnit, Charlie."

Eri quietly finished her coffee in the cargo bay. Ash ran up as Eri placed the cup down in her usual spot outside the engine room. Even within just a couple of weeks, she had shown massive improvements with her fitness and no longer wheezed when she finished her runs, though she still seemed winded. Her boots and pants were covered in mud, and she made streaks and left globs all over the floor as she slowly walked in circles for her cooldown. Her hair and arms dripped with rainwater, making the mess even worse.

"Ash, can you make a wet mess on another floor?" Eri asked. "You're going to make someone fall and I don't want Charlie to break his hand *again*."

Ash chuckled between breaths. "God, I wish a man would help me make a wet mess on the floor," she jested semi-seriously.

"Gross," Eri said as she rolled her eyes.

"It's easy for ya to say," Ash said as she continued to walk in a circle, "you're the perfect height for most men, and bigger tits than me. I like men taller than me, so pickin's are slim, even in the more populated cities. Hell, I was just as tall as most of the men in the militia."

Eri got closer and leaned in. "Well what about Francis? He's pretty tall and handsome—in a gruff outdoorsman kind of way."

Ash stopped and stared at Eri with a furrowed brow. "Eri, he's married with a kid. Why would I ever do that?"

"What!" Eri exclaimed with shock. "Are they going to join us on the ship?"

Ash's face showed realization. "Sorry, I thought ya knew. Did he or Charlie never mention it to ya?"

"No!" she exclaimed again, "I had no idea."

"Yeah…well…it's a whole story. Don't worry about it."

"Complicated?" she asked.

"Very," Ash simply responded.

Eri sat quietly for a moment and watched her tall sister.

"But if he wasn't?" the maintainer asked with a devious smirk.

Ash looked at Eri and quietly nodded with her eyes closed.

With the morning rain, Francis decided to unpack all of his belongings and place them in his newly finished captain's quarters. Well, technically Charlie had the captain's quarters, since they'd agreed that Charlie should have access to all the ship's systems whenever it was his shift to watch the ship overnight. The captain's quarters also allowed for many more books and shelving. Lastly, the captain's quarters were the nearest room to the armory, and Charlie insisted that he had the room closest to all the guns and armor should the need arise.

The first officer's quarters was still spacious and comfortable, so Francis didn't mind. He was a simple man who had simple tastes anyway. He didn't need bookshelves and he preferred a much more open room like the galley as his meeting room rather than the much more cramped space that the captain's quarters offered. Their exchange of rooms was mutually beneficial.

Francis opened a box and retrieved some of his clothes, hanging them neatly in the closet adjacent to his own wash closet with a shower. The captain's quarters had better accommodations for the closet and washroom, but a full tub meant nothing to him over a standing shower. Even if he preferred having a full tub, it would be too small for his tall frame. The shower was too short as well, but he was accustomed to squatting and bending over in the shower just to get all of his body and hair wet.

He finished the first box and moved onto the second box, where he found a suit that he hadn't worn in years, some other formal attire, and his old dress uniform. He slowly pulled the dress uniform out of the box and stared listlessly at it, then gazed at his ribbon racks. Many of the awards had multiple oak leaf designations to show how many times he had received the award.

Francis had three campaign medals, each with a star to signify that he fought there twice: Kusa, Ankara, and New Tibet. He had the Isolde Revolutionary War Medal, the Frontier Defense Medal, the Good Conduct Medal with two oak leaves, the IFSA Ground Forces Achievement Medal with three oak leaves, IFSA Ground Forces Commendation Medal with two oak leaves, the White Cross with one oak leaf, signifying he was wounded twice, and the IFSA Ground Forces Moon—the third highest award—with an oak leaf and a V designator for valor. Above the ribbon rack stood his assault infantry badge signifying that he was a trained shock troop.

He started the war as a private first class and finished his tenure with the rank of first lieutenant. His first Moon was accompanied by a battlefield commission, giving him the rank of second lieutenant, and his second Moon came only with regret, guilt, trauma, and a pity promotion to first lieutenant.

He stared at the dress uniform with a bittersweet nostalgia. He was proud that he'd served in the IFSA Ground Forces and fought for the liberty that he enjoyed, but the cost that came with that freedom often weighed heavily on his shoulders, exactly where his rank sat.

Francis had been thrusted into leadership without a mentor or guidance from seasoned veterans who had already served stints in the Federal Navy or Federal Marines before joining the revolution. Many of the more grizzled and seasoned veterans were cold, distant, and unwelcoming of new leadership or new peers. They saw them merely as the newest people to fill coffins and never took the time to properly mentor anyone. The military leadership that emerged from the war consisted of mostly men like Francis who proudly took on the role, but often fell short or were so unprepared for their position that they became toxic to their subordinates.

Charlie's experience in leadership was much like his own, and their common experience had helped them to bond after the war. Francis knew that his cousin had burned his uniform, but it wasn't out of hatred of IFSA. Instead, Charlie simply hated the war altogether. He joined the Federal Navy out of a sense of patriotism, became disillusioned, and then broken as a double agent.

"The bastards gave me a fucking medal that you deserved, and all I had to do to earn it was kill my friends," he once said.

Francis didn't find out until just a few months ago that the medal that Charlie received was the IFSA Star, the second highest award available to military service members. Charlie kept his service a closely guarded secret for a long time, but after the events that led to him losing his arm, he'd opened up, albeit slightly and with minimal explanation, about the things he did in the war, specifically joining the Federal Navy and defecting after the Isolde Massacre, or, as the Feddies named it, the "Isolde Incident."

Charlie knew that the Federal Navy was aware of the massive civilian populations in the cities that they bombarded from orbit, and he was vocal about it. Even Feddies who moved out into the Frontier would get at least a mouthful from Charlie whenever they called it an "incident." At the very worst, Charlie would require multiple men to pull him off the offender, who would surely have a broken eye socket by the time he was removed.

Besides his defection and work as a double agent at Federal Naval Intelligence headquarters on Bhutan, Charlie said little else about what he did in the war. The closest thing Francis ever heard in terms of specifics was when he finally started seeing a psychiatrist and therapist about his trauma and learned that talking about his experiences with like-minded people helped him heal. He tried to get Charlie to follow suit, but his cousin only replied with, "I don't think anyone wants to hear about me killing my friends."

Unlike Charlie, Francis did not suffer from constant nightmares or the occasional panic attacks accompanied by flashbacks, and even then, Charlie said he only had occasional nightmares until Tristan and Christie betrayed him.

Francis instead suffered in silence, spending many nights at the end of a bottle with a loaded pistol in his hand. While Charlie was haunted by his actions, Francis had extreme survivor's guilt. Every time he made a bad call or pushed a position recklessly, it was never he who suffered, but his subordinates. He often asked

God why he had to live when so many young men and women had died on his behalf. The alcohol and pistol were the results of the silence that followed the question. Of the few times they ever talked about the war, Charlie simply said, "Better to be a fuckup than a monster…"

That was Charlie's way of vocalizing that he envied him.

Francis finally pulled away from his uniform and placed it far into the back of the closet to hang, forever memorializing his achievements and failures. He moved on to another box. This one was for his nightstand. He opened it and immediately frowned. He slowly removed a picture frame from the box and gently rubbed it with his thumb.

In the picture stood a younger and clean-shaven Francis in a tux next to a beautiful tan woman in a bridal gown. They were flanked by four groomsmen and four bridesmaids. Despite being so close to his cousin, Charlie wasn't in the picture, nor at the wedding. At four years his junior, Charlie was still attending high school during the wedding. Charlie and Francis had met at some family functions and talked, but they didn't really know each other until after the revolution. He had sent an invitation out of kindness, but he knew Charlie would RSVP "no."

Feddie schools usually ended two to three weeks later than Frontier schools. Just three days before the wedding, Francis had attended his graduation with the University of Venture. He had a dual degree in art and graphic design and had planned on being an artist in his free time while he worked as a graphic designer for money. He was always good with a brush and even better with a small paint knife. Oil painting was his favorite, and he had even made some beautiful works before he graduated. Two days after the wedding, the Frontier Systems parliament in Persephone on Isolde declared independence.

If things had worked out as intended, he would have celebrated his tenth anniversary with Maria four months ago. Instead, he and Charlie spent the day together. Despite his seriousness and severity, Charlie always tried to maintain a positive attitude whenever Francis's anniversary came around. Though he tried to cheer Francis up, it only reminded him when things were simpler and happier, especially for Charlie.

Charlie never treated his son, Francis III, "Trey," as just his cousin's son. He always acted like an uncle around him and even called Trey his nephew. After the Armistice, Charlie officially immigrated to the Frontier. He visited often from Patagonia, four days away by FTL, to spend time with Trey. The boy seemed to melt away Charlie's hard and abrasive exterior, and the man would smile from ear to ear whenever they were around each other. However, whenever Trey was ever threatened, Charlie's explosive anger would return like a volcanic eruption.

Francis still remembered the time when they celebrated the first anniversary of Armistice Day in 3192. The City of Venture had held a massive festival in downtown area that had a bunch of parks all connected to each other. The crowd was so dense that it seemed the entire population of the Frontier had come to celebrate. A man even taller and significantly more muscular than Francis had bumped into Trey as he was holding Charlie's hand. At the tender age of four, any bump and fall would make him cry, but Charlie didn't care if it was for attention or not. As soon as Trey began to cry, Charlie pounced on the man and started beating him senseless. It took Francis and three other men to pull his cousin off the man, who was twice his size.

Francis had asked him one time why he was so protective of Trey and other children, and he simply said, "Enough innocent kids died in the war."

"I wish I had been there," Charlie said from the doorway. Francis suddenly snapped out of his memories and saw the stern first officer with a cast over his left hand, leaning against the doorframe. He smiled slightly as he looked at the wedding photo. "I was actually just thinking about Trey the other day. Little shit will be nine in three months."

"Yeah…"

"Sorry, I shouldn't have said anything," he apologized quietly, "I just miss him a ton. Maria, not so much. I never liked her."

"I know ya never liked her," Francis grumbled. "Ya say it any time she's mentioned."

"Yeah, well…at least she only figuratively stabbed you in the back; my bride-to-be *literally* shot me in the back." Charlie looked away pensively. Something else was on his mind, but he was not saying it. Francis had learned by now that if he didn't say it, it was not worth talking about.

"How long until your hand heals?" Francis asked.

"Three days as long as my body doesn't start attacking the SCR and Doc's blood. The hospital doctors aren't as optimistic though. They think my GD will flare up no later than the day after tomorrow. Woe to us few who must heal the natural way."

"I'm sure you've enjoyed the short recovery time though," Francis commented.

"My rib's almost completely healed," he replied, "and the cut and stab are already just scars. Back before SCR, the rib would have taken six weeks, the stab about a month, and the cut three weeks to a month. I'm practically a walking museum of older medicine."

Francis snorted with a smile. The few times that Charlie would jest, it was often self-deprecating.

"I should go help Eri," the first officer said as he left the room awkwardly. Something was definitely on his mind, but he was trying to ignore it, or in the very least keep a good mood in front of it.

# Chapter 26

Charlie was walking down into the cargo bay when Ash returned from *Fire Arrow* with a fresh change of clothes after her shower.

"How'd the hospital visit go?" she asked cheerfully.

"Well aren't you bright this morning," Charlie remarked, "What put you in such a fine mood?"

"Just finally seein' some progress with the vest," she replied. "I may even try out the heavier vest tomorrow."

"Don't start running with that vest until the smaller vest doesn't add anything to the effort you need for the run," Charlie advised, "otherwise, you're just going to injure yourself. You'll get there eventually, but don't rush it like I did."

She slowly nodded in defeat but she seemed to understand.

"Did you see the post out there?" he asked.

"Yeah," she replied slowly, "just dunno if I'm ready for it just yet."

"No one's ever ready to purposefully skin their knuckles or break their hand," Charlie rebuked. "It's not about hurting yourself, but overcoming the instinct to avoid it. Only do as much as you're comfortable with, then go just a tiny bit more. Before you know it, you'll punch it with force, look at your bloody knuckles, and simply do it again."

"Ya make it sound so easy," she said nervously.

"It's only as hard as you make it. Just like running, you have to become uncomfortable in order to progress and become stronger. Remember: strength of mind and body—"

"Comes from overcoming your limits."

Charlie smirked.

"Keep practicing and start on the post sooner rather than later. Procrastination and stagnation are the—"

"Causes of most avoidable failures."

"At least you listen well," Charlie remarked proudly. "You make for a decent protégé, Tall Hands." That was a much stronger compliment than he usually gave. Ash looked at her feet and smiled bashfully.

"Alright, now go help the captain with whatever he needs," he commanded, "I need to help the grease monkey."

"I heard that," Eri said distantly from the engine room.

"Why don't you stop eavesdropping and get the drive core ready?" he asked jokingly.

"Well maybe if you'd actually be useful in here, I wouldn't have to listen to your lectures all the time," she retorted jovially.

Ash chuckled as she ascended the stairs. Charlie walked into the engine room where he saw Eri waiting, feigning impatience.

"Finally!" she exclaimed in jest as she handed him the binder full of paper, "I was starting to age waiting for you to finish your lecture with Ash."

"Well, if I ever have to give you one, I'll be sure to make it a long one," he said as he began reading the instructions. "Thanks again, for earlier."

"Wow, the first officer finally shows more graciousness," she said sarcastically. "Today really is a day of firsts. Maybe he'll smile for me today, but I think I'm being too optimistic."

Charlie looked up from the binder and glared, causing her to giggle. She didn't notice until it was too late that the glare was not playful by any means. His demeanor had changed.

"Anything to keep your hysterical tears away."

Eri gasped. His words were below the belt, and he clearly realized it when he looked away with shame.

"I'm sorry," he apologized quietly, "that was uncalled for…"

She noticed his voice was pained and his expression was solemn.

"Something's wrong," she concluded.

Charlie sat down on the floor against the wall. "I don't want to trouble you about it," he said quietly.

Eri descended from the drive core. "It's no trouble," she said truthfully, "talk to me."

Charlie sighed and looked down. "No, let's just get back to work. Sorry again. That was cruel of me to say, and I know you're embarrassed about everything that happened yesterday. You don't deserve that kind of treatment, especially from me."

Eri could see that his swift apology meant none of his ire involved her, and that he recognized his mistake. It was good enough for her, though his words still stung. She also knew that something was truly troubling him, but she didn't press the matter. The maintainer knew that if he refused twice, he wasn't going to give in on the third time.

"As long as you don't talk like that again," she said authoritatively.

"I won't," he said softly. He quickly got up and handed her the binder. "I'm sorry, I need a minute." He walked out without saying another word.

She peered out of the engine room's doorway and saw him light a cigarette at the edge of the ramp, staying out of the rain. The cigarette slowly released smoke as he looked out pensively. He took another slow drag, looking at the ground, seeming downtrodden. He then removed a folded pamphlet out of his pants pocket and read it as he inhaled another puff of smoke. Eri had seen pamphlets like that before at the hospital. They were typically informational pamphlets that educated people on certain diseases and conditions. Did he learn something at the hospital? What did they discover while fixing his hand? Whatever it was, he was deeply concerned and had failed in his attempt to hide it.

She managed to pull herself away from the doorway before he looked back. It made her wonder, but she knew better than to be nosy, especially with him. She read the instructions and continued her work. A short time later, the first officer returned. He tried to cover his concern with his usual icy severity, but Eri could see through the veil. For some time, he just read the manual, and she followed the instructions.

A few hours passed as they worked nonstop. The rains ended and the contractors arrived a short time later. The noisy sounds of the workers completing their tasks turned into a low drone. Finally, the workers stopped, and they could hear the clanging of feet on the metal floor as most marched out for lunch. They were in the middle of removing a part to rearrange and reinstall, so they both decided to soldier on past the usual lunch break. Before they knew it, the footsteps returned. They had worked through lunch.

Eri had only one more part to remove before she could make the necessary changes, but the bolts were very close to another part. Her ratchet did a lot of the work, but she couldn't reach the final bolt.

"God damnit!" she exclaimed as she threw the ratchet, making a loud clang against the wall and a bang against the floor.

"Just can't reach it?" Charlie asked.

"No, and this is the best angle to get it. I either need to buy a longer arm for the ratchet—which I don't think there is a longer one readily available—grow my arms, or undo all the welds so we can separate these sections."

The first officer stood up, retrieved the ratchet, and walked over to the ladder to get atop the drive core, where Eri sat. He ascended, but Eri shook her head.

"You may have longer arms, but there is no way you're going to be able to reach this," she said. "My arm was all the way down in there, up to my armpit, and I couldn't reach. Your arms are too big for the gap and will never get as low as mine."

"Just let me see," he demanded calmly. He sat next to her on the drive core and peered down the thin gap. He pushed his arm down until it was wedged.

"See what I mean?" she said.

"I do, but I have a party trick that may just work," he said as he gently set the ratchet down on the drive core. "If I lie down, I should be able to reach it, but you're going to need to help me."

He scooted very close to her, making Eri shyness flare with his proximity. Charlie lifted his arm as if presenting it to her.

"You're going to need to disassemble my arm, I'll walk you through it," he said as he looked at her. "I won't be able to do it with a broken hand."

"Okay," she said nervously.

With Charlie's instruction, Eri had managed to remove Charlie's thumb, index finger, pinkie finger, the plates that made the palm and top of his hand, and the plates to the forearm. She had never seen a cybernetic prosthetic arm like his, and she finally understood what Charlie meant when he said that it was heavily customized and modified. The arm below the elbow was now essentially two long, articulable rods that connected to his middle and ring fingers, and the control panel was attached to a chassis connected to the rods.

"Ok," Charlie said, "now you need to press the CPCR button. After that, you need to pinch the bottom and it'll slide off. After that, the hard part."

Eri slowly moved to press the button on the control panel. It made her want to disassemble the entire thing and look at its inner workings. She pressed the button and the panel hissed and popped, but it only shuddered on its housing. He then tilted his arm so that she could pinch the last latch holding the panel to the chassis, which she managed to pull out. The panel could not be removed completely, as it was attached to a power cable that slithered up into his arm's bicep. Charlie straightened the arm out.

"Okay, so now take a small flat head and depress the locking mechanism on the bicep next to the elbow. You'll then have to do the same thing near the shoulder."

Thankfully, there was a small flat head on the ladder, and she leaned backward and grabbed it. She could feel her tank top riding up on her torso and exposing her midsection, and she quickly pulled herself upright before she made things awkward. When she was back to her original position, she noticed that Charlie was looking away respectfully.

*Shit, too late…*

She quickly took her mind off of it. Disassembling his arm had already taken about fifteen minutes, and she was getting hungry. She managed to pop the bicep plate off and saw a power cable coupled just above the elbow were the bicep used to be. Charlie shifted as Eri put the bicep plate on the pile of other plates in a box on the ladder.

"So now for the hard part," he grumbled. "First, press the PNCR button. Then, you're going to need to disconnect the power cable, and it's very tight, so you're going to need to pull as hard as you can. Just make sure you hold on to the power cable after you pull it off because that's the only thing keeping the control panel in place."

Eri pressed the button and heard a clicking sound. She then gripped the power cable and pulled, but it wouldn't budge. She grabbed with both hands, Charlie leaning back to help her. Still, it would not budge.

"Fuck," she said, "you weren't kidding about how tight it is…"

"Put your foot on my leg and use it as leverage if you need to."

Charlie shifted again and lent his left thigh as a base for her to use. She straddled the metal arm awkwardly, her right foot pushing hard against his thigh as she leaned back. Eri then closed her eyes and yanked as hard as she could, using the leverage and her weight, groaning and grunting, the effort causing her to breathe heavily. She bit her bottom lip to keep the pain away from her fingers gripping the textured coupler.

"What the *fuck* are ya two doin'?!" Ash cried out in horror as she saw her sister moaning with Charlie's right arm between her legs.

The sudden shouting frightened Eri and she jumped, causing the power cable to finally free itself. She fell backward onto the drive core. Charlie was also startled by the sudden yelling and looked over his shoulder at Ash.

"You scared the fuck out of me, Tall Hands!" he shouted. He turned and looked at Eri, his tone much softer with concern. "Are you alright?"

Eri groaned as she got up, dazed. She had somehow managed to hold on to the power cable, and the panel dangled from her hand.

"I can't believe ya two!" Ash said. "And on the top of the drive core like a couple of degenerates!"

The two looked at each other in confusion. *Degenerates? What is she talking about?*

The realization hit them both simultaneously, and they roared with laughter.

"It ain't funny! It's disgustin'!" Ash shouted as she stormed out, her face red.

Her words only made the two laugh harder. Eri giggled harder than she had in years as Charlie bellowed. Tears rolled down Eri's cheeks from her laughter and Charlie tried to catch his breath. Of all times, Ash had to walk into the engine room at that very moment.

"She…she thought…" Eri managed to utter between gasps, but she wasn't able to finish her sentence before once again giggling loudly. She didn't know how long they laughed, but any time one tried to speak, they both cackled. Finally, the two managed to calm down, their abs and sides sore from the laughter.

"Anyways," Charlie said as he slowed his breathing, "now that the shit show is over, I can get this bolt undone."

Eri tried with all her might to stop snickering, but she could only manage for a few moments. Charlie took a deep breath to return to normal.

"C'mon, let's focus," he pleaded. "Hand me the ratchet."

Eri finally opened her eyes and exhaled loudly to push the remaining laughs out of her chest. She placed the control panel with the rest of the arm parts, wiped the tears from her eyes and cheeks, and handed him the tool. The two rods that connected to his middle and ring fingers separated and twisted, which allowed him to tightly grasp the end of the ratchet like a claw. It was both horrifying and fascinating to the maintainer.

Charlie got down onto his stomach and reached. His tongue stuck out slightly as he tried to get the ratchet on the bolt. Finally, it was seated and ready to loosen. Eri pulled upward on the large part that she needed to remove so it wouldn't put too much weight on the bolt. Charlie pulled on the ratchet and it creaked, warping slightly as he put force on the end of the long arm, but the bolt remained immovable. Finally, the ratchet lurched with a loud snap. Charlie gasped and looked at her with shock. She sat there silently in horror, hoping he wouldn't say the next words.

"I think I broke the bolt," he said sheepishly.

"Sonofabitch…" she moaned.

"I'm just fucking with you," he said jovially as he finished loosening the bolt.

"You fucking asshole!" she exclaimed with relief and anger. "You scared the shit out of me! That's not funny, Charlie."

Charlie chuckled as the claw moved rhythmically back and forth, the ratchet clicking as he reset the tool. "It was pretty funny seeing the sheer terror on your face," he admitted.

Finally, the bolt was free, and the two moved the part off to the side.

"Well, now we just need to put the arm back together and we'll take a break," Charlie said proudly.

"Is it going to be as much of a pain in the ass as it was disassembling it?" Eri groaned.

"Not as bad actually. It's easier to push in than it is to pull out."

Eri snickered. "Not the first time I heard a man say that to me."

Charlie shook his head with mild disappointment. "The power cable is still a pain."

"Fine, let's put it back together," she begrudgingly said as she descended the ladder.

Charlie put the claw rods together and twisted them with mental commands to reset his arm back to a normal position as Eri grabbed the panel and started to push in the power cable. The two stood tall on the floor and pushed against each other with their leg strength. Just as Eri felt the cable start to push inwards, Francis barged into the room.

"Charlie," Francis said sternly.

Instinctively, the first officer turned his body, but stopped pushing with his legs, causing him to fall backward, Eri landing on top of him with a grunt. Thankfully, Charlie managed to react fast enough to hold onto Eri and keep her steady. If he hadn't, she might have hit her head on the metal flooring.

Eri couldn't help but snicker and got up.

"That's twice now," Eri said between giggles.

"What's this all about?" Francis asked with a growl as he put his hands on his hips. "Ash was so flustered that she had to go outside for fresh air and said it had to do with ya two, so what happened? Why are ya two laughing?"

Charlie managed to control himself for a moment. "To be honest, I don't know whose side of the story would be funnier to hear: ours or hers," the first officer replied. Eri burst into laughter again.

"Well if ya two are just going to giggle like teenage girls, then maybe I'll just ask her," Francis said angrily, clearly still confused with the whole situation.

"Here, Francis," Charlie said as he turned to the captain, "help me put my arm back together so Eri here can get some air herself."

"Maybe I should smoke a cigarette and keep Ash guessing," Eri cackled. "I hear a lot of people smoke after."

Charlie closed his eyes and tried to control his laughter. "Well, Captain, I think the ship just got her first inside joke."

Eri left the room, cackling loudly.

The captain shook his head and started reassembling Charlie's arm. To Charlie's surprise, the captain needed no instruction from the first officer.

"I'm surprised you remember," Charlie said. "You've only helped me do this once."

"It's such a pain in the ass, it's hard to forget, 'specially with that power cable," Francis replied.

Charlie started chuckling, "Well I'm sure Eri will never forget either."

"Can ya please tell me what the fuck is so funny?" he pleaded.

"Can't now. I want to hear your reaction when you ask Ash her side of the story."

Francis shook his head as he returned the rest of the parts back to their designated spots. He closed the access plate to the control panel with a flourish, and Charlie started testing his arm to ensure that everything functioned as it should.

"I guess I'll go ask Ash then if ya won't tell me," he said defeatedly. "It better be worth it."

Charlie smiled. "Oh, it's worth it. I know you'll understand our side immediately and laugh."

"Hey," Francis said as Charlie moved past him toward the cargo bay, "good to see ya smilin' again."

The first officer smiled and nodded before he walked away.

# Chapter 27

Eri cackled through the cargo bay as she walked outside into the sun and felt its warmth. *Silver Bow* was already starting to get hot inside, and the slight breeze outside in the sun felt significantly better. She lay on two crates, letting her fair skin soak up some sun. She enjoyed this kind of weather, but she could only enjoy it in short spurts without getting sunburned. She breathed deep and closed her eyes, the sun penetrating her eyelids and making her vision orange and red rather than black.

The workers were walking back and forth to finish the HVAC, water, and extra electrical work. Their footsteps clanked and clunked up and down the ramp. Despite the ruckus, the sun's warmth and the light breeze coming off the coast soothed her.

Then her stomach growled.

She sat up and looked at the time on her tool when she smelled the familiar scent of Charlie's choice of cigarettes. After looking around, she noticed him standing off to the side by Ash's truck, once again pensively looking at the ground as he inhaled the smoke. Though she was glad to see the stern first officer smile and laugh earlier, she knew that it was only a temporary medicine to whatever plight he was going through.

She wanted to help, even if it was in a small way, and what better way than to have a nice lunch break? She thought about *Indigo* and how she hadn't gone to eat there in a while. She loved their food and its proximity to the beach was ideal for a peaceful moment for Charlie to enjoy.

She got up from the crates and walked over to the first officer as he flicked his cigarette toward a pile of scrap metal.

"Hey," she said, "I just realized I haven't eaten all day. You hungry?"

Charlie looked out into the distance and then back at her. "I could eat. What are you thinking for lunch? All the food is gone already, so we'd have to go out and get some for ourselves."

"Even if there was food, I'd rather go get some seafood. You like seafood?"

"Very much, actually," he said as he faced her.

"Great. I know a place only locals know about. Kind of a hidden gem. I'll take you there."

Charlie gestured toward Ash's truck and Eri jumped in the driver seat. As she adjusted the seat and mirrors to her liking, she saw Charlie composing a message to Francis on his tool to let him know that they would be gone for lunch. Once adjusted, she turned on the truck's power cell and lowered the top.

"You may like the rain, but the sun is my thing," Eri said with a smile as she grabbed a pair of sunglasses out of the center console. They drove for a while with the top down, the wind and road noise the only sound between them. Charlie glanced over at her a few times, observing her fiddle with her hair to find the perfect way to keep it from hitting her face in the wind.

He wouldn't let his gaze linger for long, though. While he found her demure, beautiful, and intelligent, he saw her as only his friend. The thought of being more than that had crossed his mind early on, but he wasn't ready for a relationship. He'd probably never be ready for a relationship after his past two.

Sometimes he wondered if he was cursed when it came to women. Both of his previous relationships with women that he loved ended in tragedy, and his heart had grown acrid and cold since becoming an adult. He would manage to find himself in a woman's bed from time to time, but the idea of a relationship rather than simply finding ways to satiate his male urges frightened him at times. It wasn't the commitment that frightened him, but two things that kept him away. The first was the idea of Tristan using the relationship against him. The other was what the doctors told him that morning.

What confused him though was that she was, somehow, still single.

He was more than willing to be friendly to his crewmate. He enjoyed her company and her strong care for others, even if unwanted. He could see that she felt duty bound to care, and he respected her devotion to making others happy. What really cemented his friendship with her was her keen mind and how quickly she was able to read people after only a single lesson. He planned on asking her if she wanted to people watch with him the next time they went out to the bar with Francis and Ash. He thought it would be quite fun to examine people together like he used to so many years ago with Zoreah.

"Something on your mind?" she asked as they drove through the city's center.

Charlie turned and looked at her, slightly dazed as he came out of his thoughts. He blinked a couple of times and looked back out the side of the truck. "Yeah, but nothing worth talking about."

They finally arrived at a parking lot next to the beach. Eri chose a spot and shut off the truck. They got out, and Eri walked over to a food stand painted in a beautiful bluish purple. Charlie followed quietly, still absentminded.

"You're going to love this place," she said as she turned to him with a smile.

The two waited in line for some time, taking in the aroma wafted by the ocean breeze. When they finally got to the order window, Charlie looked at the menu. Eri, however, had other ideas.

"Hey! Can I get two lobster rolls with garlic butter, two fish tacos, one side of fries, and two Mendisas, please?" The woman behind the counter gave her the total, and Charlie pulled out his wallet. Before he had a chance to pull out the cash to pay, Eri slapped his metal hand down authoritatively.

"This is my treat, put your wallet away," she demanded.

Charlie smirked slightly and returned the wallet to its normal place. The two stood by the pickup window, Eri swaying happily as she clasped her hands behind her back. A short time later, their order was ready. Eri grabbed one bag along with one of the pilsners and Charlie grabbed his.

"We'll eat here and then go back," Eri said as they walked back to the truck. "Might as well enjoy the beach while we're here, right?"

Charlie finally understood what she was doing. She had taken notice of his downtrodden demeanor in the wake of the news he received that morning while in the hospital and was trying to raise his spirits. Once again, Eri was showing how much she cared, even if she was trying to be subtle about it. Gestures like these were what initially stopped him from keeping her as far away as possible.

He often kept people much further than arm's reach because of his trust issues and guilt, but he let his guard down around her at times because of her kind nature. He knew it and allowed it, but only briefly. Whenever he felt she got too familiar or too close, he would push her back to arm's length again.

Eri got up on the truck and sat on the back of the cab where the roof panels sat underneath the back panel. The breeze gently caressed their backs as the sun warmed their faces.

"Try the lobster roll first," she demanded.

Charlie obliged and silently took a bite of the sandwich. The lobster was perfectly cooked and seasoned. The sauce that smothered the meat was packed with roasted garlic. An exceptional sandwich. He hummed with delight and satisfaction as he took in the flavors. Eri smiled as she heard and saw his approval and continued eating. Charlie then opened the pilsner and took a sip of the beer. Nothing truly special, but it had a lightness to it that complimented the richness of the garlic and butter sauce.

He moved on to the fish taco while Eri sat the fries between them and took a few. The taco had an excellent flavor of citrus with a slightly spicy kick. The meat was flaky, juicy, and tender, and the lettuce was crunchy and fresh. He believed the meat was mahi-mahi, one of his favorite fish. He took another drink from his beer as he tried the fries. Seasoned well, but not on the same level of flavor as the sandwich and taco.

He lifted his beer with a slight smile and looked at Eri, waiting for her to toast with him. It took her a moment, but she moved quickly once she realized. She held up her bottle in return.

"To the ship's first inside joke, may there be many more," he softly but jovially toasted. Eri chuckled as they clinked the bottoms of their bottles and drank.

"Thanks for taking me here," he said after a brief pause.

"Wow," she said jokingly, "a thank you, twice in one day?"

He glanced at her through the side of his face and smirked, then looked down at the bed and quietly drank the rest of his beer. The two sat there silently and slowly finished their food and drinks.

The two returned to *Silver Bow* sometime later. The workers scurried about the ship, moving crates, panels, and various other things. They immediately went back to work in the now sweltering engine room. The temperature in the room was not nearly as high as it was in the days preceding the monsoon rains, but the humidity that came with them made the room feel hotter, and both sweated profusely for the rest of the afternoon.

While Charlie waited for the maintainer to finish removing a part, he flipped through the pages of the binder, wondering how much more work was involved to get the engine prepped for the overclock feature. His eyes widened more and more as the pages continued. When he finally reached the end, he placed one of his fingers in it to mark his place. He then went backward in the binder to see where they had started. The outlook was grim.

"Eri, I don't know if we're going to finish this anytime soon…"

"What makes you say that?" she asked without looking away from her work.

"Well, I just went to see how far we've gotten into the section versus how far we have to go. It doesn't look too good."

Eri removed the part and looked up at him indicating the difference in pages. From what it appeared, they were only a quarter or one third through the setup.

"Francis told me that he wanted this done by end of day, the day after tomorrow. There's no way we'll get this done by then unless we also work well into the night today, tomorrow, and the next."

"Then it sounds like we'll just have to work well into the night to get it done," she said with a shrug.

"I don't think you understand how much work this is, Eri," he clarified, "Every waking moment besides meals would have to involve working on it. That's too much work for you."

"Well I'm glad you're actually acknowledging who is doing all the work around here," she joked.

"Eri, you'll—"

"Be fine," she interrupted. "Now what's the next step?"

Charlie smirked, admiring her tenacity and work ethic. He looked down at the manual and read the next step.

Eri continued to work as Charlie read the instructions to her, one by one. Before they knew it, they had progressed much further than he'd anticipated. Though the outside air started to cool and the noise from the workers had ended, they continued. The engineering compartment remained hot despite the cooler air starting to seep in from outside, and the two simply continued to sweat. Before long, Francis and Ash announced their presence.

"Hey ya two," Francis said happily, "Kai went to the casino, but we're goin' to get some dinner and drinks, ya wanna join us?"

"Can't," Eri replied, "too much work to do in too little time. We'll be in here for a while."

Francis looked at Charlie, who simply waited for them to leave. "Are ya hungry? Do you want us to get anything for ya?"

"Nah, we both ate pretty late in the afternoon. I know I won't be hungry for at least a few hours. What about you, Eri? Need any food?"

"Nope," she answered as she loosened a bolt, "when you get a second, Charlie, I'm going to need the fourteen mil socket."

Charlie looked at the captain, waiting for him to ask or say anything else before he grabbed the socket.

"We'll see ya later then," Francis said with a shrug. The captain and security officer left and the first officer and maintainer got back to work.

Eri and Charlie continued to work as the night wore on. Occasionally, Charlie would light a cigarette as he waited patiently for Eri to finish removing or placing a part. She noticed that he was smoking less frequently while working with her despite the long periods of boredom for him. She wondered if he did it for her sake and to not fill the room with smoke. She wouldn't have minded; many maintainers smoked while they worked and she had smoked a cigar on occasion, so it never bothered her.

Charlie often lifted the heavier parts with his metal arm to help, or would hold bolts for Eri, but the job was mostly just for her to complete, though Charlie often offered to assist her when he could. Between, he simply read the instructions, which helped Eri more than Charlie would admit. His ability to read and understand the material helped her work more efficiently.

At one point in the night, she realized that she needed Charlie's claw again. She helped him disassemble the arm and started chuckling as she began.

"I swear to god, if Ash walks in here while we do this again," she said as she clicked one of the buttons on the control panel, "I'm just ending it for the night because I won't stop laughing."

Charlie was able to reach the part with the claw and gently removed it. She reassembled the arm and immediately went back to work.

The two soldiered onward, working until they heard laughter and footsteps. They both stopped and realized if Ash and Francis had returned from the bar, it was very late. They looked at each other in shock and woke their tools to see the time. It was just past eleven. Charlie set the manual down on the floor and walked out into the cargo bay as Ash and Francis finished their ascent up the cargo ramp.

"Are ya two *still* working?" Ash asked in shock.

Charlie scratched the back of his head. "I guess we lost track of time…"

Eri walked out of the engine room, disheveled and sweaty.

"Oh my God, ya *have* been working this entire time," Francis said in astonishment. "I never thought I'd have to say this as captain, but I'm going to have to order ya to stop workin' for the night."

"Can we at least finish this last part?" Eri asked. "We're almost done." She may have wanted to finish, but her stomach protested loudly enough for everyone to hear. She looked down at her feet, her face turning bright red.

"I think your empty stomach is even orderin' ya to stop," Francis remarked jokingly.

"It's late, Eri," Charlie agreed, "I'll take you home."

The first officer walked out to his car, the maintainer dragging her feet with embarrassment. The two got into the car and drove off. The streetlights passed by as they silently headed back to the apartment. Charlie glanced over at her halfway to the apartment.

"Are you as awake as I am?"

Eri sighed with frustration, "Yeah…"

"How about a late bite to eat? This time, it'll be a hidden gem I know and it'll be *my* treat."

"Ten shen I've already been there," she said confidently, "but I'm down for that."

"I can almost guarantee you've never eaten at this place, or knew it existed," he replied.

Eri looked at him with narrowed eyes. "Hundred shen, then?"

Charlie snorted. "Sure, but I don't need your money," he retorted, "instead, you have to do maintenance on my arm. I'm pretty sure the servos have something stuck in them. Felt a hitch when I pulled that transformer out for you."

"Well if we're betting with work, then I'd rather make it worth my while," she replied with a smirk.

"What do you have in mind?" he asked as he pulled into the apartment complex.

"You teach me how to fly *Fire Arrow*," she wagered resolutely.

He slowly turned to her as he came to a stop in front of the apartment. They locked eyes, their wills fighting against each other.

Charlie said nothing and only lifted his hand for a handshake. She silently obliged and opened the door.

"I'll be back in about thirty minutes," he announced.

"You can start teaching me how to fly once we finish the drive core," she said as she went to the door.

Charlie returned just as he said, freshly showered and changed into clean clothes. Ash had returned by then and her truck sat in the driveway. He didn't wait for her to emerge and instead started honking the horn, knowing it would embarrass Eri. Shortly after he honked, the door was thrown open. She closed the door and Charlie honked again.

"Stop honking, asshole!" she loudly whispered. "You're going to wake up the neighbors!"

"Fuck it," he retorted, "it's not like they're going to have you for a neighbor much longer."

"It's not about that," she said as she got into the car, her hair still damp, "it's about being nice. I know it can be really hard for you sometimes."

Charlie snorted and drove off. He was wearing the same kind of clothing he always did, but Eri was wearing different street clothes than he was used to seeing her in. Before, she always wore a simple shirt with pants, but she instead wore a spaghetti strap that was just short enough to show some of her abdomen. He didn't want to give away anything, so he didn't warn her that it would be much colder where they were going.

They drove for a short while, Charlie glancing over at her as she confidently sat in the seat, observing her surroundings. Her exposed chest rose and sank with her breathing and her fair skin shimmered in the light of the passing streetlamps. It was like a transformation every time she changed out of her coveralls.

Her confidence waned as he took a familiar route. She looked around nervously, realizing that they were heading back to the ship.

"Are we going back to *Silver Bow*?" she asked. "If you're going to take me to the ship's galley, that doesn't count and the bet is off."

Charlie chuckled. "That's actually kind of a clever," he admitted, "I wouldn't have thought about it."

"So are we going back to the ship?" she asked nervously.

"We have to take *Fire Arrow* to this place," he clarified. The answer clearly bothered her, he could see it. He smirked deviously.

They arrived at the ship. Francis stood in the cargo bay and waved as they passed. Charlie must have informed him of their little bet. The way Francis waved made Eri more nervous that she would lose their friendly wager. The two exited the car and got inside *Fire Arrow*. She eyed him as he grabbed his duster and donned it before getting in the pilot's seat. It was cooler outside, but it wasn't *that* cold. Why would he wear it? Was it a bluff, or did he actually need the duster? The more she thought about it, the more butterflies entered her empty stomach.

Charlie started the engines and VTOL system and immediately lifted off, not even asking Corinth control for permission. He flew southeast toward the shallow mountains at the edge of town opposite of the beach. She felt a little more confident with the direction. She had been to a few of the restaurants out in the mountains with Ash whenever they went on hikes in the past.

Charlie flipped a switch and pressed a few buttons on his console. Above his head, the communications monitor said *"CMLP2."*

"Corinth Mines Landing Pad Two, this is Foxtrot Alpha Three-Nine-One-Three, requesting permission to approach and land, over."

"FA Thirty-Nine Thirteen, CMLP2, I do not have you on my schedule, over."

"Roger, Pad Two, this is an unscheduled flight. We are requesting landing for one hour to get some Carol's, over."

Carol's? *What's that place? I've never heard of it!*

There was a short silence over the radio.

"FA Thirty-Nine Thirteen, you have permission to land on Pad Two for one hour, over."

"Roger, Pad Two, on approach."

The first officer gracefully approached the landing pad on top of the cliffs that the mines dug into. The landing pad was made for smaller ships, far too small for *Silver Bow*. He landed *Fire Arrow* softly on the pad and powered down the ship to auxiliary.

He got out of the pilot's seat and pointed at her with fake concern. "Oh, do you not have a coat or jacket? It gets cold and windy up here at night."

Eri sneered as she folded her arms. "So, we're getting Carol's, huh?" she asked.

"You forgot who you're talking to," he said with a grin, clearly seeing right through her lies. "Perhaps you could enlighten me on the type of food they serve at Carol's."

Eri's looked away with frustration, her arms still folded.

"That's what I thought," he said. "You can do maintenance on my servos tomorrow evening after work."

"Yeah, yeah," she replied with annoyance as the ramp lowered. The night's chill hit her as wind pounded against her exposed skin. He put his hand on her upper back and ushered her to the elevator. They got inside quickly and Charlie pressed a button for many floors below them. The elevator hummed as they descended and warmed Eri's skin from the chill.

The elevator finally came to a stop and the doors opened. As soon as a crack appeared between the door, her nose was filled with the aroma of green onion, sesame, garlic, and chili. There were a few night shift workers in the small food court, where she could see the sign for Carol's not too far in front of them. Charlie led the way and Eri followed with curiosity. Unlike Eri, Charlie allowed her to look at the menu, but she didn't bother.

"I ordered for you last time, you do the same for me," she said happily.

"How well can you handle spice?" he asked.

"I can handle some spice, but not a whole lot," she admitted.

"It's not traditional, but do you want meat?"

"Oh, uh…let's just go with the classic. Chicken."

Charlie nodded and walked up to the counter, Eri right behind him and looking around his shoulder. There was a man behind the counter who silently waited for their order.

"Let me have two re gan mian, one with chicken at a three and one with steak at a seven. I also want two classic bao buns, and two of that iced cherry green tea that you make." The man behind the counter gave him the total, and he paid with cash, as he always did. "Can you also let Carol know that Charlie Menillo is here? I know she's in the back making those alkali noodles right now." The man nodded and promptly left.

*Bao buns! I haven't had any in forever! Did Ash tell him that I liked bao, or is this just a huge coincidence? I've never had green tea though...*

She followed him over to the pickup window, and they waited patiently. After a short time, a woman in her late fifties, perhaps early sixties shuffled out from the kitchen.

"Charlie, darling! How are you, sweetie?" The woman rushed at him with her arms wide open, ready to hug. Surprisingly, Charlie bent down to the little woman and reciprocated. She had never seen him happily hug anyone before, and yet this little old woman just got the easiest hug out of Charlie.

"How are you, Mama?" he asked softly as he pulled away. A genuine smile emerged from his face.

*Mama? That can't be his mom...*

"Oh, same old, same old," she said with a wave of her hand. She glanced over at Eri and quietly gasped. She turned to Charlie with a look and nudged him with her elbow. "And who is your cute little girlfriend here?"

Charlie chuckled nervously and rubbed the back of his head. "She's just a friend, Mama," he reassured her. "This is Eri—she works on the ship with Francis and me."

"Hello," Eri greeted awkwardly.

"She's a cutie," she said to Charlie with another nudge. "Why the hell are you keeping her in the friend zone? You should be asking her out."

"Carol..." he growled through his teeth. Eri giggled and noticed a slight red coloring to Charlie's cheeks. Charlie blushing was probably the last thing she expected to see that day. Carol was starting to embarrass him, like a doting aunt who couldn't read a room.

"I'm just saying, you haven't been with a woman in years, and it's time you got back in the saddle. I know that Christie girl broke your heart, but you can't sulk forever."

"Drop it," he commanded with a glare.

"Where are my manners?" she asked rhetorically as she extended her hand, "Carol Sho-Chang."

"Eri Bezek," she said with a smile as she shook Carol's hand. "So how do you two know each other?"

"Through a wonderful woman in Athens named Michelle," she replied.

"Wait…*the* Michelle?" she asked Charlie.

"The very same," he replied.

"It was a little over three years ago, I think. I was getting all ready for my youngest daughter's wedding and I was so indecisive that my appointment ran into Charlie's. He was there getting a suit for some special occasion. You should have seen him; he was so nervous that he looked like a teenager getting his first tux for a school dance."

"Carol…" Charlie growled again as Eri giggled.

"Anyways, we talked for a little while as Michelle worked with both of us and I let him know about my humble restaurant here in the Corinth mines. Ever since he's been in Corinth, I've seen him at least once a week."

"That's really sweet, actually," Eri said with a smile. Charlie glanced away.

"Oh, well here's your food," Carol announced as two bags appeared at the pickup counter. "Give me another hug, dear," she said as she leaned in toward Charlie. They embraced again lovingly. "Are you going to take her up to the roof? Such a romantic view of Corinth from there…"

"Carol…" he snarled as she cackled and playfully slapped his chest.

"If you want some advice, dear," Carol said as she handed Eri her bag, "you're going to have to make the first move."

Charlie snatched his bag with a groan and marched toward the elevator. Eri giggled as Carol cackled at his embarrassment. She followed Charlie as he breathed deeply, trying to regain his dignity. He pressed the button and stared at the doors, waiting for the elevator to return. It was endearing to see Charlie that way, even if it was at the expense of his dignity. She was glad to see yet another side to him.

The doors opened and they quietly got inside the elevator. Charlie pressed the button for the roof. He sat his bag down and removed the duster. He awkwardly put it over Eri's shoulders, warming her instantly. The mixture of the leather and the body heat that had been stored inside was soothing and made her feel safe.

He sighed deeply. "Of course Carol had to ruin it with her insinuations…"

"I like her," she said as she instinctively pulled the duster closer, keeping the warmth inside the coat. "She is like that aunt that loves on everyone but doesn't understand what 'discreet' means."

"Yeah," he agreed, "and she often overshares."

"Why do you call her 'Mama?'" she asked.

"A conversation for another time."

Eri nodded as the doors opened, the cold breeze hitting her face. She had been so concerned with getting out of the cold wind earlier that she hadn't even the incredible view of Corinth at night.

"How romantic," she said sarcastically. Charlie rolled his eyes as he sat down. Eri sat down next to him, ensuring that the duster kept her warm. The landing pad was a peaceful refuge, but not necessarily quiet. The wind blew strong enough to make noise in her ear, and the machinery working at the mine overnight created a constant drone.

"Have you ever had re gan mian?" he asked.

"I don't know what that is," she admitted.

"Dry noodles," he replied as he took his bao bun out of the bag, "it's from Carol's family's homeland back on Earth. It's a simple dish loaded with flavor."

"Well, I know bao buns very well," she said as she pulled hers out of the bag, "my mother used to make them when I was young."

"You'll like these then," he said as he took a massive bite.

Eri bit into the bao. All the familiar textures and flavors came back to her. The dense yet airy dough was just as she remembered, and the filling was sweet and savory with just the smallest hint of spice on the back end. It wasn't the same as having her mother's bao, but Carol made a close second. She apprehensively tried the iced cherry green tea, and its quality and taste surprised her. It was just the right amount of sweetness.

She noticed Charlie had already finished his bao and was starting to fiddle with his noodles, plumes of steam coming off the dish in the cold air. He glanced at her and then refocused on his bowl.

"You have to mix the ingredients yourself," he instructed. "The difference between good and great re gan mian is the noodles, and Carol makes the best alkali noodles."

She finished her bao and sipped her tea as Charlie took his first big slurp of noodles. He closed his eyes and hummed with pleasure. He clearly loved the noodles, and Eri hoped she would feel the same. She began to mix the ingredients on top of her noodles just as Charlie was finishing his. He always ate fast, so it was not unusual for him to finish so quickly.

Charlie drank some of his tea and leaned back on his hands, taking in the view. Eri finished mixing the ingredients and took a slurp. Charlie's assessment was spot-on: simple but packed with flavor. She could taste the green onion, garlic, sesame, and chili oil. Her mouth tingled and burned with the spice. It was almost too much for her, but she soldiered on. If she could barely handle a level three spice, she would die trying Charlie's level seven.

She took another slurp and looked at Charlie. His expression was slowly shifting from contented to somber. Whatever was on his mind earlier that day, it had returned. She continued eating her noodles and picked out the pieces of chicken, enjoying the juicy meat. Once she finished her noodles, she finished her tea to help mitigate the spice. Her lips and mouth tingled. She looked around and noticed a bin near the elevator. She grabbed the bags wordlessly and threw them away. Charlie hadn't moved or said anything since he leaned back, but she noticed him shifting slightly.

She sat back down next to him and took in the view, trying to keep his solemn demeanor out of her mind to enjoy the peaceful moment and wrapped the duster tightly around her body to stave off the cold breeze. The lights throughout the town were distinguishable enough for her to figure out the streets and intersections. In the distance, she could see Bullseye! and Blackout on opposite sides of town. It was too dark over in the junkyard, so she couldn't see *Silver Bow*.

Charlie finally broke the relative silence between them as he sat up. "Thanks again for earlier," he said softly, "I know you were trying to cheer me up."

She looked over at him. He had a frown that cut into his face, and his eyes looked out into the distance at nothing.

"You looked like you could use some cheering up," she replied as she continued to fidget with the duster nervously.

Charlie didn't respond, his frown and distant stare still etched onto his face. He was deep in thought.

"I have traumatic encephalopathy syndrome," he said. "If you remember the first day we met, I had an appointment with the doctor. I got the results back this morning when they pinned my hand."

"What's that?" she asked with concern.

"TES is a type of brain damage caused by trauma. It can lead to dementia, depending on the damage."

Eri's mouth opened slightly with shock. She saw the pain on his face and wanted to give him a comforting hug. News like that would be difficult to hear, and even a hardened man like him needed a reassuring embrace after hearing news like that. She dared not move though.

"Is it treatable…or fatal?" she asked.

"It can be both," he answered with a shrug, "again, just depends on the damage."

"And how extensive is *your* damage?" she asked nervously.

Charlie slowly turned his head and looked at her. His blue orbs radiated fear and helplessness. His gaze stabbed her like knives. She already knew his response wasn't going to be hopeful.

"They gave me ten to fifteen years on the outside," he replied with a trembling voice, "They suspect seven."

"Charlie…" she muttered sadly, "I'm so sorry…"

It took everything in Eri not to run to him and hold him.

"Yeah…" he replied. He slowly looked out to the view of Corinth. "I haven't even told Francis yet…"

"Too hard to say?"

"Too difficult for *him* to hear," he said, "I'm all he's got left, and he me."

Eri's lips pursed as she saw him silently deal with his own mortality. To know that you most likely won't live to see your forties…it would have crushed her.

"Anyways," he said as he collected himself, returning to his normal seriousness like the flip of a switch, "we need to leave. I only requested an hour." He stood up, grabbed his tea, and lowered the ramp to *Fire Arrow*.

Eri couldn't believe how stoic the man was—even after hearing about his impending doom, he never once wavered. She would have cried for hours after telling someone, yet here he was, getting inside *Fire Arrow* without even a sniffle. She followed him inside the ship and he raised the ramp.

The inside of *Fire Arrow* was warm. He had kept the auxiliary systems running while they were outside, so the interior remained at a comfortable temperature. She removed the duster and placed it gently on the bunk. Charlie restarted the drive core and began his preflight checks as if nothing happened.

They flew away and Eri checked the time on her tool. It was one in the morning. She started to feel sleepy, more than likely caused by the food now nestled comfortably in her tummy. She suddenly had an idea.

"Hey Charlie?" she asked.

"Hmm?" he hummed as he looked over his shoulder.

"It's pretty late now and I would rather get as much sleep as possible. Can I sleep in the ship tonight? I'd rather make up for the commute with more sleep."

Charlie nodded once and looked back out the wind screen. "Just make sure you ask Ash to bring you some work clothes. I'm sure you wouldn't want to work on the engine with what you're wearing right now."

"Right," she said as she composed a message for Ash.

They landed a short time later. Charlie shut down everything except for auxiliary and took his duster off the bed.

"If you need to, you can adjust the temperature on the console on the left side," he said as he lowered the ramp.

"Oh, no, this is your bed," she said nervously, "I can sleep in my new quarters on *Silver Bow*."

"It'll be too cold inside the ship, and I'd rather you have some relative privacy since all the doors are still open in the living quarters," he replied. "Just sleep here and I'll sleep on a cot in *Silver Bow*."

Eri shifted uncomfortably. "Okay, thanks." Charlie walked down the ramp. "Charlie?" she blurted. He slowly turned around. "If you ever need to talk about it…"

Charlie didn't move or say anything. He simply looked at her distantly. He finally looked down and nodded as he left.

# Chapter 28

Ash sipped from her beer as Francis mirrored her. Both had just finished their dinner, but the recent events with Jessik, Charlie and Eri in the engine room, and Charlie breaking his hand had sobered Ash in a way that she never thought was possible. She was starting to shy away from hard liquor and mixers and opted instead to follow Charlie's example of simply having a few beers for a mild buzz and leaving it at that. The last thing she needed was to be drunk when the crew needed her most.

Since she and Francis had been talking more during their off time, they had talked about his drinking habits and how much he used alcohol to keep his demons away, but Francis had started to also stay away from liquor and followed Ash with simple beer. Liquor was reserved for celebrations now, and she was glad that talking with the tall and handsome captain was starting to help him change for the better.

Francis chuckled. "I know it probably looked horrifyin' from your perspective, but it's still funny as shit."

"Not that god damn funny," she grumbled as she looked away. "Looked like your cousin was finger blastin' my sister from the top of the engine."

"Well, *they* thought it was funny as shit," he replied with another chuckle.

"Yeah, yeah…"

"It all worked out in the end though," he said as he sipped his beer, "saw Charlie actually smile for the first time in a long while."

"The more ya tell me about him, the more I start to see the little things," she said as she watched the bubbles rise. "The thing with his arm—his brother and fiancée tryin' to kill him—it makes a lot more sense why he's so damn guarded. The fact his parents never showed affection to him and why he's so cold and distant but does his best to tell me that he's proud of me. Him tellin' ya that he had a lot of regrets in the war and then him tellin' me to not fail like he did…it gives me perspective that I need."

"I'm just tellin' ya what I know," he explained. "Still don't know half of the shit about Tristan and Christie and how that all went down."

Ash sipped her beer and looked at the frosted glass distantly. "He told me the other day that in order to be a good guardian, I had to be a monster sometimes. Ya know what that's about?"

"Besides him havin' to do shit for Jessik? Dunno."

"What did he do for Jessik before y'all started buildin' the ship?"

Francis sighed heavily as he looked at the table. Ash could see in his eyes that he was gathering his thoughts and fighting against his own guilt. He had mentioned before that Charlie worked for Jessik to keep the don away from him and his dad, but he had never gone into any detail.

"My dad accrued almost half a million shen in gamblin' debts. He went to Jessik for a loan to pay back the bookies, and Jessik asked for interest in return and for my dad to do some jobs for him. One of which was storin' some of Jessik's and his dad's products. They were big sellers for hard drugs, and he wanted to expand his family's empire onto Venture. He told Dad one day that he needed him to start payin' off his debts, and he was so ashamed that he asked Charlie to help him."

Ash watched him quietly. She could see on Francis's face that Charlie's situation with Jessik still weighed heavily on him. She wanted to hold his hand to offer him some strength. Despite knowing he was married, she was starting to feel something for Francis, and she knew a lot of it had to do with his gentle nature. She remembered Charlie quoting something the morning the drive core came in. Something about being violent making a man gentle. Despite being a hardened heavy assault infantry veteran of the war, their talks revealed a big softie under that smile of his.

They had spent so much time together both during the day and in the evenings that she'd started to notice the small changes in his smile, and when the smile was fake or real. It was usually fake when the smile was big. Whenever he only showed a little of his white teeth, she knew that it was genuine.

"So after that, Charlie would go to Athens once or twice a month and help Jessik with simple drug runnin', then he started bringin' the shit back to Venture, where Dad would store it to be retrieved later by Jessik's small drug operation. About a year and a half ago, 'bout six months after he started running drugs on Dad's behalf, one of Jessik's men learned that Charlie was an infamous merc that the White Rabbits hated. They only knew him as the Red Boa."

"Ya mentioned that he worked as a merc for Tristan and Christie, but ya never told me that he had a reputation," she remarked.

"Only with the White Rabbits mostly. Other merc bands knew of him, but they didn't really know much beyond that. Once Jessik found out, he made Charlie an enforcer. That's…that's when I noticed Charlie startin' to act different."

"What'd'ya mean?"

He looked at her. "He started pushin' everyone away after that. Started callin' himself a monster."

"Havin' to hurt or kill people ya got no hate for will do that to ya," Ash replied. "He did it to protect ya and your dad though, and that was probably the one thing that kept him going."

"Dad did a lot for him after the incident with the grenade, and I think Charlie just did everything he could to keep Jessik away. It…it started to wear on him a lot. Between workin' for Dad, doing Jessik's dirty work, and trainin' to be a Frontier Commando, he didn't really—"

"Commando?" she asked incredulously.

Francis chuckled. "Yeah. How do ya think he got all those commando field manuals? The tactics he taught ya? Commando trainin'."

"So what happened to the commando shit?" she asked.

"That's…a sore subject with him. After he got out of the hospital and started workin' for Dad, he met the head of commando trainin' school. They talked at length about some of the shit he did in the war as a defector, and the guy recruited him. Charlie was so hell-bent on revenge that he just wanted to get the trainin' and then leave before it was too late. After a while, he started to like it and wanted in, but he was kicked out of the program."

"What for?"

Francis sighed. "I'm sure you've noticed every now and then he'll have a few days of bad sleep and then suddenly be fine one day."

Ash's shoulders slumped. "He takes drops, doesn't he?"

"Yeah, how'd ya know?"

Ash looked away and could feel the frown on her face. The thought of her mentor abusing drops to sleep better made her feel low. Her mother, Catrina, abused drops all the time when she was growing up and eventually died from an overdose mixed with alcohol.

"My mom…she took drops."

Ash saw Francis's face change from curiosity to empathy. "So ya know what it's like then."

"Yeah…but he's only shown a couple of signs. Figured he just had a good night's sleep."

"He has bad nightmares about what he did in the war and the shit he did for Jessik. Won't tell me what, but he does. Keeps him up at night."

"Mom took drops after Dad left with Eri's mom when she got pregnant. Said she needed them to fall asleep 'cause she was always used to a warm body bein' in bed with her. Started out simple as that, then she started takin' 'em right after work to 'unwind' after a long day. Spent many mornin's callin' Mom's work and tellin' 'em that she wasn't feelin' well and needed to take a sick day. She lost a lotta jobs that way."

"Well, pretty much what happened with Charlie," Francis explained. "Came back to Venture from Athens one day, had a terrible panic attack, took the rest of the day off, then took a lotta drops. So much that he missed his trainin'. Woke up to dozens of messages and missed calls from his trainer. Last one told him to not bother."

"Damn."

"He told me the day before I met y'all was because he had to beat up and threaten some old folks who opened a shop in Jessik's territory. They didn't want to pay protection money, so he had to beat 'em within an inch of their life. Had to tell 'em that if they didn't pay, he'd visit their families. Said it fucked 'em up more than just killin' some guy who messed with the wrong people. Dunno why though. Maybe 'cause they was just some old folks tryin' to open a shop in their retirement, maybe somethin' else."

"A monster to protect the ones ya care about…" Ash said distantly.

"Y'all want another?" the waitress asked.

"Yeah, just one more for me. How 'bout ya, Ash?"

"Yeah, just one more."

The waitress nodded and left.

"So if your momma couldn't hold a job well with the drops, I remember ya sayin' that ya had days where ya hardly ate except at school."

"Yeah. When I turned fifteen, I was allowed to work, so I worked after school so I could buy food for myself. Was sick of Mom usin' our grocery food for drops and shit."

"Explains a lot about ya, actually," Francis said with a very slight smirk.

"Whatcha mean?"

"Just really independent, gotta chip on your shoulder, always tryin' to prove you're capable."

"Yeah, well, no one really gave me a chance to show what I could do. I give a shit, ya know? People just don't care if ya give a shit, only if you're good right off the bat. Just wanted someone to believe in me, is all."

"Charlie believes in ya," he replied.

Ash noticed that Francis said only Charlie's name. She wondered if Francis had his doubts about her.

"And what about ya? Do ya believe in me?"

He shrugged. "Charlie's the one that recruited ya. He's the one that matters. I'm just the pilot and the captain. He says you're a good fit, then you're a good fit."

"Why do ya trust him so much with hirin' people if ya own the business and are the captain?"

"Besides the fact he can read people? He's smarter than I am, and got a lot better schoolin'. I trust his judgement."

"But didn't ya say that he felt a lotta guilt about the war 'cause of the decisions he made?" she asked.

"The decisions he *had* to make," Francis clarified. "Charlie told me on a few occasions that he was stuck between a rock and a hard place a lotta times, and both choices weren't good ones."

"So it's not so much he ain't confident in himself, but just havin' to make decisions that he regrets makin'?"

"Yeah, exactly. Shit, I'm the one that ain't confident in himself."

"Look, Francis, ya may have a really dark and troubled past, but that shouldn't be a reason why ya don't trust yourself. Have we had our disagreements about some of your decisions? Yeah, but that don't mean you're a bad leader or nothin', just that we don't see eye to eye. Ya understand people's strengths and weaknesses well, which is why we've talked so much. Ya know I feel completely useless compared to Charlie and have my own self-doubts, but you're always there encouragin' me. That's a good captain, Francis."

"Don't feel like it sometimes," he said. "I rely on Charlie a lot to offer advice."

"He's first officer," she explained, "he's supposed to offer advice."

"Yeah, well—"

"Stop beatin' yourself up. You're doin' fine as captain so far."

He nodded distantly and she could see the apprehension in his eyes. He needed some cheering up.

"C'mon. I'll let ya beat me in darts."

"*Let* me?" Francis let out a barking laugh. "We're playin' cricket then."

"Thanks for givin' me some more context about Charlie earlier," Ash said as they drove back to the ship in her truck.

Francis looked at her from the passenger seat. "Yeah, no problem. Just remember what I've said about keepin' it under wraps. Charlie don't like me talkin' about him without his permission and shit, but I can tell ya just wanna make him proud and need that little bit to help."

She smirked. "I know lately conversation has been a lot about Charlie, but I appreciate ya helpin' me with this."

"I don't mind, Ash," he reassured her.

"I mean it, Francis. You've been a big help. Actin' like the captain ya say ya ain't. Shit like our talks are what make ya a good captain."

He shook his head. "Just makes me a good person, not a captain."

"Why are ya so hung up on sayin' ya ain't a good captain?" she asked with a tinge of annoyance. "This hafta do with the shit ya did in the war?"

He looked away from her and out the window. She knew that it was a touchy subject with him, but she also knew that if she just pressed a little more about it, he'd open up. He already felt guilty about pushing people away in the past six years, so she understood how to get him to open up.

"I just…" He sighed as he looked out the window. He was fighting against himself. "I just never make good decisions and I get people killed, alright?"

"So it *is* about the war," she said. "Look, not everyone can make the right decision all the time, Francis. Ya did the best with the orders and info that ya had. Nothin' wrong with that."

"A lotta times people died because I just didn't take a little longer to assess the situation or scan the terrain," he argued.

"Ya don't know that, Francis. Ya can't say for certain that even waitin' was a better idea. Ya may have even caught the enemy off guard because ya made a quick decision. Ya can't question your choices like that when ya have no idea how things woulda turned out in the other scenario. All ya got are theories."

"Ya don't need to try to make me feel better," he grumbled.

"I'm not, Francis, but ya gotta look at the bigger picture. Just 'cause shit happened in combat don't mean that ya ain't a good captain or a good leader."

"Soundin' just like Charlie…"

"Ya ever think that's maybe because we're both right and ya just don't wanna believe it?"

Francis sighed heavily and continued to look out the window as they stopped at a light.

"Francis," she said, "look at me for a sec." She saw his eyes in the red light look down before he finally turned his head to her. "You're a good leader 'cause ya help others and ya work just as hard as everyone else. Ya ask people to help and they do it 'cause we know you'd do the same for us if we asked ya. Never had a leader do that; always delegated work to some random asshole and sat on his ass.

"Ya know that someone can do somethin' better than ya, so ya let 'em do it instead. Charlie told me that a sign of a good leader is someone who can look at themselves in a mirror and utilize other people's strengths to cover their weaknesses. Ya do it, and ya don't know it."

The captain looked down and nodded.

Ash chuckled. "Well, at least this conversation was barely about your cousin," she said as she drove through the intersection. "Let's talk about somethin' else though."

"Like what?" he asked.

"How 'bout some more funny stories of ya and your friends in high school. The last couple ones ya told me were pretty damn funny."

# Chapter 29

The next day started with a mild shower that lasted for only an hour. The workers would come much earlier with such a short rain. Francis gathered the crew in the cargo bay for an easy start to their day.

Eri, despite going to bed later than usual, was anxious to start on the drive core. So, in the middle of Charlie giving Ash some advice on security during an exchange of cargo and cash, she got up from the crate and walked into the engine room. As Eri left, Charlie quickly finished his explanation with the security officer, took a long drag from his cigarette, and flicked it out into the mud before finally going into the engine room.

"You didn't have to come help," she said as he entered, "I just wanted to get started."

"I can't help that much anyway unless we need the claw," he said with a shrug, "but at least I can still read directions to you while you work."

"As long as you keep being the same useless asshole," she joked. Charlie pursed his lips and looked off to the side with shame.

"Oh, don't give me that pathetic look," she said. "You need to rest that hand anyways. I don't think Kai could deal with you rebreaking your hand twice."

Throughout the day, Charlie read instructions and assisted Eri as much as he could. Mercifully, nothing required getting into tight spaces, so Charlie was able to keep his arm assembled. Ash walked into the engine room twice to retrieve the first officer to get his help with the construction of the medical bay, and both times she announced her presence before peering around the corner, which only made the two laugh. Francis had already explained to her what really happened the day before, but Ash didn't seem to entirely believe the explanation.

Charlie simply returned to the engine room both times and continued doing his work with the maintainer after each instance of being pulled away. Eri knew that he would be often pulled away during the normal workday, so it never perturbed her.

She and the first officer seemed to have bonded well. She had also found herself thinking of *Silver Bow* as home more than her apartment with Ash, and she wanted to finish the drive core as soon as possible so they could finally install and run the life support systems. After that, she could live on the ship full-time.

Though the past three weeks had been full of frightening and exciting events, Eri noticed that Charlie seemed more relaxed than when she first met him. His less stern—albeit still serious— demeanor made working with him easier. The past two days had felt normal, but only relatively. Despite having what felt like a routine morning, something seemed off about him, but not in the same vein as the day prior, when he was dealing with the news of his TES. He was not as motivated or full of his endless energy, which worried her slightly. As the morning continued, his sluggishness seemed to get more and more severe. She thought that maybe it was just the lack of sleep getting to him.

Up until yesterday, Charlie had often seemed annoyed with her. It was a nice change, but she didn't quite understand how they had managed to bond. What confused her more was how they had managed to become friends enough for him to confess his condition to her. He had reminded her that morning that Francis and Ash didn't know and that he wanted to keep it that way.

It wasn't unwelcome by any means. In fact, she was quite glad that she finally had a male friend again. Though he was abrasive and as cryptic as they came, and often self-destructive, she continued to see glimpses of a calm and gentle person who only tried to do the right thing. Perhaps that's what ultimately drew her to him: despite all the terrible things that he' gone through—whatever they were—he still tried doing what he thought was right, even if it required him to do wrong.

"You listening?" he asked her. She snapped out of her thoughts.

"Sorry, spaced there for a moment," she replied shyly.

"What was the last thing you heard?" he asked.

Eri scratched her head. "I don't even think I heard you at the beginning," she admitted.

Charlie sighed with frustration and looked at the time on his tool. "Well, it's about lunchtime anyway, and I'm exhausted. Let's just take a break for lunch and resume after."

The crew adjourned for lunch shortly after. Some of the workers stayed on-site and ate prepared meals while others left to go find food elsewhere. Eri was listening to Ash tell story about her days in the militia when the security officer seemed to notice something wrong with her mentor. Charlie was typically the first one done with his food, followed closely by the captain, but he had barely touched any of his lunch.

"Ya okay, Charlie?" Ash asked with concern.

"Just a little sluggish," he replied, sweat beading on his forehead.

"Or it's your Garner's disorder finally flaring up," Kai said as he went to feel the first officer's forehead. "I am going to get my bag."

"What's Garner's disorder?" Eri asked as she watched Charlie stare listlessly in front of him.

"GD is a rare genetic autoimmune disorder that pretty much attacks anythin' foreign in the body," Francis explained, "his immune system is probably fighting off Doc's blood and the SCR. The only reason he was even able to get a blood transfusion from him was simply because of how much blood he lost the other day. His blood has finally overtaken the Doc's by volume and now it's beginnin' to kill it all off."

"Which means he will be back to healing slowly and being lightheaded for the next couple of days as his cells try to replace the ones they are attacking," Kai interrupted as he took Charlie's temperature and other vitals. "As I suspected," he concluded, "you are running a moderate fever, Charlie. You need to lie down and rest and let things take their course."

"To hell with that, I've got too many things to do," he said as he got up.

Eri pushed down hard on his shoulder, forcing him to sit back down on the crate. "The hell you are," she retorted, "if you want me to fix that servo that's been bothering you, you either rest off your fever in engineering by *only* reading me the directions or you go to *Fire Arrow* and sleep. Useless, or less useless? Your pick…"

Charlie sat there meekly like a scolded child. "Fine," he grumbled after a moment, "I'll read instructions."

Charlie's submission clearly shocked the rest of the crew. Ash's eyes went wide with disbelief and Francis's jaw was halfway to the floor. Even Kai leaned away from the maintainer.

"So is Charlie actually sick, or just feverish?" Eri asked as if nothing happened.

"W-Well," Kai stammered, "his body thinks it is sick, so he is running a fever as his immune system is working overtime. If you are asking if he is contagious, then no."

"Will he experience any flu-like symptoms?" she clarified.

"He may have flu-like symptoms," Kai answered, "it simply depends on how much his body fights the supposed infection."

"Thanks," she said kindly as she turned to the first officer again. "You throw-up once in the engine room, and you sleep on the *Fire Arrow*, understand?" The crew once again stared with incredulity as Charlie sheepishly nodded his head in acknowledgement. "Would it be better if he had some soup instead of this?"

"Uh…yes," Kai replied, "a liquid diet is always best while the body fights sickness to help ease nausea and ensure that the patient stays hydrated."

"Ash," she said, "go get some spicy soup for the sick first officer, please."

Ash quickly stood and walked toward the truck, leaving in the vehicle.

"Captain," she asked sweetly, "can you get a cot and place it in the engineering bay against the outer wall for Charlie?"

Francis stood up and shook his head with a smile. "Maybe ya should be first officer instead of him," he remarked with a laugh.

Charlie sat on the cot as he rested against one of the pillars that lined the walls. He ached and was sweating profusely with his fever as his body attacked the very things that were helping him recover from the last week's worth of ordeals.

"Alright, what's next?" Eri asked as she finished replacing a part.

"You know the only reason I'm letting you boss me around is because you're extorting me with the servo servicing," he said sarcastically.

"No, you're letting me boss you around because I know that you don't want to feel useless, especially after what you learned yesterday."

Charlie looked at the end of the cot. She was right. Once the TES progressed, he would start going through the stages of dementia. After some time, he would barely be able to do anything for himself.

The first officer slowly started to read the instructions and Eri followed them. After a short while, Ash announced that she was entering the room. Eri stopped what she was doing and put her hands on her hips.

"It was funny the first couple of times, Ash, but now it's just annoying."

"Temper, temper," Charlie muttered weakly. Eri leaned around the drive core and glared at him.

"Jesus, ya look like shit," Ash blurted as she saw Charlie. "I think you're paler than Eri right now."

"Hilarious," Eri deadpanned.

Ash brought the bowl of soup to Charlie and gently handed it to him. He held it meekly and sat it down in his lap.

"How much do I owe you for the soup?" he asked.

"On the house," Ash replied with a smile.

"You're working on the post, I see," he remarked as he noticed her scraped and bruised knuckles.

Ash looked at her hands. "It didn't last long. My hands really hurt."

"They will for the first few sessions," he replied with a slight smile.

"Hey, it's great you two are bonding, but I need him to read the next step," Eri said from the other side of the drive core.

Ash smirked and left the engine room. Charlie read the instructions and then opened his soup. He slowly consumed the soup between reading the steps, but he started to become nauseous as it filled up his stomach. He closed the lid to the half-eaten soup and set it on the floor.

"Was the soup good?" Eri asked from the far side of the room as her ratchet rhythmically clicked. He was used to walking around the drive core and shield generator to keep her in sight, so it was strange to him to hear her voice, but not see her.

"Huh?" he asked.

Eri emerged from the drive core. "I asked if you liked the soup."

"Oh, yeah," he responded as he stared blankly into the distance.

Eri walked over to him. He weakly lifted his head and looked at her as she reached out to feel his sweaty forehead. "You're burning up, Charlie," she concluded. "It might be too hot in here for you. You may just need to lie down in *Fire Arrow* anyway…"

He slowly shook his head as he managed to smile slightly. "I'd rather feel hot than have the fever chills. Do you need me to read the next step?"

Eri smiled slightly in return.

"Take a nap," she said softly as she took the binder, "you can help me after."

Charlie sighed slightly, but didn't fight back. He slowly lay down on the cot. As Eri turned away, Charlie spoke.

"I only let you boss me around because you care," he admitted.

Eri turned to him. "You've been stubborn around plenty of people who care, and to me," she argued. "Don't you remember the morning after Jessik's guys beat you to a pulp?"

"I do, but that was for different reasons. I'm stubborn around people who only care because that's what they were taught to do in that situation—or fear that someone will be angry at them for not taking care of someone. You care…because you care. You're a kind and gentle soul."

Eri blushed slightly at his words. "The fever must be really getting to you if you're saying shit like that," she said jokingly.

Charlie's eyes grew heavy as he chuckled. He quickly fell asleep.

Charlie gasped as he jolted awake in the hot engine room. He sat up as he desperately inhaled air, his chest feeling like he had held his breath to the point of suffocation. Eri held his metal hand and patted it gently. He looked at her wide-eyed as his breathing slowed. Her concerned expression told Charlie everything he needed to know.

"I'm here," she said gently, "did you have another nightmare?"

"I thought the term 'fever dream' was just a saying, not a real thing," he admitted.

"The way you were rolling and kicking on the cot for the last twenty minutes, it must have been one hell of a fever dream."

"Yes and no," he said slowly, "I can hardly remember it because of how weird it was."

Eri slowly released his metal hand. A wave of lethargy crashed into his body as he reached for his forehead. He had become lightheaded again. His body was already killing off the doctor's blood.

"Do you even want to go back to sleep after that?" she asked, noting his expression.

Charlie slowly closed his eyes. "I feel so weak now…"

Eri felt his forehead. "Maybe you should go back to sleep."

"How long have I been out?" he asked.

"Couple hours now," she said as she checked the time on her tool.

"Then I'm not going back to sleep," he replied as he rearranged himself to lean against the pillar again. "Hand me the manual."

Eri slowly handed Charlie the manual. Despite her worries, Charlie managed throughout the rest of the day. Once the workers had finished most of the medbay, they left. The crew members came into the engine room to find Eri hard at work as Charlie read instructions. Kai checked on Charlie's vitals and gave him some over the counter pain meds to help with his body aches and broken hand.

Francis decided to have everyone join Charlie in the engineering compartment to have dinner. He wanted something that was appropriate for the first officer, so he got the entire crew some pho. Charlie didn't eat much of his pho, but he graciously accepted what he could.

After dinner, the captain told Charlie to sleep in *Fire Arrow* while he helped Eri with the drive core for the rest of the night, but Charlie stubbornly refused despite how weak and sickly he was. Eri shooed the captain away and told everyone to simply let them work.

For a few more hours, Charlie read from the manual as he sipped on water. The work had become routine and the two managed to converse about various things, one of which was their childhoods.

"I just never had such a thing," Charlie said, "my parents were never the type to show affection or anything of the sort. I got more hugs from other parents than my own."

"Is that why you called Carol 'Mama?'"

Charlie nodded. "She's more of a mother than my own, even after three short years."

"That's horrible!" Eri exclaimed.

He shrugged. "I got all the affection I needed from my friend's parents. I hardly ever felt like I was my own parents' son, more of just a person living in their house. It didn't bother me though. They were boring people who cared only about their work and couldn't carry a conversation further than simple pleasantries. Sometimes I even wondered how my brother and I were even conceived. They hardly showed affection to each other."

"I can't imagine what it would be like," she said somberly, "I've only known affectionate and caring parents. I can't even count the amount of times my father said, 'I'm proud of you.' I can understand why you never mention it. I don't know what's worse: dead parents or ones that hardly existed in the first place."

"'It is the infirmity of our nature always to believe ourselves much more unhappy than those who groan by our sides,'" he quoted whimsically with heavy eyes.

"What's that from?" she asked.

He slowly turned to her with a smirk. "*The Count of Monte Cristo*, of course."

"You must *really* love that book to be able to quote something relevant to the conversation without even skipping a beat," she concluded.

He looked at his feet somberly. "If only life had a happier ending…if only I had sixteen years…"

Eri looked at him with sadness as he once again came to grips with his own mortality. To know that you only had fifteen years at the absolute most—it was difficult to know that every day was truly another step toward death.

"You still haven't told Francis, have you?"

He shook his head. "I don't know if I'll tell him any time soon," he replied. "He can't have that constantly on his thoughts while he tries to get the business going. I just want to do as much as I can before my mind betrays me…so let's get back to work."

Charlie's time helping didn't last much longer than that. The lethargy and lightheadedness from his fever and his body attacking the doctor's blood made him fall asleep after reading instructions, but woke with a jolt, his eyes opening instantly. He took a breath as Eri awkwardly held his shoulders.

"It's alright," she said softly as she released him, "You fell asleep and I was just trying to make you comfortable before you got a crick in your neck."

"I'm fine, I can keep helping," he said as he shifted.

"Just go to sleep," she said, "I'll just have an earlier start tomorrow. You need your rest and I would rather let you sleep longer than you trying to fight through your fever."

Charlie nodded and pulled himself down onto the cot.

Eri turned off the lights in the engine room and stopped at the doorway. "Goodnight, Charlie."

# Chapter 30

Charlie's fever continued the next day and his weakness continued for another day after that, but the duo managed to get the overclock feature finished. On the same day they finished the drive core, the workers also finished setting up the life support systems. For the first time, Eri could sleep in her own bed on the ship. She wanted to move in the night they finished, but Charlie insisted that she take the next day off to move all her belongings instead.

"That's tomorrow's problem," he said, "tonight, I'm going out for the first time in a week, and you're coming with me, Ash, and Francis."

"Are you going to be okay with your lower blood count?" she asked with concern.

"It'll be the easiest way for me to get drunk," he replied with a devious smile. "There's a reason you've never seen me drunk. It takes a lot."

"He can practically drink anyone under the table," Francis said as he entered the room. "While ya two get showered and dressed, I'll get life support runnin'. Charlie, I know ya wanna get drunk, but don't overdo it. Ya gotta oversee the installation of the weapon systems tomorrow. They'll finish the armory early so the next couple of days will be your show."

"Of course," Charlie replied confidently.

"Alright then. Ash is waitin' for ya outside, Eri. Go home and we'll meet ya there in about half an hour. Make sure ya and Ash wear somethin' for a nightclub."

"We're going to a club?" she asked.

"When Charlie actually goes out to get drunk or, in my case, we really want to celebrate, we go to clubs, so make sure you dress up pretty well."

The two men arrived at the apartment as Eri was drying her hair with a towel as best she could before she simply allowed it to dry on its own. The men rang the doorbell and Ash answered. She opened the door and simply stared at the sight in shock.

On the meagre front porch, Francis was wearing khaki casual slacks associated with Venture fashion. On Venture, pants were often quite formfitting and tapered past the knee to accentuate thighs and calves. He had an off-white button-up shirt with the top two buttons undone, showing an undershirt. The sleeves on the button-up were rolled up tightly and neatly just above his elbows, revealing his hairy arms.

Francis also wore the typical thin brown leather bands found in fashion on Venture that wrapped around the highest part of the bicep to accentuate musculature. Resting on his arm was a brown trench coat, not needed at the moment as they stood beneath the roof of the porch.

Ash couldn't help but stare at the smiling captain. He had even taken the time to get his beard touched up. He was smiling that genuine smile of his, and she couldn't help but smile back at him. He was nothing short of handsome, and those chestnut brown eyes of his had a soft look. The one thing she found most mesmerizing about them was how they had such distinct, visible lines that came from his pupils, like spokes on a wheel. The lack of light outside in the dark and the bright light of her apartment's common area made his eyes stand out.

That was when she noticed the hint of a cologne; wood and spice. Francis had no idea, but that was the combination she liked the most on a man, and she melted under the scent. She also knew that it would only smell better as the night went on.

*Of all the men I like, why'd ya hafta be married?*

While Francis wore typical club wear found on Venture, Charlie had a completely different look. He wore black leather boots that rode hallway up the calf with gray linen pants tightly tucked and bloused into them. The pants were slimmer in fit than what Charlie typically wore. His shirt was also made of linen and was a very light gray, almost off-white. The shirt seemed as if it were simply wrapped around his torso and tucked into his pants, with his arms pulled through the sleeves. The sleeves were quite strange to Ash.

Where Venture fashion always accentuated muscle tone, Charlie's sleeves seemed to do the exact opposite. The sleeves were large and baggy at the top, but quickly tapered to an elastic band at the wrist. The clothing looked both loose and tight. On top of everything rested a strange navy blue cloak that opened on his left side, obscuring his right half until his right boot but leaving his left side completely exposed. The opening was held together by a silvery clasp just over his left armpit. There was a strangely beautiful asymmetry to it. The collar of the cloak was thick, like a loosely fitted scarf and obscured some of Charlie's neck.

Ash and Eri both wore typical club attire for Magna Graecia. Ash, being taller than many women, wore simple western-style brown leather boots with denim pants that went up to her waist, but were slightly loose around the legs. She wore a sleeveless white shirt made of a synthetic material that was embroidered around the high neck, complimented by a thin brown chiffon kimono that went down to her mid-thigh. Eri wore a flowing blue cocktail dress that ended just below her knees and had a square neckline.

"Glad to see ya two understood what I meant," Francis said as Charlie looked around in the rain and smoked a cigarette. The water that landed on his clothing beaded off the fibers.

"I dunno if Charlie understood," Ash whispered as she leaned toward Francis. She didn't care if Charlie heard, she just wanted an excuse to get a better smell of Francis's cologne.

"Hexham fashion," Francis said plainly with a nod of his head toward Charlie. "They get so much rain their fashion is designed around it."

Ash shrugged and turned around to Eri. "Ya ready to go to The Quarry?"

"Oh, so ya already know where we're going?" Francis asked.

"It's the only true club in town," Eri replied, "not too hard to figure out if you're telling us to dress nice. Everything else that claims to be a club is just a really loud bar with a dance floor."

Francis chuckled. "Fair enough. Let's go."

The women grabbed their raincoats and locked the apartment as Charlie flicked his cigarette into a puddle out in the street.

"Do you think we'll even get in?" Eri asked apprehensively as they walked to the car in the rain.

"We'll get in just fine," Charlie said confidently, his clothes still strangely dry.

"I doubt it with that Feddie clothin'," Ash replied as she got into the back of the car with Eri.

The four parked across the street from The Quarry some time later. The line waiting to get inside wrapped around the building under makeshift coverings that kept the patrons dry during the monsoon season. Eri saw the length of the line and her shoulders sunk, knowing that they might get in sometime after midnight, but more than likely not before.

"There ain't no way we're getting' in," Ash said defeatedly.

"Wait here," Charlie said as he got out.

"Watch this," Francis said as Charlie shut the door and made his way across the street. He immediately walked up to one of the bouncers and spoke in his ear. The bouncer leaned back in shock and said something to the first officer. Charlie reached for something under his cloak and flashed it at the bouncer, whose eyes widened more. He then opened the door to the VIP entrance. Charlie turned and signaled them to join him.

"How the *fuck*...?" Ash exclaimed quietly.

The three got out of the car and crossed the street. Charlie waited for them by the door, then led the way inside. The music thumped as they entered the VIP section of the club. The red light changed the color of Charlie's navy blue cloak to black as they made their way to a table. He led them to a round booth table in the corner. Francis and Ash sat next to each other with Eri and Charlie on the ends. The dance floor was filled with patrons as the music continued to bump and thump. The VIP section was a sea of red while the dance floor and bar were a blanket of black with only the underlit bar top and the dance lights of various colors illuminating the rest of the club. A woman wearing a short dress with a low-cut neck that left little for the imagination walked up with menus.

"Hiya!" she greeted bubbly over the music, "What can I get for ya?"

"Hyperlane," Eri said.

"Just a Klekit for me," Francis said. Klekit was a carbonated soft drink.

"Hyperlane," Ash said.

"Dry Dredge Number Five, neat," Charlie said, "and three Lady Killers for me and the ladies."

The waitress left and Francis glared at Charlie.

"What?"

"I told ya to take it easy," he said angrily.

"And I will," Charlie replied, "just wanting to start the night off right."

"What's a Lady Killer?" Eri asked.

"No, the question we should be asking is 'how the fuck did ya get us in the VIP section?'" Ash said before Charlie could speak.

Charlie ignored Ash's question. "It's a specialty shot they make here," he said as he lit a cigarette and pulled an ash tray close to him. "You'll like it, it's got citrus and whiskey in it."

"I don't like whiskey…" Ash lamented.

"And you don't want to know how I got us in here," Charlie finally replied to Ash.

"Why not?"

"I already told you that you don't want to know," he reiterated.

The waitress came back with their drinks and promptly left. Charlie picked up his shot glass and held it up.

"To the final stretch," he said, "may our girl fly soon."

"Here, here!" Francis said as they all touched their glasses. Charlie threw back the shot and licked his lips. Eri tried the shot. It had a sweet, then sour flavor with a hint of whiskey in the back end.

Sweet, then sour, then bitter, just like a bad relationship. Lady Killer.

"I like it," Eri said happily. Charlie nodded with a smirk. In the red light, his blue eyes turned black, and they looked back at her like polished hematite stones.

"It's alright," Ash replied with a slight grimace caused by the whiskey aftertaste.

Charlie took a drag from his cigarette, his seemingly black eyes fixated to something near the bar. Eri saw his eyes narrow right before he stood up and grabbed his whiskey. "I'll be right back," he said as he walked over toward the bar.

The crowd cheered as a famous song made by a local artist started to play.

"Ash! It's Stinger! C'mon, let's dance!" Eri said cheerfully.

Ash smiled and scooted out of the booth to join her. The women asked Francis to watch their bags as they scurried away. The two joined the others on the dance floor, the beat making them both energetic.

The women whooped and hollered in their fun until the song ended. As a slower song came on, two tall men approached the women and started conversation, but Eri suddenly caught Charlie out of the corner of her eye. He was at the bar talking with a very young woman, possibly even too young to be in the club.

Charlie walked over to the bar. He had seen a familiar face and was so shocked that she made it inside that he wondered if she perhaps had a deal with the bouncers. He was curious if she had taken his words seriously from a week before.

The young woman was at the bar gently caressing a young man's chest with her finger, saying sweet nothings to him. Unlike the other day, she was much better dressed, though she wore even more revealing clothes.

"Beat it," Charlie commanded, "she's underage."

The young man's eyes widened at Charlie, looked back at the girl, who whirled around. Her eyes smoldered as she finally saw Charlie's true, unbruised face.

"You said you were twenty-two," the young man croaked at her.

"She graduated high school three months ago," Charlie clarified as he flashed his bounty hunter badge from underneath his cloak, "beat it."

The young man hurried away with his drink.

"Thanks, asshole," she bemoaned.

"What are you doing here, Wei-Lu?"

"I'm working, Daniel," she replied plainly.

"This is Jessik's territory. You think that's wise while the Sun Scorpions have no leadership?"

"It's exactly why it works," she said as she drank her vodka tonic, "no one would suspect it."

"I thought I advised you to get out."

"You also told me to have a plan, and I don't fuckin' have one yet. What's with the clothes? They require far too much of my imagination. Maybe you will let my imagination take a break and let my eyes do the work instead?"

"I'm almost a decade older than you, Wei-Lu," he said as he finished his whiskey and signaled to the bartender.

"The law says I'm an adult, so what's the problem with two consenting adults having a good time?" she asked seductively.

"The problem is—Dry Dredge Number Five, neat, for VIP twelve—is that I prefer experienced women who have been with more than just hormonal teenagers and who know not to be clingy after sharing their bed."

"I've been with older men," she argued.

"Still out of the question," he replied, "what I'd rather talk about is what products you have."

"You need some fruit already?" she asked with surprise.

"Nope," he said as he shook his head and took a sip of his whiskey, "drops."

"You surprise me," she said with a raised eyebrow. "You want lucid or dark drops?"

"Dark drops, just one glass worth."

"You don't want to dream of me tonight?" she asked playfully as she caressed the top of her breast.

"You got it or not?" he asked.

She sighed loudly enough to show her frustration. "I'll do you a solid in exchange for something else."

"And what would that be?"

"You take a full glass, and when I get out, you give me more than a kiss," she said as she leaned in close. He remained still, staring into her brown eyes. "I can't think of any better payment than riding you all night."

"I'd rather pay cash," he said as he revealed a wad of Frontier shen.

"I'll even call you master, and let you put it wherever you like," she whispered in his ear. "I'll even consent to ropes and whips, if you're into that. I'm not afraid to share either."

She nibbled his earlobe, then pulled away from his scarred ear and stared him down. They locked wills for a moment as they both refused to look away. Despite the offer, Charlie wanted no part of her fantasy of wanting to sleep with a killer like him. Without looking away, he slowly put the wad of cash in her cleavage.

She slowly looked away and discreetly gave him the eye dropper full of drops. "I guess I'll just have to settle for that kiss, though I think you won't be able to hold yourself back once you do. You seem like the kind of man that refuses women because you can't control yourself."

Charlie's eyes had never left hers as he leaned toward her ear and gripped her forearm.

"You get out and give me a good enough kiss, you just might find out," he rasped.

She turned to him, but he moved away before she had a chance to react. He quickly walked away and back to his table. He didn't mean any of it, but if it was motivation for her to get out, it was worth playing with her feelings.

Eri and Ash stood on the dance floor with the two men. Both were tall and had well-built physiques. They were clearly from the nicer part of Corinth and each wore button-up shirts and slacks. One had his sleeves rolled all the way to his armpits, while the other simply had the sleeves pulled away from his wrists. Ash had started up some idle conversation, but Eri was still eyeing Charlie out of the corner of her eye.

The first officer stood in front of a young woman wearing low-cut silver dress that went down to the middle of her thighs and a push-up bra. She didn't need that kind of bra; she had large enough breasts to begin with.

Between the people moving about on the dance floor and trying to maintain the conversation with the man in front of her, Eri could only catch a few glimpses of the first officer. The thing she noticed more than anything was his deep stare into the girl's eyes after he seductively placed money into her cleavage.

*Is she a prostitute?*

"So what do you do for work?" the man asked.

She snapped out of her curiosity and looked back at the tall, muscular man in front of her. "I'm a certified maintainer."

"A mechanic? Wouldn't have ever guessed that," he admitted. "What made you decide to do that?"

"My father loved restoring old cars," she said nostalgically, "and nothing much else really interested me in school. I just always wanted to work on ships. You?"

"I'm a White Rabbit," he said proudly.

"What's a white rabbit?" she asked with confusion.

"C'mon…the White Rabbits? It's Corinth's own PMC."

Eri looked down. *PMC? What's that? Should I know what that is?* "I'm sorry if I sound stupid, but I don't know what a PMC is," she finally admitted.

"Private military corporation. Mercenaries?"

Eri slapped her forehead with embarrassment. "Yeah…duh…"

"It's alright," he said softly, smiling at her shyness.

"So, I've never talked with a merc before. What exactly do you guys do?"

"Whatever we get paid to do," he replied plainly. "Sometimes we just guard some rich guy while he's in town, other times we help police raid a gang's compound, other times we're paid to train the local militia. Most of us fought in the war, so we got a lot of experience."

"Interesting," she lied. It was exactly what she guessed. Soldiers who simply wanted more pay than what the militia, IFSA Marines, or IFSA Ground Forces gave. She knew that he was not explaining everything he did. Charlie was practically a mercenary for Jessik, though not necessarily willingly, and she knew that merc work was often dirty work. "Do you guys have a military-style rank structure?"

"Yeah, but I'm too new so I'm just a PFC right now."

"Honest. That's respectable."

"No use in lying about my rank," he said with a shrug. "If I had said captain, would it have impressed you?"

"Me?" she said with a sly grin as her eyes raked over his body. "Not really."

"Not everything has to be about status," he said wisely.

She gently held his muscular forearm. "Yeah, that are plenty of other qualities that a woman looks for…"

"Well if you say it like that," he began as he got closer, "then I'd assume you'd be more than happy to let me buy you a drink and see how the night goes?"

"My drinks are already paid for, but I'd be happy to see how the night goes," she said as she looked up at him, still caressing his forearm.

"Well, who's paying for your drinks?" he asked, jokingly gesturing that she'd hurt him. "I'll let them know that I can take the rest of your bill."

"If you insist," she said with a shrug. She turned around and saw Charlie and Francis chatting at the table. At some point in her conversation, he must have returned from the bar. She pointed at the two men. "Those are my bosses. They're paying for our drinks tonight."

The man looked at them, and just as he was about to walk over, Charlie brought the drink up to his lips, revealing his metal arm. The first officer turned and looked at them. Eri turned back around, but the man paled and stood frozen.

"You alright?" she said.

"You work for the Pit Bull?" he asked, voice quavering.

"Pit Bull?"

*Charlie being my little Pit Bull here in Corinth is a good start.* She remembered Jessik saying that a week ago.

"No way, girl, I'm not getting involved with that," he said as he quickly retreated into the crowd. "C'mon, Sanders, the chicks are with the Pit Bull."

The other man looked at Ash in fear and retreated with his friend. The two women stood there in confusion.

*Is Charlie's reputation with Jessik really that infamous? Is that how he got us a table in the VIP section?*

"What the fuck was that about? Who's the Pit Bull?" Ash asked angrily.

"Charlie is…" Eri said as she looked at the first officer. "You remember Jessik calling him 'dog' and 'doggie?' I think he's got a reputation that the mercs know about."

"And they're White Rabbits, not the kind of guys to back down from a fight," Ash added. "They both are twice Charlie's size, and they didn't even wanna talk to us after they found out we were with him…what kinda shit has he done that would make men like them run with their tails between their legs?"

"Probably the same stuff he did a week ago…"

"Now I'm too fucken curious," Ash said as she marched over to the table. Eri followed.

The two approached as Charlie was saying something to Francis, a slight smirk on his face.

"—starting to feel it though," Eri heard Charlie say.

"So what the fuck did ya do?" his protégé asked Charlie with her hands on her hips.

Charlie slowly turned and looked at her. The two women could see that the alcohol, for once, seemed to affect the first officer.

"Context to that question would be helpful," he said, "and a little less attitude goes a long way."

"We were just out on the dance floor with two insanely hot White Rabbit mercs when they found out we were with ya and they practically tripped over themselves to get away from us. They called ya the Pit Bull."

Charlie signaled them to sit at the table. The two complied as Francis scooted to let them enter the booth comfortably. The women waited nervously across from Charlie to hear the explanation. He signaled for the waitress and ordered three more Lady Killers and another glass of whiskey. He drank the rest of his whiskey and lit a cigarette.

"Ya might wanna slow down," Francis advised.

"I'm just now starting to feel it, Francis," Charlie argued as he released smoke out of his nose, "I'll be fine for a few more drinks."

"So are ya gonna explain it to us or not?" Ash asked.

"Patience," Charlie said with his hand up for emphasis. The waitress returned with the drinks. Eri didn't even wait and slammed back the shot. Charlie snorted and raised his glass toward her. "Cheers, I guess…" Ash simply slid her shot over to Eri, who quickly took it.

"This is Jessik's territory," Charlie simply said as he took a long drag from his cigarette. "The regulars and staff know who I am. The regulars know me by my clothes and metal arm, of course. I wear the same thing to the club so people won't forget me."

"That's great that ya finally explained how ya got us a table in the VIP section, but that don't explain how two men who would tower over ya and are three or more weight classes higher than ya would look like they saw the galaxy's most deadly assassin," Ash grumbled.

"Because the White Rabbits also know that I used to be a Pit Viper back in the day when I was a merc. Pit Viper, Pit Bull, quite poetic, honestly."

"You never told me that you were a mercenary. Where's your tattoo?" Eri asked with apprehension.

"They're always on the right shoulder," Charlie replied. "If I have to explain to you how that's an issue, you're less observant than I thought."

"Okay, so who are the Pit Vipers? How come I ain't heard of 'em before?" Ash asked.

"They don't exist anymore," he replied, "but I was second-in-command, and four years ago, the Pit Vipers were the bitter rivals of the White Rabbits. Those two must have heard stories about me in that old merc group fighting against them. I was infamous among the White Rabbit ranks, and after a few battles against us, the White Rabbits no longer took jobs that were opposite of the Pit Vipers. In short, if I were still in the Pit Vipers, my armor would show dozens of little white rabbits on my tallies."

"Tallies?" Eri asked.

"Symbols that mark kills," Ash explained, "Mercs often paint symbols of their kills, especially of other merc groups, to frighten their opponents."

Charlie took another drag of his cigarette, looking at both women as he exhaled the smoke through his nostrils. "Why do you think Jessik wanted me to be his personal attack dog for so long? He found out through one of his lieutenants, who was once a White Rabbit, about my merc days and how good I was, so he forced me to work for him to pay off Frank's debts."

"So what happened to the Pit Vipers and how come I ain't never heard of them despite your…exploits?" Ash inquired.

"We were a short-lived merc group," he replied as he stamped out his cigarette in the ashtray, "it crumbled and fell apart only after a year and a half, and we operated strictly in the border regions."

Charlie sipped his whiskey, his face becoming flush from the alcohol. He got up and announced that he would be back shortly from a bathroom break. When he left, Eri saw Ash look at Francis with a pained expression.

"You already knew about this, didn't you?" Eri asked them.

"Yeah," Ash replied, "but ya know how Charlie is. Don't want no one knowin' about his past without his permission."

"So you asked questions to things you already knew so that he wouldn't suspect it," Eri concluded aloud. Ash nodded, then Eri looked at Francis. "If Charlie ever finds out, he'll be pissed, Francis."

"Don't worry about it," Ash said dismissively. Francis never looked away from his Klekit.

Charlie walked through the dance floor, weaving between the dancers, toward the bathroom. At about the halfway point, a woman fell into him. He caught her to prevent her from falling to the floor, but quickly recognized that she'd only feigned falling. He gripped her wrist tightly, but not enough to hurt her.

"Put the wallet back," he commanded as he pulled her up to her feet.

"You're smarter than you look," the woman admitted. She was a beautiful redheaded woman with long, straight hair that went down beyond her shoulder blades. Her eyes were a bright and piercing green that returned the same hard stare he gave. She lifted his cloak and slowly put it inside the concealed pocket.

"I'm surprised you know where the pockets are on a Hexhamite cloak," he said with slight pride, "you ever been?"

"Oh yes," she said with a flick of her eyebrows, "it's winter right now, and the entire city would be covered in half-melted snow."

"You lived there," he said, curious now. "What neighborhood?"

"Manchester," she said with a smile.

"Newcastle," he said with disbelief, "when did you go to high school? We might have known each other."

"Graduated in 3183," she said plainly.

"3187," he replied with a shake of his head.

"Just a baby," she said with a fake gasp as she rubbed the silvery clasp. "What brings a young Hexham man like you out to this mining town?"

"Was just about to ask you the same thing," he said as he got closer. "What would an educated Hexham woman be doing in a club in Corinth working as a pickpocket?"

She looked into his eyes. "I just like doing it from time to time," she admitted, "I'm a materials engineer for the mining corporation. I left the Federation after what happened on Isolde during the revolution. Will you answer *my* question now?"

"I'm rebuilding a ship. I'm first officer and security chief for a freighter…and I also left the Federation after Isolde."

"As many expats did," she said. "What are you doing later? I was about to leave and head home."

"Sounds like you could use a nightcap to enjoy the overnight rain with a fellow Hexhamite."

"Monsoon season is my favorite time of year here," she replied slyly, "and I've yet to find someone who appreciates it as much as I do." Her eyes looked deeply into his, then his lips. "Did you get all those scars from the war?"

"No," he replied as she got closer to him.

"Mysterious," she remarked as she opened his cloak and peered at his zinc-carbide hand, "and that?"

"After the war," he answered.

"They definitely tell a story," she said as she looked back into his eyes. She subtly lifted her chin towards him. "I'd love to hear the tale."

He smirked and leaned in. They kissed slowly and he could taste the floral notes of juniper berries. Gin. The last time he had kissed a woman with gin on her lips, he still wore the Federal uniform. A wave of nostalgia hit him, but he shoved it deep down as he tried to enjoy the moment.

"Then I'll meet you outside in about five minutes."

The three sat at the table quietly. Ash sighed with frustration as she realized that Charlie's presence meant that none of the mercs would dare go near her, ruining any chances of having a man take her back to his place. Going to the club without a night spent in someone else's bed felt like a waste.

It wasn't all bad though. She was sitting next to Francis and could smell the middle notes of his cologne. She finally understood why they were called "the love notes." She found herself leaning toward him to get a better sniff.

Her mind drifted as she started to worry about the captain's cousin. He was still dealing with a low blood count, and the alcohol would definitely catch up with him faster than anticipated.

A notification came up on Francis' tool. He opened it and saw it was a message from Charlie. He tilted the holographic screen and showed Ash the message.

Charlie: Don't wait up for me. Bill is paid. See you tomorrow.

"Ya two wanna get out of here?" Francis asked as he closed the message.

"What about Charlie?" Eri asked as she finally lifted her head from her drink.

"He won't be joinin' us for the rest of the night," Francis hinted.

"Must be with that girl he was talking to at the bar earlier," Eri concluded aloud as she drank the rest of her whiskey sour.

Ash checked the time on her tool. "We could still get a round or two of darts at Bullseye! before we head in for the evenin'."

"We could, or we could join Kai at Cutters," Francis suggested. "He's enjoyin' a cigar there right now and it'd be a nice gesture to include him even though he declined the club."

"I'm okay with havin' a cigar and beer," Ash replied. "Eri?"

She looked at Ash, and the security officer could see her sister was deep in thought about something, probably the news about Charlie being an infamous merc.

"I'll go without the cigar, but I'll join," Eri finally said.

The three left and got into the car. They needed to drive only about six blocks to Cutters, the cigar bar in the downtown area. Francis turned around and started to head that way. Ash sat up front in the passenger seat while Eri looked out the window, watching the rain splatter against the window. The car took a left and stopped at a light. Ash looked around to keep herself occupied and noticed a very familiar cloak walking down the street.

"Look, it's Charlie," Ash announced, "he gave his cloak to some woman and he's walkin' with her in the rain over on the sidewalk."

"Ya should embarrass him," Francis said mischievously.

"Don't embarrass him!" Eri demanded as she tried to see the first officer. "Just let him enjoy the rest of his evening."

"Fuck that, he ruined mine with his stupid reputation," Ash said as she lowered the window. The light turned green and she leaned out, gave her best sarcastic Feddie accent, and shouted, "Oh, yes, dear lady, won't thoust taketh my cloak!"

The two turned to see Ash giving Charlie the finger as she cackled.

# Chapter 31

"Friends of yours?" Millie asked as the car drove away.

Charlie smirked. "Yeah, some of the crew."

She turned her head slightly to see him from under the hood, but she ensured that her hair would remain dry. "How long will you be in Corinth before you leave?"

He glanced at her. "A week," he replied. He looked at her again, and she was still eyeing him. "Why did you ask for my cloak? You and I both know what that means."

"And yet you gave it freely," she retorted. "What does that say about you, Charlie?"

"It was mostly because it's still raining and you had conveniently lost your raincoat."

Millie giggled. "Yes, such a tragedy."

"So you were testing me?" he asked with a raised eyebrow.

"Just wanted to see if you had commitment issues, or if you were the kind of man to give it anyway despite what the gesture means."

Charlie looked forward as they approached an intersection. "So you aren't interested in that kind of relationship?"

Millie chuckled. "I just learned your name ten minutes ago. Let's see how things go tonight before I even consider such a notion as an exclusive relationship."

Charlie also chuckled. "Fair enough, but I'm not much relationship material at the moment, for obvious reasons."

"And yet I sense there's another reason," she remarked. "What exactly is going on in your life that keeps you away from a relationship?"

They stopped at a crosswalk and waited for their time to cross. Charlie looked at her again and noticed that she was still watching him.

"Let's see how things go tonight before I explain," he echoed.

She nodded quietly and finally looked away. They walked for another five blocks and conversed to learn more about each other. Both obviously were attracted to the other physically, her eyes being the first thing that caught his attention, but Charlie wanted to make sure that she wasn't some sort of honey trap from Jessik. Things seemed to fall in place too easily, so he asked her questions that would help him read her to see if she was lying.

To his surprise, Millie O'Donnell, the materials engineer, was just a woman who seemed willing to take a chance with a disfigured man. It surprised him, but a few women had said to him before that they liked scars, or, in the very least, were unbothered by them.

They reached her house in midtown, and she invited him in. She took only a few steps inside, then stopped and remained still. She was signaling to him that she wanted him to remove the cloak for her. It was expected for the man to do so on Hexham, and she was maintaining the tradition. He reached around and gingerly unclasped the cloak, and Millie pointed to a coat rack. He sauntered over and hung it on a spare hook as she walked over to a wet bar and made herself a gin and tonic.

"Would you like one as well?" she asked.

"Sure," Charlie replied as he looked around. The large, open room had a polished, rust-colored concrete floor that gave it a kind of utilitarian and industrial feel, and much of the furniture followed the trend. He slowly walked over to a couch and gingerly sat as she finished their drinks.

"Boots," she commanded.

Charlie nodded and removed his boots as she joined him on the couch. He pulled his second boot off as she placed his glass on a coaster on the coffee table in front of them.

"Were you a sailor or marine?" she asked as she sipped her drink.

"Sailor," he answered as he reached for his glass. He sipped it and held it in his metal hand.

"And you graduated high school right after the Parliament declared independence."

Charlie nodded. "I was a naïve patriot then."

"Did you see a lot of combat?"

He shook his head. "Was only in combat once in the entire war. I was a desk jockey on Bhutan."

"Usually, men would be less open about that if they're trying to spend the night with a woman."

"And yet I'm already in your house," he replied as he sipped again. She seemed satisfied with that remark.

"What did you do in the navy?" she asked.

Charlie shook his head. "That's all you're going to get out of me about my wartime history. Where did you get your degree in materials engineering?"

"Vienna Tech," she replied plainly.

"Impressive," he said, "that's a very good engineering school. You're obviously very intelligent."

She smiled and looked away from him as she sipped her drink. "Did you go back to school after the Armistice?" she asked.

"No. Became a bounty hunter after a short stint working as an entry-level data specialist."

"Well, that explains the badge that I felt in your cloak," she replied with a giggle. "I was worried for a moment you were a deputy or police officer."

He shook his head. "Always had a complicated relationship with cops. Being a bounty hunter and mercenary will warp your view of them."

"A mercenary as well?"

He nodded.

"What PMC?"

"The Pit Vipers. You've probably never heard of them."

"I haven't," she admitted. "Were you a desk jockey with them as well?"

He shook his head. "No, but let's talk about something else."

"Don't like a woman asking you about your history?"

"Don't like anyone interrogating me about my past," he explained. "Mine isn't pleasant, and not a good icebreaker for a beautiful woman who invited me back to her house for a nightcap."

"So, what should we talk about then?" she asked as she finished her drink.

He finished his drink as well and placed it back on the coaster. He looked at her with a devious smirk. "How about your favorite position and if you like your hair being pulled, Miss O'Donnell?"

Millie tried to project a calm demeanor on her face, but the subtle pink coloration in her cheeks told a different story. Despite being drunk, Charlie could still see the fine details in her body language and expression.

"You're quite forward, Mister Menillo," she responded with a mask of calm.

"I just wanted to see how you would react," he said as he faced his body toward her, "but I do want to know, before we get started, that this is actual attraction, not some fetish for a man with scars or prosthetics."

She shook her head. "Let's just say I have a morbid curiosity about you." She stood and sauntered over to him, and he rose from his spot on the couch.

She looked into his eyes, then to his mouth. He leaned forward and kissed her gently. They both may have been forward earlier, but he felt compelled to be gentle with her in her house. Given how she reacted to his question earlier by not answering, she obviously preferred intimacy in the bed, but liked it rough if the mood was right.

As he kissed her deeply, he could feel her breathing intensify. He pulled away to look into her beautiful eyes. As he opened his mouth to say something to her, the power went out.

"Well that makes things—"

Before Millie finished her sentence, Charlie noticed that lights from nearby houses were still shining through the windows and blinds. He quickly covered her mouth and shushed her.

"Quiet," he whispered. His eyes flicked to the front door, then to her back door. "All the other houses have power, which means yours was cut."

Millie tried to pull away, but he pulled her closer and shushed her again. His hand had not left her mouth, and she started to struggle.

"Stop," he whispered. He listened intently, then heard a creak. "It's not safe here," he told her. "Go into the garage."

As he released her, swift footsteps sounded in the hallway that led to another part of the house.

*Who the fuck?*

Charlie grabbed Millie and threw her down to the floor between the couch and coffee table. She grunted as she landed, and Charlie turned to face the attacker as he unsheathed his knife from under his shirt.

The man was already in striking distance by the time he unsheathed the knife, and the attacker immediately knocked it out of his hand. In the dark, Charlie could see that the man wore a balaclava to cover everything but his eyes along with all-black attire to hide in the darkness. An assassin. The question was whether or not the assassin was from the FIA or from Jessik. The man's fighting abilities would show.

*Of course this asshole waits until I'm fucking drunk.*

The assassin lunged forward with a knife to stab him in his right lung, but Charlie grabbed his wrist. He felt so slow and sluggish fighting drunk. He tried to perform the disarm—the same one that he taught Ash—but the man twisted and contorted to break free.

The assassin tried to slash at Charlie's face, but he leaned away and tried to kick the man in the groin. He was so off-balance that he barely made contact with the heal of his foot. The man groaned and stumbled back as Charlie regained his footing.

The attacker quickly lunged with the knife to stab, but Charlie knocked the man's hand down and away with a palm strike on the wrist, following up with a turning kick into the man's left ribcage. The man shifted for another stab, but Charlie backstepped and kicked the man in his right knee from the side. The man yelped and fell to one knee.

Charlie tried to grapple the man from the side, but the assassin wildly swung the blade at him to keep a distance between them. The assassin then stood and flipped the blade around to change to a backward grip.

The man slashed, and Charlie knew he would immediately follow up with a stab from the side. Instead of doing what was expected—stepping back to avoid the slash—Charlie instead pushed the man's hand upward with another palm strike to the wrist from below. With the assassin's knife hand high in the air, he struck the man's throat with his metal hand cupped as if he were holding a glass to cause trauma to both the trachea and the carotid artery. The shock to his neck made the assassin gasp for air and drop the knife.

Charlie felt a mild cutting sensation on his left forearm as the knife fell, but he ignored it. Charlie then grabbed the man by the shirt and yanked him in for a headbutt, but he dazed himself just as much as he did the assassin. The Pit Bull was able to recover faster than the attacker, though, and he kicked him hard in the knee with his heel.

The man's leg bent backward from his knee being hyperextended, and he fell back with a pained yell. Charlie pounced and grappled with the man, eventually getting into the rear naked choke. He used his elbow to wrap around the man's neck and squeezed just enough to cut the blood circulation, but not asphyxiate him. The man swung wildly and writhed to break free, but Charlie remained in his position.

Eventually, the man went limp. Charlie immediately ensured that the man was breathing. The assassin was more useful to him alive. Charlie let out a sigh of relief when he was able to determine that the attacker was still alive and breathing.

*Amateur. Definitely not FIA unless it was just some idiot field agent fresh out of the Box.*

The first officer breathed heavily. He was extremely lightheaded from both the alcohol and his lower blood count. If it hadn't been for the current circumstances, Charlie would have easily overpowered him, even though the assassin seemed to at least know what he was doing. He just hadn't expected Charlie to be as proficient as he was, even with alcohol in his veins.

"Millie?" he called out. "You alright?"

The redhead's eyes slowly appeared from behind the couch.

"I'm okay. You?" she asked meekly.

Charlie nodded slowly as he tried to catch his breath. He glanced at his left forearm and noticed that there was a minor flesh wound from the knife. "I know you want to, but don't call the police. I need to ask this guy questions."

"Why was he trying to kill you?" she asked.

He exhaled sharply from his nose. "I'm in with some pretty bad people, and I'm trying to get out. Sorry for bringing trouble to your house."

"I'm guessing you're going to leave, then?" she asked.

"Yeah, but I need answers," he replied. "I'm going to need to borrow your car."

"What for?" she asked.

"Need to take him out of town to get those questions answered."

"You're drunk," she replied. "Let me drive. I just have a good buzz going."

"That's your decision," he said. "We'll need to make a pit stop at my ship, then take him over by the old mine."

"Okay, yeah," she replied as she finally stood in the darkness.

"I'll need some zip ties…and some bandages if you have them," he said as he grabbed his cloak and donned it.

"So how exactly are you going to get answers out of him? What kind of bad people are you with?"

Charlie glanced at her in the car. The assassin remained unconscious in the back seat, his hands and feet bound with zip ties.

"My uncle had debts with a mafia boss," he admitted. "I've been an enforcer ever since."

"Willingly or unwillingly?" Millie asked with apprehension.

He glanced at her again, and their eyes locked for a moment. Charlie looked down. "Unwillingly. Look, I like you, Millie, but I haven't had a normal life since high school."

"I can tell," she grumbled. "What have you gotten me into, Charlie? I'm just a materials engineer. I'm pretty sure that was the first time I saw an actual fight in my life."

"It was never my intention to involve you."

"Well you did, and now I have some guy in my back seat that's hogtied, and we're taking him out into the middle of nowhere."

"I'm sorry, Millie, but you didn't have to help. I'm already sober anyway."

"Well, I wasn't going to let you just take my car," she argued.

Charlie sighed. "I'd like to make it up to you."

"How?" she asked as she glanced at him. "How could you possibly make this up to me?"

"Proper date. Drinks and food with some conversation."

She looked at him. "Are you serious?"

"I said that I liked you, Millie," he replied with a shrug. "You're far smarter than I am and you seem to be a kind woman. Doesn't have to be anything serious."

"Do you honestly think trying to start things over is somehow going to make me forget that?" she asked as she gestured to the unconscious assassin.

"No, but I would like for you to see—"

"Well, you can forget it, Charlie. After I help you with this, I don't want to see you anymore. I don't want to be involved in whatever you're going to do."

Charlie looked out the window. Her words stung like acid on an open wound. He had enjoyed their conversation on their way to her house from The Quarry and their talk in her den. He could tell that she was an intelligent, beautiful woman. He was hoping to show her that night that he wasn't what others saw when they looked at him. He wasn't just some disfigured man. He wasn't just the Pit Bull or the Red Boa.

He wanted to show her that despite his gruff, off-putting looks, he was just a man like any other. Constance was the last woman to understand that.

*It's been almost a year since…*

He wanted to try something with Millie, even if it was just casual dating. He wanted to finally trust women again, but Millie clearly wanted nothing of it, and he didn't blame her. Who would willingly involve themselves in this kind of dirty business?

"There's the old mine," she announced as they approached. The entrance to the mine had been sealed twenty years ago, and nothing was around but the remnants of what it once was.

Charlie opened the door when Millie stopped the car, and he dragged the assassin out of the back seat and sat him up against a large rock. Charlie lifted the man's unmasked, limp head before shoving smelling salts up against the assassin's nostrils. The man jolted awake and looked around as the headlights on Millie's car turned off.

"Wha…" the assassin murmured as he looked around.

"Who sent you to kill me?" Charlie growled.

The assassin looked at him with wide eyes. "You're just going to kill me if I tell you."

"Maybe, maybe not," the Pit Bull replied flatly. "You and I are both just pawns in a game. I can understand and empathize with that. If you tell me, I may be sympathetic and let you go."

"Not unless you make guarantees," he bargained.

"You seem to believe that you're in a place to negotiate," Charlie remarked. "That is a false assumption. Tell me. If I decide to kill you, I'll make it quick, but I may also feel like granting amnesty. Either way, it's your choice."

The assassin shifted uneasily. "Jessik Kepov," he muttered.

"I had a feeling," Charlie replied. "What's your name?"

The assassin looked at Millie, but Charlie gripped the man's jaw with his metal hand and squeezed tightly, forcing the man to look at him.

"She's not here to mediate," he said quietly. "What's your name?"

"Lazar," he said after Charlie let go of his jaw.

Charlie nodded his head and woke his tool. He made a call to Sinister and used the speaker on his tool rather than his earpiece.

"Sinister Nightclub in Athens, Magna Graecia, who do you need to speak with?"

"Put Jessik on the phone, Nasib. It's the Pit Bull."

There was a pause as distant music thumped through the speaker. "Yeah, sure, Charlie," Nasib replied uneasily.

Charlie waited for a while and glanced at Millie once. Even in the darkness and the light rain, Charlie could see her apprehension, her fear. She looked like she was ready to run for her life, forcing him to frown.

*She's afraid of me…*

"Yeah? Hello?" Jessik answered.

"It's your favorite attack dog," Charlie said as he refocused. "I have Lazar here, and he's told me something quite interesting. You didn't try to send an assassin to kill me before I could leave your crew…did you?"

"Huh? What? I don't know what you're talkin' about, doggie. We agreed that you'd finish that job, then pay me a quarter mil. Why would I just skip on a quarter mil?"

Charlie could hear the nervousness in Jessik's voice. The mafia boss hadn't expected Charlie to survive. Clearly, he had decided if he couldn't have his Pit Bull, no one could.

"Because it was never about the money, Jessik," Charlie replied. "Knowing you, there's a few people that you can only keep in line because you use me as a threat. You're taking my offer, do you understand? I'm done working for you, and Francis won't have any more debts. Am I clear?"

"Don't you be tellin' me what to do, doggie. I only agreed to this because you forced me to. You better show up with that quarter mil next week."

"What about Lazar? Should I drop him off somewhere?"

"I already told you that I don't know what you're talkin' about, dog. I didn't send an assassin to kill you. Got it?"

"Oh, so if you didn't send him to kill me, then you wouldn't mind if I killed him then."

"What? No. I don't care," Jessik replied nervously.

"That's good to hear," Charlie replied as he unholstered his sidearm.

"Wait! No!" Lazar yelled.

Charlie shot the assassin in the kneecap, and he screamed. Jessik was quiet on the other end of the connection.

"Still with me, Jessik? I've wounded him, but you can save his life if you just tell me the truth."

Lazar fell to his side in the mud as the rain started to pick up in intensity. He moaned in pain, unable to do anything.

*Just confess, shithead.*

"Nope. Didn't send him."

"You're lying, Jessik," Charlie growled.

"Why would I need to lie to you?" he asked with disdain.

Lazar was whimpering and sobbing in the mud as Charlie waited for Jessik to confess.

"Alright, fine," Jessik replied. "I sent him to kill you. No hard feelings though. Just business. I'll let you go if you pay the quarter mil. Happy?"

"Extremely," the Pit Bull replied as he shot Lazar in the head.

He disconnected the call as Millie gasped. Charlie had forgotten that she was there. The woman bent over and vomited immediately. It must have been the first time she'd seen anyone die. Everyone vomits when they see their first killing or kill someone for the first time. Charlie was no different when he had to kill his roommate, Mashal, after he found out that Charlie was a defector and spy.

When she finished evacuating her stomach, she pointed at him with a trembling hand.

"You stay away from me, you fucking *monster*," she snarled.

Her words cut into him, but he forced his expression to remain blank. "I hope you will keep this to yourself, considering that I saved your life. He would have killed you once he killed me."

"I don't give a shit!" she shouted in the rain. "You just stay the fuck away from me! You killed him in cold blood!"

"He tried killing both of us, Millie. I couldn't let him live."

Millie looked at Lazar and shuddered, showing signs that she would vomit again.

"Just stay away from me," she repeated. She got into her car as Charlie put the hood over his head and grabbed the two spent casings from the mud to get rid of any substantial evidence. He pocketed the brass as she sped away, and he slowly started walking back to the junkyard behind Ray's Astral.

*Monster...*

# Chapter 32

Eri and Ash awoke the next morning, both reeling from their hangovers. They put on their work clothes in their apartment, and Eri realized that it would be her last day thinking of the apartment as home. It was still raining, though it had lessened in intensity. Corinth would experience flooding if the rain continued for a few more hours.

Eri made coffee for both her and her sister, and they both drank it to help alleviate the hangover. The two women quietly ate breakfast, both groaning as they tried to keep their food down. After they'd left the club, they had more drinks at Cutters, then took a taxi to Akhmed's while Francis returned to *Silver Bow.* Before they knew it, they closed down the bar long after midnight and took a taxi back to the apartment, both stumbling up to the door in their stupor.

Unlike most days, Ash and Eri didn't arrive at the ship early. They parked the truck next to the cargo ramp as soon as the clock turned to their designated start time, just moments behind the doctor. He got out of his car as they dragged themselves out of the truck.

"Oh, goodness," he said, "coffee may help with the headache, but water is the best cure for a hangover, ladies."

They both weakly nodded as they followed him up the ramp. Francis was waiting there at the top, his hands on his hips.

"Well at least some of my crew is here," he said angrily. "Have any of y'all gotten messages from Charlie?"

"He's not here?" Ash asked as she rubbed her eyes.

"No, and he won't reply to my messages or calls."

"Well, I hope he is alright," the doctor worried.

Eri sipped her coffee. "What if he's still asleep? He may have gotten so drunk that he passed out."

"If he passed out with such a low blood count, he may have gotten alcohol poisoning," the doctor warned the captain.

"Ya think ya can check the local hospitals for him?"

"I can make a few calls," Kai said.

"Have you checked *Fire Arrow*?" Eri suggested. "He may have gotten so drunk that he forgot that *Silver Bow* has life support."

Francis looked up and nodded. "Go check, Eri."

Eri marched over to the red Daniels Dart and lowered the rear ramp. Just as she suspected, Charlie was passed out on the bunk, slumbering lazily and still wearing the same clothes from the night before. She shook her head and walked up to him.

*I wonder what happened between him and that woman. Did he just leave her place in the middle of the night or did he take her back to the ship and she left early this morning?*

Eri grasped his shoulder and shook him, but he didn't stir. Out like a light. She sighed heavily and walked back to the cargo bay. Kai was over by engineering on his tool and speaking with a local hospital. Francis immediately turned to hear her report.

"Charlie is in *Fire Arrow*, but he's out cold," she explained. "I tried waking him, but he didn't even groan."

Francis nodded and looked at the security officer. "Ash, help me get him up to medbay so Doc can look at him. Eri, tell Kai he don't need to keep callin' the hospitals."

Eri nodded as the two left and she walked over to Kai.

"Alright," he said defeatedly, "I appreciate your help regardless, madam. Bye." The doctor tapped the holographic screen and put his tool to sleep.

"I found Charlie in *Fire Arrow*," she explained to him. "Francis and Ash are pulling him out now and bringing him to medbay."

"What is his condition?" he asked.

"Unconscious," she answered, "and he didn't stir at all when I tried shaking him awake."

Kai nodded with an intrigued hum. "Thank you, Erina. I will ready my equipment, then."

The doctor immediately proceeded up the port stairs and into medbay as Eri continued to wonder what could have possibly transpired the night before. Ash said that Charlie was walking with some redheaded woman on the sidewalk, but the woman that he spoke with at the bar had black hair. Stranger still, he was alone in *Fire Arrow* that morning and had passed out.

"I think your instincts are right," Francis said as he and Ash ascended the ramp with Charlie in their arms. "I've seen him like this a few times, and it was always the mornin' after. Him takin' it with his low blood count probably knocked him out cold."

"Take what?" Eri asked as they went up the port stairs.

"Don't worry 'bout it, Squirt," Ash replied flatly.

Eri knew something was amiss with how quickly Ash replied. They didn't want Eri to know something about Charlie. Probably something else that Francis had explained to Ash that she wasn't supposed to know.

After a few minutes, Ash and Francis returned to the cargo bay and joined Eri. Francis shifted awkwardly.

"Well, the weather said the rain won't stop until noon or so. Y'all can grab some of your stuff and bring it here if ya want. No pressure if ya wanna stay in your apartment until we leave, but it's probably best to start sleepin' here on *Bow* as soon as possible so ya can get used to the hum of the drive core in auxiliary."

"What did Charlie take?" Eri queried.

Ash and Francis looked at each other. "Don't worry about—"

"Don't you tell me what to worry about, Ash. What do you two know that I don't?"

The two looked at each other again, and Francis sighed heavily. He scratched the back of his head.

"Charlie takes drops every now and then," the captain said.

"Why would he take drops?" Eri asked.

"Do ya want the reasons in alphabetical order, or chronological?" Francis asked with a mirthless chuckle.

Eri looked down. Charlie had taken a combat stimulant and smoked, and a lot of people found addictions elsewhere when certain things weren't enough. Drops was just one more thing that Charlie took. "I thought you wouldn't approve, Captain."

"I don't," Francis replied, "but he always seems to find a way to get 'em without me ever knowin' until it's already happened. Everyone has their vice. His is drops. Dad's was gamblin'."

"Just wish he wouldn't," Ash said distantly. "I've seen what that shit does to people. Ain't worth none of it in my book."

"Shit, might be able to get him to stop if Eri tells him," Francis joked. "Never seen him let anyone boss him around like that."

Despite the joke, no one laughed. There was a silence between the three of them as the rain clinked against the ship's hull and splattered on the mud outside.

Eri looked up from the metal flooring. "Has Charlie's life really been that bad?"

Francis let out a breath through his nose. "Yeah, but there's no use gettin' all mopey about it right now. Ya two go get some of your things and bring 'em here while we wait for Charlie to wake up and the rain to stop."

Charlie's eyes slowly opened to the sound of rain tinging and clanging on the ship's hull above him.

"Excellent, you are awake," Kai said from Charlie's left, "How are you feeling?"

"You know how I'm feeling, Doc," he replied groggily.

"Hmm," he hummed affirmatively as he grabbed a small flashlight and held the first officer's left eye open. He flashed the light, causing Charlie to wince and try to close the eye, but the doctor's gloved fingers held back his eyelids. He waved the light in front of his eye a couple more times and observed his pupil shrinking and growing. "How many drops did you have last night?"

"I don't remember," he stated.

"You are lucky then," he replied, "you might have gone into a permanent coma with how low your blood count was last night. I took a sample while you slept, and you will most likely return to normal within the next day or two."

"Good to hear. I'll drink some water and get some food in my stomach, then."

"Not so fast, Charlie," Kai said sternly.

Charlie sighed with frustration. "What?"

Kai shifted. "There are plenty of therapies to help with addiction—"

"I'm not addicted, Doc," the first officer grumbled angrily. "I take them occasionally, mostly to get a full night's sleep."

"What do you mean?" the doctor asked.

"I mostly use them to catch up on sleep," Charlie explained. "My nightmares never let me have an uninterrupted night, so I take a few drops every now and then to mitigate that."

"You do not need drops to deal with—"

"I'm not having this conversation right now, Doc," Charlie interrupted again. "I need to get up and moving so I can direct the contractors with the weapon installations."

As the first officer shifted to the end of the examination table, the doctor put a hand between them. "Wait a moment. I want to know if you have informed the captain and Ashley about your TES."

Charlie shook his head. "Waiting for the right time to tell them, Doc."

"And when, pray tell, would that be?"

"I don't know yet," he answered with a tinge of anger.

"So I am the only one on this ship that knows about your condition?"

Charlie pushed his lips to one side. "No. Eri knows as well."

Kai blinked. "She is literally the only person on this ship who does *not* need to know about your condition, and you are telling me that she knows?"

"I needed to talk to someone about it, Kai," he explained.

"Am I not that someone?" the doctor asked with hurt in his voice.

"No," Charlie answered flatly. "I wanted to talk to someone who wasn't a damn doctor and would just talk to me about it instead of constantly trying to tell me what will slow the progression, what I should and should not do. I know it may be hard for you to fully grasp, but some people just need to talk to a *human* about their condition rather than a nagging doctor."

Kai sighed. "I know you are stubborn at times, Charlie, but you could have just told me that. If you wished to talk about your condition and terminal prognosis, I would have. It is difficult for anyone, and I understand if you would rather talk about the less scientific aspect of facing your own mortality."

"Well, it doesn't matter now," Charlie said as he finally stood. "She knows, and she will keep it secret. I hope—for your sake—that you will also show discretion."

"Of course I would!" he replied.

"Good," Charlie said in a low tone as he walked out of the medbay.

Francis walked up to Charlie's door, and it opened automatically. He saw his cousin behind the desk, silently removing rounds from a pistol magazine. His marred pistol sat on the desk with the slide locked to the rear.

"Changin' out ammo?" Francis asked him.

Charlie didn't look up from the pistol magazine as his thumb pushed the last two rounds out. "Yeah," he replied distantly.

Francis looked at the number of rounds on the desk.

*Thirteen. I thought that pistol of his held fifteen.*

He eyed his cousin, as he produced a small box of ammunition and put new bullets into the magazine.

"Thought that thing was a fifteen plus one," Francis probed.

"I is," his cousin said plainly. "Expended two last night."

"When and where did that happen? I thought ya told me before we left to pick up the girls that ya weren't carryin'."

"I wasn't," he answered. "Jessik sent someone to kill me."

"He obviously failed if you're speakin' to me," Francis remarked. "So ya killed him?"

Charlie finally looked up at him. His eyes were under the dark shadow of his brow. He looked menacing. Pissed.

"Yeah. Shot him in the kneecap, then the back of his skull."

"Why?"

"Wanted Jessik to confess that he hired the assassin. I worried at first it was one of Tristan's men."

Francis sighed heavily as his shoulders slumped. "Charlie, I don't think Tristan is gonna worry about ya."

"I'm too groggy to have that argument with you again," Charlie replied, "but I was actually glad it was just some hired killer from Jessik. I may not have defeated him if he was an FIA operative. I was still drunk when I fought him."

"Shit…wait…if ya were still drunk, did it happen when ya went home with that woman?"

Charlie looked back down at the pistol magazine and continued putting rounds into it.

"Is that a yes?" Francis asked.

"Did you need something, Francis, or are you just wanting to chat?"

"Just wantin' to get the whole damn picture for once, rather than just little bits scattered about."

"I was at her house," he muttered. "Anything else?"

"Somethin' must've happened that upset ya besides the obvious part about Jessik tryin' to get ya killed," Francis said. "Ya always acted like this whenever ya got done with a job ya didn't like. Just tell me what happened."

Charlie glared at him from underneath his brow again, but never responded.

"Fine, ya fucken stubborn shit," Francis said. "Keep your fucken secrets to yourself then. Rain'll be endin' soon, so get ready to give the contractors instructions with the weapons."

Francis didn't even wait for his cousin to acknowledge his command and stomped out of his room.

Charlie changed into clothes more fit and appropriate for work restoring a ship. He wore a plain shirt with his pants under his coveralls. He directed the different contractors on how to install each of the railgun turrets and had them prepare the front of the ship for the front-mounted beam cannons.

Condensed particle beam cannons were fickle weapons for such a small class of ship. Though on the smallest end of medium freight, a Kandahl AG-53 was not equipped with many weapons for defense, and the weapons that Charlie wanted would need to be custom-fitted and installed. With the powerful Lestour E-7 as the drive core, he could outfit the vessel with two front-mounted Nebula CK-35 beam cannons in a battery as a means to punch through the shields of pirate vessels or even frigates and light cruisers, if necessary.

In order to accommodate the cannons, Charlie had to remove much of the onboard storage in front of the engineering compartment underneath the galley. Moreover, he had to move the one viable weapon system that the AG-53 had from factory: the large missile and mine container. He decided to use the rest of the space that he had reserved for the beam cannons to have retractable missile pods that could be fired three times rather than one large pod mounted on the front that could only be fired once before rearmament.

The beam cannons would be mounted and installed alongside most of the turrets over the next three days, and the rest of the turrets, missile pods, and spare ammunition would be installed after. The railgun turrets were designed mostly as point defense systems on the AG-53, though they would also be used for short-range strikes on unshielded targets. The ammunition for the railguns could be changed on the fly with the gunner's pod on the bridge next to the helm. The railguns would be automated for point defense unless given a manual command or overridden by a person entering the gunner's pod. The missile disruption system was the standard affair with flares or chaff mines.

His ace in the hole was actually already installed on *Fire Arrow*. The large pod mounted at the top was an anti-ship torpedo. Though torpedoes were older weaponry that could be countered with flares, torpedoes fired manually and not locked onto a target would be devastating even for larger cruisers if it struck an unshielded ship. The only way to counter a torpedo fired manually would be from point defense systems hitting it at range; however, mounting it on *Fire Arrow* allowed for the torpedo to either be fired from the separated shuttle from a different direction as *Silver Bow*, or fired while still docked on the ship's top while the missile pods fired and distracted the point defense systems. It was a trick that he had learned from intelligence reports while working at FNI HQ.

Given that torpedoes were mostly out of use and considered "obsolete" because of the proliferation of particle beam weaponry, most newer capital ships would not have the necessary countermeasures to defeat it, and the torpedo could easily be replenished at the fraction of the price they used to be a decade ago. *Fire Arrow*'s nose-mounted railguns could also be used as a forward cannon, and he had already installed connections through the airlock to allow *Silver Bow* to control *Fire Arrow*'s railguns while she was docked with the mothership.

While the first officer oversaw the contractors installing the weaponry, the few that were left working on the interior worked on the armory. The armory was smaller than he wanted and couldn't accommodate everything he wished to install. He originally wanted the ship to be completely self-sufficient with small arms, complete with a reloading bench to help pass the time by making bullets at loads he wanted, rather than hauling thousands of factory rounds.

The room was unfortunately just too small to hold everything, so he instead went with more storage. If he couldn't make his own ammunition, he'd have the room to store it all, which unfortunately would eat into operational costs. The bench had been replaced by a rack of normal suits with thruster packs to allow the crew to properly conduct salvage operations if they ran across a derelict ship out in space. Once the day was complete, he would begin the long process of moving and storing all of his weapons, both innocuous and exotic, in the armory, which would be locked at all times and only accessible to him, Ash, and Francis.

As Eri used the mech to help the workers install the massive housing for the particle condensers, Ash approached the first officer.

"Alright, Eri, go ahead and release the assembly and slowly back out," he commanded as his protégé waited patiently for the task to be finished. Eri moved the mech out of the way and Charlie turned to Ash. "What do you need, Tall Hands?"

"The guys are all done with the armory," Ash said. "Just wanted ya to give your approval before I told them to help elsewhere."

Charlie nodded and walked over to Eri in the mech. "Can you supervise for a while?" he asked her.

"We just need to weld this into the frame and then install the condensers, right?" Eri asked. Charlie nodded. "Yeah, I can take over, but don't take too long. I don't know nearly as much about beam weapons as I do about other things on the ship."

Charlie nodded and signaled Ash to follow him. The security team then walked along the length of the ship as Charlie gingerly traced the hull with his fingertips. He looked up and saw the three small stripes near the top of the hull. Red, orange, and yellow. Just like a fire. Francis said that wanted to give some flair to *Silver Bow*, and what better way than to give it some color near the top where the red Daniels Dart would be docked? Since the shuttle was called *Fire Arrow*, Francis said that he would make it look like fire coming off the roof. It was a nice touch.

The two walked up the cargo ramp and up the port stairs. Halfway up the port stairs at a custom made landing, the doors for the new armory were open to him. He walked inside and inspected with a prideful smirk. Things were really starting to come together on the ship. It wouldn't be much longer until they were able to fly.

"Looks good, Tall Hands," he said. "Thanks for supervising."

"Not a problem, Charlie," she said. "If you're okay with this setup, I can tell the workers to help out with the railguns up top."

Charlie nodded. "Yeah, that would be best."

"Anythin' ya need me to do?"

"If you want to help, bring all the shit I have in *Fire Arrow* into the armory and lock it. I'll organize and inventory it later."

"Easy enough," she replied.

"After that, I have nothing else for you. Ask Francis if he needs your help when you're done."

"Sounds good," she said.

Charlie looked at the shelves, lockers, and armor racks, imagining where exactly he would put certain items, but he was pulled away from his thoughts when he realized that he had never heard footsteps leaving the armory. He turned around, and Ash was standing there, watching him.

"You're dismissed, Tall Hands," he said flatly.

"Why did ya take drops last night, Charlie?" she asked.

Charlie rolled his eyes and sighed. "Did Francis tell you?"

She shook her head. "Mom was addicted to that shit when I was growin' up. I know all the signs."

"It's none of your business what I do when it's off-hours," he replied.

"I get it, Charlie, but that don't mean I don't give a shit about ya. Did things not work out with ya and that woman that I saw ya with last night?"

"It's none of your business," he reiterated angrily.

"Kinda is though, Charlie," she argued. "I'm kinda the only other security officer on the ship, which means we need to trust each other so we got each other's back."

"Knowing the intricacies of my life won't make you a better security officer, Tall Hands, now get the fuck back to work." Charlie walked past her as he clenched his jaw and went back to the beam battery. As he marched back to his spot overseeing the construction, he saw Eri on her tool having a video call with someone. She was laughing about something.

"Well, the contractors are almost done with their break, so I'm going to let you go, Elga," Eri said as he joined her.

"Okay, sounds good, Eri. Send me a picture when it's all finished and tell Charlie I said, 'hi.'"

Eri flipped the screen around and showed him Elga on the other end. "Tell him yourself, bitch," Eri joked.

"Well, hey there!" Elga greeted him. "You look like shit when you don't wear a tailored suit."

Charlie chuckled. "Good seeing you again, Elga."

Eri flipped the screen back to herself. "See you later!"

"Bye!"

Eri ended the video call and looked at him. "You okay, Charlie? You look like something's eating at you."

"Fine," he lied. "When will the contractors be back from their break?"

"Not too long now. Probably five minutes." She peered at him again. "So, did you leave her place or did she leave *Fire Arrow*?"

Charlie's eyes narrowed. She was asking about Millie. He could see that she was doing everything she could to avoid talking about him taking drops, but she was curious about it.

He pressed his lips together. "Just ask me the real question, Eri."

She leaned back with confusion. "What do you mean?"

"You're asking if she's the reason why I took drops last night. I can see it on your face."

Eri looked away and scratched the back of her head. "I wasn't going to ask you about that, actually. I figured you took them because of your nightmares and past. I was curious because it wasn't the woman I saw you talking to at the bar."

Charlie raised an eyebrow. "At the bar?" She looked back at him, and he realized that she had seen him talking to Wei-Lu. He chuckled. "That was my supplier. Affection is one-sided between her and me."

"She doesn't like you?" she asked.

"Huh? No, I'm not interested."

"Oh…well, I saw you putting money in her—"

Charlie couldn't help but laugh. "She wouldn't take the money. Kept trying to barter for sexual favors."

"So then who was the other woman?"

"Just some woman originally from Hexham," he replied. "Things didn't work out."

"We're ready to go, Charlie!" the team lead informed him. Charlie looked to his right and saw all the contractors ready to continue mounting the beam cannons.

"Alright, thanks, Kim," he said. He looked at Eri and flicked his head towards the construction. "Let's go."

# Chapter 33

Charlie slowly lifted his arms up to let Jessik's doorman frisk him for weapons. As he had for the past year and a half while helping Frank pay off his debts, the doorman took his weapons and put them in a lockbox. It was during Sinister's hours of operation, so it had to appear like a respectable nightclub, not some place owned by the Kepov mafia family that functioned as Jessik's headquarters.

Frank was unfortunately behind on his payments again, so Charlie, as usual, was commanded to go to Magna Graecia to help Jessik. Normally, he would have been on a tight schedule, but Colonel Monnigan had kicked him out of his commando training just two months before, so he had a much freer schedule.

He sauntered inside and walked over to the VIP section. Jessik was sitting at a horseshoe-shaped booth with his arms stretched out along the top of the booth's bench. At the table was a group of women who were all giggling and laughing. The music thumped as Charlie slowly approached the booth.

Jessik looked away from all the scantily clad women and smirked as he saw Charlie approach.

"There he fuckin' is," he said as he puffed on his cigar. "Took ya long enough, dog."

"Had shit I needed to do, Jessik. I was on Svea when you sent the message."

"It's been almost a week. Svea is only five days away," he said with an annoyed face.

"What do you want, Jessik?" Charlie asked with annoyance of his own.

The mob boss looked at the woman to his right. "Can you believe the sack on him? You'd think he was the guy in charge here with how he's speakin' to me."

Charlie sighed as he waited. Jessik always had to establish that he was the one pulling the strings whenever he was around people.

"You see," he said to the woman on his left, "this man here is my little attack dog, but he's still just a dog. He can be trained with enough treats or a really good swat on the ass if he's a bad boy. Speakin' of which…Hector."

Charlie knew what was coming and relaxed his face as much as he could. Jessik liked to watch his men hit him, but it was probably the worst time of year to ask one of his goons to hit him. Charlie was angry that he had been pulled away from his yearly ritual and he'd already been feeling terrible for the past couple of weeks.

The young enforcer stepped up to him and swung. Poor Hector was the nearest person that gave him a reason to hurt someone, and he would ensure that he was in a lot of pain.

Charlie backstepped, gripped the young man's wrist, and hit his elbow with an open-palm strike. The man's elbow hyperextended as he yelped in pain. The Pit Bull then continued to pull on his wrist and kneed him hard in the stomach, which made him double over. As he moaned with pain, Charlie swiftly punched Hector in the jaw with his metal hand, making his jaw break in two places.

The table, including Jessik, went quiet. The enforcer moaned on the floor as blood oozed out of his mouth and he held his elbow. Jessik bared his teeth with a snarl and looked at another man.

"Gustov."

Charlie simply turned his head to the other enforcer with a serious expression. He only needed to stare him down to keep him from advancing. He slowly turned his head back to Jessik.

"The job. What is it?"

Jessik shifted uncomfortably as one of the women spoke up.

"If ya teach a dog to fight, Jessik, it's all it'll do. Ya apparently didn't give 'im enough of the treats."

"Maybe, but my little doggie knows not to bite the merciful hand that feeds him," the mobster retorted with a glare of his own. "Con will give ya the job orders."

"Multiple?" he asked with a raised eyebrow.

"Consider it a way to pay your debt to me for takin' your dear sweet time fuckin' gettin' here, dog."

Charlie sighed as he walked over to another table in the VIP section. It was the booth specifically for Constance and her friend Siu-Kei. The two women were in an interesting position amongst Jessik's crew. At night, they were simply there as intermediaries for giving and receiving orders from Jessik, but during the day, they were Jessik's spies. They would talk with low-level drug dealers from other gangs that tried to go into the mobster's territory, then would report on the men they'd seduced or flirted with to get information.

Constance wore black thigh-high stockings and a matching dress that barely covered her butt. Her skin stretched the fabric and above the stockings and extremely low neck of the dress. She clearly knew that her large breasts and thighs were a way to manipulate men, and Charlie was one of them. He'd always preferred the hourglass figure and appreciated a good set of thighs.

On more than one occasion, he'd spent the night at her apartment before he flew back to Venture, and she'd even convinced him to get a mod for his arm's taser to stimulate her. After she tried it for the first time, she always asked him to spend the night with her before he left. This time would be no different.

Siu-Kei was Constance's close friend, so close that they often shared men, either one at a time or together in the same room, but Siu-Kei was into a lot of kink, and that wasn't Charlie's thing. He'd tried a few things with her just to say that he did, but Siu-Kei never held it against him. Charlie was practically the only man that the two didn't share, and he wondered if it was because Constance had much more than just carnal attraction to him. The past two times that he had spent the night with her, she'd kissed him differently and even wanted to cuddle.

Siu-Kei was very much the opposite of Constance in terms of dress. She had more of a runner's figure, and often wore the very stylish red pencil dress that she wore that night.

He sat down next to Constance, and she shuffled closer to him. She smiled softly as she rubbed his right ear as always. When she first did it, he thought she was just being rude, but he found out later that night in her bed that she just liked touching his ear. It was different, and apparently she liked different. She would often kiss the right side of his face and the scar tissue on his ear. He hated to admit it, but he liked it; most women grimaced with disgust at it.

She kissed his cheek and whispered into his ear, just loud enough for him to hear over the dance floor, "How long are you staying, sweet thing? I don't want you to go back to Venture without a proper goodbye."

He turned his head to look at her. "Depends on the jobs you're supposed to give me, but I'll make time."

She smirked deviously. "Good, because ever since Jessik gave me the letter, I've thought of nothing but you."

"I doubt that," he replied semi-seriously.

"I'm serious," she whispered as she kissed his neck. "I haven't even fucked anyone else since the last time you visited. I only want *you* now."

His eyes flicked to Siu-Kei, and he could see in her face that she was watching intently. She was invested in how the conversation went, which meant that Constance was serious. Close friends were always the ones that truly gave away people's ulterior motives or secret feelings because they were just as invested, sometimes even more invested.

His eyes returned to hers, and he could see that her soft expression was sincere. He smiled slightly, knowing that something had changed. He wondered again if she had developed feelings for him, but he would wait patiently until he knew for sure.

"Let me look at the orders and I'll tell you when to expect me."

She opened the bag where she always kept orders for Jessik's enforcers and revealed his. It had only *"PB"* on the front of the envelope, obviously Pit Bull. He opened it and saw that he had to rough up two different store owners for being late on their protection money and had to kill one of Jessik's men, Thomas. Apparently, he was a rat, which explained why Jessik was so impatient. He'd kill the rat first. He knew the guy, and the man mostly worked at night and slept during the day, which meant that it was best to wait until he was asleep.

He'd be able to spend the night with Constance before he did the jobs. She looked up at him patiently since she didn't know the contents of the letters that she delivered. He kissed her on the neck, and she leaned into it.

"I'll meet you tonight at your place, unless you'd like a more private setting in my ship."

"I finally get to see *your* place?" she asked with a coyly raised eyebrow. "I could use a change of scenery. Have you ever fucked a woman in it?" He shook his head. She hummed quietly as she kissed his cheek. "Fuck me in the ship then," she rasped.

"How much longer are you going to be here?" he asked.

"Only another hour," she whispered in his ear. "What hangar?"

"Seventy-three. Knock four times on the side airlock."

With that, Charlie got out of the booth and walked out of the VIP entrance. He then collected his weapons from the locker outside and walked toward the spaceport. Halfway, he began to feel a headache, and he took a pill bottle out of his pocket after visiting a convenience store and getting himself some water. By the time he got back to *Fire Arrow*, the headache meds started to kick in. For the past few months, Charlie had been experiencing occasional migraines, so he carried pills to alleviate the symptoms.

When he got into *Fire Arrow*, he put his coat on a hangar. He scrolled through videos on his tool while he waited for Constance, and at about midnight, almost two hours since he saw her, he sent her a message asking where she was.

Moments later, he received a reply.

`Connie: Walking into the hangar right now, sweet thing.`

He opened the back ramp. Constance was still walking to the ship, but he could see that she had changed. She also had an overnight bag with her. He smirked when she walked up the ramp and peered around. He closed the back ramp as she dropped the bag on the floor and inspected the cabin.

"Despite having so little in here, I'm sure it's more expensive than my apartment," she said as she turned around. "And the bed is just small enough that we *have* to cuddle after."

He locked the ship with the access panel and sauntered toward her.

"So, what's the real reason why you haven't slept with anyone else?" he asked. "I thought we had something casual. Passing lights in the night every couple of months. Do you have a thing for me, Connie?"

Though she tried to hide it, he could see her stiffen. She didn't expect him to see through her so easily. Her sudden change in her typical confidence made him chuckle.

"Didn't expect me to see it?" he asked with a smirk. "What could you possibly like about me?" He approached closer until he could hold her waist. She exhaled heavily as he slowly kissed her neck, leaning into it again. "I won't go any farther until you tell me."

She sighed and he could hear her conflicted emotions in the sound.

"Because you've always treated me well, but it was never the kind of bullshit most men try. You don't shower me with gifts and praise to get my attention. You only try to give me a good time and treat me like a woman. You give *me* attention."

"That's not the real reason though," he said as he pulled the strap down on her tank top and kissed the top of her chest. She breathed heavier and groaned with frustration as she gingerly held his back with one hand and the back of his head with another.

"Please just fuck me, Charlie. I've waited two months."

"No," he replied plainly, "not until you tell me."

She exhaled sharply through her mouth as he continued to tease her.

"Because you're gentle," she explained. "Because I know you don't want to do all this shit for Jessik, and I don't either."

He pulled the tank top off her and removed her bra. She started to breathe hard and tugged on his shirt, but he swiped her hands away. He wasn't satisfied with her answer.

"Charlie, please," she pleaded with anticipation.

"Be completely honest," he commanded. He kissed her just below the navel, and he knew that drove her wild. Her fingers raked through his hair as she tried to resist, but she relented.

"Because you cared to know me," she admitted. He looked up at her as he stopped. He stood straight and she immediately tugged on his shirt again.

"You never answered my question, Charlie," Constance said flatly as he put his boots on. She crossed her arms in the morning light coming through the pilot's viewport.

"I can't go, Connie," he replied plainly. "I'm in much deeper than you are. If you disappear from Jessik, he'll just start relying on Siu-Kei or replace both of you. If I leave without a trace, Jessik will take all of his frustration out on my uncle—or worse, my cousin, who is innocent and ignorant to all of this. I will be happy to help you, but I'm not going with you."

Constance looked down and nodded. "I understand."

Charlie walked over to his coat and put it on. He then walked over to his locker, and he could feel Constance's sullen eyes on him.

"You told me that you did this because of your uncle, and yet how many times have you come back here from Venture because he's behind on his payments?"

"What else am I supposed to do, Connie?" he asked as he grabbed his knife and pistol. He checked for a round in the chamber and holstered it in the small of his back.

"*Leave*," she said as if it was obvious.

He spun around. "I just told you why I can't. Frank and Francis are all I have."

"And yet Frank sends you to the wolves every other month."

Charlie sighed with frustration. "Connie, we aren't in a relationship. I'm not starting a new life with you when you just now admitted your feelings after fucking me on and off for a year. What's gotten into you?"

She looked down. Her eyes darted all over the floor, but she never answered. She was hiding something.

"Tell me," he commanded.

She looked up at him, and he could see in her eyes that he was going to say something that he had never known.

"I'm married, and my husband found out about you…and how I feel."

Charlie stiffened. "Married? I've only ever seen you at the apartment."

"It's Siu-Kei's apartment, but I have the spare room there for obvious reasons. Andrew had been in the dark for so long, but Siu-Kei sent me a message about you at the worst time. That's when he found out. I got the divorce papers yesterday."

Charlie clenched his jaw. "Don't come back here, Connie. I'll help you leave the crew, but you're not welcome in my bed anymore."

She looked at him with sad eyes. "Please, Charlie."

"Don't," he growled. "Don't you dare try to justify any of it to me. If I had known you were married…I would have never…"

Charlie breathed to remain calm. He was fine with having something casual with a woman, but he never wanted to be an affair partner for someone.

"Get off my ship, Connie."

She slumped and looked at her feet. "I thought…"

"Get. Off."

Connie sniffled and straightened. "Fine," she said as she tried to appear stoic. "I'm going back to my place then."

"Just ask when you want my help, but that's all you're getting from me."

She slowly nodded and he opened the ramp for her. Not long after she left, he left the ship. He had breakfast at a small food cart, quietly fuming at the recent revelation.

*I swear I'm cursed with women…*

Charlie finished his food, threw the refuse in the bin, then marched over to the rat's apartment. Thomas would be first.

He donned his gloves when he arrived at the complex. He took deep and intentional breaths as he walked up the three flights of stairs to Thomas's door. He stopped just outside the door and took one last deep breath.

He pulled out his tablet and hacked the lock, which clicked with approval. He unsheathed his knife and quietly opened the door. Thomas wasn't awake in the common areas. He silently shut the door and tiptoed his way to the bedroom. There, he quietly turned the knob and opened the door.

The hinges squealed as the door opened, and Thomas immediately woke. Charlie rushed him and pinned him on the bed, wrapping his metal fingers around the man's throat and squeezing. He leaned back to prevent Thomas from scratching him and getting his DNA under his fingernails. The rat squirmed and flailed as he fought for his life, but Charlie was in control.

He took the knife in his left hand and slowly eased it down into the man's heart. The blade slid into his chest cavity, and he tried to scream with pain, but the Pit Bull's metal hand was crushing his windpipe.

"Nothing personal, Tommy," Charlie said quietly, "but Jessik found out you were a rat."

With those final words, he slammed the knife down while he crushed Thomas's trachea. His arms fell down and splayed out on his bed as his legs relaxed. Charlie watched the light fade from the man's eyes, and he retrieved his knife. He wiped the blood on the knife on the sheets, exited, then closed the bedroom door behind him and marched to the front door. He opened it, looked around for witnesses, and stepped out. He locked the door with his tablet and headed to the two businesses that he needed to visit.

The first business was clearly struggling. As he walked up to the storefront, he saw paint that was in desperate need of replacement and windows with iron bars on them. Athens was a nice city, but there were a few small parts that were really shitty, and this was in the heart of one of them. If it was a poor area of Athens, Jessik more than likely had a protection racquet, a drug dealer, and a pimp there.

He put his gloves in his coat pockets and walked up to the door. He sauntered inside, and there weren't any customers. That was good that they were alone. A man appeared from the back and hastily walked to the cash register.

"Can I help you?" the man asked.

Charlie placed his metal hand on the table to make a point.

"This is zinc carbide. Have you ever seen what it can do to a face?"

The man leaned back. "Huh?"

"Slow on the uptake, huh? Let's put it simply then." Charlie leaned forward. "You owe Jessik Kepov protection money, and you're late on your payment."

"P-please, I've barely made enough money—"

"Shut up," Charlie interrupted. "That is no concern to me or to Jessik. If you operate a business in his territory, you pay him money to protect you from other gangs. Jessik asks for a pound of flesh each month, and I'm here to collect…one way or another."

"Sir, please, I won't be able—"

"You interrupt me again, and you won't be able to pay your hospital bills either."

The man stiffened as he looked at the cameras.

"If you can barely afford rent, I know you can't afford the data storage off-site for your security cameras, which means that you have to store on-site. I can easily destroy or take the media storage after I show you how close you can get to the brink of death without ever having fatal wounds. So you have a choice, Julio. You either give me the protection money you owe right now, or I show you what it's like to get hospitalized from a beating and take everything I can find."

"You take pleasure in intimidating people?" he asked angrily. "Evil. Every single one of you."

"Yeah, yeah, I'm shaken from your pathetic retort," Charlie said in a bored tone. "Now pay me or I'll take what I please."

The man slowly opened the cash register and started pulling out bills. He handed the cash to Charlie, and he quickly counted it. When he was done, he looked up at the store owner.

"You're short by a hundred and forty shen," Charlie said flatly.

"It's all I got in the register," Julio said with a trembling voice.

The Pit Bull stared him down. He didn't say a word. The man was short, simple as that.

"I-I can get more next month," he added.

He waited wordlessly. The man started to shake in fear.

"W-what do you want from me?" he asked nervously.

"The one hundred forty shen you still need to pay," he said plainly.

"I have nothing left!"

The Pit Bull slowly walked around the counter and blocked the store owner from leaving. "Then you will pay in other ways."

"P-p-please…"

The man began to cry and whimper, and it only made Charlie angry. He punched the man hard in the stomach, and he doubled over with a pained moan.

"You're fucking pathetic, Julio," he said calmly. "You either need to market more or get out of your business."

The Pit Bull grabbed the man's hair and yanked his head up, causing him to yelp. He punched the man hard in the liver, and he fell down. While the man was on the ground, he stomped the heel of his boot onto the man's hand. As two of his fingers broke, he cried out in pain.

He left Julio on the ground and took four packs of cigarettes from behind the counter. He then walked to the back, removed the media drive for his security cameras, and left. As he opened the door, the man groaned and whimpered.

Charlie rolled his eyes. "Have all the money next month."

He walked away and pulled up the company that he needed to visit next. It was a small boutique for specialty pastries near the beachfront. It was an area that Jessik kept in line because he had the landlords in his pocket. Many of the businesses were successful in the area, so someone not paying into the protection racquet was someone standing in an ivory tower, thinking that the police would help them.

The nearest police station was always understaffed and too busy dealing with rowdy tourists on the beach. Even if they managed to call the police, they wouldn't arrive before he made his point. The boutique would obviously have cameras that would store data off-site, so he had to be creative. More than likely, the shipping dock for supplies wouldn't have cameras, but if it did, he would simply disable it by cutting the power.

When he got close to the beachfront, he took the alley that led to the back. There wasn't a camera that looked at the back door, but he wouldn't take any chances. He went to the shutoff for the electric company and cut the power. He waited by the door, knowing that the owners would come out this way to see if there was some mistake. He put on a balaclava to hide his face and wore gloves to not give away his metal arm. People like this would give the police a description, believing that the police would help them. An old man opened the door.

The Pit Bull rushed inside and pushed the man to the floor, making him grunt from the impact. He used his metal hand to grip the man's mouth and cheeks so he couldn't speak. He pulled the man up and punched him hard in the stomach. He groaned as he fell to his knees, and Charlie then kicked him in the head. The man was so dazed that he didn't say anything or make any noise besides the grunt.

The woman obviously heard the commotion and ran into the kitchen. Charlie knew it would happen and had already rushed to the door. When the woman got into the kitchen, the Pit Bull drew his knife and held it to her throat.

"You scream, and I'll kill him," he growled. He gestured to the man, who was finally recovering from the blow to the head. The old man looked at them wide-eyed as he realized what he was seeing.

"What do you want?" the old man asked as the woman whimpered.

Charlie's eyes narrowed. "You told my boss's messenger to fuck off the other day. You wouldn't pay the protection money that you owe him."

"Bah," the old man said with a swipe of his hand. "I'm not gonna pay into your bullshit protection racquet."

"Bill..." the woman whimpered.

"Listen to your wife, Bill," the Pit Bull warned him. "I'd hate to hospitalize an old man like you. If I have to go to the trouble, you *will* suffer."

"Then gimme an ass whoopin' and be done with it," he said angrily. "I'm not gonna pay ya anything. Pissants like ya never understand how hard I worked to get here."

"You think you're the only person to ever sacrifice and feel loss?" the Pit Bull growled. "You would have committed suicide if you experienced half of what I did."

"I *earned* what I've got and did it on my own as a poor boy in Corinth. What would a little shit like you ever understand about an *honest* livin'?"

"So be it," the Pit Bull said calmly.

Charlie punched the back of the woman's leg hard. It was with enough force to cause her leg to give out from underneath her, and she yelped as she fell. He approached the man, and the geezer thought he could somehow ambush Charlie with a knife on the counter. He tried to stab, but Charlie quickly hyperextended his elbow with a crunch. The knife fell to the floor, and the Pit Bull kicked the man hard in the knee.

The man yelped as he fell to the floor, and the Pit Bull started to pound the man in the face with his left hand.

"Pay your protection money," the Pit Bull said between punches. "Self-righteous cunt." He slapped him hard with his metal hand as the old man whimpered. "You think that just because you have money that it somehow makes you better than anyone? That virtue is somehow parallel with your bank account?"

The Pit Bull punched him again and again, and the woman begged for him to stop the beating.

"I will give you a lesson about the true cruelty of the universe." The Pit Bull punched him in the mouth with his metal hand, and all of the dental implants on the left side broke off their housings. He punched him again with his metal hand, and he broke his eye socket. "You live off the sacrifices of people like me! You will finally understand what people like me feel!"

"Please, stop!" the woman shouted at the top of her lungs.

He held his fist in the air as he panted and looked at her.

"Please…we'll pay…just don't hurt him anymore."

"I'm glad you saw reason," Charlie said as he released the man. He would need a hospital. The woman limped out to the closed lobby and pulled cash out of the register. Charlie counted the money and nodded.

"Please just leave now. We'll pay from now on."

"I know you will," the Pit Bull replied. "If you don't, I won't pay you a visit. I'll pay your children and their spouses a visit, then I'll pay your grandchildren a visit. Do you understand?"

The woman meekly nodded. Charlie headed to the exit with the money in his pocket, stepping over the man.

"And tell your husband to stop being a self-righteous cunt, or I'll have him do what I had to do in the war…and I'm sure he wouldn't like having to kill the woman he loves out of mercy."

The woman stiffened as he turned back around and walked out through the back door. He marched down the alley, removed his mask and his gloves, but as he walked out into the main road, he suddenly felt nauseous. Spit filled his mouth, and he rushed back into the alley and vomited.

He leaned against the wall for a moment and panted. He had just beaten an old man within an inch of his life in front of his wife…and he *liked* it. Before, he did what he had to do because it kept Jessik away from Frank and Francis. This time, he didn't have to put up a mask of intimidation. He *wanted* to hurt the man. He *wanted* to make the wife watch in terror. He'd relished her fearful face when he told her that he would visit her family if they didn't pay.

He had never felt that way before with any of the jobs that he had in the past year and a half. When he finally pulled himself away from the wall, he heard sirens. The police and ambulance were coming.

He walked away as fast as he could for a few blocks before he hailed a taxi and took a ride to the spaceport. For the length of the ride, Charlie felt numb.

*This…is what I've become.*

He paid the cab and slowly walked to his hangar. On the way, he bumped into a few people, but it barely registered in his mind in the moment. He just stared at the ground in front of him until he reached the back ramp and keyed in his passcode.

He walked up the ramp, closed it, walked into the bathroom unit, turned on the shower, and simply sat down on the floor. He never disrobed. He didn't even take his boots off. He just sat there as the water splashed him and stared at the wall.

The only thing he could think about was the monster that had looked back at him in the hospital washroom over two years ago. It wasn't just his disfigured body that made had him a monster. It was *him*. His rage, his hatred. He had done so many horrible things in his adult life, and he was only continuing the downward spiral.

"I'm…sorry…" he said to no one and everyone.

He let his head slam the wall behind him and screamed with sorrow.

# Chapter 34

The next four days flew by with all the work that Charlie and the crew did to get the weapons installed and mounted, but they finished on schedule. The only thing needed was to simply fly and test all the systems while in atmosphere and out in space. By then, the crew had all moved their things into their quarters and started to condition themselves to living on the ship and sleeping with the drive core humming.

Charlie, having been on ships previously, slept better than he had in months with the drone of the drive core helping him fall asleep. The nightmares continued, but he had grown accustomed to waking up in the middle of the night. Now that the ship only needed testing, Francis started implementing the overnight watch schedule. The shift rotated and the crew members who worked the overnight shifts were not expected to wake at the same time as the rest.

That morning, Charlie received a message from Sven letting him know that Ash's armor had arrived and that he also managed to procure an item from Charlie's wish list. Sven didn't specify, but it was good news, whatever it was—the wish list was extensive. The day of Jessik's reckoning was quickly approaching, so Charlie simply decided to kill two birds with one stone. He informed Sven that he would be there in two days for pickup. After, he would take care of the mobster. He had already planned out how he would do it. Everything was in place, his plan would finally come to fruition.

With each day that got closer to the two week mark from when he spoke with Asher, Charlie became more and more antsy. He was tempted to kill Jessik early, but he wanted to make sure that he did it the day before they left, just in case there were any complications. It was easier to run from the police if you had a ship that could leave the system.

Killing Jessik would be the final mark on the Pit Bull's reputation—a period that ended the last sentence in that chapter of his life. More importantly, it was to send Jessik's father, Jorgie, a warning to leave him and his crew alone…or suffer the consequences. Jessik's death would also send a certain someone in the Federation a very clear message as well, one that Charlie hoped would be very clear to his patriotic brother, Tristan.

He got out of bed and showered after seeing the good news. He was tired from the overnight watch shift, but the good news made his heart race and flutter with devilish glee. After he showered, he put on the clothes that he wore whenever he would go out, including his pistol, magazines, and knife, and went into the galley. Breakfast had already been made and Eri was still asleep from being on second shift.

Charlie poured a glass of water, reheated his leftover breakfast that Francis had set aside, and ate it quickly. He placed his container and water cup in the sink to let the day shift clean it for him. It was customary that the night shift would have fewer duties and cleaning, so small things like cleaning the night shift's morning dishes was a quickly adopted practice aboard *Silver Bow*.

Charlie descended the starboard staircase into the cargo bay as Francis finally restarted his morning workout, the first time since Frank died.

"Morning," Charlie said as his boots clanked against the metal flooring of the cargo bay.

"You're up early," Francis said between puffs as he pushed the barbell above his head.

"I got some good news just now, so I wanted to let Ash know," he explained.

"She's outside with the post," he said.

Charlie descended the ramp as the morning sun cast its light on the junkyard. He looked to his left and saw Ash staring down the post with her knuckles bloodied. She remained focused and did not look at her mentor. She sucked in air with force and pushed it out with even greater force as she punched the post. A few splinters flew off as she hit it with her other hand. She grunted with pain, then punched it twice more. Charlie waited silently, observing her.

When she finally lowered her bloodied hands, she finally looked at him.

"You're improving far more than I expected, Tall Hands," he said proudly.

"Thanks," she said as she walked over to a water bottle and poured it on her hands to wash away the excess blood. She then took some gauze and wrapped it around her knuckles to help the blood pool and coagulate to help the knuckles scab. "I'm surprised you're up already."

"I couldn't sleep after I got a message," he said as he leaned in to grab her attention. "Your armor is ready for pickup. I'll be in Athens in two days to get it."

"Excitin'!" she exclaimed, "Do you want me to come with ya?"

"No, that won't be necessary," he said with a raised hand, "I have some other business to take care of in Athens before we finally go off world, so I'd rather just go retrieve it by myself."

"Suit yourself," she said with a shrug as she sipped her water. "I'm about to go for a run, care to join me?"

Charlie smiled proudly. In just a month, Ash had become a fine soldier, one worthy of the armor she was about to receive. Not only was she a quick learner, but her work ethic rivaled even his. For once, he felt like he had accomplished something.

"Sure, I'll join," he replied. "Let me go change."

The two returned from their workout and chuckled about something Ash had said. They cooled down in the cargo bay as Eri lazily rubbed her eyes. She wore an oversized shirt and soft cotton shorts and groggily groaned as she held her coffee and descended the starboard stairs.

"Mornin', Squirt," Ash said between breaths.

"Morning…"

"I'm surprised you're up already," Ash said as she took a sip of water from her bottle.

"I slept before my shift and could only sleep for a couple of hours. I want to sleep, but my brain just wants me up, I guess."

"You'll get used to it," Charlie said as he removed the vest and dropped it on the floor, making a loud bang on the metal.

Eri slowly blinked and sipped the coffee as she sat on a crate near the two, letting the sun help her wake up.

"When are you and Francis going to start testing the ship today?" Charlie asked to break the silence.

She slowly looked at him, dark circles and bags under her eyes. "Whenever I finally wake up, I guess. He hasn't told me."

Charlie picked up the forty kilo vest and put it in the crate next to all the gym equipment. "I'm going to shower. Tall Hands, let's take a range day while the captain and your sister test out the systems."

"Alright, sounds fun," she said with a shrug.

"Wait," Eri said sleepily. "I remembered last night on my shift that I never got a chance to look at your servos."

Charlie thought for a moment and realized that Eri had never gotten the chance to fulfill her end of their little wager. They both had forgotten about it between the sickness and all the work getting the weapon systems installed.

"Huh…well, you could always do it tonight, I guess," he said, "but I have a feeling that Francis will want to celebrate after getting *Silver Bow* flying in atmosphere. We may just have to wait until we get off world."

"I'll just do it tonight," she said with a wave of her hand, "even if it means coming back early."

"Suit yourself," Charlie shrugged, "the option is on the table if you'd rather just wait a few days."

"No, let's do it tonight."

"Should I just avoid the engine room until tomorrow?" Ash asked with a chuckle.

Eri stared daggers at her sister.

Eri checked all of the drive core's systems to ensure they were working properly as *Silver Bow*'s VTOL system came to life with a loud roar. Unlike *Fire Arrow*, the ship required much more downward thrust to propel her upward.

Eri walked over to the PA system panel near the entrance to the engine room and depressed the call button.

"All green, Francis," she said giddily, "she's ready for her first flight."

"Roger, Eri," Francis replied.

The VTOL screamed and Eri felt the upward thrust for a moment before the inertial dampeners onboard stopped the pull of gravity inside the ship. She made a mental note to make adjustments to the inertial dampeners' sensitivities. Eri observed all the system monitors to see if there were any fluctuations or power spikes. The drive core purred gently as Francis put power into the engines and flew. Still nothing out of the ordinary.

"Anythin', Eri?" Francis asked over the speaker.

"Everything still well within norms," she responded.

"Alright then. I'm gonna start increasing thrust and test flight stability. If everything's fine, we'll start adding systems to the output."

She faintly heard the engines grow louder and higher pitched as he increased the output. Though she couldn't feel it, Francis's announcements of banking port and starboard made her realize that they were flying in atmosphere at high speeds. If only she could look out and see…

"Climbing," he announced.

She watched the monitors as the beautiful Lestour E-7 effortlessly strengthened its power output and gave more thrust to the engines as they fought gravity.

"Strap into your emergency seat just in case the inertial dampeners lag with inversion," he commanded.

Eri ran to the far side of the room and unfolded the emergency jumper seat with its four-point harness. She quickly buckled it and tightened the belts.

"Ready!" she shouted to the PA panel.

"Inversion in three…two…one…"

She felt the initial lurch, but the dampeners caught up and stopped the feeling of inertia—not even a nudge in one direction or another. She noticed that the engines and VTOL screamed as he obviously pulled the ship away from a crash course with the ground. The sudden realization made her sick to her stomach.

"Everything okay?" she asked nervously.

"Yup, just testin' her. She flies even more nimbly than I expected, and that E-7 has no lag with thrust output. Okay let's add the shields to the mix."

"Roger!" she shouted to the panel as she unbuckled herself. She checked the shield generator's systems and everything seemed normal. "Looks good, go ahead and activate the shields."

The shield generator came to life with a low-pitched drone. The noise raised in intensity and pitch as Francis increased output and shifted the shields from front to rear.

"How's the core?" he asked.

"Everything is fine," she said, "just a tiny dip in power output when you turned on the shields, but that's expected."

"Alright then," he replied, "I'm gonna be off channel for a sec and go over the ocean to test the cannons and turrets. I gotta ask permission and get a designated area to do it, so I'll be off comm for a while."

"Understood," she said as she pulled out the manual's second binder. She wanted to go over some warnings and cautions in the manual about the overclock system before they tested it. She quickly flipped through and read each warning and caution. Nothing seemed out of the ordinary. It said nothing about atmospheric flight, which made her nervous. What if the overclock couldn't work in atmosphere? What kind of problems would that cause?

She thought hard about the implications of testing the overclock in atmosphere, but nothing came to mind. She considered what she had learned in her school about manuals, warnings, and cautions. One of her teachers once said that the people who write the manuals are practically dictating what the engineers tried to convey with the machine. If they didn't give a warning or caution about a particular feature or situation, it didn't necessarily mean that it was fine to do. It may have just never been considered by the engineers. But surely using the overclock feature in atmosphere would have been considered, right?

*What if they never expected anyone to need the overclock feature in atmosphere, so they ignored it? What if it causes catastrophic failure?*

Even though she had practically rebuilt the drive core and installed it, she wondered if she could honestly make that call.

"Alright, we're ready to fire the weapons," Francis finally said over the PA. "Ready?"

"Yeah," she said, still distracted with her internal struggle.

"Firin' in three…two…one…"

Eri heard a loud whooshing drone and felt a slight tingle in her feet. The beam cannons caused some slight reverberations with the hull.

*Charlie would want to know about that.*

She looked at the output history monitor and noticed a small dip in output with the beam cannons, but it was still well within normal ranges.

"Okay, weapons test complete," Francis announced happily. "How'd the power look with the cannons firing?"

"Barely put a dent in the output, Francis," she replied cheerfully.

"Let's head back then."

*Silver Bow* landed softly back in the junkyard. The cargo ramp lowered as the elated maintainer came out of the engine room. Her pure excitement made her rush out, shouting with glee and running down the ramp to Charlie, Ash, and Kai. She raised her hands victoriously as she ran to Ash, jumping up for her taller sister to catch her and give her the strongest and warmest of hugs. The two sisters laughed as Ash swung Eri around.

"Proud of ya, Squirt." Ash beamed.

"Excellent work, Erina," Kai said. The maintainer quickly moved over to the doctor, who gave her a fatherly hug. As the oldest of the crew, Kai often was more like a father than a doctor to the other four.

Francis approached, and the captain softly hugged her. "Great job with the drive core, Eri. Thank ya for giving my girl the strongest and healthiest heart."

"*Bow*'s not just your girl anymore," Charlie finally said, "she's Eri's as well."

Eri released Francis and looked around him. Charlie stood there proudly with his arms folded and with a soft smile. He walked up to her and wrapped his arms around her. Unlike the last time he tried to hug her, it wasn't awkward. She wasn't going to miss the opportunity and threw her arms around his waist, resting her head on his chest.

"Thank you for rewarding my faith," he said quietly.

She pulled away slightly and looked up at him. "Couldn't have done it without you."

He released her and looked into her eyes. "No, you definitely would have. No doubts about that. You're the best maintainer we could have ever asked for."

A wave of emotion surged through Eri. Her efforts had made all of this possible. After all her hard work installing, reconfiguring, and tweaking the drive core, *Silver Bow* now flew, and beautifully at that. Charlie had *faith* in her. He had known very little about her, only asked her a few questions and spoke with her a few times before he hired her, and yet he had believed in her so early on.

She always wanted to work on ships and drive cores, but she'd never truly believed in herself. She had struggled a few times with imposter syndrome during the construction of the ship, especially while reconfiguring the E-7 to use the overclock feature, but Charlie had always held faith that not only would she succeed, but do so remarkably.

The emotion overwhelmed her, and she fell to her knees in the soft dirt, crying into her hands. Charlie knelt beside her and gently grasped her shoulder.

"What's wrong?" he asked.

"Why did you have faith in me? I was a nobody that worked on cars and winterized yachts."

"Eri," he said gently. She continued to cry both in happiness and sorrow, still not understanding why he believed in her. "You misjudge yourself. You're a far better maintainer than you believe. That beautiful silver girl right there is the proof of your abilities, and you should be proud of yourself. All of us here believed in you, not just me."

Eri finally calmed when Ash joined her on the ground and hugged her. "Love ya, Squirt," she said to the maintainer. "We didn't doubt ya for a minute."

Eri finally wiped the tears from her eyes. "Thank you…thank you all for believing in me."

Charlie stood up and opened one of the few crates still on the site, revealing a bottle of champagne. "I think it's time we christened the girl—what do you think, Francis?"

The five of them stood atop *Silver Bow* as the late afternoon sun cast long shadows. Charlie had tied a rope to the champagne bottle and ensured that it was taut and properly knotted to a mooring anchor point. He held the bottle out to Francis.

"Throw it out and it'll swing back down against her hull," he instructed his cousin. "Just don't hurl it, or it may come out of the rope and fall."

Francis held the bottle silently for a moment as Charlie joined the rest of the crew. The captain's face crumpled as he tried to hold back his emotion. After struggling for a moment, he straightened himself and looked at the crew.

"I christen *Silver Bow* in honor of my father, Frank Flores. May his spirit protect us and guide us as we travel across the stars."

With that, Francis threw the bottle over the side. The rope went taut and flung the bottle onto the hull, breaking apart with a loud pop and sending champagne all over the metal. The crew applauded, and the captain smiled with his toothy grin.

"I'll get the other champagne and flutes," Charlie said as he walked over to the airlock that led them back into the ship.

The four of them went to the galley as Charlie retrieved the champagne bottle and the champagne flutes for drinking. He popped the cork and poured the first flute for Eri, then poured the rest, starting with Francis. Kai wasn't much of a drinker, but even he partook in the special occasion.

The crew toasted to the ship a few times. They began to laugh and talk, but Charlie remained as silent as ever. Eri looked at him as he balanced his empty flute under his left forefinger, spinning it in a circle with the lightest of touches.

He stared at the glass somberly, then sat it upright before swiftly leaving the galley. Kai told a story about his time at Athens General Hospital, and for a while, Eri listened and talked with the others. It wasn't until they were out of champagne that she realized Charlie had never returned.

"Where'd our quiet first officer go?" Ash asked.

"He left a while ago," Francis said. "Maybe he's just tired and went to bed early. He doesn't like interruptin' just to let people know that he's going to bed."

"No way, too early," Ash argued. "He's probably just havin' a cigarette on the cargo ramp."

The hull began to tip and tap with the sound of rain hitting the metal.

"Or he's out in the rain," Ash suggested.

"Well, we are fresh out of champagne," Kai announced. "Are we going to continue our libations?"

"No," Francis said, "I figured we'd all have one big night out before we go off world."

Eri left and peered into Charlie's room, but he wasn't there. She checked the cargo bay, engine room, medbay, and laundry. Nowhere. She walked back into the galley, her stomach turning with worry as Francis shuffled cards on the opposite side of the table from Kai.

Francis looked quizzically at her. "Everythin' alright, Eri?"

"I've looked around the ship for the past twenty minutes and I haven't seen Charlie at all."

"Hmm…" Francis put his hand up to his bearded chin and thought for a moment, then stood up and looked up at her. "Follow me."

He exited his room and quickly walked to the cargo bay catwalk. Eri followed him, wondering what could have given him an idea. He went across the catwalk to the port side of the ship and pressed his tool against the locking mechanism for the armory. The panel beeped with approval and the doors opened. He looked inside and his shoulders slumped.

"I was really hopin' I wasn't right…"

"What?" she asked.

"Do you remember when he forced Jessik to agree to a deal?"

"I do, but what does that have to do with anything?" she asked.

"He said he'd kill the other two gang leaders for him before givin' him blood money in Athens. He leaves for Athens the day after tomorrow…"

Eri began to realize and looked inside the armory. His armor wasn't there. Eri groaned quietly.

"So he went and left without saying a word…just like what happened two weeks ago," Eri grumbled. "Why is Charlie doing this again? Is it so bad if we know he's leaving? It's not like I'm going to stop him."

Francis sighed as he looked down. "If ya want my honest opinion, Eri, it's for two reasons." Eri looked at him and waited. "The first reason is just 'cause he don't want to say the quiet part out loud. He's leavin' a celebration and happy times to kill someone."

"And the second?" Eri asked with a raised eyebrow.

"He don't want Ash to come with him. She's gotten a lot more confident in her abilities, but Charlie don't want her comin' with him."

"Why not? Wouldn't having some backup this time around be a good thing? I don't really want to find him bleeding like that again."

Francis looked down, and Eri could see him trying to find the right words. "Charlie…he's always been one to shoulder things on his own. Ya might just see it as a necessary evil to get Jessik off our backs, but it's deeper with Charlie. He's always been a martyr, takin' everythin' upon himself and keepin' others in the dark.

"I didn't know about my dad's debts until he died six months ago. Charlie had been workin' for Jessik the whole time to keep me away from his nasty business and so I'd always think highly of my dad. I confronted him about it when Jessik summoned us to Athens after Dad died, and I asked him why he was okay with doin' all the terrible shit for Jessik. Ya know what he said to me? He said 'I'm already a monster. Might as well be me.' He's got a lot of guilt, and he would rather do more terrible things himself than share it with someone as kind and beautiful as your sister."

"He would rather bear it all than let others," Eri summarized. "He's definitely got a lot of guilt."

"That, or he's got a thing for Ash and he don't want her to see him bein' the Pit Bull."

"You think so?" Eri asked. "I had my suspicions early on, but I'm not that convinced anymore."

Francis shrugged. "Sometimes I wonder."

Eri nodded and went back to her room as Francis went back to the galley. She opened the door and sat down on the bed. Her chest and stomach felt tight as she began to worry. Worrying about Charlie made her angry, and she sent him a message letting him know how she felt.

Despite feeling tired, Eri stared at the ceiling, unable to sleep. She sighed as he tool unexpectedly chimed with a notification. She woke it and saw a message from Charlie.

*At least this time, he replied.*

"I just don't understand, Francis," Ash said at the galley table. "Why would Charlie just leave without me?"

"Gin," Kai said with a smug grin as he revealed his cards.

"God damnit," Francis grumbled. He looked at Ash as he collected the cards and Kai wrote down the point totals. "Maybe he just doesn't want ya involved. He volunteered to do dirty business and he may not have wanted ya to be part of that. He took his armor too, and he won't get your armor until he goes to Athens to pay off Jessik. Maybe it's just too dangerous for ya."

"I hope it's just 'cause he don't want me doin' that shit with him. I can handle myself. Hell, he coulda just given me the rifle and I coulda provided overwatch or somethin'."

"If I were you, I would be thankful that he left you here," Kai interjected. "If he has to go assassinate a rival of Jessik's, he more than likely will have to do it in a very ruthless and cunning way. If I were a betting man—and I am—I would surmise that he spared you the dirty things that he will have to do in order to complete his job. Twenty shen on that."

"Sur-what?" Ash asked.

Kai sighed. "Surmise. It is an educated guess."

"So why wouldn't ya just say 'guess' instead of sur-whatsit?"

"Because it was an educated guess, not a shot in the dark."

"Whatever," Ash grumbled. "Regardless, he already told me a buncha times that I gotta be ready to do nasty shit to protect the crew, so why's he suddenly carin' if I go with him or not? The only explanation I can come up with is that he thinks I'm slowin' him down."

"Ash," Francis said with disappointment, "why ya gotta beat yourself up like that? If ya don't know, ask him, but don't sit here and just think of all the reasons why. *I* don't even know what the short fuck is up to half the time, so what makes ya think that ya could figure it out?"

"What do you mean by 'short?'" Kai asked with a tinge of anger. "He's only about a centimeter shorter than I am, and I am above average height."

"He's kinda got a point, Francis," Ash agreed. "Anyone is short compared to ya."

Francis chuckled. "Was hopin' maybe he heard me and would come back runnin' and sayin' somethin' like, 'won't be so fucken tall when you're on the ground.' Shithead is always remindin' me about how much better he is in a fight."

"Are you going to deal the cards or are you out of money, Captain?" Kai asked smugly.

"Alright, asshole. Gimme a minute to shuffle."

"Try not to forget your twenty shen."

Francis sighed and slapped another twenty shen on the table, which made Ash giggle. She liked seeing Francis finally lose at something. He was pretty good at cards, but Kai was just better than him. She enjoyed watching the two play off the clock, and it gave her a chance to be around Francis more.

"Ain't funny," he grumbled at her.

"It's kinda cute watchin' ya get so frustrated," Ash replied.

Francis glanced at her with a very subtle smile, but he didn't say anything.

*What was that look?*

"Don't ya have first shift tonight?" he asked her.

"Yeah, but I ain't tired a damn bit," she answered. "Couldn't sleep if I wanted to."

"Suit yourself," the captain replied with a shrug as he dealt the cards. Kai slowly organized his hand, then looked at the field. Francis quickly moved his cards around the way he wanted, then looked at her. "Ya know how to play?"

"Me? Shit no," Ash replied.

"Ya wanna learn?" he asked. "That way we have somethin' to play if we don't got four for spades."

She looked at him, and he slowly moved his cards closer to her. She couldn't help but smile softly as he grinned with that charismatic smile of his.

"Alright," she said as she scooted closer to him. Their shoulders gently rested against each other. He held his hand in between both of them and started pointing at the cards.

"So, the object of the game is to turn all ten of your cards into different groups of runs or sets of the same card. See how I got these here? Tryin' to do a run. These? A set. Kai starts 'cause I dealt. He can either pick up the discard or let me take it, and if neither of us want it, he draws from that stack in front of him. Once either of us have…"

Ash stopped listening and just watched Francis explain. He was so into it that Ash couldn't help but smile. A man passionately explaining anything was always a cute thing to see, and his gentle tone warmed her heart.

Kai waited patiently as he taught her, and when Francis finished, he gave her a strange look.

"What?" he asked with confusion.

"Nothin'," she replied, "just listenin' is all."

"What's with that smile?" he asked.

Ash snickered. "Just enjoyin' ya teachin' me is all."

In that moment, Ash realized how close their faces were. She had to fight against herself not to lean in for a kiss. He was so handsome and adorable in that moment. His brown eyes looked at hers, and she felt like even he was tempted to kiss her.

"Ready, Captain?" Kai asked cordially.

He turned his head and looked at the doctor. "Yeah. Ya pickin' up?"

*Shit. What am I doin'? He's married, Ash. Stop tryin' to get his attention...*

# Chapter 35

Charlie smoked a cigarette with his visor raised on his suit's helmet. He only had to wait a little while longer to get to who he needed to find the leader of the Cobras, Yufei Tong. He had lied to Jessik about knowing the man's location, but he'd already sent a message to Rock Solid's leader, Moise Louamba, to go into hiding for his own protection from Jessik. It was a good lie to get him to comply before Asher let him in on the secret. Charlie was going to kill Jessik and end the Kepov mafia's grip on Magna Graecia to allow Asher's gang, the Sun Scorpions, and Rock Solid to take what was left in the aftermath.

He slowly released smoke out of his nostrils as he waited in the foothills of the mountains where the mines were, overlooking a rundown warehouse where he would meet with the Cobra lieutenants. He had managed to get the contact ID to one of Tong's lieutenants and had sent out a message to him saying that he had information about Jessik's plans for the Cobras and wanted to meet the lieutenants in secret to deliver the information.

It was a lie. Jessik wanted Yufei dead, but only because the mafia don wanted Corinth for himself. Yufei was still going to die, but because Charlie wasn't going to let the Cobras exist anymore. Only the Sun Scorpions and Rock Solid would be on Magna Graecia.

The Cobras had already heard about Moise and Asher supposedly dying, so if the Pit Bull came to them saying that Jessik had plans for the Cobras, Yufei couldn't pass up the opportunity to at least hear the Pit Bull out. If Jessik had plans for the Cobras, then perhaps it was a strategic alliance. After all, the Cobras supplied some of the younger prostitutes to Jessik's gang for a premium.

The Pit Bull said that he would meet the lieutenants personally with the assurance that he would be alone. It sounded nice on paper that it was a peaceful offering, but Charlie never said that he would be unarmed or in one of the best suits of armor money could buy.

Yufei and the Cobras knew that they couldn't pass up the opportunity to hear the Pit Bull out, especially if the information came directly from Jessik. In the very least, Charlie guessed, the Cobras would come to the warehouse to take a shot at glory for themselves and try to kill him as a warning to Jessik to stay away from Corinth. Either way, Charlie knew they would show.

Once the lieutenants arrived and he dispatched them, Charlie would immediately go for Yufei. He couldn't let the man go into hiding, so he had to be fast and efficient. A man like Yufei—the biggest human trafficker in this sector of Frontier space—could not live, and he wasn't going to trust Asher or Moise to kill their old ally.

Lights appeared at the end of the lone road that led to the old warehouse. Charlie took a final drag of his cigarette and threw it into a pile of rocks. He lowered the visor and raised the armor plate as he exhaled through his nostrils, and an alarm went off in his helmet. The internal environmental controls inside the helmet immediately sucked the smoke out of the exhaust vents in the back of the helmet, causing it to belch behind him like a cremator.

He quickly jogged down the hill with his T-13 automatic rifle and ensured that a round was chambered. When he reached a wall that had been crumbling for decades, he listened to the men gather. Rain started to fall and clink against his armor as he heard cars pull up one at a time with a man getting out and starting conversation with the others. All of them seemed to be ready, and a couple wondered where the Pit Bull was and if the monster would be late.

*I've been here the whole time. Gangsters are always too confident. Not a single one has searched the building or the perimeter to see if it was a trap.*

The fifth man finally arrived, and the other four jeered at him.

"What's this asshole doing here?"

"What are ya gonna do? Balance the Pit Bull's sheets for him?"

"You're a fuckin' accountant. Go back and crunch more numbers for Yufei."

"If we have to start shooting, you either run or make yourself useful as a meat shield."

Charlie shook his head at the snide comments, but he knew exactly who would be his target for interrogation. The accountant, whoever that was.

"Has he shown up yet?" the obvious accountant asked meekly.

*Why the hell is this guy one of Yufei's lieutenants?*

"Nah, but we're still about five minutes early. Knowing an asshole like the Pit Bull, he'd make us wait ten minutes before he showed up."

Charlie smirked inside his helmet as he decided to add some dramatic flair to the situation. He turned on his shield and walked around the corner.

"Or I've been here the whole time," he said through his suit's speakers as he appeared in front of them. All of them stiffened at the sight, and he could see in almost all of their expressions that they were all on the verge of panic. "So which one of you is the accountant?" he asked sternly.

Frightened, the other four men immediately pointed at the man that he suspected. The man wasn't necessarily meek by any means, but he was definitely not gang material. Charlie slowly approached all of them, and they all reflexively took a step back.

"What's wrong?" Charlie asked. "I thought Cobras were the toughest gang in Corinth, yet all of you look like you're happy that it's raining so I don't see the puddles of piss in your pants."

"What do you want, Pit Bull?" one of the men squeaked out.

"First, let's play a little game that I like to call, 'do what I say because I have advanced armor with shields and you have fuck all.'"

All of the men shifted uneasily, though two had their hands ready to retrieve a pistol. Charlie had no idea why the idiots believed that they even had a chance against him, but it mattered little.

"Let's start with the accountant," Charlie said. "Go ahead and tie your shoelaces, pencil neck."

The accountant slowly knelt down, and as soon as he started retying his laces, Charlie lifted his rifle and opened fire on the other lieutenants. One managed to unholster his pistol before he was killed, but the rest all fell before they could react. The accountant held his hands up in surrender, and Charlie turned off his shield. He glanced at the number of rounds in his magazine through the viewport; he still had half of the magazine left.

Charlie approached the man as he cowered. He didn't say anything, but the clunking of his armored boots made the accountant tense more and more as he got closer. The man's hands trembled as Charlie knelt next to him.

"I find it quite amusing that you five idiots decided to meet with me with only pistols on your hips," Charlie said through his suit's speakers. "What did you morons expect when meeting with the Pit Bull?"

"I was just told to meet with the other lieutenants here," he replied quietly. He hadn't lowered his hands.

"What's a little shit like you doing in the Cobras?"

The man finally looked at him for the first time, but when he saw the armor plated helmet and rifle, he looked back down again.

"Didn't have any choice. It was that or be killed. It's how Yufei gets his recruits. Congratulates you when you graduate high school by giving you a choice to join or die. Didn't feel like dying at eighteen."

"And how old are you now?"

"Twenty-three," he answered. "Spent the past five years doing what I could to just get in Yufei's good graces so I could do something cushy."

"Like being his treasurer."

"Yeah…"

"Interesting. Where can I find Yufei?"

"You're just going to kill me anyway whether I tell you or not," the accountant replied. "So just get it over with already."

"You had no choice in the matter and you know what the Cobras do, yet you'd rather have one last act of loyalty? I spared you already. What's to say I won't spare you again?"

"You're the Pit Bull. No one survives."

"Plenty of people have seen my face and lived," Charlie replied plainly. "Who's to say you'll die or live? If you give me what I want—and don't interfere with me killing Yufei—I might spare you."

"Might," he said astutely.

"That's your choice, but if you don't tell me or if you give me bad information, I *guarantee* that you will die, but not after I see if you'll give up the information in exchange for a quicker death. I know all sorts of ways to make someone's death take hours. I'd rather not have to hear your screams tonight and would rather just kill your boss, so why don't we cut the negotiations and you just take my offer?"

The man kept his head low and slowly lowered his hands. He considered for a moment and finally looked up at Charlie.

"I will if you don't kill me."

"I can't guarantee that if you give me bad intel and it turns out to be a wild goose chase," Charlie replied. "But if you provide accurate information, I'll strongly consider letting you live."

The man gulped, then slowly told him the address and a few details about the house. Charlie put the information into his map through the armor's access panel for his tool. It would be about a fifteen-minute drive, an hour and a half on foot.

"Thank you for the information," he said calmly. "Now, you stay here until I am done with Yufei, and I'll let you know if you get to live."

The man nodded and sat on the pile of broken bricks in the rain. Charlie stood and walked over to a car. The moron had left it running and unlocked. He shoved himself into the driver seat with his rifle leaning against the front passenger seat. As he readjusted the seat to be able to fit properly with his armor and shield generator pack on, he received a message on his tool.

He opened the message through his suit's interface. It was a message from Eri.

Eri: I'm so mad at you right now, and I'm
not staying up waiting for you tonight.

He smirked and typed a reply message.

Charlie: Since you're so worried, I'm still
alive and unhurt at the moment.

Charlie drove off and headed to the address. He kept his helmet on because he had no idea what he was going into, and the accountant could be stupid and warn Yufei. Charlie hoped that he was smart enough to realize that his best option was to stay still and quiet.

After five minutes of driving, he received another message from Eri. He quickly opened it and glanced at it when he was at a red light.

Eri: Be careful, please. I'm worried.

Charlie marked the message as read and drove for another eight minutes, then turned onto the road to Yufei's house. He slowly progressed down the road toward Yufei's house. Like Asher's, Yufei's headquarters was the nicest for a kilometer in each direction. As he drove the speed limit down the road, he saw two guards out front. Neither had a rifle, so more than likely they only had knives and sidearms. The overnight monsoon rains started to fall heavier as he approached.

Still in his armor, he turned the cruise control on, grabbed his rifle, and turned on his shields. The accountant had told him that Yufei had at least five guards in and around the house at all times. He smirked deviously.

It was going to be a bloodbath.

Charlie turned the wheel to have it crash against the house's stoop, threw open the door, and jumped out. He rolled on the concrete just before the curb, stood, and shot both of the guards twice in the chest with his T-13 before the car stopped at the brick and concrete stoop. He rushed up the stoop as they fell to the ground and he kicked in the door at the deadbolt. The door crashed open to reveal a guard already heading down the hall in front of him to see what was happening.

Charlie quickly fired twice in the man's chest and once in the head. The guard had managed to fire once and hit his shield. A door flew open upstairs. He immediately dispatched the man upstairs, conducted a tactical reload, and continued clearing the downstairs.

As he turned the corner from the den into the kitchen, a man with a knife tried to ambush him. He blocked the kitchen knife with his arm as the blade scraped against his armor with a terrible screech. Charlie kicked him in the groin, then shoved his rifle barrel under the man's jaw. When he fired, pink mist sprayed from the top of his head. Some of it hit the ceiling, some of it landed on his helmet.

He continued to search the downstairs, but nothing. He then stormed up the stairs, and a guard in the hallway fired his shotgun as soon as Charlie came into his view. The buckshot exploded into sparks on his shield as the pellets spalled, causing tiny pieces of metal to hit the ceiling, floor, and walls. Charlie immediately returned fire with two shots in the chest. He pushed open the first door, but no one was inside. He moved to the second room, and as he opened the door, another shotgun blast hit his shield with a shower of sparks and spalling. Annoyed, Charlie shot him in the neck.

He moved to the last room, kicked in the door, and saw that Yufei was inside with two high-school-age girls cowering in the corner. The girls were covering themselves however they could. Yufei fired his pistol and hit his shield. Charlie shot him once in the gut.

The man fell to the ground, dropping his gun as he clutched at his wound. Charlie kicked the pistol away as he approached.

"Fuck…" Yufei mumbled as his hands trembled.

Charlie slowly turned his head to the two naked girls trying to cover themselves. "Get your clothes on and leave."

The girls nodded quickly, grabbed their clothes, and rushed out of the room. Charlie knelt down next to Yufei Tong as he moaned with pain. He slung the rifle, unsheathed his knife, and slashed the man's leg. Yufei looked surprised, but he didn't cry out in pain.

"Huh," Charlie said with amusement. "I must have hit your spine as well."

"Who are you?" he asked with terror.

Charlie opened his helmet so Yufei could see his face. "I'm the Pit Bull. Perhaps you've heard of me."

"Fuck…" he murmured again as he started to cry.

"I unfortunately can't stay long, but I want you to know that Asher isn't dead, and neither is Moise. You're the only gang leader in Corinth that I'm actually going to kill…and I'm going to make you suffer before you pass. Child sex traffickers like you don't deserve prison. You, and your entire bloodline, deserve to be extinguished from the universe."

"Please…" he begged.

Charlie took his knife, shoved it into Yufei's mouth, and slashed outward, splitting open the man's cheek. He yelped in pain as the blood started to trickle down his face. The man moaned weakly.

"Shut up," Charlie said calmly. "Society doesn't benefit from men like you somehow 'reforming' in prison. Your only option is death, and I'm here to ensure that."

Charlie drew his five-seventy-five magnum revolver, Darling, from her holster and fired once in the man's groin. He knew the bullet would turn his dick into mincemeat. Unsalvageable and unrecognizable. Blood splurted onto Charlie's armor. Yufei couldn't feel the bullet because his lower spine was severed, but he shouted with horror all the same.

"I won't let you have children raped for degenerates," Charlie growled. He fired Darling into the man's elbow, then again in his other elbow. The gang leader screamed in agony as his arms began to gush blood from both arteries. He'd bleed out soon enough.

He holstered Darling and stabbed Yufei in the gut on his left side. The man cried out as Charlie held the knife's hand grip with both hands, and slashed open his stomach with the serrated part of the blade. What was left of his intestines started to spill out of the massive cavity. He yelled, and Charlie wiped the blade on a dry spot on Yufei's pants.

He sheathed the knife and stared at the man blankly.

"No one will miss you."

Charlie left the man there to die on the floor and closed his visor and armor plate on the helmet. He swiftly walked out of the house, marched to a random car, retrieved his tablet from the dump pouch he used for empty magazines, and hacked the car's locks and ignition. He pulled away and headed back to the abandoned warehouse near the mines.

When he returned, the accountant was still there, listlessly sitting under a covered area out of the rain. Charlie grunted with approval when he approached, and the man looked up with anticipation and fear. He walked up to the man and towered over him.

He let the man's anxiety grow. As his chin quivered, Charlie let out one chuckle.

"If I see you trying to restart the gang," Charlie said through the suit's speakers, "I'll do far worse than what I did to Yufei. Understand?" The man nodded. "Good. Now get out of here before I change my mind, bean counter."

The man quickly scurried away, and Charlie began the long walk back. He'd take the time to let the monsoon rains wash the blood off him.

Everything was falling into place. In two days, Jessik would join Yufei.

# Chapter 36

Ash sat in the helmsman's seat on the bridge, half-asleep and trying to stave off boredom. She finally understood why Charlie had so many books to pass the time. There was little to entertain herself. Even scrolling through videos and news could only hold her attention for so long. Maybe she would ask to borrow a book from him.

The proximity alarm beeped at her from the console. She jumped out of the seat and ran to the armory. Why now? Who could be trying to get into the ship, or trying to steal what very little was left outside? She impatiently tapped her foot, waiting for the armory door to unlock. The panel beeped and the doors flew open with a hiss. She grabbed one of the shotguns and made sure a shell was chambered.

The ramp lowered.

*Fuck! Please be Charlie comin' back...*

Out in the rain stood a fully armored man holding a rifle and waiting for the cargo ramp to lower. It was the first officer in his armor, the same kind of armor that she would start wearing soon.

"Thank Christ it's just ya comin' back," she said with relief. "I was hopin' it was just ya and not some asshole." She lowered the shotgun and sighed.

Charlie removed his helmet as he walked up the ramp and closed it with the control panel. He began walking up the stairs to the armory, where Ash put the shotgun back in its place.

"I thought I told you to always have at least your sidearm on you while you're on duty," he said with a scowl, the armor dripping with rainwater.

"I'm sorry, I just forgot," she said defeatedly.

"Not good enough," he growled as his armored hand gripped her shirt, "we're going to be out there in unfriendly territory in just three mornings. You have to be on your guard at *all* times with at least a pistol at your side. No excuses, no mistakes. You are security for this ship, Tall Hands, act like it." He pushed her away slightly as he released her shirt. His sudden outburst frightened her.

"So I'm guessin' if you're in your armor and with a T-13 that ya killed the other two gang leaders," she said quietly.

"I did," he said as he unloaded and cleared his rifle in the armory. He set the rifle down on the cleaning table along with his pistol and the massive, painted revolver that he called Darling. He looked at her. "Where's your pistol?"

"It's in my room," she replied, looking down at her feet.

"God damnit, Tall Hands," he replied with icy disappointment. He put his helmet back in its spot on the armor rack. "You will carry your pistol at all times from now on." He dropped the shield generator onto a small table. "I don't care if you're in the shower or sleeping naked, you will have that pistol on your hip or thigh, do you understand?"

"Understood…"

Charlie unlocked and removed the armored gloves off his hands. He looked at her.

"What do you want, Tall Hands?" he asked with annoyance.

"Just wanna know why ya didn't ask me to help. I thought you'd want my help."

The first officer sighed. "I didn't want you involved. This was my responsibility and my idea, so I was going to do it myself. I don't need you doing such nasty business. I'd rather you kill people that are trying to hurt the crew, not a bunch of thugs who are uninvolved. Jessik wanted to carve away at the gang territory in Corinth, and I just gave it to him so he would leave us alone."

"But ya coulda used backup, Charlie," Ash replied. "I know ya don't want me involved, but I want to protect your six. Even if that just meant stayin' outside and makin' sure no one came."

"I didn't need nor want your help, Tall Hands," Charlie replied plainly. "You've never had to do this kind of shit, and I didn't want you to ever have to. It's not what I hired you for and it's not what I want you to do. I've been doing shit like this for years.

Just another job for Jessik, but there won't be any more after tonight."

Ash looked down. "That's the only reason? Not 'cause ya think I'm not good enough in a fight, right?"

Charlie rolled his eyes as he unhooked the codpiece from the lower and upper portions of this armor.

"No, Tall Hands," he replied gently. "Now go put your pistol on and resume your overnight duties."

"Right," she replied.

"And don't let me catch you without your damn sidearm again," Charlie barked as he closed the armory.

Eri awoke to the sound of her door's access panel chiming. Someone was requesting to come into her room. The realization hit her quickly, and she wondered if it was good or bad news.

She threw the sheets off of her, rushed to the access panel, and pressed the open button. The door flew open and revealed Charlie standing there in his nighttime clothes; he wore a simple tank top and sport shorts. She sighed with relief as she looked at him angrily.

"So I was right to assume you were asleep," Charlie replied. "Good thing I didn't call you when I was on my way back."

"Can you ever just let people know that you're leaving to go somewhere?" she asked angrily. "If you had at least sent a message when you left, I wouldn't be this pissed right now, Charlie."

"You all were having fun and I was on a tight schedule," he replied with a shrug.

"So then send a message when you're on the way toward wherever you were going, Charlie. This is ridiculous that I don't hear a thing from you until I send you a message!"

"Look, I'm sorry," he said with raised hands, "I just didn't want to dampen the mood. You were all enjoying yourselves and celebrating. Besides, you didn't notice that I was gone until almost an hour after I left."

"I didn't notice because I thought you just went to your room, not off the ship! And why is this all about you thinking that you'll bring the mood down? You leaving without a word is what brought the mood down, Charlie. If you had told us, things would have been easier tonight. Do you really think of yourself so lowly that you believe you're a detriment to everyone else's mood?"

Charlie looked away. "I just didn't want anyone to worry about me or ask questions, especially Ash. I didn't want her involved in this shit tonight."

"Yeah, and you could have just said that to her instead of making her doubt herself all night. Have you even told her that it had nothing to do with her skill level?"

"I told her about fifteen minutes ago," he replied.

"Good," she replied. "Why do you think so lowly of yourself, Charlie? I understand you may feel guilty or remorseful about the things Jessik made you do over the years, but that shouldn't define who you are."

"Goodnight, Eri," he said with a tinge of anger. He didn't wait for her response, and immediately walked toward his room.

"Charlie…" she pleaded.

The first officer walked into his room. The doors shut, and the locks activated with a clank.

The next morning, Francis dragged his feet into the galley, and his eyes widened. His cousin stood there cooking breakfast with his sidearm poking out of his pants, the shirt tucked behind the pistol's handgrip to ensure quick retrieval.

"When did ya get back?" he asked quietly.

Charlie looked over his shoulder and then refocused on the food. "Just a little after midnight."

"I'm guessin' ya went to finish the job for Jessik," he concluded.

"Everything for Jessik is almost in order," he said.

"What about the quarter mil?"

"Handled," he answered. "He'll receive my gift tomorrow when I'm in Athens picking up Ash's armor. We should leave first thing the next morning just in case Jessik has any ideas. I'll do a full watch that night. I'd rather be ready if he wants to try anything."

"As ya wish," Francis said as he sat down at the table. Charlie made a plate for his cousin and set it in front of him.

"Soon, we'll be rid of him, Francis, I promise."

"I hope so," he said reluctantly.

"Morning," Eri grumbled as she rubbed her eyes.

Charlie silently filled a plate for the maintainer and sat it on the table for her. He then filled a container for Ash, placed it in the fridge, and made a plate for Kai. He walked into the bridge and gave the doc his breakfast. The first officer then returned and walked through the galley toward the living quarters.

"I need to get some last minute supplies before we leave Magna Graecia. I'll be back in a few hours and we'll commence the vacuum tests when I return," he said as he marched to his room.

Eri sat down at the table and looked at the cup of coffee that Charlie had already poured for her. She sat down and slowly started to eat her food.

"He finished the job last night," Eri said to Francis.

"Yeah," the captain said quietly. "Told me he came back after midnight, but he seems determined. He told me that he's gonna give Jessik the money tomorrow."

"I just wish he would have let us know before he left last night," she said. "Really brought the mood down for the rest of the night and I hardly had any sleep before he returned. He woke me up to let me know he was safe and back, but that didn't make up for it. Made me sick to my stomach knowing that he was going out and killing again."

"Charlie will do what he needs to in order to protect the crew," Francis explained, "If that means he has to leave in the middle of a celebration to kill people, he'll do it."

"It's one thing to do anything and everything protect the crew," she explained. "I understand that, but for him to just kill more people for a mob boss…how are you okay with this, Francis?"

"I'm not, but Charlie is doin' what's best for the ship and the crew, so I'll never berate him for it."

"Hasn't he already done enough? He's almost died doing stupid jobs for that creep. We should just leave and not give him the money."

"He's doin' this 'cause Jessik has a father named Jorgie, Eri—and he's got a lot more influence, power, and resources. Jessik would ask his fatass dad to have us hunted down, and Jorgie never allow us to find safe harbor. He's payin' off debts and givin' him blood money in exchange for our safety and autonomy."

"Jessik's…dad?"

"Yes, and he controls a hell of a lot more than just Magna Graecia."

Eri paled.

Charlie returned three hours later. Ash had just woken up by the time he arrived. The test was simple: do exactly what they did the day before, but this time Charlie would also inspect the hull for leaks while the ship was in high orbit. If everything went well, no welds would need to be replaced. If any welds required replacement, they could hopefully fix them the next day while Charlie was in Athens and *Silver Bow* would leave the morning after.

Thankfully, the test went smoothly, and *Silver Bow* was ready for her maiden voyage. Eri still had not tested the overclock feature and she told Charlie that she wanted to double-check everything before conducting the test. The cousins didn't mind. Francis didn't plan on taking any dangerous jobs until they had done a couple of easier, less risky ones to get the crew acclimated, which gave them plenty of time to conduct the test.

Charlie, on the other hand, already had ideas for their maiden voyage, ones that didn't sit too well with Francis. The captain, however, had little choice since all of his contacts had no need for freighters at the moment. They needed to test the overclock sooner rather than later, and Eri said she would do it near their first destination. Charlie wanted to go to Rock Island.

Rock Island offered many opportunities that otherwise would be unavailable to them in more civilized towns and cities, one of which were exorbitant bounties. As a certified bounty hunter, Charlie could take Ash as his official apprentice with the guild and they could use their skills to hunt down some of the worst criminals in the Frontier. Many wanted criminals gathered at Rock Island, but many bounty hunters did not dare to stalk their prey there, as most found their way inside gangs that protected them in large sectors of the station.

Charlie wasn't fazed by that, and he wanted to see if Ash was as fearless as he was in that kind of situation. If her performance satisfied him, he wouldn't need to take another full-time security officer aboard and would instead only hire the occasional mercenary when the need arose. Some of the bounties on Rock Island were as much as some jobs that the crew would take on, so the spoils would be shared just like any other, though Charlie and Ash would take a larger cut as part of their hazard pay.

In the meantime, Francis would go and find work, whether transporting people or cargo, that paid well enough. Whether the captain wanted to admit it or not, Charlie's choice of Rock Island would be the best short-term solution.

Charlie remained reclusive for the rest of the day. He sat in his room with the door closed and locked. Ash and Eri went to the beach for the afternoon and Kai left with Francis to procure some more supplies for the medbay. Francis and Kai returned only after a couple of hours, but Ash and Eri didn't return until it was dark.

Charlie's absence had clearly affected the crew's dynamic despite him often being silent when they were all gathered. While they tried to pass the time, Charlie called the doctor over the intercom and asked to meet him in the medbay. The doctor left, but the three that remained quickly decided that they would just retire for the night.

Eri went to her door, but she hesitated. She wanted to borrow a book from Charlie and see if maybe reading would help her pass the time. She waited by his door for him to return from the medbay, but grew impatient after a while. She decided to simply ask the first officer if she could borrow a book from his room and leave. Perhaps he would allow her free access to his library.

She turned the corner leading to the medbay, but stopped near the entrance as she heard Charlie speak to Kai with a rather frustrated tone.

"Look, I know you want me to use the prescription, but I don't want it. They make me drowsy in the morning, they slow my reaction time, and they can be habit-forming."

"And drops are not habit-forming?" Kai asked condescendingly.

"Don't speak to me like a child, Kai. I'm trying to have an honest conversation with you about having a small supply of drops available to help me *relax* and sleep."

"And I refuse to partake in such practices. You either use the prescription that I will write for you, or you simply get drops on your own time and with your own money."

"The prescriptions are terrible and I would be paying you for the prescriptions anyway!"

"That is not my problem," he stated simply, "and you should not take drops with your TES. It will only exacerbate it and accelerate the degeneration."

"I don't care!" he exclaimed. "I just want what little life I have left to be comfortable, is that too much to ask? Is it really that bad when I'm terminal already?"

"Look, Charlie," Kai said, "I know the past week has been difficult for you with your mood swings, especially when you think about what Millie said to you, but you should not be so quick to resign yourself! The hospital doctors may have diagnosed you, but I am certain your prognosis is not as grim as they say. They may even be incorrect in their diagnosis. If you do not alter your self-destructive habits, then you *will* be terminal, but if you stop abusing all these narcotics, you have a fighting chance."

"I'm not going to simply limp along with brain damage for the rest of my life avoiding any and all danger for the sake of living longer."

There was a short silence.

"Eri!" Charlie shouted.

The maintainer froze. Did he know she was there?

"My quarters, *now.*"

She quickly walked back toward his room as her stomach turned. She waited there nervously for him to follow her down the hall, but she didn't see him. He instead took the other way around the medbay to his room through the cargo bay's catwalk. He stomped on the grating and turned the corner. His eyes were lit like a blazing inferno as he glared spears and swords toward her. He pressed his tool against the control panel and it beeped approvingly. The doors clicked and flew open with a hiss and he stormed into his room.

"Get in here and lock the door," he commanded.

Eri knew she was in significant trouble. His voice was loud, yet low with authority, and his breathing was deliberate. She meekly pressed the close and lock button on the interior control panel, and the doors shut and clicked behind her. He had his back to her and pointed at the chair in front of his desk without ever looking at her.

"Sit," he commanded.

Eri slowly sat down and felt compelled to explain herself. "I'm s—"

"I don't want to fucking hear it!" he shouted as he spun around. His explosive rage caused Eri to tense up and grip the arms of the chair. She had never seen him like this, and it terrified her. Her hands started to shake with anxiety.

"When is it ever appropriate to eavesdrop on a private conversation between a doctor and his patient?"

"Well, I—"

"That was fucking rhetorical," he growled as he shot to the edge of his desk. He walked around it and stood over her menacingly. His eyes darkened as he tilted his head down in the overhead light.

"I would like to believe I'm pretty loose with my rules and ask only moderate compliance given that we're just freighters, but there is one rule that I do not allow any bending or breaking, and that's the *sanctity* of privacy. The only reason the medbay doors were even open was because neither of us expected you or anyone else to be eavesdropping and would respect our privacy."

"Look, I—"

"I'm. Not. Finished." Charlie got close to her face with a hard scowl. Eri leaned away from him in fear. "For someone who claims that her sister is nosy, you seem to continually demonstrate that *you* are the nosy one. I trusted you with private information, but apparently, I misplaced that trust. I confided in you with a terrible secret and for *once* let my guard down and allowed myself to be vulnerable around someone, and you spat in my face."

Charlie slowly stood straight and walked back to his side of the desk. He placed both hands on it and leaned toward her. "I don't care how good of a maintainer you are. If I hear another person on this crew telling me that you tried to eavesdrop on a private conversation again—especially when it comes to the matter of doctor-patient privacy—I will kick you off this fucking ship at the nearest mooring and without severance under the morality clause. Do you understand?"

Eri's lip quivered. "Yes…" she replied in a quiet and trembling voice.

"You stood there for half of our fucking conversation and not once even dared to move away or even announce your presence. Your shadow was cast out in front of the doorway and it moved not even once."

"I didn't know that you knew—"

"And you think that absolves you of guilt? Do you know the definition of 'integrity,' Eri?"

"It's—"

"Rhetorical, again. Integrity is the act of honesty and doing what is right, even when you believe no one is watching. You failed every part of that definition. If I can't trust you to mind your *fucking* business, why should I trust you with the drive core? And you wonder with *total bewilderment* why I never open up to anyone or talk about my issues?"

He scoffed with disdain. "I thought you were my friend, Eri, someone that I could trust—someone I could finally be honest with and explain myself without worrying about the consequences—but now it only makes me wonder if our friendship was just a ruse to get more information out of me."

Eri looked down and tears fell from her eyes. Charlie stood up straight and sighed as she quietly cried. Silence fell upon the room like a thick quilt, Eri's sniffles the only noise. Charlie turned around, walked to his shelves, and removed a book from his collection. He took the small book in his hand and dropped it on the table in front of her. The loud slap made her jump and gasp.

"Start with that one; if you like it, I have other recommendations," he said defeatedly.

Charlie knew the whole time why she sought him out. She looked up at him. His face was stern but no longer wrathful and severe.

"Wipe your face, collect yourself, and get out," he commanded plainly.

Eri slowly stood up as she wiped the tears from her cheeks, her breath still uneven. "I'm sorry," she muttered quietly. She looked at the book. It was *Lord of the Flies*.

"Don't do it again," he replied sternly, "I don't want to have this conversation again and I don't want to be like this to my crew, but I will be a disciplinarian if I must."

"I just wanted—"

"I don't want to hear it."

Eri looked down again and wiped another tear from her face. "Sorry…" With that, she turned around and left the room.

# Chapter 37

Charlie awoke early the next morning and gathered his things. Eri would still be on shift, but he didn't want to speak to her at the moment. He knew he was harsh with her and she deserved an apology, but he just wanted to keep on schedule. Apologies from both of them could wait. The crew wanted to have one last hurrah before leaving Corinth, which meant he needed to be back by dinner. He grabbed two duffles with all of his supplies and left his room, quickly descending into the cargo bay, then lowered the ramp and watched the top of the stairs, hoping Eri would take too long to realize what he was doing and wouldn't be able to catch him. No one appeared as the ramp finished lowering.

He descended the ramp and pressed the button to raise it, swiftly marching to *Fire Arrow* next to the ship. He got inside and dropped the bags. He turned on the drive core, engines, and VTOL. As soon as he received permission from Corinth tower control, he lifted off and headed for Athens. He turned on autopilot and pressed the button on the pilot's seat to pull it away from the console. As the chair stopped, he noticed something placed underneath the bunk's sheets, sticking out just enough to be visible.

He turned on the cabin lights from the console and looked at the object. It was a folded paper with his name written on it. He retrieved it and opened the paper. The contents were in Eri's handwriting, something he had become familiar with while reading her notes in the margins of the owner's manual for the *Lestour* E-7.

Charlie,

I know you are probably still very upset with me, and I understand. I just wanted you to know how truly sorry I am for invading your privacy like that. I know you have a lot to do in Athens today, so I figured you would have some time to read this on the flight out or back. I'm better with writing things out like this anyway.

You were right about me. I am nosy, maybe too much. You are my friend and you placed faith and trust in me that I broke all because I couldn't just leave things alone. I'm not trying to make excuses, but I feel like you need to understand where I'm coming from.

I worry about you a lot. Between the TES, everything with Jessik, the nightmares, the panic attacks, and some of the things you've said to me and Ash, I feel like you're near a breaking point. You taught me to look at the small details, and even though you may get upset when I look at yours, it's hard sometimes not to see that you're hurting all the time. I just want to help. My problem is that I thought that if I knew more, I could help better. I was wrong.

I promise that I won't invade your privacy again, and I'm very sorry.

Eri

Charlie sat on the bunk. He knew her assessment wasn't wrong. He was near a breaking point. Even now, as he travelled to Athens, he was going to do something he thought he would never do. He had planned for it and was ready, but he would be crossing a line with Jessik. He wouldn't just kill him. He would make him suffer, and greatly at that.

He wanted to tell someone—anyone—but how could he ever explain all of his hardship, his guilt, his horrible deeds to anyone without sounding like a monster?

He *was* a monster, and he accepted that.

He had placed trust in his new friend and confided in her about his terminal condition, but he knew that if he ever explained to her what truly haunted him, she would never look at him the same again. They had become friends over the past month, and it would break him to see the horror on her face, especially if she knew what he was going to do to Jessik. Even if he'd threatened to hurt and rape her, she would say that not even Jessik deserved the fate that Charlie had planned for him.

Eri was kind, gentle, and caring, her heart pure. Despite his abrasive nature, Charlie had somehow bonded with her and often found himself calmer and at peace around her. They may have been complete opposites in some ways, but they understood each other. He once believed in the many things she still did, which made him admire her as a person, and her work ethic alongside her passion for her craft made him respect her as a crewmate. They both were very emotional people, but on opposite sides of the spectrum. Where he was hateful, spiteful, and cruel, she was empathetic, thoughtful, and charitable.

That dichotomy is what drew him to be so harsh to her the night before. Why did she have to care so much? Why care about him, a man capable of nauseating brutality? Why couldn't he push her away like everyone else?

He knew that she meant no harm, and him keeping his secrets close led to her developing a desire to know more about him and to understand his self-destruction. He couldn't blame her, not really. Francis was the same when Frank took him into their household. His cousin was also a caring person and only ever tried to help him heal. He'd seen the pain and sadness in Charlie, and had understood how self-hatred and anguish could draw a man into the darkest parts of his mind and soul.

Charlie never accepted help, and pushed everyone away. He wouldn't have to do it for much longer. With his brain putting him into an early grave, he would simply wither away and become nothing but a distant memory to what few friends and family he had. Something pulled at him, though. Between Eri's and Francis's insistence on telling his story, he felt compelled to, at the very least, keep the memory of his friends alive. If anyone deserved to be remembered, it was them, not the monster that he was.

Charlie slowly woke his tool, pensively wrote a message, and sent it to Eri. She responded almost immediately.

Charlie: Got your letter. Talk tonight?
Eri: Ok.

Charlie didn't immediately go to Athens Spaceport. He diverted course and landed near an abandoned warehouse at the farthest edge of town. He removed a duffle from *Fire Arrow* and set it down. He grabbed the other duffle and dumped the contents onto the concrete floor in the warehouse. He quickly and efficiently created a makeshift metal chair with welds and concrete screws to anchor the chair to the floor. He sat in the chair and ensured that it could hold his weight, then gripped the armrests and tried to rock the chair back and forth, ensuring that it was properly welded and anchored. The chair didn't budge. He then shifted certain contents from one duffle to the other. Satisfied with his work, he left one bag near an old metal drum that looked to be a fire pit for homeless people at night and returned to *Fire Arrow* with the other.

He took off with *Fire Arrow* and explained to ATH-SP that he experienced engine failure and was required to land for repairs. He quickly flew to his designated hangar and landed, ensuring that the dockworkers refueled the ship and had it ready.

He made his way to Sven's shop with a large envelope of cash to see what this mysterious new toy from Charlie's wish list that had become available for purchase. He walked into the shop and waited for Sven to emerge from the back.

When the man emerged, he immediately closed down shop and lowered the metal gates so no one could see inside.

"Charlie, my favorite customer," he said jovially as the metal gates lowered, "I have your friend's armor and a special treat for you."

"Let me inspect the armor first," Charlie demanded calmly.

"Of course," Sven said. "Beer?"

"Sure," he replied.

Sven returned again with a beer and a large strongbox. He opened the can as Charlie opened the crate. Charlie grabbed the beer and began his long inspection process. Even though Sven always ensured that everything was of quality, Charlie was no fool. Arms dealers like him always found ways of cutting costs, especially if it meant that the customer wouldn't be able to live long enough to get angry with him. Satisfied, he closed the case.

"Let's see this new toy," he said.

Charlie drank a few large gulps from the beer, an amber lager, and a brand he enjoyed. Sven returned with a devious grin and a large case similar in size to the armor's. Intrigued, Charlie pulled the armor off the counter to allow Sven to set it down.

"You're going to love her," the arms dealer said with a toothy grin as he unlocked the case. He lifted the lid and Charlie gasped.

"Is that…?"

"The Specter M-110 Anti-Materiel Rifle," he said proudly. "Ground forces and marines called it the Blockbuster, with good reason."

"I'm well aware of her reputation. It's why I had it on my list. How the fuck did you manage to get one out of the Federation?" he asked with astonishment.

"Some guy smuggled it out, but every buyer that he went to didn't understand exactly what this twenty-seven millimeter beauty actually was, or wouldn't pay him what he thought was proper. One of them sent him to me, and I paid a pretty penny for it."

"Does it have any rounds? It's not like there's a Specter factory in the Frontier for me to get some…"

"Only the four rounds in there, unfortunately," Sven lamented, "but I'm sure you're smart enough to figure out a way to make or get your own."

"No one knew about the M-110?"

"That, or they just offered an offensively low number."

"This thing can kill a man with full shields at two kilometers," Charlie remembered aloud. "I saw it in the war. Feddie snipers were efficient and deadly with them. Does she have a replacement barrel?"

"Sorry, this is all I got, but I knew you'd appreciate her more than any of my clients."

"You mean I'm the only one who would actually know what she was," he corrected jokingly. His eyes flicked from the twenty-seven millimeter rifle to the arms dealer. "How much?"

"Thirty."

Charlie shook his head. "You already said so yourself that I'm the only one who would actually appreciate the beast. Twenty-five and you have a deal, especially since she doesn't have a replacement barrel and only has four rounds."

"Fine, twenty-five." They shook hands, exchanged the cash for the rifle, and Sven reopened the shop. Charlie left with the two massive cases in each hand and made his way to the spaceport. He reached his hangar for *Fire Arrow* and lowered the ramp, placed the cases down on the floor next to the bunk, then stared at the M-110's case. He hungered to fire the weapon. He had seen its deadly precision efficiently disable vehicles, cut men in half, shoot through concrete barriers to kill men on the other side, and take down a VTOL transport with an accurate shot to one of its engines.

If he ever had the chance to use it, he would do it in a heartbeat. This weapon alone would strike fear into the hearts of all his enemies, including Tristan. His firearm collection now felt nearly complete for the possible battles ahead.

He woke his tool and looked at the time. Jessik wouldn't arrive at Sinister with his crew for another hour. The wave of emotion that surged within him was palpable. He may be a monster, but he'd never felt this kind of feeling before. He relished the idea of executing his plan and exacting his revenge. He couldn't help but think of a well-known line spoken by Edmond Dantes from *The Count of Monte Cristo*.

*How did I plan this moment? With pleasure.*

He closed his eyes and breathed deeply. He tensed his muscles and relaxed them. He knew what he had to do, and he would do it gladly.

The only thing that made him nervous was the fact that Sinister was in an area with a lot of cameras, and being near a large apartment complex made planning the raid tricky. Unlike his assault on Yufei's house, he couldn't run in with armor, especially with a suit as recognizable as his.

He would have to play smart to keep cops off his tail. He would need to fight Jessik's guards in clothes while preventing his face from matching in facial recognition in police databases.

He would only be able to bring his pistol, his knife, Darling, and a couple party favors to give himself an advantage. He had trained for it with Colonel Monnigan. Now, it was an operation.

A guard stood outside Sinister's VIP entrance in the late morning, a sidearm on his hip. He shifted as Charlie slowly pulled into the parking lot. The guard steadied himself as the Pit Bull emerged from the vehicle wearing boots, heavy pants, a plain shirt, a long overcoat, and a plain hat. Charlie shut the door and reached inside the back seat and grabbed his duffle. He calmly closed the back door and made his way up to the guard.

"That's far enough," the guard commanded.

Charlie stood still and raised his hat to reveal his face.

"I'm here to pay the don," Charlie said. "The Pit Bull is getting out of the business."

The guard finally recognized him and beckoned him over. Charlie gently placed the duffle on the sidewalk and spread his legs for a search.

"So what's with the paint on your face?" the guard asked as he felt up Charlie's legs for weapons.

Charlie didn't respond immediately. He waited for the guard to lift himself higher, where his head was more accessible.

"It's to fool facial recognition."

As soon as the guard started to search the waistband, Charlie pulled the knife from his coat sleeve and stabbed him in the neck. The knife entered his neck right at the carotid artery, angled upward behind his jaw, slicing and stabbing up into his mouth and cutting his tongue open. He pushed the guard off the knife to prevent blood getting on his coat. The man desperately held on to his neck in a futile attempt to stop the bleeding as he gurgled. He would die of blood loss quickly. Charlie calmly wiped his blade on the man's pants to clean it and put it back in its sheath as the light began to fade from his eyes.

Charlie then opened the duffle. Not a single shen was inside. Instead, he pulled out his two party favors: flashbang grenades. He smiled like a hungry demon as he pulled the pin on one, keeping the spoon held in place so he could prepare. He removed his sidearm from its holster as the guard's gurgles softened and faded, the man's pool of blood soaking into the concrete.

Charlie readied himself at the door and remembered his training. He took a deep breath, released the spoon, and kicked the door in. He threw the flashbang out onto the floor, turned his eyes, and held a hand over one of his ears. There was a split second of terrified screams before the grenade went off with a thunderous pop.

He turned and shot the first man in the head, then turned to his right and shot through the door at about chest height. There was always someone right there. He quickly sidestepped to his left. One man who was only slightly dazed by the concussion raised his pistol, but Charlie shot him once in the chest and then finished him off with a shot just below his right eye.

Xi, the big man that used to rough up Frank when he was still alive, poked over one of the VIP booths with his pistol. Charlie immediately rushed to one of the VIP booths as well to use as moderate cover, but he knew most bullets would be able to fly through it. Xi fired at him as he dove behind the small wall as splinters flew above his head.

The Pit Bull dropped the pistol and immediately reached for his revolver, Darling. If anything could penetrate through four booth walls, it was the painted beauty. He pulled back on the hammer and fired through the wall at about the height Xi would be squatting. He holstered the revolver, picked up his pistol, and poked around the corner.

As soon as his eyes could see around the booth's wall, he saw Nasib and Hector running with Jessik, dragging him with their arms locked with his. He shot Nasib in the back, forcing the enforcer to immediately fall and bring Jessik with him. Jessik falling also made Hector fall, and the little shit scrambled to get Jessik to safety.

Charlie stood to get a better firing angle, but saw George, the asshole who broke Francis's arm six months ago to "welcome" him into the gang, with a small submachine gun.

*Holy shit!*

Charlie immediately dropped to the floor and became as small as possible as George dumped a magazine into the booths to keep him pinned. Charlie couldn't waste any time. While splinters flew all around him, he quickly retrieved his second flashbang and pulled the pin. This time, he didn't hold the spoon and instead let the fuse cook before throwing.

*One…two…three!*

Charlie chucked the flashbang towards Jessik and his remaining enforcers, and it popped midair. George would be blinded by it for sure, but Jessik and Hector more than likely would just be momentarily stunned by the concussion.

Charlie stood as he drew Darling and saw George reeling from the flash and concussion with his head turned and his arm up at his eyes. Charlie shot through his arm, and the five-seventy-five magnum penetrated through his arm and skull.

The Pit Bull charged Jessik and Hector. As he turned the corner, he saw Hector on his back and pointing his pistol directly at Charlie.

*Fuck.*

Hector squeezed the trigger, but nothing happened. The fucking idiot forgot to chamber a round. Charlie pulled back on Darling's hammer, and shot Hector in the forehead as he screamed, "Wait!"

Jessik was on the ground with his hands up in surrender. Charlie holstered his weapon and hit him hard over the head with his metal hand, knocking him out cold. Charlie closed his eyes and breathed deeply. The hard part was over.

He removed handcuffs from his belt and cuffed Jessik's hands behind his back, just in case he woke up faster than expected. He put Nasib out of his misery, then dragged the don out to the car that he stole and threw him in the back. The guard outside was long dead and in a pool of his own blood.

Charlie had to be quick. Even though Sinister was near the edge of town, he was still in the city, and someone would be calling the police after hearing all the gunfire. He rushed inside, collected all of his shells and what was left of the flashbangs, placed them in the duffle, and threw the bag in the car. He turned on the car and hastily drove away.

Jessik awoke sometime later. He had been gagged, stripped of his clothes, and strapped to a chair in the middle of a massive, empty room. He breathed heavily as he looked around and tried moving, but his bindings and the chair wouldn't budge. His breathing intensified as he saw a man standing in a strange uniform inspecting the clothing's seals for tightness.

"You're finally awake," the Pit Bull said. His voice was calm with a slight note of happiness leaking out.

Jessik made noises from behind his gag.

"Oh, the getup? It's amazing what you can buy at a medical supply store all under the guise of making a costume. It's a biohazard suit designed to keep everything off me. Can't leave a trail for the police or get your filthy blood on me. I'm sure you understand."

Jessik continued to struggle and make noise.

"You know, Jessik, I've been planning this for a couple of weeks now, and I have to say, you're struggling a lot more than I expected. Consider me impressed. I thought for sure by now you would be crying and trying to beg for mercy and forgiveness. I thought being naked would have frightened the shit out of you, but I guess I can't always be correct in my predictions."

Charlie slowly revealed various tools and items from the duffle. Jessik may have been screaming from behind the gag and struggling with his bindings, but Charlie could see that he was terrified, not angry. Jessik had seen his attack dog being serious, stern, and angry, but he had never seen him calm.

Charlie slowly looked up from the duffle and looked Jessik in the eyes. "Do you know why you're here? Why I'm going to kill you?"

Jessik grunted behind the gag. His eyes widened with realization.

"Did you honestly think I would just threaten you and let you go after the mess I made at Sinister? Oh, no, no, no." Charlie stood up and approached him, his footsteps squeaking and swishing from the biohazard suit's materials. "I'm going to kill you, *slowly*, because you crossed a line, Jessik. You can order me around all you want because my moral compass is completely fucked up—has been since I was nineteen—but when you threatened to rape and kill my friend in front of me, all to simply make me compliant, your life was forfeit.

"It didn't have to be this way, Jessik, but in your hubris you wanted to cut costs and corners, so you decided to use the threat of raping and murdering my friends as a cudgel. Even if you had just had your guards beat me, but left them alone, I probably still would have done the job and you'd see the sun tomorrow."

Charlie walked over to Jessik and stood over him. "I find it quite funny that you call me the Pit Bull. You see, the pit bull was originally bred to be a working dog meant to attack and pin people, like a Malinois, but in the twentieth and twenty-first centuries, the pit bull got a nickname that stuck. It's called 'the nanny dog' because they are *fierce* protectors, but gentle around those they care for.

"The problem is that pit bulls require a lot of training and exercise to be that gentle, and you unfortunately trained yours to fight, hurt, and kill others, so I have no choice but to show you exactly how far down I've gone. I have a crew now, and I will protect all four of them like the moniker that you so fittingly gave me."

Charlie leaned in close to Jessik's face, his eyes dark with bloodlust. "Did you really think you could control a man who was trained by Frontier commandos and had become so infamous as a mercenary that the White Rabbits put a quarter million bounty on his head? Did you honestly think I was *ever* intimidated by you? Francis and Frank may have been, but surely you understood that I was never like them."

Jessik's breathing intensified and Charlie heard warm liquid splatter on the floor. He leaned back and looked at the ground.

"You've already pissed yourself, Jessik," he remarked. "That's good though. I'd hate for your piss to get on me. Now, your shit is a whole other story. No one ever mentions how dead bodies just *evacuate* the bowels as the muscles relax, and it's never a normal kind of shit smell either. It's that putrid, acrid smell of diarrhea that would make a fly gag. Thankfully, I have a nice mask to keep the smell out. I'll show it to you later."

Jessik began to whimper. Charlie immediately backhanded him with his left hand.

"Quit your whimpering, you fucking coward. I haven't even told you how this is going to work. I only have a few hours before I need to head back. The crew wants to do a bar crawl tonight as their last night out on Magna Graecia, and they'd start to worry if I don't get there before dinner."

Charlie returned to his duffle bag and revealed a black knife. He extended the blade from the handle.

"Remember this? You stabbed me with it. To me, water under the bridge, but you threatened to use it on my friend, Erina. You remember what you said?"

Jessik trembled as Charlie approached, pointing the knife in his direction.

"You said that you would rape her until you went chafe, then you would take the knife and continue her 'greasy cunt' all the way up to her mouth and split her open in front of me. Do you remember that? Blink twice if you remember."

Jessik blinked quickly.

"Good, because I want you to know that what I will do to you will be *far* worse. You see, I can't just kill you; your father would simply send his goons after me and harass me forever while I just try to make a living in the waning years of my short life. I have to send your father a message, and the message will be loud and clear. It will tell him that if he ever threatens or hurts my crew, I will exact it upon his fat meatsack tenfold."

Charlie walked back over to his bag and pulled out two vials and a syringe.

"This is a red combat stim—you might know them as 'fruit' because of their bright colors—it's supposed to really amp up your senses and brain activity. The problem is that if you use a red one, pain is multiplied." He filled ten milliliters of the red fruit into the syringe. "Combat stims only last for about thirty minutes, so I need to use it sparingly." He inserted the syringe into Jessik's vein and pushed the contents inside. The man's eyes rolled as the combat stim flowed through him. "I want you to feel every bit of pain, Jessik, but if you're in too much pain, you'll just pass out, so I need to make sure you stay *wide* awake, which is what *this* is for." Charlie removed ten milliliters from the other vial into the syringe and inserted it as well. "This is epinephrine, adrenaline. It will keep you awake while I do my work. Enjoy these last moments of ecstasy, because after I'm through with you, you'll *beg* me to kill you."

Charlie returned the syringe and vials to the bag. He grabbed a few more tools and staged them near the chair. He revealed Jessik's knife again.

"I'm going to tell you what I'm going to do, that way there won't be any surprises. First, I'm going to break all your fingers and toes with that hammer down there. You see, the human body has over two hundred bones, and a large number of them are just in the hands and feet. Once I'm done breaking every bone in your hands and feet, I'm going to take those pliers over there and pull out each of your fingernails and toenails, one by one. After that, I'm going to carve that nice little message for your disgusting father on your chest.

"Then, I'm going to make a few precise cuts down the length and along the circumference of your arms and legs, and I'm going to peel the skin off like I'm pulling tape off a roll. After that, I'm going to castrate you. I'll take your balls first with a nice flick of this knife of yours. Then, I'm going to slowly push this knife down your urethra, splitting your dick open like a banana peel as I push. Once I get into your pelvis, I'm going to slice up and stop right here below your sternum. I'm going to open you up and let your guts fall out onto the floor. And just as you're about to die from blood loss, I'm going to put the knife back in the hole where your dick is supposed to be. Questions?"

Jessik struggled and whimpered, tears flowing down his face. Charlie put on his gas mask and cinched the hood around it tightly, forming a seal to keep the blood off him.

Three grueling hours later, Charlie had finished his work. The warehouse stank of blood, piss, and shit. Jessik was dead, brutally murdered at Charlie's hands. He removed the clean suit and threw it into an empty duffle along with all the tools he used. After removing the clean suit, he was only wearing his underwear, and he quickly put his normal clothes back on, inspecting them for any blood.

He took the duffle and slowly walked back to the ship. It would take him about an hour to walk back on his route, even with a taxi's help. He had used Jessik's shirt to get the paint off his face and had thrown all items that he wasn't wearing into the duffle. It now contained all the evidence of his crime, and he would throw the bag out the airlock in his low orbit flight.

Fifty-seven minutes later, he arrived at his hangar, no one the wiser. He placed the duffle in the airlock and took off toward Corinth. Halfway through the flight, he opened the outer airlock door and watched the duffle get sucked out into the vacuum of space and burn up in the atmosphere, destroying everything inside. Any evidence now, if the cops actually cared about catching the mafia don's killer, would be circumstantial.

# Chapter 38

Charlie returned with *Fire Arrow* at the very end of his expected window of return. It was near dinnertime. For the first time, he would have the small Daniels Dart dock on top of *Silver Bow*. He slowly hovered the craft over the much larger Kandahl AG-53 and aligned the airlocks before descending. The landing gear touched softly on the upper hull, but to the people inside the freighter, the hull would have sounded like it had collapsed under *Fire Arrow*'s weight. Both ships were fine though, and the airlock created a seal.

Charlie hadn't used the lower airlock in quite some time. He lifted the appropriate panel and revealed the hatch. He pressed the open button on the access panel and the hatch opened with a loud hiss.

Charlie grabbed one of the crates and descended the ladder, which terminated on the catwalk in the cargo bay next to the medbay and his quarters.

"Welcome back," Francis said happily with his hands on his hips, "did things go well?"

"Jessik won't be bothering us anymore," Charlie said distantly.

Francis's shoulders slumped as the weight of the mobster finally left his frame.

"You owe me," Charlie stated in a low tone as he walked toward the armory.

Francis followed him. "Ya wanna be reimbursed for the quarter million?"

"I don't care how you repay me," he replied as he unlocked the armory with his tool, "whether it's cash, favors, or whatever, you owe me." Charlie entered the room and dropped the case on the floor then exited. "I've sacrificed too much for you *and* your father, and I want at least something in return." Charlie started to ascend the ladder back to the shuttle.

"Name it," Francis said.

"A fucking 'thank you' would go a lot farther than you'd think," Charlie growled from *Fire Arrow* as he retrieved the second case and descended the ladder. "You and your father both. Men who owe the world, yet when someone bails them out, the words 'thank you' suddenly don't exist in their vocabulary." Charlie scowled at the captain as he passed him on the catwalk, his tall and thin cousin's eyes affixed to the floor in shame. The armory opened again and Charlie placed the second crate on top of the first. He returned to the catwalk.

"Charlie," Francis uttered when the first officer reached the ladder, "Thanks…"

He looked at the captain, his expression blank and distant, patiently waiting for something else.

"I don't know if I'll ever be able to pay ya back, but I'll do what I can."

Charlie remained silent as he looked at his cousin, then snorted and ascended the ladder. He returned with a duffle bag and also placed it in the armory, Francis was wordless and still on the catwalk. After dropping the duffle inside the armory, Charlie locked the door with his tool. He stepped in front of Francis, silently demanding his attention. The captain looked at his shorter cousin.

"I know you'll never pay me back," he growled, "no matter how hard you try, it'll never be enough. Do you know how many innocent people I had to kill to keep that piece of shit off your back—and your father's? How many people I was forced to pummel because they couldn't afford their protection money? I still think about an elderly man that I beat to an inch of his life as they tried to start a small business in their retirement years, all because your father was behind on his payments.

"Do you know what it's like to slowly allow your moral compass to erode just to keep your family safe? I forgot, you're a *peaceful* man now, letting me do the monstrous things on your behalf. Unlike you, I'm willing to do *whatever* it takes to keep my friends and family safe."

Francis remained still, his shame seeming to envelop him like crude oil on skin.

"For two and a half years, I've done nothing but clean up your father's mess, and now I'm done with it. I'm just glad you have the temerity to not gamble like he did, but if I ever find out that you've accumulated a gambling debt with a mobster, you're on your own."

"I'll transfer the quarter million to your account," the captain said meekly.

"No, don't you fucking dare take away from the ship's expense account or from the emergency fund for the crew," Charlie commanded, "I will not have you shuffle that money away from the crew or the ship. None of them were part of this and were only victims. One day, I won't be around, and you'll need to be the survivor and leader that I once knew rather than whatever bullshit you've decided to become."

Charlie stormed off toward his quarters, leaving the captain alone with his shame and sorrow. The weight of all that he had done in Frank's name had finally slid off his back and shoulders, but he couldn't help but feel his anger rise as he wondered how long Francis would have allowed Charlie to be Jessik's attack dog if he'd not finished it all that morning. Did Francis and Frank even care about what the don had made him do? Did they take advantage of his selflessness? Charlie gripped his desk as he grinded his teeth.

The door opened with a hiss, and Charlie looked up with dark eyes shrouded by the shadows his furrowed brow created. He'd left the door on automatic just in case one of the crew needed to speak with him. His expression softened as he saw Eri standing in the doorway. She was wearing a crimson skirt with crimson heels, a cream spaghetti strap, and a maroon hooded cloak made of synthetic fibers. She was obviously ready for the bar crawl that night, but prepared for the expected rain later. The darker reds on her outfit, combined with her fair skin and wavy, brunette hair made her hazel eyes pop.

Whether Charlie wanted to admit it or not, he recognized that his friend was striking in red, just like when he saw her at the wedding reception. If Michelle knew and understood one thing, it was that the color of clothes could make the eyes more pronounced and give a completely new definition to their beauty.

Despite everything, he was happy that Jessik would never hurt Eri or the rest of the crew. His grip on the table loosened and his cheeks raised with the slightest of smiles. Even though his cousin and uncle may have left him alone to deal with Jessik to help pay off their debts, he would never have to worry about Eri being under his shadow. He and Ash would protect her, no matter what. Her earlier transgressions faded like a distant memory and any anger he still had for her disappeared.

"Did everything go well?" she asked, avoiding his gaze with shame still lingering from the night before.

"Jessik won't be a problem from now on," Charlie replied softly, his smile becoming more pronounced as he realized that everything had been worth it.

"Can I come in?" she requested meekly.

"Of course," he answered.

She slowly entered the room and sat down in the chair across from him. She had yet to look at him.

"I just wanted to say—"

"You've already said enough," he interrupted her with a hand raised. She finally looked up with a frown as he stood up straight. "I should be apologizing for acting the way I did. No one should have to fear their leader, and no one should have to be afraid of their friend. To be honest, I didn't sleep well last night because I kept thinking about how scared you were. I promise that I will do everything I can to make it up to you. You should feel safe around me, not terrified."

Eri pursed her lips in an attempt to remove her frown.

"When are we leaving for the bar crawl?" he asked after a long silence.

"In about thirty minutes," she replied, "there's going to be rain again tonight, so make sure you wear something to keep you dry."

"Lock the door on your way out then," he requested. "I'm going to shower and change."

Charlie stood in the shower as the warm water dripped on him endlessly. He had remained there for a long while, letting the warmth embrace him and the water wash away his sins. He may not have gotten any of Jessik's blood on him, but he still felt like he was covered in it. Somehow, he could still smell it.

Even after all the carnage he had seen in his lifetime, the gruesome job he'd executed that day stood out for him. It was a necessary evil to keep Jessik and his father Jorgie away from *Silver Bow*, but he had never seen that much blood before, not even when he was bleeding out in the staging yard. He often wondered if that sight bothered Eri from time to time, like his memories of the elderly couple, his roommate Mashal, or Zoreah leaking into his thoughts. He wanted to ask, but it wasn't his business, and the question was probably too personal.

He slowly shaved his face, washed his hair, and lathered his body in soap, but no matter what he did, he could still smell Jessik's blood. It hung in the air about him and it made him feel sick to his stomach, not because of what he did, but because of his disdain for the creature. The don had committed horrible atrocities on innocent and not-so-innocent people for decades. He had hurt, murdered, and raped dozens, if not hundreds. His blood even stank like an acrid solution of acid.

Charlie was not proud of his actions, but the more he thought about how many opportunities he had to kill the man, it made his skin crawl as he realized how long he had allowed the man to control him and commit evils. In the shower, as the hot water began to turn cold, he swore he would never allow that to happen again.

*You're next, Tristan.*

The first officer finally shut off the water and began to dry himself as he saw the panel on the wall light up from the door's intercom.

"Charlie? Ya coming?" Ash asked through the bathroom panel's speaker.

"Shit," Charlie whispered as he approached the box, water still dripping off him and onto the tile floor. He had been in the shower for half an hour. Time had slipped away in his thoughts. He depressed the talk button. "Sorry, I fell asleep in the shower," he lied. "What bar are you going to first? I'll take a taxi and meet you there."

"We're goin' to McGillan's," she replied.

"Alright, I'll be there as soon as possible."

Charlie walked away from the panel and continued drying himself, the mirror in the bathroom completely obscured by condensation. He put on his underwear and looked at the clothes in his closet absentmindedly. He put on some waterproof boots, plain pants, a white undershirt, and a dark gray Henley tunic without buttons, then rolled the long sleeves up to his elbows.

He removed his Hexhamite cloak off its hanger, but when he was about to put it on, he smelled something familiar. He pressed the soft waterproof cloth up to his nose and breathed in. The cloak still smelled like Millie's perfume. Sadness rushed through him as all his thoughts lingered on her disgusted voice.

*You stay away from me, you fucking monster.*

Millie was the first woman that Charlie had ever considered dating, even if casually, since Christie. Before he could even get things started with her, she saw the Pit Bull. For the past four years, Charlie had only known violence and had learned to accept himself as a monster. Christie encouraged it, so when Millie called him a monster, it hurt him in a way that it never had before. The first woman that had interested him since he had been betrayed by his brother and fiancée showed fear and disgust, and he realized in that moment how far he had really gone.

It's one thing to be called a monster by some shop keeper he didn't care about, it was another to hear it from a woman that he liked. He sighed heavily.

*Monster.*

That's what he was, and that's what he would be. He wanted one woman to see who he once was, the Charlie that clawed to the surface while being pulled down by the phantoms of his past. The Charlie that Zoreah knew. The optimistic, altruistic Charlie that joined the Federal Navy out of a sense of patriotism and morality, not the Charlie that hurt and killed people because it kept the pain of loss and regret down a little longer.

He slowly donned his cloak with Millie's perfume still lingering. A few cigarettes would make the scent disappear.

Eri sat on the end of the crowded bench next to Kai on McGillan's busy patio. The crew hardly ever went to the pub because it was constantly crowded. Many of the miners were of Irish descent one way or another, and the Irish from Earth had held on to their heritage far more than other long-gone nationalities. While many other nationalities only existed in food, dance, clothing, and names seven hundred years after humanity started colonizing the stars, the Irish retained much of their traditions and culture, especially their language, devotion to Catholicism, and music. Some still even had their accent.

The primary colony for the Irish was the planet Nova Hibernia, now a planet in IFSA on the border with the Federation. Many Irish saw it as their new homeland, but some still found new areas of the galaxy to colonize, and Corinth on Magna Graecia was one of them. The mines offered opportunity, and a large contingent from Nova Hibernia left to start new lives.

As Irish folk music played over the speakers in the crowded pub, Eri stared at the message displayed on her tool. It was from Rojer Mishra, an old boyfriend of hers from maintainer school. She had fallen in love with him, and the day that she wanted to confess, he ended things between them without warning and ghosted her.

Now, he was contacting her after two years.

`Rojer: Hey. I hope things are well with you. Send me a message when you are free. I want to talk about some things with you and apologize how things ended. I miss you.`

Why now? Why after two years of complete radio silence and breaking her heart would he want to apologize and tell her that he missed her? She had to date two separate men when she was living in Athens with Ash just to get over him and the sudden heartache. Their unexpected breakup was what made her start to believe men found her unattractive whenever they saw her in her coveralls. The day before Rojer left her, he saw her dirty and in her school-provided coveralls, and it was the only explanation she had for his sudden change.

"Hey, y'all, make some room for my friend here," Ash demanded to the group of patrons sharing the bench with the crew. Eri looked up and saw Ash getting closer to Francis and another patron shifting to allow Charlie to sit next to her sister. He was wearing that dark blue cloak of his, and a few patrons seemed to take notice. The Irish hated Hexhamites because most of them came from the United Kingdom back on Earth. Even over a thousand years later, there was still bad blood between the Irish and British.

Charlie sat down wordlessly and looked down at the table. Something was on his mind. A waitress came by a short time later and gently placed her hand on the absentminded first officer. He quickly flicked his head to her.

"Oh, sorry, love," the waitress said, "didn't mean to scare you. What would you like to drink?"

Charlie looked away in embarrassment. "Just startled me is all. Two double Jamesons."

"I'll be back soon, love," she said as she walked away.

The waitress returned with his two glasses of Irish whiskey.

"Well, now that we're all here with drinks," Francis said as he stood up with a raised glass, "to a new beginnin' and new adventures."

"Here, here!" Eri cheered. The five of them toasted and drank. Charlie wasted no time and took both of his. He stacked his glasses and set them off to the side. While Eri masked her problems behind a happy face, Charlie didn't seem to care about hiding it.

The crew started up conversation, but the first officer remained reclusive and distant, lighting a cigarette. Ash noticed her mentor being icier than normal and leaned toward him. She whispered something in his ear, and Charlie glared at her. She conceded with raised hands and started talking to Francis.

After the rest of the crew finished their drinks at McGillan's, they moved onto Cutters as the evening sun lowered near sunset. Charlie apparently had gotten cigars for all of them, and the first officer seemed to know what kind of cigars the sisters liked, but they never mentioned it to them. Ash seemed incredulous that Charlie knew the exact brand and type of cigar that she liked, but Eri knew it was just more of Charlie's skill working for him. It made her remember that Charlie somehow knew she liked midnight snacks, but she had still been unable to figure it out.

Unfortunately, she never got the chance to ask a question because Ash and Francis started asking her for recommendations for the next bar since it was her turn to pick. McGillan's was Ash's request and Cutters was Kai's. Charlie would be after Eri, and Francis would pick the last one.

While she decided, her eyes kept drifting over to Charlie, who was still distant and quiet, even more than usual. He wasn't just deep in thought, something was eating at him.

After Cutters, Kai took a taxi back to the ship. Ash showed her disappointment that Kai once again refused to have more than a few drinks with them by calling him "chickenshit." The four were walking towards Eri's choice, Bullseye!, when Charlie's stomach growled.

"You know," Eri started, "Indigo is still open for an hour. You could take a taxi and get a couple lobster rolls with garlic butter."

"Well that was the most unsubtle hint I've heard all day," Charlie said, "let me guess, you'll come along and protect me?"

"The beach can be a really dangerous place at night," Eri said sarcastically as she held back laughter.

Charlie looked at Francis and shrugged. "I'll message you when we are leaving the beach." Francis nodded and the group split. Charlie hailed a cab and the two got in. The taxi drove for a while to Indigo and the two looked out the window, observing their surroundings. The taxi ride was relatively short to get to the beach, and before long, they stepped out of the car and smelled the familiar aromas from two weeks before.

Charlie ordered the same food he had last time, but Eri was not nearly as hungry as before and only got a single lobster roll with a beer. When their order arrived, the two immediately opened their beers and walked to the beach, which was now glowing under the three-quarter moon.

They walked and ate. Every time Eri noticed Charlie's silence, she tried to speak, but the words never escaped her lips.

# Chapter 39

The two arrived at Bullseye! a short while later. Ash and Francis were already playing darts in their usual spot. Eri started to head to the bar top where Charlie usually sat, but he diverted course and picked a table in the corner away from everything. Intrigued, she followed him to the table. The waitress walked over to them as they sat down.

"What would you like, hon?" the waitress asked Eri.

"Whiskey sour, please," she said with a smile.

"And what about you, Stump?" she lovingly called the one-armed first officer.

"Old fashioned," he replied.

The waitress left and Charlie leaned back in his seat, lighting a cigarette. Despite keeping up with everyone in drinks, he had yet to show any signs of it affecting him. His tolerance frustrated Eri, who absorbed alcohol at a normal rate.

"You know, I never really got to see you drunk back when we went to The Quarry," she hinted to the first officer. He looked at her and smirked.

"Are you going to pay for that amount of alcohol?" he asked.

"If you won't back out of it," she replied, "but you have to drink every shot I put in front of you."

"You act like I won't," he chuckled as he took a drag from his cigarette.

"I'm just laying down the ground rules," she said as the waitress returned with their drinks. "Excuse me, Maria, can you also get Charlie a shot of white tequila?" Eri placed a twenty on the table, indicating that she was paying for it.

The waitress took the twenty and pocketed it. "Sure, hon. I'll come back with the shot and your change."

Charlie sipped on his old fashioned as the waitress left, flicking his cigarette in the ashtray. His expression hardened as he gazed at the ember on the end of the cigarette.

"Alright, what's on your mind?" she asked.

Charlie looked up as Ash cheered in victory across the bar. Eri could tell that he wanted to say something, but he stopped himself, staring pensively at her.

"What?" she asked shyly, looking away from his gaze.

"Sorry," he said as he resituated himself, "zoned out there for a moment."

The waitress returned, placed the shot on the table, and left.

"So what's on your mind?" she asked again.

Charlie took the shot, licked his lips, and tapped the ash off of his cigarette. He looked out into the bar.

"I should be over the moon right now," he began. "I should be grinning from ear to ear knowing that Jessik won't be a problem anymore. Yet..."

Eri waited as he inhaled more smoke and slowly released it out of his nose.

"And yet I can only look back and see all the terrible shit I've done over the past two and a half years and how much all of it turned me into..."

Eri frowned as she saw him struggle with his emotions and guilt. He didn't have his usual cold and serious demeanor. She could see the pain in his dark blue eyes and the deep lines on his face.

"Jessik tried to have me killed the night we went to The Quarry. Sent an assassin. He failed, obviously, but when I killed him..."

Charlie sipped his old fashioned and took another drag from his cigarette.

"Millie called me a monster...and I knew she was right."

"I'm assuming Millie is the woman that left the club with you," Eri said. Charlie slowly nodded. "That's why you took drops that night. You're ashamed."

He looked down and extinguished his cigarette. "She was the first woman in three years that made me want to actually date. I've had a couple of flings, but nothing substantial. Women don't want to date a monster. They're happy to share a bed with one every now and then, but men like me aren't boyfriend material. Hearing her call me that…it gave me the perspective that I needed."

Eri sipped her whiskey sour, and Charlie mirrored her.

"So what have you been trying to hide all evening?" he asked.

Eri tilted her head. "I thought you said you controlled your skills around me."

"I do, but your emotions were very visible when I joined the table at McGillan's."

Eri sighed and shook her head. "You don't want to hear about it. It's stupid."

"Better than me talking about my guilt," he retorted.

Eri sipped her whiskey sour again. "About three years ago, while I was in my last year of schooling, I met a guy named Rojer. Handsome, tall, and really funny. He and I were in avionics together and the only open spot in the class was next to me on the first day. By the end of the first lecture, he asked me out on a date. We were both so compatible, and he was a great lover too. He just…understood me, you know?

"After two weeks of pure bliss being with him every minute outside class, he suddenly broke it off. Said he wasn't ready for a relationship and took someone else's spot on the far side of the room from me. Never said a word or even looked at me for the rest of that semester. The worst part was that I was going to tell him after class that day that I loved him."

"He finally contacted you again," he concluded. "That's why you were looking at your tool."

Eri looked away. "I'm over him…but when I read 'I miss you,' I felt giddy for a short moment. Then, I was mad at myself. I don't want to be that kind of girl that just runs back into an old ex's arms, especially with how he treated me. Yet…"

"You never got the closure you wanted and you're tempted anyway."

She looked at him. "A little, but a lot of me just wants to ignore him."

"Then ignore him," he replied. "Take it from me. Life is too short to wonder, and life can be cruel as well. Ignore him and find someone else."

She smiled at him. "I appreciate your perspective."

"You probably shouldn't to take my advice," he replied, "I've had terrible luck with relationships."

"And now that the cynical first officer has returned to the table, let's get him another shot." Eri waved down the waitress and ordered Charlie another shot. As the waitress left, Ash and Francis walked over.

"There ya are," Ash said happily, "how long have ya two been here?"

"A while," Eri answered with a smile, "we were just letting you two play your game and chatting."

"Did ya order another drink?" Francis asked. "We were actually just about to go to Akhmed's."

She looked at Charlie. "You chose Akhmed's?"

He smirked. "Figured we could go where it all began."

She smiled and looked at the captain. "I just ordered a shot for Charlie. I can finish my whiskey sour and we can go after."

"Cool," Ash replied warmly, "where should we go after that?"

"I don't have a preference," Francis answered. "Eri kinda already picked my choice, so I'll leave it up to y'all."

Eri thought for a while and sipped on her whiskey sour as the waitress returned with Charlie's shot.

"I have an idea," Eri finally said as Charlie quietly threw back the shot glass. "Let's go to Blackout. We could dance and get a lot of cheap shots."

"Sounds like a plan," Francis said with his toothy smile. "It's rainin' outside, so I'll get us a taxi while ya finish your drink."

"I'm going to walk," Charlie finally said. "It's only five blocks away."

"Suit yourself," Francis replied with a shrug.

Eri could see that Charlie needed to talk more.

"I think I'll walk with him," Eri said, "we'll catch up."

"Ya sure?" Ash asked with apprehension.

"I've got the poncho. I'll be fine."

"Cloak," Charlie corrected quietly. "A poncho only opens at the top and bottom. A cloak is clasped together, even if it goes down the length from end to end like yours."

Francis chuckled and walked off.

"Don't take too long!" Ash commanded happily as she followed the captain.

Eri quickly finished her drink while Charlie sipped his old fashioned.

"Speaking of cloaks," she began, "I saw that you gave Millie your cloak that night. Didn't take you for the helpless, romantic gentleman type. It was kinda cute, to be honest." Charlie glared at her. "Don't like being called cute?" she asked.

"No," he answered flatly as he finished his drink.

Eri giggled as she got up from her seat. "C'mon, let's go."

Charlie paid his bill and walked out with her. The rain was coming down in steady, large drops. Eri squirmed a little when the rain hit the lower part of her skirt, calves, and shoes. She was trying to be a good friend by walking with him. Charlie obviously noticed her discomfort and signaled to a cab to pull forward.

"Oh, no, I'm fine with walking!" she told him.

"Shut up," he replied. "You can't fool me."

Eri's shoulders slumped as the rain tapped on her hooded cloak. "I'll walk with you if you want to walk in the rain," she explained.

"I know you will," he said, "and I appreciate you trying to be a good friend, but you don't need to do that."

The taxi pulled up, but when Charlie tried to open the door, she put her hand over it to keep it shut.

"I've made my decision, now start walking before I just start doing it myself," she replied authoritatively. She stared at him, daring him to try to be more stubborn. He pulled his hand away from the door. "Start walking, asshole," she commanded.

Charlie snorted and started walking, waving the cab away. Another group of people quickly rushed into the summoned cab and took it from them. They walked together on the sidewalk as the rain slapped against their clothes.

After about a block, Eri had become accustomed to the rain slapping against her lower legs and feet. Cars drove by and the streetlights illuminated their path as they walked next to many recently closed stores or small restaurants close to closing time. She knew that her friend could use a companion on the walk to keep him away from his somber thoughts, so she tried to make conversation.

"So where are we heading tomorrow?" she asked excitedly.

He turned his head and looked at her. His cloak may have had a hood, but he kept it down to let the rain hit his head and wet his hair. "Rock Island," he answered.

"What's that?" she asked.

"It's a deep space station on a large asteroid about eighteen hours away from here. It's a good place to start our business."

"What kind of work will be there?" she asked.

"Mostly bounty hunting work for me, but we may find some work for cargo or personal transport. It's not the safest of places, though, so you won't go off ship unless your sister or I are escorting you."

"I'm very capable," she argued.

"Don't care," he replied plainly, "I'm head of security, and once we've been there a few days, you'll understand why anyone going off ship needs an escort."

"Is it really that dangerous? Why would we go there?"

"It has the *potential* to be that dangerous in the places that we'll visit, but it offers a lot of opportunities to get the business started before we go to more…civilized places. Rock Island has twelve sectors, and only three are relatively safe. The crew will be allowed in those three territories with an escort; only Ash and I can go to the other nine, and we'll be *very* well-armed. Don't worry though, we probably won't be there for long."

Eri looked forward anxiously. If Charlie thought it was dangerous enough to require a security escort to leave the ship, then it was definitely a place she didn't want to be alone.

"I know what you're thinking," he said in a gentle tone as he looked at her, "but I'll protect you, no matter what."

She looked at him and could see on his resolute face that it was a promise he planned to keep. Her worries melted away in the rain as she thought about what he had done already to protect her. If he was willing to go through so much to protect the crew, she had no doubt he and Ash would keep them safe.

They arrived at Akhmed's shortly afterward. Francis and Ash were both sitting at a table in the smoking section waiting for them. Ash was cackling at something.

Eri lowered her hood as Charlie removed his cloak. He held out his hand to take her cloak. She unclasped it and rested it on his outstretched arm. They joined the captain and the security officer at the table. Ash and Francis apparently had already ordered them drinks and were waiting for them at the table.

"About damn time," Ash said with feigned annoyance.

"Yeah, yeah," Eri replied jokingly as she sat next to her sister.

"Ya know, I was just thinkin'," Ash said to all of them, "that police lieutenant said he wanted to see the completed ship before we left. Maybe he can come and take pictures of us before we take off!"

"I doubt he'll be available," Charlie said quickly.

"Well, I'll send him a message and see. When are we headin' out?"

"Judgin' that we'll all probably be hungover tomorrow, let's have a later start than normal," Francis answered. "We'll leave three hours after wakeup."

Charlie looked away distantly as Ash sent the message. He took a large gulp from his old fashioned as Eri drank from her whiskey sour.

"Is that the Andre fellow you've been messaging?" Eri asked deviously, trying to embarrass her sister.

"Maybe…" she said as she pulled her tool away from the prying eyes of her sister. Eri giggled.

Eri signaled the waiter and asked for two shots for Charlie.

"Ya feedin' him shots tonight?" Francis asked with a chuckle.

"I never got to see him drunk the other night," she said, "I'm not going to miss the opportunity."

"I honestly have no idea where the fuck it goes," Ash said as she put her tool to sleep.

"It's a mystery to us all," Francis replied.

The waiter returned with the two shots. Charlie looked at them listlessly for a moment, shrugged, then cleared his throat to get the others' attention. He threw back each shot, one after the other, and began chugging the rest of his beer.

"Now we're fucken talkin'!" Ash hollered.

The four left and went over to Blackout in a taxi to end their evening. Charlie was finally starting to feel the alcohol as they entered the windowless bar and dance room. The typical music was playing with deep bass and thumping, fast rhythms. He hadn't been in the bar since he first met Wei-Lu and bought his combat stims. Eri excitedly picked a table near the dance floor.

Francis and the women ordered lighter alcohol chasers with the specialty shot that night running at a two-for-one discount. Charlie obliged them and got a strong drink along with a shot.

"And jus' keep comin' over this way with those shots," Ash yelled to the scantily clad waitress as she handed her a twenty, "we're gonna be feeding him shots all night."

The dance floor lights flashed as the beat dropped and the crowd erupted with excitement and energy. The waitress came back and gave them all their drinks and shots. They all raised their shot cups, touched them together, and drank.

"Alright, let's go dance," Eri commanded all of them as she pulled on Charlie's metal arm. He remained planted and shook his head.

"Not a dancer, remember?" he reminded her.

"Then what happened at Huang's wedding reception?" she asked snidely.

"A one-time thing," he said sternly.

"Wait, Charlie danced with ya?" Francis asked with shock.

"Bullshit!" Ash exclaimed in disbelief.

Eri smugly woke her tool and scrolled through her pictures as Charlie glared at her. She stopped on the picture and stared into his eyes. They were obscured by the low light, but the random flashes from the dance floor occasionally illuminated her hazel irises. She flipped the holographic screen around with a flourish of her fingers and showed them the picture that Elga took. Before the others could get a closer look, she minimized the screen with her palm.

"Last chance," she told Charlie, "dance with us, or they get to see it."

Charlie's eyes narrowed as he stood, pressed his lips together, and leaned close to her, trying to make her nervous with his proximity. She, however, proved to be more stubborn than anticipated and stood her ground. There was a long silence between them as the music blared in their ears.

"I don't give in to blackmail," he said sternly. He straightened himself and drank from his mixer. "You may have gotten me to dance if I was drunk enough later tonight, but now you lost the chance."

Charlie sat down in his seat in defiance.

"Let me see the picture!" Ash demanded.

Eri eyed the first officer, then smugly showed the picture to them.

"Aw!" Ash exclaimed sarcastically. "He *is* human!"

"Well I'll be…" Francis said in disbelief, "this was at your friend's weddin'?"

"Yup," she answered with a smile.

"Well, he can watch our stuff while we dance," Ash suggested as she joined Eri.

"Fuck it," Francis said as he joined them, "I'm already startin' to get drunk, might as well let ya two see me dance."

The sisters squealed with excitement and dragged the captain to the dance floor. Charlie sat at the table and drank his mixer quietly. He closed his eyes and felt the music hit his body, the loud booms of the bass causing his skin to shudder slightly as the air compressions wafted over him. He pulled a cigarette out of his pocket and as he retrieved his lighter, a flash appeared to his right, producing a flame for him to use. With the cigarette in his mouth, he traced the feminine hand up the arm and saw a familiar face.

"I was wondering if they were ever going to leave you alone," Wei-Lu said with her chest puffed out, pointing her cleavage at him. Her eyes were affixed to his, her brow lowered and her eyes full of desire. Looking only into Wei-Lu's eyes, he leaned forward and lit the cigarette with her lighter. He exhaled the smoke and leaned back in his chair as he put his lighter away.

"Working again?" he asked casually.

"Bills don't take a day off," she said as she leaned closer to him, "but I could take an hour or two off if you'd rather do something other than dance."

"How about taking off forever?" he hinted.

Wei-Lu straightened up and looked at him with frustration. "You really won't give me what I want until I get out, will you?"

"That's kind of how quid pro quo works," he said sarcastically.

"Well what if I told you that I'm seriously considering your offer?"

"I'd say you were full of shit," he answered, "you like the money too much despite not understanding that if you don't get out soon, you'll never be *allowed* to leave."

"Well…I am," she said as her typical seductive persona dissolved. She held her arm with her other hand and slumped down. "I heard there's a war coming, and I don't want to be caught in the middle."

"Do you have a plan?" he asked.

"Not really, but I have some money saved up."

Charlie looked away and thought for a moment. He returned his eyes back to her and could see her sincerity in her vulnerability. She wasn't trying to trick him just to sneak a kiss. She genuinely wanted to get out. He sighed reluctantly.

"What kind of skills do you have, besides selling drugs and getting men between your legs, I mean."

Wei-Lu shrugged. "I just got out of high school, remember?"

"Can you shoot?"

"What? Like a gun? No."

"Can you fly a ship?"

"No!"

"Do you know how to cook?" he asked in desperation.

"Do instant noodles count?"

Charlie's looked out to the dance floor, but couldn't see Francis or the girls. He finally turned back to Wei-Lu, who looked worried.

"Daniel, you told me that if I ever needed your help, you would offer it. I need your help."

*I know I'm going to regret this…*

"Fine," he said finally, "I have a ship that's heading to Rock Island tomorrow. It's in the junkyard behind the astral dealership. You know where that is?"

Wei-Lu nodded quietly.

"Be there at nine with everything you can carry with you. We'll figure out what to do from there."

"So I just have to leave Corinth behind? What about my friends?" she asked. "I've got younger friends stuck in the gang and they rely on me."

"I'm not a charity service, Lu," he replied, "just you, and you're going to work-off your debt to me. You're going to basically be a janitor on the ship while we find you a place to start over."

"I can't just leave my friends behind," she argued.

"That's my offer," he replied sternly as he took a drag from his cigarette. "Make your decision by nine or we *will* leave without you. Friends come and go, but you only get one life, and when you're presented an opportunity to make a change, you have to leave everything behind and take it."

Wei-Lu stood there silently, her face still showing fear and worry. She finally nodded in affirmation.

"Lu, I left my homeworld, my family, everyone, to start a new life. If you want to live safely and never worry about pissing off a psychopath gang boss, you need to be willing to leave it all behind. Take the rest of your night off and go get ready. If you decide to stay because of your friends, that's your business. I won't come looking for you. You have to make this decision yourself.

"I knew someone who was too deep, and she refused to leave because she was married and tried to work things out with her husband. When Jessik found out that she considered leaving his crew, he had her husband killed. Gang leaders will use your friends against you and discard them without a second thought. You have to be selfish when you leave a gang. If you don't, the people you care about will be hurt to keep you around. Don't be late tomorrow."

Wei-Lu's almond eyes finally returned to his, and he looked at her resolutely. Her lip trembled before she wordlessly walked away.

Charlie sat at the table, pensively drinking his mixer as the shot girl came around and sat four shots on the table. The first officer handed her some cash. He looked at the shots and wondered if he should bother telling Francis about Wei-Lu. If she boarded *Silver Bow* without his prior knowledge, he would be furious, but if he told him and she never showed, he wouldn't hesitate to send out the crew to find her and bring her aboard regardless of her decision.

Francis's fatherly instincts would not allow such a young woman to be left behind, even if she made the choice to stay. Charlie knew this, and it weighed on him. Wei-Lu had to make her decision, and she had to live with that choice. She may be barely an adult, but she was an adult all the same. Charlie wouldn't make that choice for her and she had to live with the consequences of whichever direction she took.

He couldn't blame her if she chose to stay with her friends. He had lost many of his own friends, and he had vowed to never lose one again if he could help it.

The thought of the friends he'd lost and his vow to keep them safe made him think about Johan and his disappearance. He hoped Johan was safe, but he feared the worst. The idea of yet another person from his old team dying made his stomach turn.

"When did the shots get here?" Ash asked, pulling him out of his thoughts.

"Oh, not too long ago," he replied.

The three grabbed their shots and drank.

"I think that's the last shot for me tonight," Ash said with a grimace.

"Perfect timing," the shot girl said as she returned. "I got another round for you guys!"

The barely dressed woman put down four more shots and took drink orders. Charlie's mixer was almost gone, so he ordered another. Francis and Ash were already drunk, so they chose to slow down and ordered beers. Eri, who was more confident and bubblier in her drunkenness, ordered another whiskey sour with a smile and flushed cheeks.

Ash and Francis handed their shots to Charlie, both no longer wanting to party as hard.

"Gimme thah," Eri demanded as she grabbed one of the surrendered shots, "I'm not gonna let you drink three. We'll share."

"You sure?" the first officer asked with mild concern despite enjoying her inebriated confidence.

"Just this once," she said with a smile, "I think these'll be my last shots of the night too."

The two took their shots, Charlie still only showing mild signs of alcohol in his system.

"I just don't understand," Eri said as she licked her lips. "How the *fuck* are ya not drunk yet? I've been feedin' ya shots since Bullseye!"

"I've just always had a high tolerance." He shrugged.

The shot girl returned with their drinks, and Francis told her to only bring two shots for the next round as he handed her more cash.

The four sat at the table and chatted between each other, telling stories of their lives and allowing the alcohol to take full effect. Charlie finally started to feel tipsy as the shot girl returned with two more for him. Ash whooped and hollered with excitement.

"I think those last two are going to send me over the edge," Charlie admitted.

"Yes!" Eri said drunkenly, "we finally getta see drunk Charlie!"

The four continued to drink and talk as the music changed to something mellower.

"I'm gonna go home," Francis said as he got up, "Still gotta wake up in the mornin'." He chuckled as he fumbled with his raincoat. Ash followed suit. "You two youngins gonna stay here?" he asked.

"Just a little longer," Charlie answered with a smile as Eri swayed in her seat. "I still have overnight watch, after all."

"Ugh!" Eri groaned with frustration. "Why can't we jus' close this place down?" she asked the first officer.

"Because we're adults with responsibilities, Eri," Charlie replied with a chuckle.

The two left the younger crewmates. Eri was deep into her inebriation while Charlie was just beginning to feel his.

"Tell me more abou' Rock Island," she requested whimsically.

Charlie sipped his drink and looked at her. Her eyes were heavy, cheeks flushed, and she had a smile so permanent only sleep and sobriety would remove it.

"What do you want to know?" he asked.

"Ya said it was a space station on a comet, right?"

"An asteroid, but yeah. It's a completely independent place and doesn't have representation in the IFSA Parliament. It's a place with very few laws and has no official government. The twelve sectors are all stacked on each other like a skyscraper and built into the face of the asteroid. The top three levels are where tourists and normal people go. The bottom nine are basically headquarters and strongholds for various gangs and crime families, and they police their own sections. For the top three, the Red Castle merc group patrol like police and are paid tribute by the other nine sectors, along with tolls and fees for docking and people who live there to maintain order. A lot of people go there for new opportunities or as their first stop on their way to a new life, but most never leave. It's a very crowded space station and people practically live on top of each other."

"Sounds interestin'," she said as she rested her head on his shoulder. Normally, he would be annoyed by it and ask her not to do that, but his own inebriation loosened his restrictions on personal space. The two sat quietly for a while as Eri continued to rest her head on Charlie's shoulder.

"I'm sorry," she eventually apologized.

Charlie turned his head and looked at her in confusion. "For what?"

"For tryin' ta get ya ta dance," she muttered. "I was jus' tryin' to keep yer mind off the redhead callin' ya a monsder and thought dancin' would help."

He smiled and rested his cheek on the top of her head. "I appreciate you trying to cheer me up. You're a good friend, Eri." He lifted his head and drank from his mixer.

"Can I ask ya somethin'?" she murmured.

"Sure," he replied calmly.

"When ya look at me, do ya only see my coveralls?"

"Huh?" he asked in confusion.

Eri finally lifted her head up to his level, but she didn't pull her body away. Her face was close to his, though her heavy eyelids concealed some of her eyes, and her flush cheeks and mouth somehow formed a frown.

Her change in mood caught Charlie off guard. Before he knew it, she had her hands on the back of his chair and on the edge of the seat, and was leaning into him with pouting eyes.

"Well," she started as she looked away, "e'er since I b'came a maintainer, guys jus' seem ta either wanna be my friend or jus' wanna take me home for only one night. Iz like the coveralls are man repell'nt or somethin'. I jus' feel like guys can't get past it and they only wanna *girlie girl*. Is that how y'are?"

"Maybe I'm missing something," he said as he turned to her. Her eyes looked up at him again. "Are you asking if I'm only your friend—and not more—because you fix engines for a living?"

"Hrmm," she said, "not jus' *you*, but *any* guy. I dunno. I jus' feel unattractive sometimes b'cause of the uniform and it makes me wonder if you're only friends with me b'cause the coveralls make me unattractive to you and other guys..." She looked away again and sat back in her chair. "I dunno what I'm tryin' ta say..."

Charlie smiled. She wanted to make sure he hadn't just put her in the friend zone because the coveralls and dirty work made her less attractive to him.

He would be lying if he said she was unattractive, but he didn't want to give her the wrong impression either. She was his friend because she cared and listened. She was his friend because she could see past his coldness and understood him as only a friend could. He respected her for her abilities as a maintainer, and it had never crossed his mind that it would make men less attracted to her. It never made her less beautiful to him after all. In fact, the first time he was truly caught off guard by her beauty was when she was in her coveralls and with only her bra on. Her explanation of how other men saw her finally explained why she was still single despite her beauty and demure personality.

Starting something casual with her had crossed his mind a couple of times, but it was not her profession that held him back. What kept him away initially was the pending TES diagnosis and Francis's no-fraternization policy. When they became friends, the thought never crossed his mind again.

The dynamic between them as friends felt far more natural to him anyway. She made him feel like he could talk about his past without judgement, and he liked that he could express his feelings without anything else complicating the issue.

Unsurprisingly, his inebriation removed many of his inhibitions as he saw her sitting there, beautiful and shy, lacking confidence that she should otherwise have. The thought of kissing her crossed his mind, but that would be taking advantage of her in her drunken, vulnerable state. She didn't need or want her friend to prove that he found her beautiful with an unwarranted kiss; she wanted validation that their friendship was sincere and not simply because he found her unattractive as a maintainer. The alcohol made it difficult for him to put it into words, and it only made the temptation stronger.

"I'm your friend because you and I understand each other," he finally said. "I'd lie…I'd be lying if I said you were unattractive." Her eyes widened as she looked at him. He felt strangely shy and looked away. "You're actually really beautiful…"

"Really?" she asked.

"Yes, really, Eri. You really *are* my friend, and I hope you find someone who will look past your coveralls. You deserve it. But I need a friend like you far more than I need a lover right now.

Things have been…really difficult for me lately. You were right to say that I need to talk to someone."

Eri smiled with quivering lips, then hugged him tightly, probably trying to get it done as soon as possible before he pushed her away. He gently reciprocated to her obvious surprise.

"Thank you for being the friend that I need," he said quietly.

She shoved her face in his shoulder with a smile.

"Alright," he said, making it known that he was done with the hug. He stood up and grabbed their outerwear. "Let's go home."

She looked up at him from the chair. "Yeah…home…"

# Chapter 40

The taxi came to a stop at the bottom of the hill that led to *Silver Bow.* The monsoon rain was starting to slow, but it would not end for a while. Charlie gave the driver money and got out as Eri cackled with laughter from a joke she told him. It wasn't that funny, but Eri's laugh made him chuckle. The two exited the vehicle, and he could see that Eri was having difficulty maintaining her balance with her heels. The first officer, barely drunk, helped her remain stable as she walked across the road. She stopped at the curb.

"Shit…the hill's all muddy," she slurred.

"Here," he said as he squatted in front of her, "I'll carry you up."

"Oh, my hero!" she said with a laugh. She gasped suddenly. "You shoul' carry me in yer arms! I've ne'er had a guy carry me in his arms!"

"Just get on my back, god damnit," Charlie commanded.

"Fine, dick," she replied as she wrapped her arms around his neck and put her weight on him. She squealed with excitement as he stood up, putting his hands on the back of her knees and holding her legs up. She started giggling as he began to carry her up the hill.

"Giddy up!" she yelled jovially and laughed. He carried her up into the cargo bay and slowly released her. Her heels clicked down on the metal and she regained her balance. "Sush a gentl'mun," she murmured as she struggled to take her heels off. Charlie walked over to the panel near the cargo door and closed it for the night, the mechanisms whirring loudly as it lifted towards its locked position.

"Soun's like the servos need main'ence," she remarked. "Wait! Did I e'er do yer servos?"

Charlie chuckled. "No, you haven't."

"Shit…Well, take yer arm off. I'll do 'em right now."

"How about we do it tomorrow on the way to Rock Island?"

"N'kay," she said in defeat. "Don' lemme ferget."

"I won't," Charlie reassured her.

"I'm fuggin' wasted," she admitted.

Charlie chuckled. "Yes, you are, Eri."

"Will ya stay wiff me tonight? I don' ever have a good night drunk…" Eri looked down, and he could see that she was embarrassed and scared.

Charlie sighed as he looked at the drunk maintainer. "Sure," he conceded, "you can sleep in my bed. I have overnight shift, so I'll watch the systems from my desk."

"Th'nks," she said, her chin pressed against her chest.

"Go change into some night clothes and I'll watch over you tonight."

"N'kay," she said as she stumbled up the starboard stairs. Charlie quickly removed his muddy boots in the cargo bay by the drains and followed her up the stairs.

"My door will be unlocked," he told her as he went toward his quarters. She leaned against the wall for balance, and Charlie shook his head as he watched her go into her room. He went into his quarters and changed into a new set of clothes. He wore a plain blue button-up shirt, black pants, and suspenders. He wore his shoulder holster for his sidearm, and as he rolled up his sleeves, he realized that Eri had yet to return. It shouldn't have taken her that long to change into night clothes.

He turned on the ship's monitoring systems at his desk and walked out of his quarters. He approached her door, but before he could knock, he heard her vomiting. Charlie opened the door with his access code and saw her weakly coughing over the waste bin in her room. She had replaced her skirt with the cotton shorts that she had worn in the mornings, but she had yet to change out of her top.

He walked in and helped her as she retched another time. She moaned with disgust after she finished evacuating her stomach, and he could see that the effort weakened her.

"It's alright, c'mon," he said as he helped her onto her feet.

"Shuln had those last two shots," she mumbled as he gently helped her to her feet.

"It's alright, I got you," he reassured her quietly. "Where are the rest of your clothes?

She weakly pointed to a small pile of clothes and he grabbed them. She leaned against the wall for support, and her eyes closed as her state worsened. He escorted her over to his room and into the bathroom, setting her clothes on the vanity.

"Yer fuggin bafroom iz nice," she complimented with a slur.

"Wash out your mouth and finish changing. If you need to throw-up, toilet is right there."

"N'kay…"

Charlie closed the door that led through his closet into the bathroom to give her privacy as he walked back to her room and collected the bag now full of her vomit. He sighed as he took the bag to the waste disposal hatch and threw it in. He went to the galley, replaced the liner, put it back in her quarters, locked her door with his code, and went back to his room. The doors opened with a hiss and she stood there, swaying next to the bed.

"Room's spinnin'" she announced quietly.

"Need some help?" he asked.

"Nah…jus' some water…"

Charlie opened a cabinet next to his desk and pulled out a glass. He went back into the bathroom and filled the glass with water. He returned and saw her sitting on the edge of the bed, her gaze distant as she continued to sway. He sat next to her and handed her the water, which she drank quickly, gasping for air as she finished the glass.

"Th'nks," she murmured as she handed him the glass.

"Go to sleep," he commanded gently. "I'll be at the desk if you need anything. I have a bin right next to the desk if you need it."

She slowly turned to him, but she was so intoxicated that she couldn't even focus her eyes on his.

"Yer too good ta me," she said as she caressed his cheek.

Charlie quickly pulled her hand down, stopping her from doing something she may regret. "Go to sleep," he gently requested again.

She blinked slowly and nodded. Charlie got up and helped her get underneath the covers. Within minutes, she was peacefully asleep. Charlie watched her drift into sleep and shook his head. He knew she would have a horrific hangover in the morning.

Charlie's overnight shift went smoothly. Despite sitting in the dark instead of his normal routine, he managed to stay awake and alert. He wasn't worried though. Jessik was dead, after all.

The rains had ceased for a few hours by the time his tool's wakeup alarm sounded and he silenced it. Eri's also sounded a short time later and he fumbled through the sheets to turn it off. He managed to find her left arm and silenced it with a gesture. Eri slept through all of it. He shook his head and put the covers back on her as she remained still.

*I don't envy her head when she finally wakes up.*

Charlie opened his door with the soft open and close feature, and he snuck out of his quarters. He readjusted his suspenders and shoulder holster with his sidearm tucked into it as he walked over to the galley and began to make a hangover hash.

Kai walked into the galley first with a spring in his step, carrying items with him. Charlie, despite not experiencing the other symptoms of hangovers, had dark circles under his eyes from the dehydration. The doctor walked over to the first officer's water glass and poured the contents of one of the packs that he had.

"Good morning," the doctor said cheerfully as he finished pouring the packet. Charlie was distracted with stirring the food in the skillet, so by the time he noticed, he couldn't protest. The first officer quickly made a plate for the doctor and placed it in front of him along with a cup of hot water for his morning tea.

"Ah, hangover hash," Kai remarked nostalgically, "Reminds me of my younger years in Med School. I took the liberty of putting a hydration packet in your water."

"I saw," Charlie said in disgust, "I hate the taste of that shit."

"A better hangover cure than a pile of fats and carbohydrates," he said as he pointed to his food, "though I do admit that there's nothing quite like a hangover hash after a long night out."

The doctor placed a tea bag into the hot water and steeped it as Charlie filled himself a plate. He ate while he started a new batch. He sipped the water with the hydration packet and grimaced.

Francis slowly walked into the galley, eyelids heavy, back bent, and his arms limp at his sides with dark circles under his eyes.

"Good morning, Captain," Kai said cheerfully.

"None of that shit, Kai," Francis commanded groggily. "I'm too fucken hungover for that right now."

Charlie placed a glass of water with the hydration powder already mixed with it and a mug of coffee in front of the captain.

"Sweet, Lord, thank you for givin' me a cousin who don't get hangovers," he prayed aloud.

"He still gets hangovers," the doctor corrected him, "he just doesn't experience any of the symptoms."

"Shut up, Doc," the captain grumbled. Charlie chuckled as he continued making Francis's batch. While he waited for the ingredients to cook, he quickly ate the rest of his plate.

"Whatever happened to your little self-imposed rule of 'leaders eat last,' Charlie?" Francis asked as he looked at the first officer's plate.

"Oh, that shit doesn't apply when everyone on the ship will be waking up on their own time because of hangovers," Charlie said with a chuckle. He put the contents of the skillet onto a plate and handed it to Francis.

"When did ya two get back?" Francis asked his cousin.

"A little after midnight," Charlie replied as he prepared more ingredients for the next batch.

"So not too long."

"Mornin'," Ash groaned with closed eyes and disheveled hair from the galley's entrance.

"I honestly think I looked better than you when I lost my arm," Charlie remarked. "I would have for sure thought you closed down the bar last night with how shitty you look."

Ash slowly opened her eyes and glared at the first officer, he turned around and started a batch of hash for his protégé.

"It's because I cracked open a bottle of Korzech after I got back," she mumbled as she walked to her chair at the table. "Wanted to celebrate my last night on Corinth a little more, and before I knew it, I was huggin' the toilet."

"Oh, so you were the one going to the main bathroom in the early hours of the morning," Charlie concluded. He placed a water glass in front of her and then a coffee mug.

"Oh, thank *God* you're bein' merciful about the coffee rule today," Ash said. Charlie chuckled as he continued making Ash's batch of hash. "Is Eri still asleep?"

"Yeah, she's in my bed right now.".

"Excuse me, *what*?" Francis asked in anger.

Charlie looked around confused. "She's in my bed, asleep," he reiterated.

"Why is a *subordinate* of yours in *your* bed?" Francis asked angrily.

"The first time she ever got really drunk at fifteen, she inhaled some of her vomit and she almost died, so now she forces people to watch her while she sleeps if she gets drunk," Ash reassured the captain. "Besides, Suspenders here is into redheads anyway."

Charlie slowly looked over his shoulder and glared at her through the side of his eye.

"I had overnight watch, captain," Charlie finally said. "I was monitoring the ship from my desk and making sure she slept soundly. Even if she tries roping people into watching her at night when she's drunk, I would have watched her anyway. She was very far gone by the time we got back."

"She got hammered?" Ash asked with a smirk as Kai quietly put his dishes in the sink.

"Oh, yes," Charlie replied with a chuckle. He put Ash's hash onto the plate and gave it to her. "She may not wake up for a while. I had to carry her up the hill because she was wearing heels and could barely stand up straight." Ash snorted as Charlie finished the last of his water with a grimace. "Make sure you two drink all of your water. That shit tastes nasty, but you'll feel better in a couple of hours."

Charlie poured the last packet into a glass of water and left the galley. He walked to his quarters and the doors opened quietly as he approached. Eri was still peacefully sleeping in his bed in the dark. He looked at his tool to check the time.

*Eight…Wei-Lu has one hour…*

The first officer hoped she would come, but he wasn't optimistic. He saw how she reacted to him offering only safe passage for her and not her friends. If she was as smart as he thought she was, she would leave without them; however, if she was as resolute as he was about protecting friends, she would never show.

Just in case, he sent her a message saying that she only had one hour left to get to the ship. He put his tool to sleep, hoping to see a message from her. He sighed as he sat quietly in the dark room, the light from the desk's screen the only thing that illuminated the room.

The peaceful maintainer had not moved an inch since she first fell asleep. He happily smiled at her and watched her for a while, the lack of sleep starting to affect him. He stared at her as time passed and his mind finally quieted. His brain often worked constantly, but he had found a moment of peace and took advantage of it.

His brain finally restarted its normal clamor of thoughts as he blinked. He hadn't simply sat with an empty mind for so long, it felt alien to him.

Eri finally stirred and groaned. Charlie woke his tool and checked the time.

*8:49? Where did the time go?*

He stood up and walked over to her as her eyes slowly opened.

"How are you feeling?" he asked as she rubbed her eyes.

"Like shit…" she mumbled.

"Here," he said as he grabbed the glass and held it in front of her, "Tastes terrible, but it'll help with the hangover."

Eri slowly rose from under the sheets and looked around in the dark, the bright light on the console making her squint. Charlie turned on the lamp behind the head of the bed near the door's access panel and she groaned in pain.

"Turn it off," she demanded sleepily.

"It's almost nine," he replied. "You need to get up."

"Nine?" she asked in shock.

"Don't worry, you're fine," he reassured her as he held the glass next to her. She slowly retrieved the glass and sipped from it and grimaced.

"Ugh, I gotta get the puke out of my trash," she said as she put her hand up to her face in both embarrassment and pain.

"No need. I took care of it."

"Thanks." She finally looked at him. "Are you wearing suspenders?"

"You seem surprised by that."

"Not really, it's just…you're probably the only person I know that can actually pull them off," she muttered.

Charlie chuckled as he held his hand out to help her up. She stood up from the bed and drank some more of the water. She grimaced again and looked up at him with a pained smile.

"Thanks…for everything last night."

"You're welcome," he said with a smirk. "Now go shower and get ready. Your breakfast is in the fridge. Can't start our maiden voyage on an empty stomach."

"Alright," she mumbled as she made her way to the door.

"Make sure you drink all of that," he commanded. She slowly nodded as she left the room.

Eri managed to wake up after she showered and changed her clothes. She made her way to the galley where the rest of the crew were waiting for her and greeted her cheerfully. Ash snickered as she saw her sister wince at the noise. Charlie had already reheated her breakfast and gave it to her. She quietly ate as she finished the last of her water, the rest of the crew chattering about various things. She noticed a large travel cup of coffee slide in front of her, the smell of vanilla rising alongside the steam. She looked up and saw Charlie wink. She smiled and continued eating, sipping on the coffee as she finished her food.

"Hey!" Ash said happily after checking her tool, "Andre is gonna be here in thirty minutes to see us off! We should ask him to take a picture for us so we don't have to use a timer!"

Charlie's heart sank from the sudden announcement. He should have replied to Ash much earlier, which meant something had changed. A change Charlie knew that meant trouble.

*He must know about Jessik. Fuck!*

He reverted back to his days working as a double agent and immediately changed his demeanor to hide his fear and worry. He had done it so many times that it only took a brief moment of focus. He breathed in deeply.

"Great," Charlie said with fake enthusiasm. "We should all get ready then and meet him outside the cargo ramp."

"Sounds good!" Ash said as she got up.

"Hold on," Francis said angrily as Eri finished her food and sipped her coffee. "Eri, why are ya dressed like that?"

The maintainer looked puzzled.

"I don't understand, Captain," she said.

"Ya know *exactly* what I'm talkin' about, Eri!" he growled. "How can you call yourself *Bow*'s maintainer wearin' somethin' like that?" The crew was silent as Francis showed anger on his face and walked over to Charlie. "Did ya approve this?" he asked the first officer angrily.

"Uh…yeah, it's fine, Captain." Charlie used his skills and looked closer at Francis, and saw subtle clues that his cousin's anger was fake.

"No, it's not," he growled as he opened a cabinet and retrieved a large box. Charlie smirked and looked at Eri, but he could see that it only confused her more. "Ya need to wear somethin' more appropriate." He put the box in front of her and opened it.

Eri's mouth gaped as she saw the contents inside the box. Folded inside the box were two sets of coveralls in a light gray with red stitching. The left breast had a patch that said "Erina Bezek" and the right with an embroidered patch for the ship. Francis had made custom coveralls just for her.

"You fucking asshole! I thought you were actually mad at me!" She pulled the first pair of coveralls out of the box, and her face crumpled as she looked at it. She gently rubbed her thumb across the embroidered patch with a stitched depiction of *Silver Bow* with its name on top.

"Do you know how hard it was to keep that secret!" Ash said with excitement. "I saw them a week ago when they were finished."

"I'm honestly surprised you managed to keep your mouth shut, Tall Hands," Charlie remarked.

"I can keep a secret!" she replied in her defense.

"Barely," Francis chuckled. "Go get rid of those things and put your new uniform on," he commanded happily.

She put down the coveralls and ran over to Francis, giving him a hug. He gently wrapped his arm around her and gave her words of encouragement. She grabbed the coveralls and ran towards her room to change.

"I was wondering when you were going to give them to her," Charlie said, "but I wasn't expecting you to reveal them like that."

Francis stood tall with his hands on his hips, revealing his toothy grin. "I just wanted to have a little fun with it."

# Chapter 41

The crew stood at the top of the cargo ramp as a police vehicle arrived at the base of the hill. The staging area no longer had any crates and it looked baren. Ash smiled, Eri beamed in her new coveralls, Kai stood stiffly, and Francis stood tall with his hands on his hips. Charlie showed a cold and stern demeanor as he checked his tool, but underneath he was close to panic.

*Half-past nine and no messages. Wei-Lu decided to stay after all...*

Andre exited his cruiser and waved as he made his way up the muddy hill. He smiled happily and shouted greetings to them. Charlie put his tool to sleep and could see that Andre was putting on a mask, which troubled him.

*If he knows, why isn't he doing something about it? Is he waiting for the right time to arrest me? I may have to disable and disarm him if it comes to that.*

The crew walked down the ramp and greeted him calmly. Charlie watched his protégé, and as he suspected, her smile and demeanor softened even more when Andre got close to her. They flirted a little when they first spoke, and Charlie knew that they probably continued flirting in their messages to each other.

Andre greeted Charlie last, and the first officer purposefully extended his metal hand. Andre looked him in the eyes and shook his hand without flinching.

"I'm surprised you weren't taken aback by the arm, lieutenant," Charlie said with narrowed eyes, "you hadn't seen it until now and most people don't expect a metal hand."

Charlie played his hand and subtly explained to him that he knew that the lieutenant knew about his arm, which meant he had seen camera footage of him.

"Well when you've had to shake hands with murders in interrogation rooms to gain their trust like I have, you aren't phased by much."

*What's he waiting for? Why not try to arrest me now?*

The two parted, still staring into each other's eyes.

"So, this is *Silver Bow*," Ash said without noticing the quiet battle between the two men, "complete, and ready to launch. I can give ya a tour, if you'd like." Charlie's gaze remained fixed on Andre, but he saw Eri rolling her eyes and looking at him in his periphery. She scratched her coverall's pant leg with her nails loudly to get his attention. His eyes flicked to her, and she subtly changed her expression to silently ask him what was wrong. He didn't answer and returned his gaze to the lieutenant.

Charlie remained still and watched Ash give him a tour as Francis sauntered over to his cousin.

"Don't worry, I already talked to Ash," he reassured Charlie. "I told her not to let him go into the armory or anyone's room. I know how ya are with police."

Charlie grunted in acknowledgement, his eyes still watching Andre.

"Relax," Francis requested, "she can handle it."

Charlie slowly looked away and walked down the cargo ramp. At the base, he removed a cigarette, lit it, and looked at the police cruiser. While Francis and Kai waited in the cargo bay, Eri walked down to the first officer. She stood next to him as he took a drag from his cigarette, staring out into the distance with him.

"What's going on?" she whispered, "What's got you so spooked?"

His looked at her through the side of his eye. "If he was off-duty, why is he in a cruiser and why did he take so long to respond to Ash?" he whispered.

"You think something's up?"

"I hope not, but I think something is," he said as he looked away from her and took another drag.

"Captain Flores, this ship is magnificent," Andre said as he descended the stairs from the living quarters. "I hope you all can do so well with such a small crew."

*He's hinting that he's going to arrest me.*

"Well, once things start pickin' up, I'm sure we'll hire more crew," Francis said.

"Yeah…once things start picking up," Andre said distantly but loud enough for Charlie to hear. "You got to pick up all the pieces before you become whole."

*They definitely found Jessik's body. Is he going to tell them?*

"Would you mind takin' a picture of all of us out by the front?" Ash asked excitedly.

"Sure!" he said with fake enthusiasm, "Let's all go together."

Charlie flicked his cigarette into a junk pile, exhaled the smoke out of his nose, then started walking towards the front of the ship. Eri tried to keep pace and walked beside him.

"Why do you think he's here then?"

"May have something to do with Jessik," he replied quietly. He hoped that Andre wouldn't tell the crew what he did to Jessik.

"Do you think he may have found out that you used to work for him or that you killed those gang leaders?"

Charlie breathed deeply as he came to a stop. "I hope not."

"Yeah, perfect!" Ash shouted from behind them, "That'll be a great shot from there!"

"I'm not going to let him arrest me," Charlie whispered to Eri. "If it comes to that, I'm going to have to incapacitate him and we're getting out as fast as possible."

Eri's face twitched slightly. "Ok I'm with you if anything happens."

"I really hope I'm just being paranoid," he said as the rest approached.

"Me too," she admitted.

The police lieutenant stepped a few paces away and lowered himself as low as he could go to get a picture of them with *Silver Bow* in the background. After a few pictures, Andre returned the tablet to Ash. They exchanged a few words, and Ash promised to send him a picture. Kai shook the man's hand and promptly left. Eri shook Andre's hand, and Charlie could see that Eri was hiding a lot in her expression. The lieutenant wished her well with a smile and turned to Francis.

"Well, Captain, she's a beauty. I wish you all safe travels and good fortune as you start your new business."

"Many thanks, lieutenant," the captain said as he walked away.

Andre approached Ash again and shook her hand cordially. She smiled softly and reciprocated. "I hope things go well for you, Ashley, and I hope to see you again."

Ash smiled. "I hope to see ya as well. I'll let you know the next time we come back to Corinth or Athens."

"Yes, please do," Andre said as his demeanor switched. "Mr. Menillo, before you leave, I have a few questions to ask you about the incident two weeks ago—just want to see if there's a pattern or connection with another crime that came across my desk."

"Certainly," Charlie said calmly. "Sorry, can you give us a minute?" he asked Ash.

Ash quietly walked away. Charlie noticed Eri was waiting by the cargo ramp, watching intently. When Ash was out of earshot, Charlie spoke.

"So what questions can I answer to help you with your investigation, officer?" he asked.

"Cut the shit, Menillo," Andre growled. "I know it was you."

"I don't understand, officer."

"You went to Athens yesterday and killed Jessik in cold blood...*brutally*."

"That's a horrifying accusation, officer, I hope you have proof."

"I saw your fucking face on CCTV footage wearing a paint pattern that confuses facial recognition software. The only people I've ever seen do that are professional assassins. This time though, I knew the person behind the paint."

Charlie started to see what was going on. Andre wanted him to know, but he wasn't going to arrest him. Charlie didn't understand why he wouldn't arrest him if he knew Charlie was the one. He probed to find out why.

"I hope you aren't insinuating that I'm a murderer, lieutenant, unless you plan on arresting me," he said calmly. "Otherwise, I'd have to make a formal complaint."

"Fuck you, Menillo," he snarled as he got in Charlie's face. "I don't care if you killed that lunatic, you had *no right* to take the law into your own hands and you definitely made that man suffer. You think you're helping people get justice? You think you're doing the world a favor? All you're doing is making life harder on all of us. Now we have to start from scratch with whoever replaces him."

"Whomever," Charlie corrected.

The lieutenant's jaw clenched in rage. "I despise vigilantes like you more than the actual criminals. At least when they commit crimes, they aren't self-righteous about it. Do you know how many of my fellow officers were happy about what you did, regardless of the brutality?"

"If you find yourself in the minority in your department, perhaps *you're* the one who is looking at the world from a twisted perspective, not the other way around."

"The only thing that's twisted is your morality," he spat. "If Athens had the balls to go after self-righteous pieces of shit like you, this world would be better, but I've been told to just wring my hands and do nothing."

"Maybe because it has nothing to do with Jessik and it has everything to do with me," Charlie supplied.

"What the fuck are you talking about?"

"Have you looked up my name in a background check?" Charlie asked flatly. "It might be illuminating why no one seems to care."

"You come back to Corinth, and I'll kill you myself."

"I don't take threats *lightly,* lieutenant," he responded flatly. "You've already seen what I'm capable of, after all. Why don't you go ahead and put on your face again, walk back to your cruiser, and do your job? I'd hate for more vigilantes to do all the work for you and all your fellow officers."

Andre breathed deeply to suppress his rage. His face contorted and he stared into Charlie's eyes. "Stay safe out there, Mr. Menillo."

"You too, lieutenant," Charlie replied, "but you may find that my background check has all the information that you need."

Andre turned around and glared at Charlie, who returned only a blank stare. The man scoffed and walked away angrily. The police lieutenant walked by the sisters and acted like nothing happened.

"Safe travels, Ashley," he told the security officer softly as he passed by them.

"Be safe," Ash replied softly as she gingerly waved at him. The sisters whispered to each other as Charlie approached them, and Eri quietly giggled.

"Let's get the girl flying," he said to them. The women excitedly ran up the ramp, Charlie marching behind them. He stopped and eyed the lieutenant getting into the cruiser. They looked at each other with disdain before Andre finally got inside his cruiser and left.

"What are you doing?" Charlie asked sternly.

Eri quickly looked away from her tablet with confusion.

"Go up to the bridge," he commanded with a smirk, "You deserve to watch from up there."

"That's ok, I want to do this," she said as she continued her work.

Charlie walked over to her and gently gripped the tablet. "Go," he said again but gentler. "She's your girl too. You deserve to watch as we go into space and then into FTL. None of this would have been possible without you."

"That's not true," she said as she looked down. "Any maintainer would have gotten her flight-ready."

"Yes," he replied as he gently lifted her chin with his finger, "but only someone as hard-working and as talented as you would have gotten her heart working as efficiently and as quickly as you did." He moved his finger away and smiled. "Go up to the bridge. I'll be down here without the windows."

Eri looked at her feet and quietly complied with a smile of her own. Charlie grabbed the headset on the wall panel and turned it on as she left the compartment. She then quickly walked to the bridge as she could hear Charlie speaking on the intercom.

"Captain, engineering," he announced through the speaker, "pre-flight checks are complete and all systems are green. You are go for launch for *Silver Bow*'s maiden voyage."

Francis, sitting at the helm, pressed the intercom button. "Roger, engineerin', beginnin' launch."

The captain put thrust into the VTOL and it roared to push the ship off the ground and fight gravity. The four on the bridge watched the sky slowly turn from a bright blue to black as the captain skillfully piloted the grand machine out of the atmosphere.

He pushed engine thrust to maximum as they left speed restrictions, moving at thousands of kilometers per hour. The large wings whirled closed, no longer needing their lift and control through the atmosphere. As the ship flew past Magna Graecia's moon, Virgil, he turned on the navigation system and plotted a course to Rock Island. Eri's stomach filled with butterflies as she knew the time was near.

"Engineerin', *Silver Bow* actual," Francis said through the intercom.

"Go ahead, actual," Charlie replied.

"Course to Rock Island has been set in Navigation and FTL is spoolin'."

"Copy, actual, FTL drive is spooling. Ready on your mark."

Francis looked over his left shoulder to face Eri. "Ya wanna do the honors?"

Eri smiled and walked over. She held her hand over the lever that started the FTL drive.

"On my mark, Engineering. Three…two…one…"

Eri threw the stick forward and the engines and drive core made a high-pitched squeal. The crew cheered as the ship cut a hole through spacetime with blue energy.

"Next stop, Rock Island."

# Epilogue

"Control, this is Surveillance Two," GL-5 whispered into his earpiece. He couldn't believe that he just saw two of the crew from *Silver Bow* again after seeing them only a few weeks before.

The last time the *Silver Bow* was moored in Moscow, the crew was extremely busy, and the few times that one of the FIA surveillance teams had a chance to capture Subject Three from Operation Hercules, either TM-9 back at headquarters had waved them off, or they simply lost the chance before TM-9 was able to respond.

"Go ahead, Surveillance Two," the controller responded robotically in his earpiece.

"I have eyes on Subject Three and *Silver Bow*'s maintainer, Erina Bezek. They are currently entering Frontier Wholesale. Please advise."

"Continue following Subject Three and Bezek until we receive information from HQ in Bhutan, Surveillance Two. Report any strange activity, change in pattern, or if any crew members join them."

"Roger, Control," GL-5 replied. He looked at his partner, AT-5, as he muted his comms. "This is going to be another wild goose chase. I hate how TM-9 doesn't allow us to take an opportunity when it's right in front of us."

"You know how he is," AT-5 replied with a shrug. They walked over to a café across the street and down the road a little from Frontier Wholesale and ordered coffee. They both silently waited for their coffees, surrounded by Frontier accents, and GL-5 hated having to use that accent all the time this deep into rebel territory.

GL-5 also hated coffee. He just wanted a breakfast blend of tea with some milk and sugar, but that was the fastest way to blow his cover.

Unlike most of the people in the FIA, GL-5 was actually from Earth, humanity's homeworld. Before Precipice became the heart of the Federation, Earth was the economic epicenter of human territory in the Milky Way, but he was born a few centuries after Precipice had already become humanity's new seat of power.

Earth now was but another world, and mostly a graveyard. The hundreds of cities on it were now in a constant state of decay, as the majority of Earth's population left to explore the galaxy. He was from a nation once known as Canada, though the nation states of centuries past had lost their meaning ever since the creation of the Federation four hundred years ago. He'd lived in Toronto before going off to the University of Precipice, and many of his childhood memories involved playing in abandoned structures.

Now he was spending his days in Moscow on Rus, and it was just as cold there as it was in Toronto. He was acclimated to the cold because of it, but that didn't mean he liked it.

Their order was called. They grabbed their coffees, took a table by the windows, and resumed their conversation with whispers.

"I get he's extremely methodical and wants to make sure that the capture goes right, but you can't honestly believe that he isn't *too* controlling with the whole thing."

"Control, Surveillance Three. No changes at the spaceport. The rest of the crew are still aboard the ship."

"Roger Surveillance Three. Continue hourly check-ins if there's no activity."

"Roger, Control."

"I'm starting to wonder if those two have a thing for each other," AT-5 told him.

GL-5 looked away from Frontier Wholesale with a raised eyebrow. "What do you mean?"

"I don't know," AT-5 whispered. "Just seems like Subject Three and Bezek have some sort of relationship or friends with benefits thing going on."

"I think you're looking too deep into it," GL-5 replied. "You didn't see him try to set Bezek up with a date three weeks ago. Some married guy that lived in a house on the far side of town from here."

"See, that's why I'm leaning more toward a friends-with-benefits situation. He was just trying to let her have some fun, but they definitely have a thing for each other."

GL-5 shook his head. "They don't. They're just friends."

AT-5 shrugged. "You were able to spot YW-3 and FR-2 having a thing for each other long before anyone else, so I'll trust your judgement."

GL-5 watched the entrance to Frontier Wholesale for hours. Boredom that came with the job, but at least with how long the pair was taking inside the ship and ship parts seller, they now had a good chance of TM-9 giving the green light to capture Subject Three.

Surveillance Three informed Control during that time that Kai Ishida and Ashley Erikson had both left the ship to go and shop at certain stores near the spaceport. Francis Flores was the only one on the ship at the moment, which gave them the advantage if they were told to conduct the capture operation.

Finally, Subject Three and Bezek left Frontier Wholesale. GL-5 kicked AT-5 in the shin.

"They're moving," he whispered.

"Let's get going then," AT-5 replied. "Let Control know."

The two stood and started to walk behind them at a distance. "Control, Surveillance Two. Be advised that Subject Three and Bezek are walking along Petersburg and seem to be heading to Market Street."

"Roger, Surveillance Two. Still no word yet from Bhutan."

"Roger, Control."

Just like the last time he tailed Subject Three, the man looked all around him, constantly scanning his environment for threats. He was very careful, but they had been trained too.

When Subject Three and his maintainer friend stopped at a crosswalk at Market Street, GL-5 knew they were going to either shop or get food. As they crossed the street, Subject Three glanced his way, and GL-5 tried to act like he wasn't looking at them. The man knew their tactics, so they had to constantly change how they followed him.

"Head across Market first before crossing Petersburg," he said to AT-5.

AT-5 nodded, and they watched Subject Three from their peripheries. The target and Bezek crossed Petersburg and headed down the hill on Market. GL-5 saw them enter a shop of some sort. When he and his partner got across Petersburg, they walked across Market again and walked over to a bench near the intersection.

"Control, Surveillance Two," he said over his comms quietly. "Subject Three and Bezek have entered The Toasted Baguette, probably getting lunch."

"Good timing, Surveillance Two. Bhutan has just authorized the capture of Subject Three. All others are secondary and optional. Surveillance Three, stay by the hangar, but do not reveal yourselves to the crew. You are there strictly to stop Subject Three from leaving. Surveillance One, you are ordered to go to Canal Street and stop Subject Three from escaping. Infiltration team, your orders are to immediately get to *Silver Bow* and board without detection."

All the teams sounded off affirmatively, and the radio continued with chatter from the various teams taking their places or conducting their assignments. It was now or never. Months of training for this one moment.

"Let's go see where they're at in the sandwich shop," AT-5 suggested.

"No," GL-5 replied, "we need to wait."

"We need to make sure that he's not onto us," AT-5 argued.

GL-5 sighed and nodded. They walked down the street and as they passed the windows, saw Subject Three and Bezek eating inside. The pair returned back to the bench that they'd started from at and waited.

After a while, the two exited. Bezek tied her shoe and looked down the hill to her right, and Subject Three lit a cigarette and looked to his left.

Right at them.

*Shit. He's onto us.*

The crewmates walked down the hill of Market Street toward the spaceport, then cut across Market Street when they had a chance. GL-5 could tell that they were walking faster than normal.

"Control, Surveillance Two," GL-5 whispered into his earpiece. "Subject Three and Bezek are heading back to the ship, and they seem to be walking quickly. They may be onto us."

"Roger, Surveillance Two. All teams, capture operation is a go."

After following them for about a block, Bezek took a left down an alley toward Canal Street.

*Shit. Well, Surveillance One will be able to capture her.*

Subject Three immediately sprinted away.

"Charlie Menillo!" GL-5 shouted as they gave chase. "Come quietly and you won't be harmed!"

*End of Part 1 of the Jalisco Incident*

*Part 2, Medina's Back, releasing December 2025*

# Acknowledgements

I am so glad that I have such an energetic and enthusiastic support base already, and I hope that this series will garner (pun intended) more encouraging fans and readers.

A few supporters of mine that I want to thank are my beta readers Thomas Morgan, James Marquis, and, as expected, my wife Sarah Coffman. I would also sincerely like to thank my immensely invested friends, Matt Elliott and Tim Henson.

A special thanks to my editor, Courtney Andersson. Without your suggestions and feedback, this novel would not be as polished as it is. No novel is complete with an author alone. Much like the process of creating a sword, the author shapes the sword so that the editor may sharpen and polish it.

Thank you, Jeff Brown, for helping me create such a unique and appropriate cover for my book and helping it come to life.

Last, but certainly not least, you. Thank *you*, reader, for taking the time to read my debut novel. Whether you love the book, hate it, or think it's just alright, I appreciate your support and feedback.